RØBIN

Lady of Legend

ROBIN

Lady of Legend

THE CLASSIC ADVENTURES OF THE GIRL WHO BECAME ROBIN HOOD

R.M. ARCEJAEGER

PLATYPUS PRESS

PROVIDING QUALITY BOOKS

Cover design by R.M. ArceJaeger
www.rmarcejaeger.com

Cover art by Chris Rawlins

Published by Platypus Press
Mountain Ranch, CA 95246
www.ajplatypus.com

Visit www.ladyoflegend.com for deleted scenes, contests, games, and more!

Also available as an eBook.

Printed in the U.S.A.

Library of Congress Control Number: 2013912219

ISBN-13: 978-0-9837317-2-6

FOR MY FAMILY
AND MY GOD

YOU ARE MY
EVERYTHING

CONTENTS

⚹ 1 ⚹

AN UNEXPECTED GIFT

ROBIN DASHED through the sweltering fields towards the house, her skirts hiked up to her knees so she could run faster. Behind her someone gave a surprised shout, but she ignored the hail and raced on, her feet churning the sun-baked dirt into dust. Before her stretched a golden path that led through the manor garden and on to the main entrance, but she ignored the carefully carved trail and leapt over the rows of vegetables and herbs instead, crushing several in her haste; she did not slow down until she reached the manor kitchen.

A blast of heat and smoke greeted Robin as she edged her way inside. Within the oppressive yellow haze bustled half-a-dozen servants, too intent on preparing vast platters of meat and pulling loaves of steaming bread from the ovens to notice her arrival—or so Robin thought.

As she slipped into the corridor, however, she glimpsed one of the kitchen girls ducking out after her. Without being told, Robin knew she had gone to inform Darah of her return.

Traitor, Robin thought without rancor, quickening her pace up the newel staircase that led to the upper story. She had barely reached her bedchamber and begun to tear off her sweat-soaked overdress when Darah, the housekeeper, strode into the room.

"Out again all day!" came the immediate berate. "Never mind I have yet to fit your gown and your sister will have to greet the guests for *your* party because *you* are still not ready, and I—oh, what am I supposed to do with you, Robin?" she demanded, catching the girl's hands in her own and *tsking* over the bow-brightened calluses.

"Send me to my room without supper?" Robin suggested hopefully.

The woman's reply was a cuff on the ear. "Don't be pert."

To Robin's annoyance, Darah ordered her to soak her hands in cold water while she arranged her hair. The house-keeper's touch was brisk and aloof, as it always was, with none of the soft tenderness that was all Robin could recall of her mother.

Lady Locksley by all accounts had been one of those rare people whose spirit was as beautiful as their features were exquisite. Her death in Robin's fifth year had struck the whole manor hard; in some ways, it had never recovered.

Lord Robert of Locksley certainly had not. The maids might reminisce about what a doting father Sir Robert had been before his wife's death, but Robin could not remember that man. The father she knew was the one who preferred to ignore his children, immuring himself in the workings of his estate while Darah managed their upbringing. That was why his summons that morning had been so unnerving.

"Try this on," Darah commanded, interrupting Robin's thoughts. Without waiting for a response, she pulled a dress over the girl's head, expertly avoiding her coiffed hair. Robin absently shrugged into the costly folds, her mind already refocused on that morning's strange meeting.

The dawn sun had barely begun to engolden the sky when Sir Robert's manservant had appeared at her door, announcing that Lord Locksley wished to see her. Such a summons — the first in her memory — had stunned Robin, and it was with a sense of misgiving that she had gone to see her father.

The door to his solar had been open, but Robin had still hesitated a moment before stepping inside. Back when her mother was alive, it had been the family bedchamber; after her death, Robin and her sister had been moved to the small solar at the opposite end of the house and were forbidden to set foot inside their old room again.

The passing of the years had since dimmed Robin's memory of her childhood chamber until all she could recall of it were wisps and shadows. As she waited for her father to acknowledge her presence, Robin seized the opportunity to look around.

Two tall windows spanned the far end of the room, their panes of translucent horn allowing the sun to fill the room with a honeyed glow. A majestic oak bed stood against the eastern wall, opposing a rectangular fireplace whose smoke was carried away by a chimney carved with reliefs of dancing hunters and leaping stags. There was a small table with the leavings of breakfast still upon it near the fire, and a little stool nearby as well. The only other furniture was a table and bench beside the bed, where her father now sat writing.

As Robin gazed around the room, she strained eagerly for some small remembrance of the warmth and joy she had been told once existed there — but the chamber remained a stranger to her; cold ashes where a blazing fire once burned.

It is a handsome room, if sparse, she decided at last, trying to dismiss her disappointment by pretending it did not matter . . . much as she had learned to do with her father. She supposed the room reflected its lord well in that way.

After what seemed like an eternity, Lord Locksley pushed away his papers and turned toward his daughter; his blue gaze as he regarded her was inscrutable.

"It is your birthday today. You are what, seventeen?" he inquired of her abruptly.

"Eighteen, my lord," she corrected politely.

His gaze sharpened. "So old? And so tall. Almost as tall as I am, I think. That could be a problem. Still, you are strong, which is an asset not many girls can claim."

Robin nodded, mystified by this line of discourse.

"No doubt you are wondering why I sent for you," her father continued, returning to his papers. "I have a surprise for you. The details still need to be worked out, but I feel confident that after tonight, everything will fall into place. Consider it my birthday gift to you. Not many girls have your good fortune."

Robin patiently awaited further explanation, but her father seemed to have forgotten she was there. "Sir?" she ventured at last, when it became clear he did not intend to say anything more.

Scowling up from his work, he dismissed her with a wave of his hand.

Knowing better than to interrupt again, Robin gave him a dissatisfied curtsy and left the room, feeling more worried and confused than she had been before.

Darah sighed. It took Robin a moment to remember that it was now afternoon, not morning, and another moment to comprehend what had the housekeeper so worried. "Just as I thought: the dress is too short. Well, there is no time to fix it now — you will just have to wear it like that."

Robin gazed down at the gown in question. The linen was a handsome wine-red — a color that brought out the red highlights in her golden hair and the deep blue of her eyes. Its hem fell just above her ankles, which was what had Darah so dismayed. Aside from this shortcoming, the dress was perfect. The skirts were full, the waist was narrow, and the top exposed her throat in the latest fashion. It was the dress of a lady.

Robin hated it.

She suspected the dress would have bothered her less if not for the expectations that went along with it. Unlike her flamboyant cousin, Will Gamwell, Robin disliked social gatherings. She detested dressing up and she abhorred small talk, but most of all, she hated — hated! — dancing.

As though her thoughts had summoned the older boy, Will Gamwell suddenly poked his head into the room. "Are you ready yet?" her cousin demanded. He stepped inside the doorway, caught sight of her, and whistled. "Gads, Robin, you look like a lady!"

Then he ducked back out again to avoid the pillow Robin threw at him.

The party was everything Robin feared it would be. Minstrels played gaily from the musician's balcony at the back of the room, their music barely audible over the heavy chatter. Smoke rose from thick tallow candles and the wide hearth fire, casting a dark blue tinge across the whole assembly. Four trestle tables spanned the front half of the Hall and were laden with delectables that disappeared as fast as the servants could replace them. The second half of the manor Hall was filled with dancers.

Robin hung back in the shadows, hoping to avoid notice. She could not avoid Darah, however, who constantly appeared at her side, pushing her into the candlelight and more often than not into a man. To Robin's dismay, these men then felt it their social obligation to ask her to dance — some of them placing their request with more eloquence than others.

"Ah, Robin, Robin, ye're still growing. Soon no bed will hold ye and who will have ye then?" Lord Grenneth cackled merrily, already drunk. He grabbed Robin and pulled her onto the rush-strewn floor. "Dance with me."

For once in her life, Robin was glad of her height because it meant she could breathe the fresh air over Lord Grenneth's head, rather than his wine-drenched breath.

Her other dance partners were not much better — they were much shorter than she, and in general paunchy; all were impaired.

"I cannot bear much more of this," she confided to Will as he stole her away for an estampie. Sir Geoffrey, whom she had been partnering, looked disappointed — he was a full head shorter than Robin and had done nothing but stare at her chest the entire time.

Not that there is much there to look at, she thought.

"You are doing very well," Will reassured her as he led her through the gentle dance. It was the only respite she was to have all evening.

When the song ended, Robin saw an unfamiliar man with squinty eyes catch her gaze; he started towards her.

"Stay with me, please," she begged her cousin.

Will had seen the man, too, and his eyes were full of pity. "I cannot," he said. He sounded truly regretful. "I promised your sister the next dance."

"Marian will understand," Robin said, but she let him go.

"Lady Robin," a deep voice breathed behind her, and she reluctantly turned around to face the speaker.

He was taller than most men — almost as tall as she was — with a broad build and thick shoulders. His face was strong, with high cheekbones and a cloven chin. He was not young, but neither was he old. She might have found him handsome, if not for his eyes. They were small and black, with a sharp gleam that made the hairs on the back of her neck start to prickle. Robin had to fight down the urge to flee from that lupine stare.

Stop it! she scolded herself for her unreasoned reaction. *You do not even know him.*

"Lady Robin," the man repeated, grinning slightly.

"Sir — ?" she began, casting around her mind for an identity.

"Phillip. Just Phillip."

Robin raised a skeptical eyebrow. Her father never invited commoners to his feasts. Nevertheless, she returned his smile politely.

"Shall we?" he asked, extending his hand. His palm as he took hers was clammy.

The music was another estampie. Robin wished it were a ductia or a jig—some such dance that did not require her to stand so near her partner.

She moved to step away; he closed the gap between them.

The crowd jostled behind her. He pulled her closer. His breath was hot and smelled strongly of Brown October. She tried to step away, but his arms trapped her. The wolf-gleam was back in his eyes. "What do you think you are doing?" she hissed, surprising herself with the anger in her voice. Strangely, her ire seemed to please him.

"This," he smirked, and without further warning, kissed her squarely on the mouth.

Robin's eyes went wide, but for a moment she was too stunned to react. His lips, loose and wet, suffocated any protest. Gathering her senses, Robin tried to pull away, but the man held her tightly against his body. In desperation, she reached out and snatched at his hair, pulling his head back with a snap.

Phillip let her go, his face contorting with fury. For a moment, she thought he would strike her. Then a change spread over his features and to Robin's astonishment, the fury in his eyes altered to a sort of cunning humor. She followed his gaze over her shoulder and saw her father watching them from across the room, an amused smile on his face. It was the last straw. Her cheeks crimson with humiliation and rage, Robin fled the room as calmly as she could, holding her head high so as not to reveal her distress. Though she did not look back, she knew that Phillip was laughing.

Darah did not permit Robin to rage in her room for long. Indeed, Robin had barely slammed the heavy door shut when it burst open again and the matron strode inside.

"Return to the feast at once," she commanded fiercely. "Your absence insults your guests."

"Their *presence* insults *me!*" Robin shot back.

"What a ridiculous notion. Stop acting like a child and return to the feast, I demand it."

Indignation and hurt flared within Robin, yet it was clear she would get no sympathy from Darah regarding Phillip's assault. And indeed, why would she, when her own father so blatantly approved of his actions? In a voice so heated it could have tempered steel, Robin announced: "I do not give one twit what you or anyone else demand, I *refuse* to set foot amongst that crowd of drunken, debauched lords again!"

Five minutes later, two lackeys deposited a struggling Robin into the servant's passage just outside the Hall. The instant her feet touched the ground, she grew quiet. The screen separating the passage from the Hall was very thin, and a scene here would just mean further shame. Straightening her gown and ignoring the stares of the kitchen cooks, she stalked resentfully back into the Hall.

A young lord espied her entrance and promptly headed in her direction, his hand outstretched to ask for a dance. Robin glowered at him and he checked himself abruptly, gazing at her in confusion. When she intensified her scowl, he decided not to dance with her after all and turned away.

For a moment, Robin felt ashamed of herself, but she was too angry to let the feeling last for long. *Darah may have made me come back, but I will not dance again,* she promised herself, glaring at the assembly from her perch against the wall. *I care not how many lords I insult.*

She noted bitterly that Phillip was now sitting with her father on the dais, talking to him with great enthusiasm. As she watched, he seized a shank of chicken from a passing servitor's tray and began to gnaw at it as he spoke, sending bits of flesh flying.

Robin shuddered and looked away.

At least the other guests seem to be tiring, she observed with relief. *Soon all of this will be over.* But even though several lords had begun to drift into wine-dazed stupors where they sat, not one of them made to leave, nor would they until her father gave the traditional birthday toast.

Robin did not have to wait long, though she endured each delayed minute with rising impatience. Finally, Lord Locksley rose to his feet; grabbing an empty goblet, he banged its base loudly against the oaken table.

It took several tries before enough of the assembly noticed and fell quiet to make projected speech worthwhile. When he had their attention, her father raised his cup in salutation. His words as he spoke were only slightly slurred.

"Good evening, good evening my fine friends. No finer in all of Nottinghamshire!"

A roar of agreement met his statement.

"Thank you for coming to help celebrate the eighteenth birthday of my eldest daughter. She has grown up nicely, has she not? If she were a horse, she would bring me a fine profit—she has as many hands to her height as she has years to her credit!"

Laughter broke out across the room. Robin flushed from her corner. Why now that he had chosen to distinguish her, did he feel the need to embarrass her? It was better to be ignored.

Lord Locksley's mood turned sober. "However, she is not a horse. She is a young woman who has grown up almost without my noticing—certainly without my help. It is not fitting that a young woman should dwell with her father forever. Indeed, some of you have indicated that I have postponed this day for far too long.

"I cannot claim that the house will be quieter with her gone, for she has rarely seen fit to stay within its walls. But it certainly will be different. Happy birthday, Robin. I give you now the greatest gift a woman can hope to receive."

He paused for a moment to catch his breath. Robin clenched her hands until they turned white, almost ill with foreboding.

"Lords and ladies, it is my pleasure to announce the engagement of my daughter, Robin of Locksley, to Phillip Darniel, the Sheriff of Nottingham."

Robin froze in horror as Darniel rose to stand next to her father and the room burst into delighted applause.

2

PLIGHTED

"HOW COULD YOU NOT TELL ME!"

Robin's enraged exclamation startled her father, who had been gazing into the solar fire in deep contemplation while his manservant laid out his nightclothes. Both men turned to stare at the furious girl.

Robin felt herself flush, but she held her ground. She had dashed upstairs as soon as the last of her well-wishers would permit, determined to have a word with her father. Now, the anger and fear she had suppressed at his announcement surged forth unchecked: "Did you think I would welcome a surprise like that? — it was no gift! You should have told me!"

Lord Locksley considered Robin for a long moment before at last giving his servant a small nod of dismissal. Only after the man had left did he address his daughter.

"I will forgive your intrusion this once because I can see that you are upset. I did not reveal my plan to you, Robin, because I did not want to raise your hopes in case the Sheriff refused to have you; he made it a condition of the match to meet you first. I was worried that he would not want a bride taller than himself, but fortunately, he was willing to overlook that fact."

"Fortunately!"

"Yes, quite; though I *did* refrain from mentioning your affinity for the longbow, knowing you will, of course, renounce such a childhood fixation once you are married."

"Father—!" Robin nearly shouted, but then stopped and bit back the words she had been going to say. It would not do to lose her temper again. She must stay calm and make her father see reason.

"Father," she began anew, "surely this match cannot meet with your approval? I may not have met the Sheriff before tonight, but I have heard of him. He is a cruel man who cheats his subjects mercilessly."

Her father shrugged. "You should know better than to heed peasant talk."

Rather than argue the point, Robin hastily switched tactics. "Furthermore, he has a daughter nearly as old as I am."

Sir Robert of Locksley waved his hand through the air as though to brush away her concerns. "A man may grow weary of widowerhood no matter how old his children are. I have contemplated taking another wife myself."

"You have? But . . . wait a moment, that is not the issue here!" Robin cried, losing her tenuous hold on her temper.

Her father's heavy fist slammed against the chimney. "Why are you so resistant, Robin? I thought you would be pleased. Darniel may not be a lord, but he is rich—"

"At the expense of his taxpayers!"

" —and he is fast becoming a very powerful man. You cannot hope for a better alliance."

"Then why does he want to marry me? Surely a man with such . . . such *attributes* can have his pick of any woman. There are plenty of lords with richer estates and prettier daughters than I."

"The Sheriff craves a connection with the king," Sir Robert patiently explained. "We are his cousins, after all. And while it is true that you are much plainer than your sister, you are the eldest daughter and custom dictates that you must marry first."

Unaware of the insult he had just paid, he continued: "Robin, I am not a fool—I know exactly why the Sheriff desires this union. But he has promised to treat you well, and I expect he will hold to that promise, which is all any woman can ask."

"Are girls to be bartered away then like nags at market day, for naught more than the promise of good treatment? You lied when you said I was not a horse; I am nothing to you but a filly you can sell, never mind the character of the buyer —"

"Enough!" Lord Locksley's face was purple with rage. In spite of herself, Robin took a step back. "Enough. I see now how remiss I have been, letting you run around for years like a wild boar and permitting you to take up the bowman's art. Darah warned me that such negligence would have repercussions. You seem to think you are a man, with a man's right to choose his fate and to speak his mind. You are not a man, not even a boy. You are nothing but a girl, and it is high time you faced that fact. If it takes a husband breaking you to him to teach you your place in the world, so be it."

Stunned, Robin made one last plea for clemency. "Please, Father . . ."

His words thundered through the room. "The contract has been signed! In one month's time, you will marry the Sheriff of Nottingham."

Tears of bitterness welled in Robin's eyes, scalding her like fire. With the last vestige of pride she possessed, she turned on her heels and strode away before her father could see them fall.

Robin refused to come out of her room the next day or the day after that. On the third day, they sent Marian to talk with her.

Robin had been lying on her bed, wondering morosely if there were any chance Phillip Darniel might die of consumption before their wedding night, when Marian's soft knock broke through the gloom of her self-pity. She looked up to see her sister hovering just outside the doorway, her hands clasped in front of her and her eyes fixed on the stone floor as though afraid Robin would send her away if she met her gaze. Marian's meekness irritated her sister, but then Marian had never been one to rebel against the expectations of others — that had been Robin's purview.

Father is right, she thought without bitterness, breaking off her scrutiny and flopping over onto her back. *Marian is the beauty of the family.* With long brown hair, solemn blue eyes, and a petite yet womanly figure, Marian at fourteen was already more lovely than Robin could ever hope to be. In contrast, Robin's hair was flaxen and thin, her frame lean and tall; even the hue of her eyes was different. No one seeing them together for the first time would suspect the two girls of being sisters.

"Darah sent me," Marian began hesitantly, taking a tentative step into the room. "She thought you would rather see me than her."

Well, Darah is on the mark there.

Taking Robin's silence as permission to continue, Marian went on: "She wanted me to tell you how lucky you are, marrying the Sheriff. She says she never thought anyone would want you at all. She says — "

"Are you going to keep repeating what Darah said?" Robin demanded testily. "Because if you are, you can get out. Now."

Marian swallowed hard and fell silent.

"Maybe . . . maybe he will not be so bad," she ventured at last. "He is rather handsome, even if he is old."

"Are looks all that matter to you?" Robin asked in disgust. "I have heard enough stories from people I trust to know that in spite of his beauty, the Sheriff is a beast, not a man: stories of friends arrested without reason, of cracked ribs and cracked pates for nothing more than a misconstrued glance. He cares not if people are too poor to pay his taxes — in fact, he *rejoices* when they cannot pay, because then he can evict them from their land and seize it for himself. How do you think he got to be so rich?"

"Oh, Robin," Marian burst out. "I am sorry! I feel just awful for you."

"If you are trying to cheer me up, you are doing a miserable job," Robin muttered, but she sat up to face her sister at last.

Marian did indeed look wretched, her pretty face twisted in sympathy for her sister.

"It will be all right," Robin said, indicating with a pat that Marian could sit down beside her on the bed. "I will think of something."

"Well, there is nothing to be done, is there?" Marian asked pragmatically as she sank onto the coverlet. "The contract has been signed."

"Not by me."

Marian took a deep breath. "I would not want to marry him myself," she confessed, looking slightly shocked at her own daring, as though she had just spoken a great blasphemy.

Robin laughed without mirth. "Well, you shan't have to, shall you?"

"Is he *really* as bad as people say?" Marian asked quietly.

"Worse, probably."

Her sister shuddered.

All at once, Robin felt guilty. Marian was only fourteen, what could she know? Then again, most noblewomen were married by that age; Robin supposed she should be thankful that Lord Locksley's self-centered preoccupation had spared them the inevitable nuptials for so long. It occurred to her that having already arranged one marriage, Lord Locksley might decide to marry her sister off as well, and possibly to someone far worse than Phillip Darniel. (*Not*, Robin thought privately, *that there is likely to be anyone worse.*) No wonder Marian looked stricken.

"It will be all right," Robin repeated, wrapping her arms around her sister's slender shoulders. Her words were as much for Marian's comfort as for her own.

Their comfort was short-lived, however — Darah walked in.

"Ah, Robin!" she said brightly, interrupting the scene of intimate commiseration. "Your father wishes to discuss with you the comportment for the betrothal ceremony."

Robin ignored her.

"Now, Robin!"

"You had better go," Marian whispered, pulling out of her sister's embrace.

"If I were a boy," Robin protested angrily, rising to her feet, "no one would try to make me marry someone I did not wish to wed." That was not true, of course — at least, not when it came to lords — but Robin did not care. A boy could forgo his inheritance and apprentice himself to a trade, or hire himself out as a soldier if he did not like his potential mate. What options were there for a girl?

"You are not a boy," Darah told her bluntly, prodding Robin towards the door. Robin barely noticed. Her father's words and Darah's assertion formed a discordant duet in her head: *You are not a boy. You are not a boy.*

No, she thought, *but I could be.*

"Thank you, Marian," Robin called to her sister as Darah shoved her into the hall, her mind already conceiving a plan. "I feel much better now."

The betrothal ceremony took place three days later.

It was held in front of the manor so that the peasants who lived on Lord Locksley's land could witness the rite without having to enter the house. Will Gamwell thought it was foolish to make them come at all — the ceremony was, after all, little more than a formality since Lord Locksley and Phillip Darniel had signed the marriage contract several days before. Nevertheless, it was customary for the intended couple to publicly exchange oaths of fidelity and to state aloud the financial recompense should either of them break the engagement. Will supposed Lord Locksley wanted his people to observe this promise from their soon-to-be lord, never mind the inconvenience.

Will tugged at his scarlet collar and looked around again for his cousin, but failed to espy either Robin or her sister. His uncle, however, he could clearly see standing on the steps leading up to the Hall, talking quietly with the friar. Next to him stood Phillip Darniel, looking resplendent in a rich purple tunic and black hose. It did not seem right to Will that so horrible a man should appear so royally confident and calm. As for Lord Locksley — did he not realize the type of man he was consigning his daughter to?

Since the day Will had arrived at the manor thirteen years ago — an eight-year old boy reeling from the loss of his parents and uncertain of his welcome in a household that had recently suffered a loss of its own — Robin had been his constant companion. The two of them had been as light and shadow, inseparable. Even when Will had begun his training to be a woodward — one of Lord Locksley's private foresters — Robin had been there beside him, insisting that she be taught as well. Now, it was another she would have to follow, another whose words would be her law and master. That the Sheriff would be that man was almost unbearable.

"Here they come," someone said. Will turned his head and saw the women's train materialize from around the gabled east corner of the manor. As soon as his gaze locked on Robin, he frowned. There was something peculiar about her. It could not be the dress; it was the same one she had worn at the party. Neither was it the expression on her face; her visage was blank, and she looked to neither side as she walked. It was her whole demeanor, he realized — the way her shoulders stooped forward just a little; the way she took small, measured steps, not the long strides he was accustomed to seeing. Everything about her bespoke one thing: resignation.

Will felt as though someone had punched him in the gut. Where was the fiery girl he had grown up with? It could not be this subdued creature climbing the stairs — it could not be!

He knew that Robin had fought with her father over the match — by George, he had gone and confronted the man himself! She abhorred this union as much as he did; surely she could not have given up?

Yet it appeared that she had. Will was too far away to hear what was being said, but if he expected his cousin to put her foot down, to throw the contract in the Sheriff's face or to refuse to say her vows, he was sorely disappointed. The ceremony was over almost before it began, and Robin and her father disappeared into the Hall. A purple-clad servant who had been holding the Sheriff's horse throughout the ritual now brought it forth, and the Sheriff mounted his steed and rode off towards Nottingham without a backwards glance.

Muttering about the brevity of the ceremony, the crowd began to disperse. Rather than following his family into the house, Will ambled down the path that led to the garden, brooding over what he had witnessed.

Clearly, Robin did not intend to make a public defiance . . . unless she was waiting until the actual wedding? If so, she had better rethink her intention; Lord Locksley would consign her to a convent if she embarrassed him like that. Will needed to talk with her, to find out what she was planning. Surely, the two of them together could come up with some scheme, some hope . . . .

Robin's face flashed once more through Will's mind, her look of abject surrender filling him with a bleak despair that he hastily shoved aside.

He could not—would not—believe what that look had told him: that Robin of Locksley had given up.

3

FLIGHT

ROBIN AWOKE SUDDENLY and silently. She lay still in her bed for a moment, listening intently. Outside her window, the summer wind whistled softly. A few wakeful crickets tried to tune their wings to the same pitch as the breeze, with limited success. In the distance, a hound bayed. No noise emanated from inside the stone house.

Assured that everyone was asleep, Robin pushed back her covers and rolled out of bed, her motions silky and fluid so as not to disturb her sister. She need not have worried: Marian did not even twitch.

Yet another difference between us, Robin mused as she got down on her hands and knees and felt around under the bed. *Marian is a sound sleeper.*

After a moment's groping in the dark, her fingers discovered the bundle she had secreted there, and she pulled it out. The sack contained some food and wine, her steel and flint, a swathe of cloth, and a few jewels and coins. It also held Will's spare forester outfit, which she had ignobly filched and then pled ignorance to when he had complained it was missing.

Robin contemplated the attire for a long moment. The law forbade a woman to dress above her class, or below it for that matter, so she could only imagine what the consequence would be if she were discovered to be wearing men's clothing. Yet that danger was nothing compared to the perils a woman faced by traveling alone. And Robin's plan called for her to travel far. For safety's sake and to keep from being identified, she would have to take on the guise of a man.

Soundlessly, she slipped off her shift; taking out the swathe of cloth from the sack, she used it to bind her chest flat. It took several attempts before Robin puzzled out how to fold the cloth so it would not fall apart or bulge awkwardly. The binding hurt; she had not expected that.

Next, she pulled on Will's tunic and the woolen hose traditionally worn by men. The boots she put on were her own. Finally, she belted the diminished bundle to her waist.

Though she was completely dressed, she felt strangely naked, her attire too light after a lifetime of being encased by weighty gowns. To step out into the world like this seemed . . . indecent. Shaking off the unexpected sensation, Robin hastened to plait her long hair and stuff the braid down her collar.

Only one last thing to do. From the bundle at her waist, Robin drew out a forester's hood. The hood was designed to cover her shoulders like a very short cape, and it had a cowl that could be pulled up over her head. As Robin put it on, she discovered that it also possessed a liripipe — a length of fabric in the back that she could wrap around her neck for warmth;

it would also help to hide her face and keep the hood from slipping down.

Her disguise was complete. It was time to go.

Robin eased opened the bedroom door and prepared to step outside . . . but a surge of conscience brought her to a halt. She teetered for a moment, indecisive, and then swiftly made her way back to the bed that she had shared with her sister for as long as she could remember.

"Farewell, Marian," Robin whispered, kissing her sister lightly on the cheek. Marian stirred, but did not wake. "I love you."

Then with three long strides, she was out the door.

Robin's plan was simple: to put as much distance between herself and the Sheriff of Nottingham as possible.

She had timed her escape to perfection. The moonlight tonight was bright and would allow her to travel far while reducing her risk of ambush. While it did increase the chance that someone might spot her leaving, she doubted that anyone would be awake to see — with only a week left until the wedding, everyone at Locksley Manor was too exhausted to do anything at night but sleep.

Everyone except for her.

She had chosen her escape route with care. Leaving through the kitchen was impossible — Darah always locked the servants' entrance to keep them from sneaking in and stealing silver or food. Likewise, the door to the Hall would be locked, with a guard stationed just inside it. Nor were there any windows on the first floor through which she could escape, but Robin did not need them.

Once, when she was ten, Darah had locked her in the buttery as punishment for a harmless prank involving a new dress and scissors. Robin had spent one minute pouting and then begun to investigate her temporary abode. She had followed the buttery staircase down to the beer cellar and discovered that the cellar was just the first in a series of subterranean storage chambers. During the Manor's more prosperous days, they had been filled with beer casks and candles. Now, the rooms were filled with spider webs and fallen masonry, the thick layers of dust disturbed only by rat imprints. It had clearly been many years since another human had ventured there.

Seized with an exuberant curiosity, Robin had snatched a rushlight from its nip and set about exploring this neglected territory. Her enthusiasm soon waned, however, when she had nothing to show for her trouble except dirty hands and mussed clothes. Only in the last chamber did she find something of interest — a broken staircase and a small trapdoor at the top that, after much exertion and several showers of dirt, had opened out onto the floor of an old guard hut. Why it was there she had never found out, because she had never told anyone she had discovered it — except for Will, of course. She told Will everything.

Well, Robin mentally amended, feeling the pain of the correction, *almost everything*. She had not told him she was planning to run away. He alone had seemed to suspect that she did not intend to calmly acquiesce to this marriage, and she had not dared to confide in him and risk his trying to stop her. She had evaded his suspicions as well as she could, primarily by evading him. Robin wished she could have said farewell.

Heat filled her eyes at the thought of leaving her dearest friend, but Robin ignored the sensation, creeping down the newel staircase and into the screens passage that separated the kitchen from the Hall.

Tentatively, she peeked into the foyer. A guard sat upon a stool by the main door, his head nodding gently against his chest. The door to the buttery lay within his line of sight, but if she were very quiet, she would not disturb him.

Robin focused on edging open the door as silently as possible; she was so intent on this that she did not notice the guard suddenly start awake, nor see his keen eyes flash in her direction.

At last the door opened, and Robin let out the breath she had not realized she had been holding. Hastily, she glanced at the guard, but his sleep seemed sound. For a moment, Robin allowed herself to look past him, filling her sight with the home that was home no more. Then taking a deep breath, she squared her shoulders and disappeared into the buttery.

The guard waited one minute, then another, before rising from his languor and following Robin into the dark.

Robin emerged from the old guard shack covered in dirt and with a few bumps and bruises she did not have before, but on the whole very pleased with her escape.

As she stepped out onto the manor grounds, she felt her breath catch. How often had she peered from her window at night to see these lands stretched out beneath her? But never once had she been allowed to stand outside like this, alone in the dark, and to feel their calm serenity all around her. Robin gazed about in wonder.

Silvery moonlight made the air shine as bright as a hundred rushlights, washing out the stars with its glow. Beyond the edge of the yard, past the stables and the barn, the acres of planted grain gleamed white in the night, their stalks billowing softly in the warm summer breeze. In the distance, Robin could make out the outline of cottages on the opposite side of the river — the homes of the peasants who tilled her father's lands. Beyond those dwellings stood the dark trees of Sherwood Forest.

Robin turned around one last time. Against the shimmering air, her father's house stood disapproving and black.

I do not need your approval, her soul challenged back. *Not now, nor ever again.*

With a sudden surge of energy, she began to trot towards the shed where she and the woodwards kept their spare equipment.

The shed was small — just a wooden shanty, its slats plastered with daub to keep out the rain. Robin had brought no candle, but she found that if she left the door open and untied her hood so that it fell back and no longer shadowed her face, the moon afforded more than enough light to let her see.

The woodwards kept the shanty in neat order — bows against one wall, quivers upon another, and shelves of arrow sheaves and arm bracers lined up against the third. Until now, Robin had always used blunts — headless arrows that would pierce a target butt or stun a rabbit but not kill a man if accidentally miss-shot. She reached for a sheaf of them by habit, but as her hand closed around the arrows, she paused. She would be traveling far, through unknown forests and lands. She would need to protect herself against wolves and other dangers, and to hunt for food as well.

Robin put down the blunts and instead picked up a sheaf of clothyard arrows — giant killers that could bring down an armored man with ease. The quiver she placed them in was longer than her usual one, in order to accommodate the arrows' extra length, and had a sheath attached to it for her bow. The bracer that would guard her left arm against whip-lash from the bowstring, she shoved into the sack at her waist. As an afterthought, Robin seized a packet of spare strings from the top shelf and tucked them into her sack as well.

When she turned to the east wall to pluck her bow off its prop, however, Robin felt her determination falter.

Will had given her this bow for her fifteenth birthday. It was yew—an expensive gift for any man to give, let alone one who had barely attained his eighteenth year. The pied wood was just as silky smooth as when she had first received it, and was completely unadorned except at the grip, where the bowyer had carved her name. Robin forced herself to sheathe her bow and swing the quiver across her back, stifling the urge to sob. Will would never forgive her for failing to say farewell.

Casting a final look around the shack, Robin could see nothing she might have forgotten to pack and turned to leave.

A man stood in the doorway, blocking her egress.

"What in the name of Saint Christopher are you doing?" he demanded fiercely, stepping inside.

"Will?" Robin gawked at him, taken completely by sur-prise. Her cousin glared at her grouchily, his arms crossed, but with a gleam of relief in his eyes that she found puzzling. "Will, whatever are you doing here?"

"I should think that was obvious. I followed you. The real question is, why are *you* here, and dressed like that?" His gaze seemed to take in her attire for the first time. "Wait a minute—are those *my* clothes?"

Robin blushed. "Um, yes."

"You told me you had no idea what happened to them!"

"Actually, what I said was that I had not seen them recently, which was technically true since I had hidden them away three days before you asked—why on earth are you grinning like that?" Robin demanded as Will's face split into a wide smile.

Will simply grinned broader. "I am just glad to have you back." His grin faded. "Only, I do not have you back, do I? You are leaving."

"Yes." Robin turned away so that she would not have to face him. "I know what you will say, cousin, but you cannot dissuade me. Oh, you can force me to return with you, but I promise to just run away again. You will have to watch me every second of every day, even after I am married. You had better let me go."

Will cleared his throat. "I have no intention of stopping you."

She looked at him in surprise. "Oh."

"Where will you go?" he asked instead.

Relieved that Will was not going to try to deter her, Robin told him gladly: "I think I will try for London, for the King's court. Surely, he will see a cousin. I am going to ask for a place in his household. Even the life of a lady-in-waiting would be preferable to a life as the Sheriff's wife."

"I see." The shadows made Will's face inscrutable. "London is a long way away."

"Are you trying to frighten me from going?"

"Never."

Robin harrumphed.

"I want you to take my horse," Will announced abruptly. "They will not expect you to get far on foot. It will give you a good head start. I would give her to you completely, but she is too fine a mount for a commoner and would attract attention. You had best leave her at the Blue Boar Inn — the innkeeper knows me and will recognize my horse; he will see that I get her back. You will have to go the rest of the way on foot."

"Why are you helping me?" Robin asked him, bewildered. "I thought for sure you would try to stop me."

"Have I ever been able to stop you before?" he demanded wryly.

Robin shook her head. It was too much. "Come with me," she begged, seizing him in a sudden embrace. Will gripped her tightly, burying his beard in her hair. She never knew until much later how close he actually came to accepting.

"No," he said at last, stepping out of her hold and speaking as if from a great distance. "They would never stop hunting us if we both ran away. Besides, I am on guard duty tonight — I can say that you were anxious about the wedding and went for a ride to calm your nerves. If I tell them you went out at dawn and headed north, it will give you more time to get away."

Robin nodded, a tight feeling in her throat. Will reached out as if to stroke her cheek; instead, he took her hand and led her to the stables.

Robin saddled Will's chestnut mare while her cousin readied the stirrups and the bridle. The horse, not accustomed to being handled in the middle of the night, whickered loudly and stomped in place. Will stroked its neck, murmuring reassurances in the mare's restless ears. At last, she calmed down and allowed her master to finish putting on her tack.

"I guess this is farewell, then," Robin said dully, finding herself unable to meet Will's eyes; she looked at the hay-strewn ground instead.

"Robin . . ." he began softly, but when she still did not

look at him, he sighed and unbuckled the sword at his waist. "Here," he said, "I want you to take this, too."

Robin drew back in amazement. "I cannot," she whispered, pushing the scabbard back toward him. "I know how much it means to you."

"You mean more. Take it," he urged, when she opened her mouth to refuse again. "Please. I want you to be able to protect yourself as well as possible."

Robin reluctantly closed her hands around the sheath. This was the sword that Lord Locksley had given to Will the day he had become a man, with a man's duties and rights. It was her cousin's most prized possession. She offered one last protest.

"But I do not even know how to use it."

"You know enough."

Unbidden, a memory from six years ago bubbled to the forefront of her mind, of two children practicing swordplay with shoots of cedar, and all the trouble those innocent lessons had caused. Robin shook her head. That was a memory for another time.

"Thank you, Will. I promise to keep it safe," she relented, buckling the sword onto her belt.

"I know you will." He reached out and pulled Robin's hood over her head, wrapping the liripipe around her throat just tight enough so that the hood would not fall down. For one moment, Robin saw indecision flicker deep within Will's eyes — indecision, and something else. Then with a sigh, he drew her to him and kissed her on the forehead, and in one unbroken motion picked her up and deposited her in the saddle.

"Take care of yourself, Robin," he whispered, stepping back into the shadows of the stall.

Not trusting herself to speak over the sudden lump in her throat, she merely nodded. Taking the reins in her hands, Robin kicked the horse into a gallop so that its hooves churned the grass and its strides filled the air with silver clouds of dust as she turned the mare onto the High Road to London. Though she did not look back, she could sense Will watching her go long after she had ridden beyond his sight.

Horse and rider raced across the dusky countryside, flying over the thin wooden bridge that spanned the river, past the cottages that speckled the manor land, and down the slim dirt road that was the only highway through Nottinghamshire. Once in the next county, that thoroughfare would connect with Fosse Way, and then eventually with Watling Street, after which it would be a straight ride to London.

But first, the road had to go through Sherwood Forest.

Dark trees blurred past Robin, at times no more than a black palisade streaking by on either side, at times so close that she could feel their feathery touch on her cheeks where the road was especially narrow. Sherwood Forest was immense — several days slow walk on foot, slightly more than a day by horse. The inn Will had mentioned lay two-thirds of the way from Locksley to Nottingham Town. If she could reach the inn before dawn, she could leave the horse there and disappear into the forest with no one the wiser.

Robin cast a furtive look at the sky. It had to be near dawn now. Already the sky was starting to look slightly lighter — a faint mauve rather than a deep violet. Beneath her legs, Will's chestnut mare heaved heavily, foam streaking along its cheeks and blowing up into Robin's face. Robin felt bad for riding the horse so hard, but she had to reach the inn before people began to awaken.

"Come on, girl," Robin whispered, patting the mare on her side. "Just a little bit farther. Then you can rest."

Please, let it be just a little bit farther.

The sky was a pallid blue by the time she reached the Blue Boar Inn. She rode the horse right into the hostelry's small yard; fatigued, it took nearly all of her strength to dismount. Though she could see that the door to the inn was closed, she knew that like all inn doors, it would be unlocked. She had only to enter and call out for the host, and a hot cup of cider would be forthcoming and most glorious of all, a bed.

Enough. Assuming that the innkeeper did not think she had stolen Will's horse and betray her to a soldiering guest, he would still remember her. He would be quick to realize that Lord Locksley's missing daughter and the mare's lissome rider were one and the same. Stay at the inn, and she might as well return home right now.

Shaking her head at her own wistful folly, Robin led the mare over to the water trough — the poor beast drank greedily, slurping at the water with desperate need. The mare was clearly spent, its sides heaving with every breath, its coat slick with sweat.

"Poor girl," Robin murmured.

She removed the saddle from the horse's back and let it drop to the ground, and then took the blanket the saddle had sat on and used it to wipe down the mare. Wet though the blanket was, she was tempted to take it with her, but it would be burdensome to carry and difficult to explain if she were seen with it, bearing as it did the Locksley crest. Better just to leave it here.

Leading the horse over to the hitching post, Robin tied her fast and set the saddle and blanket on the ground nearby. The mare was so worn out that she did not even try to nibble on the hay scattered by the post, but sank down onto the dirt with what might almost have been a sigh.

Guilt gnawed at Robin for just leaving her there, but she had done all that she could afford to do. Taking the horse into the stable would undoubtedly wake the stable boy, and that she could not chance. Besides, the innkeeper would be up very soon, and Will had said that he knew the horse; he would take care of her.

Now that she had seen to the mare, the adrenaline that had sustained Robin throughout her ride vanished, leaving in its place an exhaustion so complete that it made her sinews tremble with the effort of remaining upright. Only sheer determination propelled her across the road and into the boughs of the forest, carrying her through the thick under-brush until she was veiled from view.

Letting her bow and quiver slide from her back, Robin sank onto the ground. It took four tries before her tired fingers could grip her belt tightly enough to unbuckle it, freeing her from her sword and sack. With the last of her strength, Robin pulled her weapons within easy reach; she was asleep before her fingers had let them go.

☙ 4 ❧

INTO THE FOREST

SOMETHING HARD was digging into Robin's side.

"Stop it, Marian," she growled, rolling over. Perversely, her sister just seemed to jab harder. "All right, all right, I am getting up—enough already!"

Robin opened her eyes to a world that was clearly not her bedchamber. Lush green branches danced lazily overhead, dazzling against the summer sun. The sharp smell of pinesap flooded her nose, and the sweet chirruping of birds chorused in her ears.

"Oh," she whispered, recalling her flight the night before and the sad truth that she would likely never see Marian or Will again. "Right."

For a moment, Robin just lay where she was, absorbing the unfamiliar forest. At last, she pushed herself to her feet, her fingers clutching at the roots and rocks that had formed her lackluster bed.

"Whoever said sleeping on the ground was good for you was *such* a liar," she winced.

With a groan, she began to stretch as the woodwards had taught her to do, slowly but surely excising the stiffness from her limbs. When she could move freely again, Robin dug around in her sack for something to eat.

The coarse bread she drew out was by now more than slightly stale, but she did not mind. It tasted wonderful. It tasted like freedom. Exhilaration outbalanced her regret, and Robin began to laugh.

The next instant, she clapped a hand to her mouth, her glee vanishing as quickly as it had come. "I sound like a girl," she whispered against her fingers, horror-struck.

In planning her escape, Robin had not considered the pitch of her laughter or her voice, but now she realized that for her disguise to bear up, she would not only have to look like a boy, but to talk and laugh like one as well. The only question was: could she?

Feeling more than a little absurd, Robin tried to imitate the hearty bellow of Locksley's head cook, but it sounded breathy and forced to her ears. Her cousin's cheerful guffaw was beyond her ability as well. In the end, she settled on a rumbling chuckle that was deeper than any sound she had ever produced.

Trying to talk like a man proved even more difficult. No matter what she tried, her voice sounded feigned to her ears and her words stilted. A few times she thought she had finally mastered the trick of it, but then a high note would turn her hopes to dust.

Maybe I should just act mute and have done with it! she thought in exasperation. Mutes were rare, though, and pretending to be one would draw far too much attention to herself once she started passing through towns on her journey to London. Resolutely, Robin began her attempts anew.

At last, she discovered that by exaggerating her pronunciation and by speaking as though she were delivering her words from her belly and not her throat, her voice came out sounding natural and deep. True, deep for her was still rather high for a man, but since people would assume she was a boy when they looked at her, Robin thought her pitch would be low enough to avoid suspicion.

She practiced speaking in this new manner until it became instinctive and sustainable. By the time she was satisfied, the sun had sunk low in the sky and the shadows around her grown long. If she planned to travel any distance before dark, she would have to leave now.

It was barely the work of a minute for Robin to gather her things; the sun told her which way was south, and her strides as she walked through the brush were long and confident.

She felt like a knight errant, picking her way through the forest in search of adventure. Feathery bracken tickled her legs and brushed its thick fronds against her hips. Tall trees soared up above Robin's head—tapered pines with their waxy, blue-green needles; spindly birches with their peeling, white trunks; thick oaks trying to dominate the airscape; broad beech trees, and others that she did not know the names of. Shrubs and ferns filled the spaces between the trees, and where they did not, wild grasses and multi-hued flowers suffused the forest floor.

Life teemed within the verdant growth—squirrels and throstles shook the branches, larks popped out of their burrows to gaze at Robin curiously, and downy brown rabbits darted across her path and then sat, ears pricked and noses quivering, as if to ask what manner of strange creature was

this? Robin knew that eventually she would have to kill one of
those rabbits for her supper, but for now she enjoyed watching them bound.

More rarely, but most majestic of all were her sightings of
the deer that populated the King's forest. Great red harts and
smaller roe deer walked the woods with a regal air, eyeing
her condescendingly and leaping haughtily away when she
approached, as if they could not bear to be in such an inferior
presence.

You are so beautiful, she thought with awe as a russet stag
flitted through the ferns. He paused for a moment as though
sensing her thoughts, and she could swear she saw his eyes
twinkle at her through the twilight.

"And you know it, too!" she called aloud, her deep tone
startling them both.

Soon the sun had set too low for her to comfortably see,
and Robin began to look for a suitable place to spend the
night. As might be expected, the moment she considered
stopping was the moment her feet and calves started to
cramp, and the quarter-mile she walked before finding a
space sufficiently devoid of tree roots and stones felt twice as
long as her entire journey.

Fortunately, obtaining some dinner proved much easier.
Robin had barely to wander a dozen yards from her chosen
rest site before she espied a large rabbit emerging from its
burrow and shot an arrow cleanly through its neck.

Now for the part she hated. Darah had made her learn
how to skin, gut, and cook a variety of animals, in case her
husband ("Assuming," the woman had frequently stressed,
"that there *is* someone willing to marry a girl who cannot
even embroider!") could not afford to keep servants. Robin
did not mind the cooking, but she found the gutting repulsive.

"Let us just get this over with, shall we?" she suggested to the rabbit, turning it over in her hands. But when she reached into her sack for her dagger, Robin discovered that she had forgotten to pack it. Cursing herself for a dolt, she unsheathed Will's sword, but quickly found that attempting to wield the blade with one hand and hold the rabbit steady with the other was not only a frustrating task, but a nearly impossible one as well. In the end, she gave up and — muttering imprecations against all blades — tugged an arrow from her quiver and used its sharp tip to skin and gut the coney instead.

That unpleasantness done, Robin built a small fire and found a pair of sticks to spit the rabbit on. Soon the aroma of sizzling juices was wafting through the forest, and Robin had to sit on her hands to keep from seizing the meat off the spit before it had finished cooking. After what seemed like an eternity to her hungry belly, the rabbit was ready to eat. Just as she was rising to remove the meat from the fire, a boisterous voice called out:

"Ho, there!"

Robin whipped around, seized her bow, and nocked an arrow before the greeting had a chance to die fully away. The man who had entered her camp looked startled.

"Hold off," he called, raising one hand in benign defense. His other hand held a stout cudgel, which he leaned against as he watched her. His eyes were keen. "I mean you no harm, lad."

"Who are you?" Robin demanded suspiciously, not lowering her bow.

He smiled broadly, showing teeth that gleamed in the firelight. "My name is John Little. Who are you?"

"Robin," she replied automatically, and then chided herself for not having thought of a pseudonym. In fact, why was she telling this stranger her name at all?

"Well Robin, I—hey, your rabbit is burning."

"Oh!"

Dropping her bow, she seized her makeshift spit and pulled the rabbit off the fire, wincing as it burned her hands. Too late, she realized that she had let down her defense, but when she whirled back around, the stranger had not moved. He stared at her curiously.

"Um, would you like some?" she asked, self-consciously holding out the rabbit.

Without the aid of a trencher or cloth, the coney was messy to eat, but tasty enough that neither person cared. They sat on opposite sides of the fire, which allowed Robin to surreptitiously study the stranger over her food. If he noticed, he gave her no sign and let her look as much as she needed.

Robin knew herself to be tall, but this man was a giant— she might just come to the top of his shoulder if they stood side by side. Those shoulders were broad, his build muscular, yet trim. Golden hair curled tightly against his neck and glinted on his arms and formed a thick beard that framed his face. That face held a nose that was slightly crooked, faded eyebrows, and high cheekbones; his eyes were pale blue.

Robin thought she should be frightened of a man like this, but oddly, she was not. Maybe it was the way he smiled as he ate his food, or the unconscious way he ran his hand through his hair. He had greeted her as if he had nothing to fear, in spite of her nocked arrow. And he had not tried to take advantage of her distraction with the rabbit. She did not trust him, of course, but she no longer felt threatened by him, either.

"So," he said lightly, breaking her out of her thoughts, "am I to be let live?"

His facetious question made her mouth quirk up in a small smile. "I would hardly feed you otherwise."

He laughed. "Indeed, we must not waste good food." His grin was infectious, and Robin felt her own smile broaden in response.

"There, that is better. Even outlaws should have a sense of humor."

"I am no outlaw," Robin answered hotly.

"A forester then?" John asked dubiously.

"No."

John Little frowned. "Yet you carry clothyard arrows," he observed.

"Is that a problem?"

"It is if you are not a forester. Carrying unblunted arrows means you are here to hunt deer, and only the King's foresters can lawfully kill deer in the King's forest—well, foresters and nobles, but no one would mistake us for that! Where are you from, that you do not know this?"

"Oh, um, from Doncaster," she said, naming a village far to the north.

John looked skeptical at her answer, but did not press. Courtesy might dictate that travelers offer food and fire to one another, but that was where their obligation ended. If this Robin lad chose not to state his true home, well, that was his right.

"I suggest you keep your arrows in your quiver, then. Otherwise, the next person you point them at might arrest you for poaching," he advised.

"But I have killed no deer!"

"You will never be able to prove it. Those shafts will condemn you before any magistrate. Of course, that assumes the forester who catches you even bothers to take you in. Most would just shave your ears off there and then." Seeing her expression, he added kindly, "Do not take this the wrong way, lad. I am just trying to warn you, lest you get into trouble."

"Thank you," Robin said. "I will be more careful from now on."

John Little nodded. "Are you traveling far?" he asked, some part of him uneasy for the youth with the innocent eyes.

Robin shook her head. "Just to Radford," she lied, naming the next village in her path.

"I am headed there myself," he yawned. "I plan to win some provisions at their fair."

"What are you competing in?" Robin asked curiously.

"Cudgeling."

For the first time, Robin realized that the staff by his side was not a walking stick, but a weapon.

"I daresay you are going for the archery contest. I hear that the Sheriff is offering a fat butt of wine to the winner," John Little surmised.

"Erm, yes. Yes I am."

"Good. We can travel together."

Robin did not see how she could refuse without betraying her story, so she just nodded. In truth, it would be nice to have someone to travel with for at least part of the trip . . . safer, too. She could always slip away once they reached Radford.

Brushing his hair back from his eyes with a sleepy smile, John Little stood up and began to tear off fronds from a near-by fern. Once he had fashioned a decent-sized headpad, he lay down upon it with a groan. Robin copied him, trying to make it appear like she utilized fern pillows all the time.

The fire popped; Robin mused drowsily that it would die soon and she should feed it, but the night air was warm and there was no real need. Besides, she was comfortable. She shifted slightly, and a sharp rock dug into her back. So much for comfort. With a small sigh, she reached behind her and tossed it away.

"Good night, Robin," John called softly, his body a mere lump of shadow against the flickering embers.

Her reply was a sleepy whisper, "Good night."

To her delight, Robin found that she enjoyed John Little's company. He talked merrily as they walked, naming trees and animals for her benefit. Often he made jokes — he had a wry humor that he was not afraid to ply at his own expense as well as at hers. She discovered that he was a farmer from Mansfield, which explained his broad shoulders, and that he hoped to get noticed by a lord at the fair and to earn a position as a retainer. Casting a look up at John — she actually had to look up to talk with him! — Robin chortled softly to herself. *How could a person possibly* not *notice John?*

Sometimes they passed other travelers in the forest. A few, like John, were simply shortcutting their way through the Sherwood; others looked like they might be permanent residents. Fortunately, no one paid the duo more heed than it took to give a brief greeting or a nod. Robin doubted that this would have been the case had John's towering presence not been beside her, and once again she was grateful for his company; she would be sorry to part with her loquacious guardian when they arrived at Radford tomorrow.

"What is it with these accursed pebbles?" Robin griped, pulling off her boot for the third time that afternoon. "Do they see my shoe and think: *Here comes a good piece of calfskin, let us hitch a ride and see the world?* I mean, honestly!"

"Radford is hardly the world," John remarked absently. He was standing beside Robin, but his head was turned away, and he was peering intently into the trees.

"To a pebble, I am sure it is the universe and beyond. What *are* you looking at?" Robin demanded irritably, stomping back into her boot.

"There are people out there," John told her. "Hush."

She obeyed. Now that she was quiet, she could hear the rise and fall of voices, and when she looked at where John was gazing, she saw distant flashes of color between the trees.

"Foresters," he informed her quietly. "Patrolling the verge. Keep your arrows in your quiver."

"I was planning to," Robin replied, a little indignant that he thought she needed reminding. All the same, she strung her bow. "Why are we whispering? They are only foresters."

John looked at her askance. "You must have led a very sheltered life if you do not know enough to avoid the Sheriff's foresters when you can. They like to accuse people of poaching and then take their purses in exchange for not cutting off their ears or hauling them before the courts."

Robin grimaced. She hated corruption more than anything. "Surely, we can just avoid them?"

"They will have heard you ranting," John said, resettling his grip on his staff. "Avoiding them now would make it seem as though we have something to hide. If they think we are outlaws, they might decide to shoot us first and check for warrants later."

"What should we do, then?"

"What we would normally do—keep walking. If we are lucky, they will not bother us."

Such a blessing was not destined to be theirs, however—the voices kept growing stronger. Within minutes of the pair's casual ambling, the shrubbery ahead of them began to tremble and quake; with a loud snap, its limbs parted and five foresters stepped into view, looking unlike any woodwards Robin had ever seen.

Rather than wearing the brown-green garments most foresters preferred, these men were attired in deep purple livery. Each man flaunted a purple tunic and hose, along with black leather boots and a belt. A black leather quiver hung from their backs, and in addition to the bow they bore, each man wore a broadsword strapped to his waist.

Their leader moved to block the path, raking Robin and John as he did so with a contemptuous stare. He looked familiar, somehow, but Robin was certain she had never seen him before. His top lip curled up in a sneer. "Well, well, what have we here? A scion and a burly giant . . . who went and brought back David and Goliath from the Crusades?" he mocked.

"Good day to you, too," John offered pleasantly, leaning against his staff.

"What is your business traveling through the Sherwood?" the man asked, ignoring John's implied rebuke. He cast an eye at Robin's quiver and the bow clenched in her hand. "Hunting?"

"Hardly," Robin said. "We go to fair."

"The Radford fair? A green lad like you with no more marrow to his bones than a starving child — planning to compete? That is rich," the forester hooted. His companions, taking their cue from him, laughed as well. Robin felt her face grow hot.

"I *was* planning to compete, but if it is true that a town's best archers are its foresters, then maybe I should not bother. I could beat any of you. But perhaps that is why the Sheriff made you foresters—he need not fear you killing any of the King's deer except by accident."

Anger flashed in the man's eyes. "Mighty words for one so young. Can you prove them?"

"I can."

"Then defend your boast. There is a herd of deer at the end of this glade. Twenty marks say you cannot hit a hart from 300 paces, let alone kill it.

"Done!" Robin cried, reaching confidently for an arrow. Her arm was arrested midair. It was the first time John had ever touched her, and she froze in surprise. His hand was large and coarse and very strong—she could no more reach for an arrow now than she could fell an oak with a sneeze.

"Do not tease the youth," John commanded. "If he shot a deer, you would pay him back with your steel blades, not with marks. If you want to challenge someone, challenge me." He gripped his staff in warning. Robin got the impression that not many people cared to challenge John.

The forester stared at him, incredulous. "Do you know who I am?" he demanded. "I am the Sheriff of Nottingham's nephew! One word from me and the two of you would be strung up from the nearest tree, whether you had shot a deer or not."

"Oh, you are his *nephew!*" Robin gasped imprudently, as if struck by a sudden revelation. "Well, that explains your bad manners, then; I suppose you cannot help your bad looks."

The yeoman gargled in fury, and his hand seized the hilt of his sword. A look of cunning stole over his face. "My uncle has charged me with protecting the King's deer from poachers and ensuring that the King's people obey his law. You do not look like good law-abiding citizens to me," he hissed.

"Doubtless, you have forgotten to pay your taxes. We will have them from you now."

Out of the corner of her eye, Robin saw John Little tighten his grip on his cudgel, his knuckles gleaming white. Surreptitiously, she wiped her free hand on her tunic. Her fingers itched for her quiver; the sword at her hip hung forgotten.

"You are welcome to collect, if you can," John said with a grim smile.

The other foresters stepped up next to their leader. Altogether, there were five of them to her two. *Good odds*, Robin thought recklessly.

The leader feinted with his sword, and John clouted him on the shoulder with his staff. Another came in from the side, and he pummeled him in the ribs. Robin saw a third man attempting to string his bow, and she struck him hard across the face with her own; John finished him off with a crack to the crown.

The fourth and fifth foresters attacked simultaneously, their swords biting deeply into John's cudgel. As he attempted to shrug them off and free his weapon, Robin saw the Sheriff's nephew rise up behind him, his sword held aloft to deliver the killing blow.

It was over in a second. With a drowning gurgle, the purple-liveried man sank to his knees, Robin's arrow quivering through his heart.

When the others saw what had happened to their leader, those who were able to dropped their weapons and fled, leaving their fallen comrades behind. John Little stood up slowly from his defensive crouch, his gaze taking in the murdered man and Robin's shocked expression.

"Robin?"

Without a word, she turned and fled, tripping over roots and rocks in her haste to get away.

"Robin!"

John Little's voice faded into the distance as her feet pounded the dirt. Robin ran desperately, barely noticing the tree branches that whipped at her arms and face, leaving long red streaks where they struck. She was filled with a terrible anguish—the knowledge that she had killed a man who probably did not deserve to die, and whom she had provoked to his death through intransigent pride.

Panic and shame bore her deep into the forest, until her legs gave out beneath her and she tumbled to the base of a massive oak. Curling into a trembling ball, Robin allowed dark oblivion to claim her.

⚔ 5 ⚔

A REFUGE

TIME PASSED SLOWLY for Robin. For several days, she adhered to her refuge, leaving it only when hunger and thirst compelled her to. Though the overripe berries she found made her ill, she could not bear the thought of trying to hunt; her bow and sword lay where she had cast them after waking up a murderer.

She had killed in defense — logically, she knew that. But logic could not keep her from vividly recalling the sensation of her arrow slipping through her fingers, nor the forester's soft gasp as her shaft pierced his lungs, nor the way his eyes rolled up in his head and the blood trickled from his mouth as he died.

The memory choked Robin, drowning her in merciless recollection. She felt as though a large claw had seized at her insides and was tearing her to pieces, rending her with agony until she could only retch.

She endured like this for several days, her body foraging mechanically for just enough food to keep her alive, while her mind remained locked in endless replay.

Eventually, Robin's spirit began to rebel against her depression, and one morning she awoke to the realization that her stomach was hollow, her limbs had grown lean, and the dead were dead and if she did not get something substantial to eat soon, she would be too.

Slowly, Robin got to her feet. She had been lying against the trunk of a giant tree, her body cushioned by a bed of moss; thick and soft, the dark green rug gradually thinned away into stunted grasses the further it grew from the tree.

Robin looked up. A resplendent English Oak towered above her head, its trunk so broad that eight men would have failed to circle it with their arms. Massive branches, twisted and gnarled with age, shot out from low on the bole. These rugged boughs supported a broad crown that stretched across the sky like a chandelier.

There was little else in the clearing — for she was in a clearing, Robin saw — save for some hardy grasses; little else could survive in the halo of shade cast by the mighty oak.

The clearing itself was vast, with its nearest edge at least a hundred paces away from where Robin was standing. Birches and pines rimmed the glade on three sides; a low wall of rock bordered the fourth.

A small path of crushed grass traced its way from Robin's feet towards that wall. She did not remember making such a trail, but there was much that Robin did not remember about the last few despondent days. Obviously, she must have traipsed that way several times in order to have created such an imprint. Unable to remember why and curious to find out, Robin followed it.

The rock wall where the trail ended proved to be the top of a granite cliff whose mild decline led to the verge of a winding, azure stream. The sight of the watercourse below made Robin dizzy, and she realized just how thirsty she was. Instinctively, she began to clamber down the speckled boulders and thick slabs of rock, as indeed she must have done many times over the last few days, touching the stones for balance with fingers that trembled.

At last, her feet touched down on silty soil, and Robin sank to her knees, folding her hands into a leaky cup and drinking deeply from the stream. The thin water cooled the hot thickness of her tongue and helped assuage her empty stomach. Tossing back her head, Robin poured the clear, cool water over her face, letting it trickle across her cheeks and into her hair like tears.

"God, my God, have mercy on me. I am truly sorry, forgive me," she whispered.

Several minutes passed, during which time Robin stared unseeing at the bank across the stream. Finally, she shook her head hard and forced her weary mind to consider her predicament.

By now, the foresters who had survived the fight would have borne their tale to the nearest village, and from there word would have spread to watch for the hooded lad who had killed Sheriff Darniel's nephew. Disguised as she was, Robin would not get very far down the road toward London Town before the Sheriff's soldiers would surely halt her for questioning. Their methods of inquiry were rarely gentle, and her true identity would be quickly discovered. Most likely she would simply be returned home to marry Darniel, but the soldiers might decide to ask the foresters if they could identify her; if they did, she would be hung for murder.

Taking off her hood and resuming her normal appearance was hardly an option, either. Assuming that Robin could find a peasant willing to trade her tunic for a dress, Lord Locksley was sure by now to have men searching everywhere for his tall, blue-eyed, blonde daughter — he might even have posted a reward for her safe return! No one would think twice about returning an errant young lady to her father, especially if gold were involved. She would be dragged back home to marry the Sheriff or dragged off to the gallows as soon as she left the forest, depending on her attire. Neither option held much appeal.

I could just stay here, Robin thought, gazing up at the rocks that hid the glade from view. *The soldiers will cease to hunt me after a while and my father in time will give up his search; then I can continue on to London Town as I had originally planned. Until then, I can live here. There is water, and I am well able to hunt for food. As for shelter, there is plenty of wood, and time enough yet to construct one before the rains start in earnest. I can survive.*

Filled with determination, Robin began the climb back up the cliff.

Her weapons lay where she had left them, a few cubits away from the base of the oak. For a moment, Robin just stared at them, a farrago of emotion warring within her. At last, she picked up her bow stave, running her hands over it to warm it up.

She did not have the strength to hunt far, so Robin found a nearby tree to perch in and waited for something to wander by. She waited until the sun was beginning to set. Just as she was about to give up the hope of any dinner, a roe pricket poked its nose out of a bush. Robin's trembling muscles caused her to miss her first shot, but she gritted her teeth and got in a swift, second shot just before the frightened deer could bound out of range.

The deer she had managed to take down was small — perhaps thirty pounds — but it was more than enough meat for one person. The delight of knowing she would soon have a full belly was tainted, however, by the memory of John's warning against killing the King's deer.

"As a noble and a cousin to the King, I have the right to hunt in this forest," Robin reasoned defensively, startling herself with the sound of her own voice. She fell silent, but her thoughts continued:

But I am not just a noble anymore, am I? I am an outlaw, and as an outlaw, I have no rights. Not even the right to food, for though beggars may plead for a pittance or scrap, even that is barred to me now. It seems, then, that for me to survive, as a consequence of having committed one crime, I must now commit another!

This terrible irony weighed down on Robin, and it took nearly all of her strength to lift her sword and hew off a slab of the roe's rump and then carry it back to the clearing.

It took her longer than usual to start a fire, but soon the smell of roasting venison was permeating the air, lifting Robin's spirits more than she would have thought possible. Later, as she tore the half-cooked meat from its skewer and consumed it ravenously, the warm flesh did much to soothe the ache in her chest.

If I am to stay here, Robin decided that night as she lay upon her bed of moss, watching the stars glister through the branches of the oak, *I must be able to defend myself — and to do so assuredly, so I will not panic and kill someone again.*

Her aim with the bow was good; she would make it perfect. The sword that Will had given her glistened in the moonlight. She would teach herself to use it. Never again would she be helpless in the face of an attack. Never again would she kill someone when she could disarm or disable. Never again.

Robin soon discovered that it took completely different muscles to wield a sword than it did to bend a bow. She dropped the hefty weapon with a groan, rubbing her aching arms and flexing out her back.

It was never this difficult when I was learning with sticks, she reflected wearily. If only she could remember everything Will had shown her! She had not been allowed to attend his lessons, of course — she never was — but after he had finished, the two of them would go to the stables and he would show her all that he had learned, eagerly demonstrating the latest pass or riposte. Laughing, they would leap over stacks of hay, startling the horses with their clacking staves and stopping only when their weapons broke or when the hostlers came to chase them away. They had been very young.

That all ended the day Robin's father entered just in time to see her knock Will's stick from his hand and level her rod at his throat, crowing triumph. Tight-lipped with anger, Lord Locksley had taken them inside the house, whipped them both, and forbidden Robin to ever touch a weapon again. Then he had broken her practice bow in front of her. Robin did not speak to her father again for nearly a month.

"It is not fair," she had complained to Marian, picking up chips of stone from their bedroom floor and flinging them at the horn-covered window. "Father did not care when Will taught me to shoot. Why should he care about us crossing sticks?"

Marian, no more than eight at the time, just stared at her

sister with large, limpid eyes. Darah answered instead.

"A lady may take up shooting for sport, or for the good of her figure," the housekeeper said, sniffing her contempt. Clearly she did not think that such pastimes suited young ladies, in spite of society's permissiveness. "No woman has any business picking up a sword, or pretending to. That is what men are for. Your father was quite right to punish you."

A handful of pebbles hurled in Darah's direction illustrated what Robin thought of that reasoning.

For three weeks, Robin refused to go outside and play. Instead, she watched from her window as Will practiced his archery—something the law required all boys to do once they reached the age of seven. Jealousy colored her vision; whenever Will came to visit, she refused to see him.

To add salt to her wound, Darah saw in Robin's prideful confinement an opportunity to reinstate her lessons in ladyship and undertook the task with enthusiasm. Robin, however, had no desire to be polished and at best ignored her attempts, and at worst actively sabotaged her plans.

One day, after handing the girl an embroidery frame and coming back an hour later to find it still untouched, Darah had announced in resignation that if Robin would only devote as much time to her finishing as she had to her archery, she would be the finest lady in all of England.

The next day, Robin sought out her father at breakfast.

"What is it?" he asked gruffly, peering at her over an upraised pasty.

Robin took a deep breath. She was uncertain what she would do if her father refused her proposition—she dared not think that far ahead.

"I want you to let me practice archery with Will again," she explained in one explosive breath.

Lord Locksley's brows knit together and his expression darkened. Robin plunged on: "I will do everything that Darah tells me to do. I promise I will learn how to be a lady and the duties of a housemistress and such—I will not even tease Darah about it—if you will just let me practice again."

Lord Locksley frowned. In truth, he had almost forgotten about the "swordfight," and he disliked how the situation was reasserting itself. Robin was only twelve, and the precocious bravery a boy would have shown in facing him thus had no place in a woman. However. Darah *had* been nagging him for years about the girl's inclination for the longbow and her distressingly poor progress in the art of running a household. As long as Robin did not bother him, he did not care much what she did, and he routinely told Darah as much. Of course, finding her practicing swordplay was another matter entirely.

Yes, the girl had grown too wild. She needed to be taught her place in the world—a place devoid of quivers and bowmen's staves. A little lesson in humility would not go amiss. Even if she passed his test, the bargain he had in mind would please both Robin and Darah, and either way his world would return to the quiet norm he was accustomed to and liked . . . .

Robin's hands clenched into fists, but she hid them within the folds of her skirt. She wished that her father's face showed what he was thinking. Hers was like an open book, but her father's furrowed features were stoic and unreadable.

At last he spoke, his words startling Robin so that she had to work quickly to recover her aplomb.

"Very well. On one condition—you beat me at this craft of yours. Three arrows. One hundred paces. If you win, you may recommence your archery practice. But win or lose, you begin lessons with Darah immediately and without complaint. Is that satisfactory?"

"Yes," Robin said in a voice faint with disbelief. "Oh, yes."

Out on the archery range, Robin watched nervously as her father inspected his arrows with careful attention. Covertly, she wiped her sweaty hands on her skirt and then rubbed at her bow, trying to keep it warm. Since her father had broken her old bow, the practice stave she was using was unfamiliar to her. It was oak, rather than elm, and slightly too firm for her — she would need all her strength just to draw it.

Her father thrust the heads of his arrows into the ground and took up his stance. In a blur of motion, he shot. All three arrows landed so close to the center of the target that from a distance they blurred into one.

"Oh, my," Robin said faintly, before she could stop herself. She would never have guessed that her reclusive father possessed such fine aim. Indignation quickly replaced disbelief — her father had tricked her! Well, she would show him what Robin Ann Locksley was capable of!

Swiftly, she plunged her arrows into the ground. Taking careful aim, she shot her first shaft; it landed in the middle of her father's small cluster. Her second arrow also landed within that clump. As Robin raised her third arrow, her arm began to shake. The strain of bending the bow back a third time was incredible, and it took all of her strength to keep her aim steady. When at last she let go, she knew that she had shot wide. Not by much, but enough.

Without looking at her, her father walked off. Robin slowly sank to her knees, the longbow clutched convulsively in her fingers. It was all over.

The next morning at breakfast, Robin stared glumly at her lap rather than risk meeting her father's eyes. She did not even look up when the servitor came in with their food. Only when Will nudged her to eat did she reluctantly glance up to see that rather than the plate of stew she had been expecting, the servant had brought the oaken longbow instead.

"I–I do not understand," she stuttered. "I lost."

"I am aware of that fact," Lord Locksley said dryly. Robin quickly shut her mouth. "You will keep your end of the bargain?"

"Oh, yes!" Robin cried. In that moment, she could have hugged him, but he had never permitted that sort of thing before. She gave him a blinding smile instead.

Lord Locksley looked at his daughter, puzzled. "I cannot understand why this means so much to you, Robin. But you have always asked for little enough. Keep your promise, and I shall keep mine. Mayhap you will grow out of this foolishness. One can hope, anyway."

Robin did keep her promise. She endured Darah's lessons, if not enthusiastically, then at least with good cheer. Some of the lessons, like how to sew a wound, she even found interesting. Who knew that embroidery could be put to such use? In time, she even became what some might call accomplished, although she never thought of herself as such. Becoming a lady was just the price she had to pay for the hour of freedom at the end of the day, when she could take up her longbow in her hand and send arrow after arrow whistling through the air like a redbreast's sweet song.

She had never played at swords again. Until now.

Robin gazed at the blade in her hand. Welts were beginning to form along her fingers and on the pad of her hand; their angry red stare mocked her. The sword was simply too heavy—it was meant to be wielded by a man, not by an eighteen-year-old girl. Well, a twelve-year-old girl had not been meant to wield her old longbow, either, but she had learned. She would learn this, too. Ignoring the way her muscles seized up as she lifted the sword once again, Robin got back to work.

⚜

The deer Robin had killed lasted her for half a week and would have lasted longer if not for the warmth of the sun and for various unwanted scavengers, which rendered the meat unfit for consumption by the fourth day.

By this time, however, much of Robin's strength had returned and she had begun to explore her surroundings. One of the first places she examined was the rock cliff leading down to the stream, which turned out to be pocketed with various caves that stayed very cool, even on the hottest of days. These hollows would be better than a larder for storing her food, and a few rocks placed over the entrance would protect her meat from any interested creatures.

So when Robin killed her second deer, rather than simply slicing away enough meat for a single meal, she proceeded to gut and carve the deer . . . or rather, she tried to. It soon became apparent, however, that while her arrows and sword were capable of removing small amounts of meat, they were entirely unsuited to the intricate task of carving. After an hour or so of trying, Robin finally cast the shaft she was using aside and resolved to make herself a dagger.

She found a nice, oblong river rock that fit comfortably in her hand and was long enough to provide a decent blade. The stone she had chosen was even pretty — red, with cream-colored bands running through it. The harder boulders of the cliff face served as her whetstone, and after an afternoon's labor, Robin had a dagger that was sharp enough to slice a scion from a tree; she felt inordinately pleased with herself.

Reprieved of their meat-cutting duties, Robin turned her arrows back to their natural task of archery. She practiced in the fog-lit mornings and in the bright afternoons. She practiced in the windy evenings, and in the dead of the night when her targets were nothing more than wisps of shadow. Soon, she could strike her mark no matter what the conditions.

She devoted just as much time to her sword, rehearsing half-remembered lunges and parries for hours on end. Once she grew strong enough to lift the blade with one hand, she began to fence against the trees. At first, she worried that the thick wood might damage the sword; Will had paid to have the blade etched with silver dragons and fairies and other fantastical creatures, and he would never forgive her if she marred the splendid detailing. But the trees did not appear to do the etchings any harm, and after a while Robin forgot that it had ever been a concern.

When she grew weary of practice, Robin would gather the saplings she had slaughtered and carry them back to the clearing. By lashing them together with strips of deer hide and by filling the chinks with bark and river mud, Robin was able to construct the walls for a shelter. The door she fashioned from shoots and branches, and the roof from the reeds that grew by the river, padded with fronds. The result was a hut with no windows that was barely big enough for her to stretch her arms out twice in either direction . . . but it was hers.

As summer started to wane, Robin began to take long walks through the forest. At first, she had to stop often to let her feet rest, but within a few days her blisters turned to calluses and her legs ceased to ache at all. Soon the muscles in her legs hardened into slender sinew to match the weapon-wrought thews in her arms and back. This sleek strength pleased Robin, though she felt certain that anyone else would have found such brawn in a woman distasteful.

During these initial wanderings, Robin was careful to notch every other tree with her dagger in order to ensure that she could find her way back; but after a while, she no longer needed to mark the trunks in order to keep her way. By the time autumn struck the Sherwood and the leaf-casting trees turned their blades to lacquered gold, Robin knew the forest paths as well as she knew her yew bow.

Most of the time her walks passed in silence, and her thoughts turned often to her cousin and her sister: she wondered what they were doing, and if they were thinking of her. But such musings only served as painful reminders of the life she no longer had, and she did her best to push them aside, as she pushed aside thoughts of her future.

Occasionally, the silence would be broken not by chittering wildlife, but by the carefree voices or the measured steps of man. Whenever this happened, Robin would duck away into the bracken until they passed, thus avoiding their dangerous notice.

Then one night as she made her way back to her refuge from an evening expedition, she stumbled upon two men sitting by a fire, singing softly into the dark. Rather than melting away again, Robin found herself creeping forward to listen to their melodic chorus of gallant knights, of loves lost and won, and of bravery nonpareil. As she listened, she found herself thinking of another campfire and of the two unburdened souls who had once sat around it. It was only when the singing stopped and the two men prepared to go to sleep that she found she could break away. If there were tears in her eyes as she made her way home, she blamed them on the smoke.

One bright September afternoon, something transpired that would forever shatter Robin's routine. The azure sky that day had a touch of briskness to it that teased of the coming winter; it filled Robin with a strange invigoration, and she found herself roaming farther afield than she ever had before, clear to the edge of Nottingham. She had just turned to head back home when she heard raised voices, and a low, muted scream.

Robin paused. Part of her wanted to ignore the shout and hurry on her way; the other part demanded that she investigate.

"It is not my problem," she muttered, but did not move. There was something about the way the holler had emerged — as if the person had tried to refrain from crying out, but could not help himself — that kept her from simply dismissing the sound.

Another scream punctuated the air.

"Plagues and murrains!" Robin cursed. Unhooking the bow from her back, she strung it and stalked off in the direction of the ruckus.

It was not hard to find the trouble's locale — all she had to do was follow the shouting. When she judged she was getting close, Robin ducked down into the brush and crept forward the remaining distance; from her hiding place behind a tree, she peered out at the scene.

In the hollow between several flax-crowned trees, two men stood laughing with their backs to Robin, holding a third man still between them. Suddenly, the man in the middle rocked backward and would have fallen if not for the restraining grips on his arms. As the two soldiers pulled him upright, Robin saw a fourth man casually wind back his fist for another blow. Like his companions, he was clothed in purple attire.

Purple. What a stupid color to wear in a forest, Robin thought uncharitably as she contemplated her options. *Then again, the Sheriff is not known for his desire to be inconspicuous. He probably has his men wear purple livery just so they do stand out. As if their brutality were not announcement enough.*

Robin sighed. There was really only one thing to do. Glancing up at the tree she was hiding behind, she saw that it was a stately old ash with a broad base and bulbous grey arms. The lowest branch V-ed off from the trunk about four feet above the ground, and the second branch emerged a clothyard above that.

It will do.

Leaning her bow against the bole of the tree, Robin eased herself up into the first split. When she was in place, she drew up her bow and climbed into the second V. Her body was now within the lower canopy, hidden from view by a cluster of pale yellow leaves.

Robin nocked an arrow and made certain that her feet were firmly settled — one upon the tree's broad branch, the other lodged in the crevice where the trunk split in twain. Her range was incredibly short — there would be no room for error here.

Sighting just below the purple shards that flashed through the leaves, Robin loosed; without pause, she drew another arrow from her quiver and shot it after the first. Arrow after arrow fell from the sky, causing the soldiers to scatter with horrified shouts. Robin was aiming for the ground near the soldiers' feet, but the men did not know that. Thinking they were under attack and completely unprepared to defend themselves against a bowman's assault, they fled, leaving their insensible victim behind.

"That was almost too easy," Robin whispered into the sudden silence, a trifle disappointed.

When she was certain that the soldiers were not coming back, Robin climbed out of the tree. Setting her bow against its trunk, she drew her sword and cautiously approached the prone victim; he had fallen over when the soldiers had let him go and now lay unmoving upon the earth. His face was matted with blood and his nose was almost certainly broken. She thought he looked young, but it was hard to tell beneath the grime. When she nudged him with the tip of her sword, he moaned but did not move.

Robin sheathed her sword and pondered the beaten man. *Now what?* They were near the edge of the forest. She supposed she could drag him to where the road met the verge; someone would stumble across him eventually.

"This is what I get for not minding my own business," Robin muttered, deferring the problem for a moment so she could retrieve her arrows.

The force of her shot had buried the shafts so deep into the dirt that she had to dig her heels into the ground and tug with both hands to free them. Robin had just managed to dislodge the last arrow when she heard a low moan behind her.

"Och, me 'ead!" a voice soughed miserably. Robin turned around to see the young man trying to sit up.

"Easy," she told him, remembering at the last second to deepen her voice. She hastened over. "You have had a rough time of it. Try not to move."

Perversely, the youth only tried harder to get up. With a sigh, Robin squatted down and put a shoulder under his arm, helping him to stand.

"Oh. Thank ye," he said, blinking up at her. "I say, is it mornin'? The sun does seem to be risin' awful swift — I swear 'twas dark just a moment ago!"

"Yes, that generally happens when people get knocked unconscious," Robin said, stepping back to see if the lad could stand on his own. He did not fall over, but swayed from side to side like a Bacchic sailor.

"I was ne!" the youth protested, his voice cracking indignantly. Robin knew she should not laugh, but it was difficult. His weaving faded a little.

Now that the lad was awake, she could see that he was even younger than she had thought — beneath all the blood, his face was smooth and soft, with a child's translucent cheeks. He could not be more than fourteen or fifteen.

"You were, too," she said, "and you would probably be dead as well if I had not frightened those men away. Whatever did you do to merit such a drubbing?"

To her surprise, the boy smirked, then winced as pain lanced through his face. "I got a little too close t' the Sheriff's daughter, if ye know what I mean. The Sheriff 'ad 'is dogs bring me 'ere t' teach me a lesson."

"You got a little too — ?" Comprehension dawned, and Robin made a face.

"'ere, now, she ain't that bad. 'Er father is a loon, but she is kind o' pretty, ye know?"

Robin raised an eyebrow. "Pretty enough to get thrashed over?"

His eyes grinned. "Maybe so."

"Well, either that beating left your wits addled or they

were that way to start, I certainly cannot tell. But it seems you will survive, so good day." Robin picked up her bow and began to walk away. The boy followed.

"What are you doing?" she demanded firmly, when it became clear that he *was* following her. He gave her an innocent gaze. "Look, you had best be getting yourself home—your parents are probably in a stew over you."

"Ain't got no home," the boy said with an indifferent shrug of his shoulders. "Ain't got no family."

"And you think that because I saved you, you can stay with me, is that it? Well, you cannot, so . . . begone!"

Robin waited for the boy to leave, but he just stood there. She thought about drawing her sword to scare him away, but this youth had laughed off almost getting killed by three grown men—she doubted that her blade would deter him. Besides, she could hardly cut him down now, could she?

With a groan of dismay, Robin stalked off through the trees, stretching her strides as long as possible in an attempt to lose the boy. It was for naught. By the time she reached the glade, her legs were cramping and the youth was still behind her. Muttering a low curse and something that sounded suspiciously like, "Problems!" Robin limped over to her hut, went in, and with one final glare at the boy, firmly shut the door.

⚒ 6 ⚒

INCURSION

THE NEXT MORNING, Robin awoke with a vague sense of disquiet.

This sensation puzzled her; the slivers of golden light peeking through the reed roof were bright and joyous, and somewhere nearby a songbird was singing — there was nothing to cause her alarm, and yet she was definitely . . . edgy. Robin tried to put her finger on the reason as she dressed, but it eluded her. In fact, it was not until she opened her door and stepped outside that she stumbled across the answer.

"What'd ye do that f'r?" the boy asked plaintively, rubbing his side and squinting up at her from where he lay sprawled out by her door. His face was still puffy from his beating, and one eye was swollen shut, but the other blinked at her lucidly from within a vibrant purple ring. Robin quickly stepped back into the shadows of her hut, pulling the cowl of her hood up over her hair and hoping that the boy had not noticed. Blinded as he was by sleep and the sun, it appeared he had not.

"Ugh," Robin groaned. "Why are you still here?"

"Where else would I be? Can' go back t' Nottingham, now can I?" he asked plaintively.

"Do not remind me," Robin griped. "Could you not at least have had the good sense to sleep somewhere you might not get stepped on?"

His eye lit up at her suggestion. "Hey, ye'r smart!"

Robin threw up her hands in defeat.

The boy followed her down to the stream and watched in silence as she washed her face; he made no attempt to scrub the dried blood and grime off his own. Robin opened her mouth to admonish him and then closed it again.

"Not my problem," she muttered to herself.

She could not ignore the way the boy's good eye went wide, however, when she rolled aside a boulder to reveal one of her larder caves, nor the way it fixed on the cut of meat she withdrew; his gaze did not stray from it the entire climb back up the granite cliff.

The boy's stare only intensified as Robin set the cut to cook. Soon the hot juices began to pop, and each time they did, the boy would refocus his attention, absently licking his lips at the sizzling meat. Robin sighed. She had seen enough starving people in her short life to refuse to let anyone she hosted go hungry, even when they were not welcome.

"Fine," she muttered in resignation. Louder, she said, "If you want to share my food, you need to go clean your hands and face. I will not let you eat when you are so dirty."

"I am ne dirty," the boy insisted, but a steely scowl from Robin convinced him that she was serious, and with a last longing look at the meat, he scampered to do as she bade.

For several days, Robin tried to get the boy to leave. She set him to do whatever tasks she could think of: cleaning out deer bladders and using them to draw water from the stream . . . gathering firewood . . . improving her spit so that it actually turned the meat, rather than charring one side and undercooking the other . . . and of course, her least favorite task: gutting her kills. No matter what she asked him to do, the boy just flashed her a smile and scuttled to do it.

In exasperation, Robin asked how he could stand it.

"'Tis fun," he explained. "Loads funner than beggin' food off farmers or workin' their fields t' eat."

Robin stared at him in amazement, but he was completely serious.

When it came to her weapon's practice, the youth distained her fancy sword, which he called "a bloom butter knife!" but he was fascinated by her archery. In the afternoons, he would sit and watch Robin practice, cheering her as she punctured the trees with more holes than a woodpecker and bemoaning the rare shots that she missed. Once, he asked her if he could take a turn, but Robin shook her head quite firmly. She was not about to let some dunderhead use her bow.

Strangely, the boy did not seem to mind being told no. His heartfelt encouragement of her was tireless, and Robin found herself practicing even longer than usual, just so she could bask in his acclamation.

Then one morning, Robin awoke to find the boy gone.

It had rained during the night, and Robin's sleep had been fretful. The nights were turning cold, and though she had not wanted to admit it to herself, she was concerned about the youth — she could not be sure that the oak tree would provide him sufficient shelter from the frigid storm.

Several times, she had sat up with the intention of calling

for him to come inside, but each time she had stopped herself before she could. The boy had invited himself into her life and taken root there in spite of her protests; she was *not* going to share with him the privacy of her hut as well.

But though she had tried to rationalize her decision, her conscience still pricked at her that she was being selfish, making her toss and turn throughout the night so that by the time the sun rose, Robin was aching to get up.

That was when she discovered the boy was gone.

"Boy!" she called. "Um, young man!" It disturbed her to realize that she did not even know his name; he had never mentioned it, and she had never cared to ask.

Robin chided herself for worrying. *He is probably just attending to personal business*, she reasoned. *He will stroll into camp in a few minutes, just you wait and see. Then you will feel the fool for fretting!*

But an hour later, he had still not returned.

Breakfast that morning was a lonely affair, and Robin realized just how much she had come to rely on the boy's mindless chatter during meals. Now, the clearing seemed too quiet. She tried to convince herself that she was glad he was gone, that she *enjoyed* her newfound silence, but she did not quite succeed.

By afternoon, Robin's spirits had sunk into a listless melancholy.

All right, I miss him, she admitted at last, staring dully into the fire. *Dunderhead or not, he was company.* And he really was not a bad sort. He was friendly and he never complained, no matter how tedious or revolting the task was she gave him to do. She could have been nicer to him.

Enervation overwhelmed her, and Robin slumped down upon the moss that grew under the massive oak, gazing through the tree's browning branches into the dimming sky and trying to think of nothing.

A dark shadow fell across her face.

"Yahh!" Robin exclaimed, sitting up so fast that her vision swarmed with spots. When her eyes cleared, she saw the boy standing in front of her.

"Where have you—" Robin bit off her instinctive chastisement. In a calmer tone, she rephrased: "What have you been doing all day?"

"Makin' this," the boy announced proudly, holding out a bow for her inspection.

"Oh, my," was Robin's reply. Clearly, no one had taught the youth how to make a longbow before. The crude implement was misshapen, with hack marks all along its spine from the rough dagger he had used to carve it. It looked as if the boy had also tried to braid a string for it from wild grasses, which frayed down its length in every direction.

"Now I 'ave a bow, too," he announced proudly. "Now we can practice together."

"It is a very nice . . . bow," Robin said carefully. "Does it work?"

He shrugged. "Dunno. Can we see?"

Robin obligingly rose and went to fetch her quiver from her cabin. On the lad's first attempt to bend the bow, his string snapped and had to be repaired. On his second attempt, his bow snapped as well.

"Oh," he said quietly, holding the broken pieces in his hands. He looked so forlorn that Robin felt a rush of compassion for the youth.

"Never mind," she consoled. "You shall make yourself another and this time I will help you."

It took them the rest of the day, with Robin patiently

explaining how to choose the right wood, how to trim the stave, how to shape the bow, and how to weave a string. She was gratified to find she remembered all the details, and the lad learned from her eagerly. Several times when he was about to err, she was tempted to simply finish the job herself, but each time she restrained the urge and merely pointed out what he needed to correct. The end result was a bow that was not very elegant, but was sturdy and bent well. The look of pride on the boy's face when he shot the first of several off-target arrows shamed Robin for all her impatience and ill will toward him.

"What is your name?" she asked as they searched through the dusky night for the shafts.

"Will Stutley." She could not see his face anymore, but from the sound of his voice, he was both surprised and pleased by her question. "What is yours?"

"Robin," she said, clearing her throat gruffly as a wave of homesickness washed through her. *Why does his name have to be Will?*

Brushing away her wistful longing, she continued on in what she hoped was an offhand tone: "Well, Will, you cannot spend your nights out in the rain catching cold. Since you seem intent on staying here, we shall have to build you a house of your own."

Robin had to throw her arms out quickly then to keep the boy from bowling her over in thanks.

When it came to archery, Will was a fast learner, eagerly assimilating everything she taught him. Soon he was hitting his target tree every time.

He is not dumb, Robin realized, *just ignorant . . . and good-ness knows, there is a world of difference between the two!*

Now that she was no longer trying to get rid of him, Rob-in found herself enjoying Will's company. He was one of those rare people whose natures are innately simple and happy, and while his boundless good cheer sometimes grated on her nerves, more often than not she found her own mood brightening to match his.

Of course, Robin had to be more careful now that there was a boy around. She never went outside without her breast binding or hood, and she went to the stream to bathe only when she was certain that Will was asleep. When her monthly came, she worried that he would notice the girdle of river ferns and cloth strips she wore under her hose and tunic, or that her sharpened temper would trigger a realization. She need not have concerned herself. Will saw her as a man and accepted her as such, and as eccentric as she sometimes was, well, that was just Robin to him.

At first, Robin found Will's own idiosyncrasies a little more difficult to deal with, especially his tendency to disap-pear without notice for hours—sometimes days—on end. When she would ask him where he had gone, he would just shrug. He always came back, though, and he usually brought some sort of gift when he did. These offerings ranged from pheasants to spiders to pinecones; needless to say, some were more pleasant than others.

One day, Will brought something back that Robin did not appreciate to start, but which like Will himself, ended up becoming one of her greatest blessings.

She had been sitting on a branch in the old pedunculate oak, reclining against its trunk and whittling herself some new arrows with her knife. Several times, she ruined a shaft when the cold wind made her shiver, even though she was sitting in the sunniest spot in the clearing.

Robin was not looking forward to a winter without sheepskin blankets and wool clothes to keep her warm. True, she had plenty of skins saved from the deer she had killed, but she was no tanner, and the blankets she had fashioned were crude at best. Still, they would have to suffice if she and Will were to survive the cold.

Robin sighed, and her breath came out as a steamy wisp of cloud.

"It is not winter *yet*," she protested. "Give me a few more weeks of warmth at least!"

The wind just tickled her nose, as though in laughter. Robin shuddered and drew her liripipe closer around her throat.

"Ho, Robin!" a familiar voice called blithely from the trees.

With a smile, Robin slid out of the oak, only to stop short when she saw that Will was not alone.

He grinned at her broadly. "See who I brung?"

She certainly did. It was a young couple—just a few years older than she—but with faces haggard by disappointment and exhaustion. The man's thick russet beard had not been trimmed for some time, and his clothes hung loosely on his frame. He opened his mouth as if to speak, but then closed it again at the displeasure in Robin's face.

The woman next to him was pale and malnourished. Her lank brown hair was tied back with a sprig of hay, and dark shadows haunted her eyes. At Robin's approach, she ducked behind her husband, but not before Robin saw that she was clearly with child.

I will get you for this, Will, Robin vowed. *You had no right to bring them here.* With substantial effort, she forced away her scowl. "Good day."

"Good day," the man replied, still apprehensive of her displeasure. "Your brother kindly invited us to stay for a while. Normally, we would not impose on your hospitality, but circumstances being what they are . . . ." His voice trailed off uncertainly.

"Will is not my brother," Robin informed him with a bluntness that was almost rude. "Why do you want to stay here? This seems the last place a woman in your wife's . . . condition . . . should be dwelling."

"Aye, we would not be here if we had anywhere else to go."

"Explain."

Shame made the man blush. "Last year, our harvest was poor. This year, no matter what we tried, we could not get our crops to grow. It was as if our land had been sown with salt. We could not pay our taxes, so the Sheriff took our land and all that we possessed. We had to beg our way here from Harworth Town: beg for a place to sleep and for food to eat. For myself, I could not have done it, but my wife . . . . Even so, it was never enough. People do not have a lot of food to spare."

"Harworth is very far away," Robin said blandly, trying not to show how troubled she was by his story.

"Yes. My wife has relatives in Radford who we had hoped would take us in . . . but that turned out not to be the case."

"I found 'em sitting by the verge," Will chimed in. "Seemed a pity just t' leave 'em there. There is plenty o' room for 'em 'ere, and food enough, too."

"Food?" the woman asked hopefully, speaking up for the first time.

Robin sighed. "Follow me."

She seated the couple at the base of the oak, on the softest patch of moss. The addition of several logs to the fire turned the low embers into a shimmering blaze — Robin rarely let the fire go out completely, as she found it much more trouble to restart than to maintain. About to ask Will to fetch some meat, she turned to find him already skewering a shoulder of venison onto the spit.

The couple were blinking wearily where they sat — Robin wondered whether they would be able to stay awake long enough to eat the food they so clearly required. Taking advantage of their sleepy stupor, Robin seized Will firmly by the ear and drew him to the opposite side of the clearing.

"What were you thinking?" she hissed, ignoring his small yelps of pain. "The Sherwood is no place for an expectant woman! Did you even think about *asking* me?"

"I did ne think I 'ad t' ask," he grumbled, rubbing at his ear. "Ye 'ave no title 'ere."

A surge of panic shot through Robin before she realized that Will was not announcing he knew she was a noble, but was instead referring to the fact that she did not own the forest.

"Where are they supposed to sleep?" she demanded instead, still trying to recover from her scare.

"They can stay in me place," Will offered. "I can make meself another."

"It is not as easy as that!"

"Why ne?"

How could Robin explain the complications presented by a pregnant woman? Men were not privy to those mysteries — even Robin did not fully understand everything that Darah had told her. And winter was coming. What would they do when the child was born? It would almost certainly freeze to death in the forest.

Then, too, there were personal reasons why Robin was loath to share her refuge with more strangers — especially when one of them was a woman. While men might overlook each other's caprices, a woman's eyes were quicker to note discrepancies and ponder out their reason. How long would Robin's secret be safe with a woman in the camp?

All these thoughts ran through Robin's head, and she could give voice to none of them. In the end, she simply turned and walked away.

David of Doncaster (as Robin learned that he was called) and his wife Mara were not the last outcasts that Will would bring to her glade. Every other day seemed to find more people wandering into the camp, all led by the cheerful youth. Soon there were more huts in her clearing than in a small village.

A few of the arrivals were like David — small families thrown off their land for tax failure. Most of the newcomers were men who had poached the King's deer to keep their families from starving, or who had stolen someone's purse to afford their rents. When their deeds were discovered, these men had fled into outlawry, rather than risk maiming or hanging by the judgment of the courts. In the depths of the forest they found sanctuary, and in Robin's camp they found something they had feared would never be theirs again — community.

"You do not know the first thing about these people," Robin complained to Will one day, watching the industrious bustle in her once serene abode with dismay. "They could be murderers, or worse."

"Do ye really think so?" Will asked in an excited tone.

Fortunately for all, it seemed that Will's invitees were essentially decent folk, driven into outlawry by ill fortune, not by ill natures. Robin did not know what she would have done if a truly bad man had made his way into her camp.

After one of his countless excursions, Will brought back an item of particular interest to Robin — a warrant. As she took the piece of paper, Robin found that her hands were trembling. Though she had known she was an outlaw, it was one thing to know it and another thing to hold the proof in her fingers. The likeness on the warrant was not very good — a hooded figure with a sharp nose and a pointed chin — but it was all there: £20 for her, dead or alive, for the murder of James Darniel. It even stated her name — Robin. She wondered how they had known what she was called, and then remembered John shouting it after her as she had fled.

"I am now a Wolf's Head," Robin murmured softly. "Any man may kill me and be rewarded for it." The realization was sobering. She rolled up the warrant and hid it in the corner of her hut.

As winter set in, the stream of immigrants slowed to a trickle and eventually came to a halt — whether because Will had finally ceased bringing people to the clearing or because the thought of living in a frosty Sherwood was too intimidating, Robin neither knew nor cared.

She was forced to allow that the influx of people did have one advantage — they possessed a variety of useful trades. At least two or three were tanners, and the blankets they produced from her deerskins put Robin's tentative efforts to shame. A few men were carpenters, and they quickly set to work building shanties to withstand the winter winds. The vast majority had been farmers, but even they found something to do: couches of sweet rushes began to appear, sitting logs were brought in to encircle the fire, burn wood was stacked, and the spits were improved. Some men had brought their dogs, and even these were helpful, making short work of any leftover bones and entrails.

Yet Robin would not admit to being pleased with her improved circumstances, not one smidge. As a chorus of yawping mongrels woke her for the third night in a row, she silently avowed that she would rather have a wind-chilled house and her isolation than warm skins and a noisy village. Several times she even thought about leaving, but this place was hers — let the others leave; she, Robin, would stay. Besides, it was not like she had anywhere better to go.

❧ 7 ❧

OUTLAWS

ROBIN CREPT through the shimmering Sherwood, trying to minimize the squelch of the snow beneath her boots. The deer she was stalking had already eluded her several times, leaping away from her bolts like a shadow leaps from light. It was a magnificent hart — a full eight-pointer — with a brown winter coat that made it nearly impossible to see against the ghostly trees.

Something shifted to her left. There it was!

Robin silently nocked an arrow and drew the shaft back to her cheek. A slight wind nipped at her fingers; she made the necessary adjustments.

She loosed! As if forewarned, the hart sprang away, although Robin knew she had made no sound.

"Very well," she called to it in resignation, gazing after the retreating stag with unwilling admiration. "Leap and live another day. I shall have you yet!"

The stag's flipped-up tail was its only response. With a sigh, Robin unstrung her bow and walked over to pick up her arrow, returning it to its quiver. All too often of late, she had returned to camp empty-handed from one of her hunts, although today marked the first time it had been due to a miss rather than to the scarcity of game.

"I hope the others have had better luck," she murmured to herself as she began the trek back to camp. "I do not know if I can endure another night of Edra's root soup."

But as Robin neared the outlaw village, the sound of distressed voices filtering through the trees pushed all thoughts of hunger from her mind.

"There you are!" David cried, running over the instant she stepped into the clearing. Despite the frigid weather, he was sweating.

"What has happened?" Robin demanded, her mind awhirl with possibilities. "Soldiers?"

"What? No, 'tis the baby . . . 'tis coming!"

"Oh," she replied, her posture sinking two inches in relief. "Well, surely the women have things in hand?"

"Noni is still sick, and last night, Tessa took ill, too. Edra went to the Blue Boar Inn to get some herbs for them—I sent someone after her, but it could be hours before they get back. I know not what else to do!"

Robin frowned, puzzled. "I do not understand. If the women are indisposed and if you are here, then who is with Mara now?"

"No one," he admitted.

"No one!"

"'Tis not right to have a man present," David protested; he quelled under Robin's scathing stare.

"Of all the idiotic, *stupid* notions—who do you think

helped Mary give birth to our Lord? The cows?" she snapped, stalking toward his cabin.

"You there," she directed, pointing to one of the burly fellows who were lurking nearby, looking abashedly useless. "Boil some water and get me a cloth to dip in it. And you — fetch me a firebrand so I can see what I am doing. Go!" The men scurried to do as she bade them.

"And you," Robin barked to David as she stepped inside his hut. "Do something useful and hold your wife's hand." He hastened to obey her, grateful that someone was taking charge.

Robin blinked and allowed her eyes to adjust to the darkness. Outside, it was still bright, but with the door shut for privacy, just enough daylight seeped through the hut's walls to illuminate the woman lying on the floor. Mara's face was taut with exertion, her eyes shut, and her breathing labored.

"All right," Robin muttered to herself, trying to recall what the midwife had done when one of the kitchen maids had gone into labor. "First things first: see how close the baby is to being born."

Nervously, she crouched down next to Mara and began to push back the woman's skirts, forgetting for a moment how the others perceived her.

Without warning, harsh hands seized Robin and threw her against the wall. The whole shack shook and some dirt crumbled from the roof onto Robin's head, but to her amazement and intense relief, the hut did not fall over.

"No man is going to see my wife there but me!" David thundered, hastily drawing back down his wife's clothes.

"Do you want to catch the baby then?" Robin demanded, pushing herself to her feet and rubbing her shoulder where it had struck the wall. She understood David's protectiveness, but now was not the time. Besides, if he knew Robin's true gender, he would welcome her actions. But she was not ready to tell him the truth and give up her disguise, nor the freedom it permitted — certainly not over a baby!

At Robin's suggestion, David blanched. "No, no," he retracted, "you do it."

This time when she went to check on Mara, he eyed her in warning, but said nothing.

Satisfied that the baby would not arrive for a while, Robin pulled the woman's skirts back down and rocked back on her heels as she thought.

What was it Darah had said during the maid's delivery — something about first births taking a long time? And herbs, herbs to help the pain.

"I brought water," carpenter John Logan announced, opening the door to the hut. He glanced uncertainly at the laboring woman and then away again, holding the bucket in front of him like a shield. Robin accepted the water from him, as well as the thin rag he held out.

"Thank you," she said. "Send Edra in here the instant she gets back, and in the meantime, see if she has any birthwort or raspberry in that hut of hers. If she does, brew them into a tea and bring it to me as quick as you can."

"Yes, Robin," came John's automatic reply; he practically fled out the door.

Time passed. Robin had David sponge his wife's face and neck with the warm water, talking to her all the while in a low voice. She doubted that Mara, distracted and faint, understood what he was saying, but it was the comforting sound of her husband's voice that was important, not the words.

When John Logan brought the herbal tea, Robin seized at it gratefully and tipped the liquid into Mara's mouth, pouring slowly so the woman would not choke. It must have eased her a little, because some of the lines in her face relaxed, and her cries of pain became less shrill. She still did not open her eyes.

Day faded into night; someone brought a torch and placed it just inside the doorway. David had fallen asleep holding his wife's hand, and Robin was nodding off as well when Mara gave a piercing scream that brought them both to their feet.

"Mary, Mother, help me," Robin prayed, hastily pushing back the woman's skirts. The baby was coming, oh, how it was coming!

"What do I do? What do I do?" David cried, barely audible as his wife gave another scream.

"I do not know!" Robin shouted back. Outside, she heard distant voices calling something, but she ignored them. All her focus was on the crowning head.

God above, do not let me drop it.

When Edra burst into the hut a few moments later, she saw David cradling a tiny infant in his arms and Robin wiping bloody hands on her tunic, a vague expression on her face. Mara had fainted from exertion, but her chest rose and fell with ease.

Though momentarily taken aback by the scene, the healer quickly recovered her wits and strode over to the baby, taking the child in her arms to assess its condition. Robin, seeing that she was no longer needed, took the opportunity to step outside. It was a beautiful night, with thin wisps of pearl-colored clouds surrounding the moon and stars like gauze studded with diamonds. Against the darkness of the clearing, a bonfire crackled, its flames rising taller than a man and silhouetting the shapes of those sitting around it.

At the sound of the infant's first howl, these outlaws had turned as one to face the cabin, and when Robin emerged, they greeted her with a relieved hail. One man whipped out a crude set of hand pipes and began to play a joyful tune in time to the baby's wails. This, in addition to many broad smiles and ribald jokes, helped shatter the tension that had gripped the camp for the last few hours. David was well liked in the community and his concern for his wife and child had become theirs; the birth of a baby who could bellow so heartily was definitely cause for celebration.

Rather than joining the nascent festivities, Robin stayed standing just outside David's hut, looking at her hands in amazement. In the distant light of the fire, the blood on them gleamed black against her golden skin.

I should wash these, she thought, but continued to stare at her palms, still stunned by what she had accomplished.

A heavy hand clasped her on the shoulder. It was David. His voice when he spoke was thick, and there were tears shining in his eyes.

"Thank you, Robin."

She nodded, and the two of them stood that way for a while, listening in the dark to the healthy sound of a baby crying.

Winter eventually melted away and the greenwood began to prosper once more. Flowers flared everywhere — pied daisies, red poppies, and cerulean bluebells — all vying to paint the landscape their particular brand of color. Baby rabbits flooded the undergrowth, sparrow couples took flight in their primordial dance of courtship, and sundry insects awoke from their winter sleep to repopulate the verdure.

One such insect — a mosquito, Robin noticed with dismay —

was currently kissing her arm in itchy appetite.

"As if I had not problems enough," she swore, dropping the bow she had been assessing onto her lap and tugging at her sleeves in an attempt to shield her arms.

This effort proved futile, since her sleeves were worn to shreds; for that matter, most of her outfit was worn to shreds. If she did not get something new to wear soon, she would be running around in threads—*which*, Robin thought wryly, *would definitely liven up the camp after a rather boring winter*. Of course, she was not the only person there in dire need of new clothes, but she had no doubt which of them would provide the greater spectacle.

It was hardly surprising that the camp's attire was in such a sorry state. Deer that winter had proved infuriatingly elusive, and the pelts of those they had been fortunate enough to kill had been distributed among the outlaws as much-needed blankets; even the hides of rabbits and squirrels had been used for this purpose. None could be spared for new clothes.

Faced with this scarcity of warmth and meat, Robin knew the outlaws could have responded with the worst of human instincts. But years of near-starvation, combined with their expulsion from society, had merely increased their desire to aid those who shared their plight. So it was that they shared with each other the little they had, growing over the winter from a community into a family. By miracle of their altruism, no one had starved or frozen to death—not even the baby.

Robin glanced over at where Mara was sitting a few feet away, bouncing her baby lightly upon her lap and chatting cheerfully with Edra. Little Hannah gurgled happily in her mother's arms and waved her plump pink fists ineffectually through the air. Outlaw life seemed to suit the babe, who flourished even while the adults grew thin. The entire camp adored the child, and the sleepy grumbles that resulted from her nighttime cries were tolerant and good-natured.

Less tolerant were the muddy feet that shuffled impatiently in front of Robin, and obediently, she returned her attention to the bow in her lap. She peered down its shaft to make sure that there was no lateral curve to the wood. She ran her fingers over the shank to check for splits and to make certain that the wood where the arrow would rest was smooth. Lastly, she checked the hemp bowstring for fraying — its coating left the faint smell of animal fat on her fingers, rather than beeswax, as the season was still too inhospitable for *that* particular insect to make itself known.

"Let me see you bend it," Robin directed, returning the longbow to its owner. The young boy in front of her strung the bow, his face screwed up in concentration. Laboriously placing the tip by his instep, he drew the string back until his hand just touched his ear. The bow bent with a small creak, but not with the cracking, snapping sound that Robin was listening for.

"Very good," she smiled with enthusiasm. "You have made a fine weapon. You should be proud."

"Thanks, Robin!" the boy said, flashing her a grin that was missing two front teeth; he scampered off to where his friends were waiting to hear the verdict.

One more for the ranks, Robin thought idly, reclining against the bole of the oak in what was her favorite spot. She was prepared to swear that the moss here was thicker and softer than anywhere else, but while a few of the other outlaws seemed to share her opinion, no one begrudged her the spot when she wanted to rest there, deferring the place to her out of respect.

It still surprised her, the people's respect. She had not sought it, had not even noticed when it began to develop — first as simple admiration, and then altering slowly into a rare high regard.

It was clear to all in the camp that Robin was their best hunter — over the winter, she had brought in thrice the amount of game that anyone else had — and she had won the evening archery contests so often that she was eventually forbidden to compete. Those competitions had proved more effective than even Robin could have dreamed and had affirmed to the others that her ideas were worth listening to.

It had begun simply, after yet another fight between men whose winter-worn tempers had snapped — this time resulting in a brawl so severe that two-thirds of the camp had been involved by its end. Robin had spent a sleepless night pondering how best to prevent another such squabble, and at the next camp convocation, she had presented her idea — a nightly competition, which would allow the people to display their prowess in archery, wrestling, or cudgeling while at the same time releasing their pent-up energies.

"Why not?" had been the general consensus. "It is not like there is anything better to do."

The resulting upswing in the camp's mood had been as great as it was unexpected. After weeks of maddening monotony, the glade now rang in the evenings with laughter and cheers. Even better, now that the men had a valid outlet for their virility, they no longer felt the need to take their boredom out on each other. Tempers had improved, and to everyone's pleasure, the number of unsanctioned fights had plummeted to nearly zero.

Impressed by Robin's ingenuity, the outlaws had begun coming to her for advice . . . much to her consternation and to

David's friendly amusement. Several even petitioned Robin to help them improve their archery, which she did gladly, showing them the tricks to smooth flight that she had discovered over the years. Soon even the worst of the archers found their aim beginning to steady, and as they started to triumph in the evenings against veteran bowmen, more and more people sought to join Robin's lessons, until she found herself teaching half of the outlaws at once. Some of the men needed only a little refinement; some of them — contrary to the King's law — had never even touched a bow before, let alone possessed one. For such men, her first lesson was simple: learn to make the weapon that could save an outlaw's life. Only once their longbow had passed her examination did she permit them to enter group training.

The men's regard for her archery skills was evident, but as anyone would have told her, archery was the least of the reasons why they respected her. Without even knowing it, Robin had shown herself to be a leader that the people could esteem. During Mara's crisis, she alone had kept her head when others had felt helpless to act. When Thatch's hut had caught on fire, her directives had kept the blaze from spreading, and when wolves had attacked Gary Ebbot, her composed commands had kept him from losing his life. And in spite of Robin's initial misgivings about the people who now filled her once-private glade, the strong community they had formed had gradually seduced her until she could not imagine living without them. In community decisions, hers was a strong and influential voice, and whenever someone needed help, she did not balk at lending her aid.

So the outlaws liked her and respected her, and called her Robin o' the Hood, because no one had ever seen her without that particular couture.

Robin o' the Hood. I rather like it, she thought sleepily, settling more comfortably against the oak. *It sounds . . . mysterious.*

The warming sun and the friendly breeze succeeded in siphoning away her thoughts after that, and she had almost managed to doze off when a commotion at the edge of the camp roused her awake.

A small pack of young men — ones that Will Stutley had adopted as his own special friends, she noted — were making their way into camp like a band of triumphant heroes. They were laden with sacks whose contents spilled out as they set them on the ground: dried foods, oats, patched woolen blankets, and even a couple live chickens. Robin watched in amazement as the outlaws converged on the items, carrying them away until not even a grain of barley remained.

"Ye want any, Robin?" Will asked, heaving a small sack in her direction. He opened it to show her a wheel of cheese and some pasties.

"Where did you get these?" she asked, incredulous.

"Oh, some farm o'er in Mansfield," he said, surprised that she did not know. "'Twas Johnny's idea. 'E decided ne t' try Nottingham again cuz they only gots rotten stuff there af'er the Sheriff gets done wi' them, but we made a good 'aul this time."

Realization made Robin dizzy. Over the last couple of weeks, she had noticed some new items appearing amongst the outlaws — a pot here, a different pair of shoes there. She had assumed that some of the outlaws had risked going into town and had bought or traded for these things. Now, she knew the truth.

"And everyone . . . knew?" she asked, still trying to comprehend.

"O' course," he said. "I thought ye did, too, or I woulda told ye." Robin's attitude puzzled him — was she not glad that the outlaws were providing for themselves? He continued to hold out the small sack.

"Put that down," she ordered, the cold fury in her voice stunning the boy. "Go gather those friends of yours and their families — better yet, gather all and sundry. We are going to have ourselves a little talk."

Robin waited for the last puzzled stragglers to find a place to sit, putting off the moment when she would have to address the crowd. She knew in her heart that what Will and his friends were doing was wrong, but it was one thing to know it, and another thing to convince everyone else of that . . . especially when they profited from the purloinment. How could she keep them from dismissing her as a meddling fool? Somehow, she would have to find a way or else the community they had formed would become a monstrosity — wolf heads in reality, preying on those too weak to stop them.

"My friends," she began, her mind still unsettled, gesturing with her hands for them to quiet. "When Will and I welcomed you here, it was because you had nowhere else to go. You had been thrown off your lands because you could not pay your taxes, or been branded as outlaws for stealing the bread you needed to eat. Some of you defended your families against assault, and as a reward found your likenesses adorning the Sheriff's bill.

"Great wrong had been done to you, and so we allowed you to build a life with us," Robin stated. "Then today, I learned that you have become the very wrongdoers that you detest. You have stolen from people who need our help and our protection, not our larceny. What right have you to take from those who have nothing spare to give?"

"The right to survive!" one man shouted. There were loud cries of agreement. "We need supplies—grains and new clothes! How else are we supposed to get them? We have as much right to maintain our lives as anyone!"

"Yes," Robin argued, "but not by depriving others of that right! I have a plan," she continued, working through a nascent idea, "to ensure that we all get a diversity of provisions. Let me help you, and I promise you that hunger and deprivation will soon be only a memory."

"You are nothing but a lad!" Guy of Gisborne cried, rising to his feet. "A whippersnapper who cannot even grow a beard upon his chin. What gives you the *right* to make yourself our leader? If anyone is to be leader here, let it be me!"

He looked around the gathering for support, but no one met his eye. Gisborne was a strong man, both mentally and physically, a soldier outlawed for killing another in a brawl. His was the voice that most often opposed Robin's in the gathered community; he was also a bully, and the people feared him. A few men shifted, but nobody stood.

Gisborne's accusation took Robin aback. Leader? She did not want to be leader—at least, that had not been her intention. She just wanted to stop these people from hurting those who were already so oppressed. But Robin knew that if she allowed Gisborne to seize control of this moment—if she were seen to back down from his challenge—then he would sway the others to his selfish ways, and what had begun as juvenile pilfering would soon degenerate into utter mercenariness.

It would not be the first time Robin had taken charge, but when she had done so in the past, it had been because circumstances required it. It seemed they required it now, but was she the one these people needed? She was a girl, not a commander! But who better? Certainly not Gisborne! As for the rest, they were villeins, uneducated and simple, knowing only their own trade and their own affairs. Robin was of noble birth, and as such had grown up with tutors who had fed her language, science, and strategy (much to Darah's disapproval)! She could think in ways these men could not even begin to comprehend. Who better to lead them than her?

There is no one better, Robin realized. *If I want to help these people, then I will have to take charge completely. It is up to me. I can do this.*

Robin squared her shoulders, accepting the role that Gisborne had unwittingly assigned her. "If you want to continue living here, then you will have to accept my undisputed leadership," she told the congregation slowly, her voice unconsciously taking on her father's timbre of command. "There can be no more personal forays. Yes, we have a right to survive, and yes, we may need to steal to do that . . . but only for what we need to keep us fed and clothed; the rest we will give back to the populace to whom it rightfully belongs. Never again will we rob from the poor — only from the corrupt rich who have pilfered the people's monies for far too long. We may be outlaws, but we will be outlaws with honor . . . a quality not many of the Sheriff's soldiers can claim to possess!"

That assertion got a small chuckle.

"So, we just have to rob from the rich instead of the poor? That does not sound so bad," laughed Gavin o' Dell.

"Honor is more than that," Robin said firmly. "It is sharing what you have with those who have less. It is sheltering and caring for the widows, the orphans, and the sick. It is doing no woman harm," she said, recalling the many bruised cheeks she had seen in her lifetime. Her gaze happened to alight at that moment on a pair of particularly randy twins, and on impulse, she added, "And that includes not spying on them when they bathe."

Tessa, who was sitting on a log near the front of the assembly, gave a distressed cry at this insinuation. Several men chuckled—a knowing rumble that swept along the crowd. Out of the corner of her eye, Robin saw Will hang his head, smiling. Once again, she was glad that she bathed half a mile upstream before anyone else was awake.

Robin waited until the laughter quieted down, her own expression serious. When she finally spoke, her words rang with an earnest conviction that seized the outlaws' hearts. "If you feel you cannot live under my direction, then leave — no one will fault you. But if you stay, you must swear to be more than a band of thieves: you must become a band with more integrity in your bows than all of the Sheriff's servicemen, a band who will do more good for the people than any king. Choose to stay, and together we will create a legacy that your children's children will acclaim."

The crowd was silent for a moment, uncertain. Lives of honor? A legacy of integrity? No one had ever painted their lives in such noble hues before, nor even told them it was a possibility. A strange excitement began to stir within them — the desire to *be* that sort of man. They looked at Robin with shining eyes.

"*I* say," Gisborne menaced from where he stood, breaking the silence, "that you are a fool and that any man who listens to you is a fool as well. I say we just kill you and do what we want with no censure — we are outlaws after all!"

Robin's breath caught in her throat — Johnny's father

looked quite capable of carrying out his threat. For the first time since she had run away, she felt afraid.

Suddenly, David was standing there beside her.

"If you want to kill Robin, you will have to get through me," his low voice menaced, and he flexed his fingers with a wrestler's readiness.

"And me!" Will avowed, racing to stand by her other side.

Everyone immediately quieted. This was truly serious, they realized. Gisborne's threat, Robin's proposal . . . what was happening here would forever change their lives in the greenwood, and they all sensed it. Heads turned to gaze from Robin, to David and Will, to Gisborne, and back to Robin again, their thoughts in a flurry. What should they do?

It was true that they admired and respected Robin, and they esteemed David, whose innate sense of honor had made him the unofficial judge in several camp disputes. Everyone liked Will, the ambassador who had brought them to their current haven, and many of the younger men considered him a personal friend. As for Gisborne . . . well, no one wanted to be under *his* dominion. But was Robin any better to issue such an ultimatum — to demand their loyalty or their expulsion?

Robin had Will and David's support — certainly a strong point in his favor! Furthermore, he had sworn to improve their standard of living, and they knew from experience that his ideas were generally good ones; more importantly, he had never yet broken a promise to them. If anyone could guide their community well, it was he. All things considered, having Robin for a leader might be worth a try!

The murmurs of the crowd converged toward acceptance, causing Guy of Gisborne's eyes to narrow in rage. "I will not follow a mere slip of a boy!" he snarled, meeting Robin's gaze with one of unmerited hatred. His hand fell on the knife at his belt and he took a step forward; David immediately echoed his stance, followed an instant later by Will. Gisborne drew up short. "That milksop will be the death of you all!" he shouted. "Come, Johnny!" Gisborne dragged his son up from his seat by the arm; Johnny shot Will an anxious look, but allowed himself to be steered away. The crowd willingly parted to let them pass.

Robin took a deep breath, trying and failing to expel some of her tension. David and Will stepped back to her side, and she gave them both a small smile of gratitude before turning back to address the gathering in a voice that quivered with passion:

"You all came here with nothing, outlawed from your rightful place in society. You have no one else. We must band together, look to one another, protect each other and those like us. You can be certain no one else will.

"I am Robin o' the Hood," she said, using their nickname for her. "Follow me, and I promise prosperity and merry times for every person here. Follow me, and together we will make the Sheriff rue the day he named us Outlaw!"

"I will follow Robin o' the Hood!" Will cried impetuously, raising his fist into the air.

"As will I," David nodded, giving her a smile.

"I will follow Robin o' Hood," another man swore, and then another, and another, until they were all standing and proclaiming their fealty.

"To Robin o' Hood!"

"Yes, Robin o' Hood!"

And one small boy with a newly made bow: "Huzzah for Robin Hood!"

⚔ 8 ⚔

FIRST FORAY

"HOW MUCH LONGER do we have to sit here?"

"As long as it takes."

"This is boring."

"My leg is falling asleep."

"*I* am falling asleep."

Robin sighed and bit back the urge to hush her men yet again. She really could not fault them for their restlessness; it had been a long afternoon. So far a palmer, two peasants, and a courier had passed them by. None had been, in Robin's estimation, sufficiently unworthy of the cargo they carried to merit her taking it from them.

She had chosen the men for her ambush very carefully, picking them for their patience and marksmanship. There was Murray, the tanner; Lot of Lincoln, a butcher; Nicolas Sutter, ex-miller; and Glenneth and Shane, twin brothers who were, after her, probably the camp's finest archers. And of course,

Will Stutley, whom she doubted she could have left behind even if she had wanted to.

At first, it was with a jovial air that they had taken up their perches in the ash trees or crouched in the bushes that lined the High Road through Sherwood Forest. But as the hours waned by, the tedious wait began to tax even their patient fortitude.

One more hour, Robin promised them silently. *One more hour and then I will call this whole thing off as a dozy idea.*

"Do you hear that?" Murray called softly from the tree next to hers.

Signaling the others to silence, Robin listened. In the distance, the muted jangle of bit harnesses, the shrill peal of bells, and the creaking of a wagon heralded the approach of a small caravan. It would reach the outlaws soon.

From her position in the tree, Robin strung her bow, seeing in her periphery her men do the same. She hoped that they would remember the instructions she had set them; she had been very firm.

"No killing," she had emphasized that morning. "None of you has killed a man, but I have. It is a bitter thing, and I hope I never need do so again. Aim your arrows for a shoulder or a foot; for most, your threat will be deterrent enough. But if something goes wrong and you must strike mortally, then strike hard and see that there is no need to strike again. I would rather have them dead than you."

"Aww, stop it, Robin, yer makin' us blush," Will had quipped, pretending to wave off her concern. The others had laughed, and that had been the end of the speech. For Robin, though, it was far from a laughing matter. She hoped they would remember her words.

She could see the caravan now: four men-at-arms and a large, laden wagon. A yellow canvas sheet was thrown over the top of the cart and bound by thick ropes. Whatever lay underneath must be heavy, for two tawny horses were needed to pull it.

The man driving the cart was clearly a merchant: his green-and-yellow silk jacket was cut in the mercantile style and trimmed with fur, and a blue silk cap perched upon his head to match his bright blue hose.

Like all nobility, Robin had an instinctive dislike for the merchant class, who frequently profited through the use of faulty scales and who sold their goods to a needy public for far more than they were worth. True, some merchants were honest, but in poor Nottinghamshire, such men were few and far between and they often had to struggle to maintain their existence against their more ruthless competitors. This merchant's clothes and guards attested to his wealth — only a rich man could afford four men to escort him through the Sherwood.

Those guards — two at front and two at back — were sitting comfortably upon their horses and peering into the forest as they rode, their expressions reflecting their tedium.

Of course they look bored, Robin mused. *Four guards are more than enough to deter an outlaw or two.* Suspicion and distrust kept most outlaws from joining together; these guards had clearly never encountered the sort of unified band that currently lay in wait for them. The thought made Robin smile.

Out of the corner of her eye, she saw Murray nock an arrow. "Wait," she hissed, knowing full well that he could not hear her. The words were more a prayer than an honest command.

The caravan was below her now, the gaze of the guards skimming right over the green-leafed ash in which Lot was hiding, past the bracken where Nicolas lurked, and beyond the trees where she and Murray dwelt.

The twins were still hidden from view in the their own ash trees several rods ahead, but Will was leaning dangerously far forward out of his. If the guards chanced to look up . . . .

A few more seconds, Robin pleaded. *Just let the wagon get a little bit further . . . .*

"Now!" she cried, leaping from her tree. Lot and Nicolas quickly followed, echoed by Glenneth and Shane. As per her plan, Murray and Will stayed where they were, covering the ambush from above.

The horses, startled by the abrupt appearance of half-a-dozen men, reared up in consternation, squealing loudly as their riders tried to wheel them around. Three of the guards drew their swords; one of them raised a large crossbow, aiming for Lot. Robin placed an arrow through his shoulder before he could shoot, causing him to drop his weapon.

The other guards turned in their saddles, cursing loudly as they examined the ambush. Robin had planned it well. Shane and Glenneth stood several yards ahead of the caravan and Nicolas several yards behind, their drawn bows allowing them to threaten the guards while their distance kept them out of danger from horse and blade. Murray and Will covered the ambush from the treetops, their whoops of glee marking their positions but their height keeping them out of jeopardy. Lot and Robin were by far the closest to the caravan, but the guards did not dare attack them with so many arrows aimed in their direction.

"What are you waiting for?" the merchant blustered. "Kill them!"

The guards ignored him.

"What do you want, archer?" their leader demanded, still struggling to control his mount.

Robin gave him an amicable smile. "To help you. It is clear that you have traveled far and are no doubt weary. Good yeomen that we are, we are here to relieve you of your burden."

"And of our lives?" he asked, stone-faced.

"Just your weapons. Unless you prove difficult. I do hope you do not prove difficult."

The guard considered, but he was in no position to defend against this ambush and he knew it. With a grunt of assent, he tossed his sword onto the ground.

At Robin's signal, Shane and Glenneth darted over to pick up the weapon and those of the other guards as they followed suit.

"I should stomp you flat," one of them muttered rebelliously, flinging his blade to the ground.

Shane mirrored Robin's grin, his eyes gleaming in merriment as he indicated the ready archers with a sweep of his hand. "You are welcome to try."

Meanwhile, Robin approached the merchant, who glared at her fiercely and primed his horses to bolt.

"I would not do that if I were you," she advised as he raised his whip. "Unless you want a sheaf of arrows in your back."

"Churl!" the man bellowed. "Brigand! You are nothing but an honorless, gutless, low-account thief!"

"Did you hear that, men?" Robin asked, pitching her voice to carry.

"We heard, Robin!" Murray shouted from the trees. "Shall we teach this varlet a lesson?"

The merchant squared his back, steeling himself for the arrow that would end his life. He did not look the least bit repentant.

"Aye, we shall," she agreed after a moment's consideration. "But not in the way he expects. Gentlemen, let it never be said that Robin o' the Hood and his men are honorless thieves. You will dine with us tonight. Come!"

Robin hopped into the wagon and seized the reins from the startled merchant. "I am afraid there is not room up here for two. You, my good sir, will have to walk."

For a moment, he looked like he was going to refuse — then with a loud oath, he dismounted, glaring dourly.

Turning her gaze from the merchant to the rest of the assemblage, Robin saw that the guard she had wounded was reeling in his saddle. In the stress of the moment, she had forgotten about him!

At her direction, Lot helped the man dismount from his horse and cut the arrow from his shoulder, using the guard's tunic as a rude bandage. Then he and Glenneth settled the wounded man onto the back of the wagon; the guard gave a small groan but made no other sound, his lips locked white against the blood loss and pain.

A queasy feeling of guilt settled into Robin's stomach. *Blast him anyway for making me shoot him,* she thought defensively. *Why could he not just surrender peacefully?*

With a nod, Lot indicated that he had done everything he could for the man — further aid would have to wait until they reached camp. Robin nodded back to show that she understood and turned the cart into the forest, leading the way; the others followed closely behind her.

All activity stopped in the camp when Robin rode in accompanied by four guards, a disgruntled merchant, and her cadre of archers.

"A feast!" she ordered blithely, leaping down from the cart. "Set a beast to cook. We have guests!"

With a bow of welcome, she indicated for the confused convoy to settle themselves at the base of the central oak. This they did with laudable self-possession, refusing to show overt discomfort at finding themselves in what was clearly an outlaw camp.

"What is going on, Robin?" David asked, appearing at her side. "I thought you were going to bring us a pretty purse, not a whole caravan."

"Now, David, would you have me refuse them our hospitality?" she asked, clapping him on the shoulder. "After all, we are not common thieves who take what has not been earned. Trust me," she said, lowering her voice. "We will get their purses yet. But I will not have it said that we are nothing but disgraceful brigands who prey on others for sheer profit. We must be more than that, or we will quickly go the way of Guy of Gisborne."

Shifting her attention, she snatched a gaping lad by the elbow as he edged in for a look. "Fetch Edra and tell her one of our guests has an arrow in his shoulder—ask her to tend to it, please."

"Now, gentlemen," Robin said, striding over to the seated men. "You have had a trying journey, I am sure. Perhaps some entertainment to help you relax?"

Not waiting for an answer, she beckoned over John Logan and Richard Bentworth, who agreed to her request to wrestle for the pleasure of their "guests."

At first, it seemed that Logan would win without difficulty, for he was a big, burly man whose large stature lent him strength; but though Bentworth was smaller, he was also craftier, and he shrewdly evaded his opponent's clutch time and again.

Such was the skill of the two wrestlers that the guards soon forgot their situation and found themselves cheering on the powerful display; even the wounded man managed a ragged whoop, startling Edra, who was in the process of dressing his wound, and earning himself a stern rebuke. Only the merchant appeared unaffected.

With one last tumble, the wrestlers stopped, and the approving guards shouted their acclaim as the sportsmen helped each other to their feet and bowed.

"Shane, Glenneth! Show these men what you can do with a longbow," Robin called before the applause had a chance to die down.

A young boy scampered to mark a piece of bark on a birch tree at the far edge of the glade, and the twins took turns shooting at the target, their arrows breaking off pieces of the bark until all that was left was a sliver of mark; they unstrung their bows with satisfied smiles.

"There is but an inch left," Robin said, gazing at her guests with a neutral expression. "Do any of you care to try to mar the mark?"

The head guard stood up. Without hesitation, Shane handed him his bow and stepped back to watch.

"You can barely see the target!" one of the guards protested. Their leader ignored him and restrung the bow. Accepting an arrow from Glenneth, he nocked it to the string and with one smooth motion, pulled back the bow and shot.

"Just shy!" called the boy who still lingered by the mark.

"No one can make that shot," the leader averred, returning the bow to Shane.

"No one?" he asked lightly, looking at Robin with an expectant smirk. Pride fluttered through her at his unspoken assumption, and she obligingly stepped forward and strung her yew bow. Giving the target the briefest of glances, she drew back an arrow and loosed.

"God's Teeth!" cried the skeptical serviceman in amazement as her shaft split the faint white mark in twain; two shards of pale bark fluttered their surrender to the ground.

Robin allowed herself a small smile as her men cheered her shot, joined after a moment by the astounded acclamation of the guards. Though her face flushed hot with pleasure, she did her best to appear unaffected by the praise.

"Now, we eat!" she cried to mask her emotion, indicating with a sweep of her hand that viands should be brought.

The guards, ravenous after the excitement of the afternoon, seized eagerly at the meat they were given, delighting in its consumption and ignoring the hot juices that burned their hands. The merchant alone turned his head away from the food, although he could not keep from licking his lips as the delicious aroma wafted around him.

"Surely, you are hungry?" Robin asked. "I know this is not the sort of fare you are accustomed to, but it will do you good to eat."

His lips curled in disgust. "Even if you were a lord in your hall, I would not eat your food. Do you think I have fallen for this act? What sort of sadistic game is this, that you would taunt us with the semblance of kindness before you kill us and take what is ours?"

"You misunderstand," Robin said, taken aback. "We have brought you here as guests of this, our greenwood inn. If we were going to kill you, we would have done it already."

Glenneth chuckled; the merchant glared.

"You claim we are thieves, but how many times have you taken advantage of your customers?" Robin continued. "Can you honestly say that those robes on your back and the jewels on your hands were not paid for by selfish — if not fraudulent — dealings? We may take from you today, but only what you have taken unfairly first, and what we purloin will go to help those you have wronged. We do not take out of a misplaced desire for profit."

The man was silent, but his face glowed red. The guards, delighting in their meal, did not notice the exchange.

Once everyone had consumed their fill, Robin stood to address her guests, raising her voice for all to hear. "Good sirs, you have supped with us and been entertained by us. You would find a less hospitable reception even in a lord's hall." She shot the merchant the briefest of glances. "It is only just that you replace the viands we have expended on you and provide payment for your entertainment. I think . . . this . . . should cover it."

She withdrew the iron strongbox she had seen under the wagon's seat. One blow from the hilt of her sword broke its lock, and she opened the box to reveal a profusion of gold coins.

"You cannot take that!" the merchant cried, a note of panic arising in his voice for the first time. "Those are the taxes I owe the Sheriff! It will beggar me to replace those."

"Somehow, I doubt that," Robin remarked blandly. "But in the meantime, think on its absence and consider well the impact of your greed." She handed the chest off to David, who was standing close by. "Come, the hour grows late; men like yourselves should not spend the night in the Sherwood —

you might fall into the company of truly dishonest persons. Mount your steeds — we will lead you back to the High Road."

"What of our weapons?" asked a ginger-haired guard as he climbed onto the horse Glenneth held.

"A gift we are honored to accept," came the shameless reply.

Robin drove the cart warily through the forest, trying to avoid the deeper brush that would snag the wheels as she led the group on a mazelike circuit back to the main road.

From now on, I think it would be wiser to simply blindfold our guests on the journey to and from camp; that way it is certain they cannot find their way back, and I will not have to waste so much time devising a detour!

By the time the group gained the road, the land was awash with the last rays of twilight. The instant Robin disembarked from the wagon, the merchant leapt up into the seat and whipped his horses into a canter, not waiting to be accompanied by his failed guards.

Shaking their heads, his escort started down the road after him, but after a moment, the head guard wheeled his mount back around and returned to address Robin.

"You are a strange one, Outlaw. You could have had our lives and all our goods many times this day — instead, you fed us and entertained us, and now you let us go. Why?"

Robin looked him solemnly in the eyes. "Because we are *not* murderers or selfish brigands — we are only humble men, trying to earn our living in a world that has stolen that living from us. Yes, we must put a price on our hospitality so that we and needful others might survive, but we bear you no ill will and would not have you bear us ill will, either."

"The Sheriff shall hear of this, you know."

Was it Robin's imagination, or were those words spoken less as a threat and more as a warning?

"I hope that is true," she told him. "And make certain he hears, too, that our inn will welcome *any* traveler who passes through the Sherwood with ill-gotten gains."

The guard's face was in shadow, so Robin might only have fancied that his mouth curved into a slight smile as he turned his horse back up the road, kicking it into an easy canter that quickly caught him up with the others.

Upon her return to camp, Robin found the outlaws surrounding the chest of gold, their eyes shining as bright in the firelight as the coins themselves. To her relief, David was standing guard in front of the chest, his watchful gaze ensuring that no eager person made off with so much as one coin.

"It is all here, Robin," David told her when she approached.

She cast the crowd an easy smile, as if she had never doubted its restraint. "Wonderful. Give every man, woman, and child a piece of gold."

Cheers greeted this instruction, and Shane and Glenneth had to step in quickly to keep the people from trampling David. Yet even once the monies had been handed out (the twins kept a stern watch to ensure that no one tried to come back for seconds—Alan Haxey had to be sent away three times), there was still a sizable amount left over.

Robin counted out ten gold coins and deposited them in the sack at her hip. The rest she left in the chest.

"David, in the morning I want you and Will to take the rest of these coins and go into town — Ancaster, this first time. Start at the outskirts, with the poorest hovels, and give each family twenty shillings worth until you run out of money. Be wary of trouble and make sure no one follows you back."

Will was shaking his head in amazement. "Twenty shillings?" he protested. "'Tis half a year's wages! Ye only gave us one coin!"

"Those people need that money a lot more than you do," Robin told him sternly. "*They* still have to pay the Sheriff's exorbitant taxes, and for most they are nearly impossible to afford. Besides, if we have many more days like today, we will soon have more than enough money to meet our needs — even receiving only one coin each! Do not begrudge the poor their share of the yield."

"What is your intention for those?" David asked, indicating Robin's makeshift purse.

She glanced ruefully down at her patchy tunic. "It seems to me that our band's most pressing need right now is new clothes. Tomorrow, I go to Lincoln Town to buy our uniforms."

"Uniforms?" Will's eyebrows shot up in alarm. "Ye ne'er said nothin' 'bout uniforms!"

David grinned at the youth's dismay. "I like the idea. Uniforms will tell the Sheriff that we are not just a bunch of discontents — we are Robin Hood's men: champions of the poor, heroes to the needy, opponents of the greedy — "

"We get the idea," she said, interrupting his teasing.

David chuckled and knelt by the chest. Taking off his cap, he began tucking into it the monies he was to disperse. "Just choose a color other than that hideous scarlet that is in style," he enjoined, looking up. "We may be your men, but that does not mean we want to go around looking like a robin redbreast."

"No, red is hardly the proper color to define an outlaw of Sherwood, is it?" Robin mused. "I will be sure to ask for something more appropriate."

⚔ 9 ⚔

LINCOLN GREEN

THE STREETS OF LINCOLN TOWN were still busy, even
though the sun had begun to set in a blaze of crimson and
gold. Robin glanced at the fiery sphere in rueful reflection; the
sun had been at the same height, but on the uprise, when she
had set out from Sherwood Forest that morning.

Nottingham would have been a much closer walk, or
Radford, or any of the other small villages that dotted the
landscape, but they did not have a tailor such as Lincoln
Town was reputed to possess. This man did his own dyeing,
and his expertise with hues was rumored to be so great that
he could make a man practically disappear against the foliage
of Sherwood! Such a valuable talent would be well worth
Robin's journey.

As she wandered through the streets in search of the tailor's shop, Robin kept her eyes open for a quiet hostelry that
would not object to her ragged attire and where she could

—after her business was done—buy herself a few hours' rest before starting back home once again. At last, a dilapidated structure with a tawdry yard caught her eye. It was called *The Pilgrim's Rest*, and from what Robin could glimpse of the inside, her shabby appearance would not give the innkeeper any qualms.

Robin managed to find the tailor's shop just as the sun was winking its last rays upon the horizon. The store was an unassuming wood-and-stone structure with a tiny dirt yard bordered by a post-and-rail fence. Robin stepped through the open door into a small room; a thin workbench laden with cloth clippings and steel shears lined one wall, opposed by a wooden model and shelves burdened with fabric on the other. A reed screen curtained off the back of the shop from what was most likely the house proper.

"Hello?" Robin called. "Is anyone here?"

"Be with ye in a moment," a man's voice shouted from the back.

"How can I help ye?" the tailor asked, materializing from behind the screen. He was a small, grizzled man with a bent back and eyes creased into slits from years spent poring over cloth by dim tallowlight. Upon seeing Robin, his eyes narrowed further with suspicion.

In her threadbare tunic, her hose with too many holes, and her head hooded even indoors, Robin knew that she looked far from reputable. Indeed, the tailor's expression gave voice to his doubts: Clearly this customer was in need of new clothes, but could he pay?

The tailor's gaze took in the bow and quiver on Robin's back and the sword that hung at her waist; many men carried such weapons, but rarely was their attire so tattered. These observations spoke contradictory tales to his seasoned eye — a client to be treated with caution.

Robin read these misgivings in the man's face, but she refused to let them disturb her. "That depends. I wish to place a large order, but I do not wish its existence to become public knowledge." She let her hand rest for a moment upon the workbench. When she moved her hand away, the glint of gold remained behind.

The tailor's gaze fell upon the coin she had laid down, and his mouth tightened.

"I do not take bribes," he barked. "Pay me my due for the work I shall do, and ye need not fear what I may say."

Robin took a deep breath, embarrassed by the rebuke, and returned the coin to her sack. "Very well, the order I wish to place is this: fifty-two outfits such as a forester might wear, four sets of ladies clothing, and seven sets of boys attire, all in that peculiar shade I hear is the very essence of Sherwood Forest."

"Its name is Lincoln Green," the tailor remarked absently, already tallying up supplies in his mind, "and I do not often receive requests for ladies clothing, not with a dressmaker in town."

His gaze sharpened; Robin feared the tailor was about to question the need for such an uncommon order, but he did not. "It will be expensive," he informed her instead. "I require payment first. You may settle in installments, if you choose."

"That will not be necessary."

Robin untied the sack of gold from her belt and handed it to him. Clearly dubious about her professed ability to pay, the tailor opened the bag; his eyes widened in surprise at the amount inside.

"I trust that will be enough?" Robin asked. She had guessed at the cost, using Darah's lectures on prices and wares to forestall getting cheated. *Someday, I will have to thank Darah . . . her lessons have turned out to be far more useful than I could have ever imagined!*

The tailor's eyes turned inward as he performed some quick calculations; after a moment, he nodded that it was. Ever an honest man, he gave Robin back one gold coin before tucking the rest of the money into his tunic. More amiable now that he had been paid, he asked for the desired measure of the clothes she wanted, which Robin did her best to provide, using the tailor and herself for a scale.

"I will need to send to London Town for more cloth, and then I will have to dye it before it can be sewn," he apprised her. "It will take several weeks to finish an order of this size."

"Then I will return every week to take what is ready," Robin said, preparing to leave. She paused at the door, David's remark flitting through her mind.

"Oh, and one more thing—throw in a suit of scarlet, will you? My size. To be completed first."

Robin managed to keep a straight face until the moment she actually handed David the first batch of clothes, and he opened the bundle to see a vibrant red suit staring up at him.

"Lord have mercy," he groaned, and Robin burst out laughing. He glared at her. "I mean it, Robin, if you did that with the whole ruddy lot . . . ."

Still laughing, Robin reached into the sack and pushed the outfit aside, revealing the layers of green underneath.

"You should have seen your face, David!" she gasped.

"It matched that tunic perfectly."

"Good 'un, Robin," Will Stutley agreed, plucking the scarlet suit out of the bag. "Can I 'ave it?"

"No, this one is mine," she answered, retrieving the outfit from him.

"Robin Redbreast," Shane called from his perch high in the oak tree. "You will stick out like a sore thumb."

"No, I shan't wear this except on special occasions . . . like the day you finally beat me at archery, Shane."

He shook his head in dismay, making those who had heard them laugh. The two youths had a casual rivalry going, which led to some good-natured gambling by the men whenever the two of them would practice together, though the stakes were never very high as Robin had yet to lose to the twin during an "official" match.

Shane pretended to scowl at this reminder. "Then you had best go change right now," he warned. "I have a feeling that tonight is going to be my night."

But as things turned out, Robin had no need to wear her red suit that night, nor any other night, much to Shane's disappointment. Instead, she reveled in her green attire, rejoicing in the feel of the soft wool against her body and in the comfortable fit of the suit. Her cousin's clothes had been just a little too tight in all the wrong places, but her new outfit was loose and airy — perfect now that it was summer, but still able to keep her warm on cooler nights.

Better still was the camouflage the new clothes provided; so long as the outlaws did not move, travelers and guards could stare straight at them without realizing they were there.

One moment a caravan might be traveling down a deserted forest path, and the next it would be surrounded by men in Lincoln Green, each with an arrow aimed at the guards. This shocking manifestation, combined with Robin's diligent planning, left sojourners no choice but to surrender. The outlaws never again had to fire a shot.

While the rich soon grew to hate Robin and her band, the poor quickly learned that they need not fear to travel through Sherwood Forest. Robin permitted attacks only on the corrupt: the abbots wearing heavy gold crucifixes, robes of silk and satin, and vitreous carbuncle rings — their wealth funded by misdirecting the tithes of impoverished peasants; the lords perched upon purebred mounts, who prospered by levying unfair taxes, even while their people starved; the merchants clothed in opulence, who rigged their scales and sold their goods for far more than they were worth. Such travelers soon found themselves the unwilling guests of Robin and her band.

Unwilling, yes, but only at first, for many of these guests soon found their rage melting away in light of the outlaws' courtesy — their captors would even apologize for having to blindfold them to and from camp! Upon their arrival, these visitors would be seated at the base of a giant oak — nick-named the Trysting Tree for this reason — and laden with ale to drink and sport to entertain while a feast was prepared in their honor.

These repasts grew along with the band's monies until guests were regaled not only with venison, but also with oaten cakes laced with honey, and with sweetmeats, quail, and pasties. Wrestlers and cudgellers would battle for their visitors' delight, but it was the archery exhibition at the close of the evening that truly astonished with its skill. When the time later came to pay the outlaws' tab, many patrons agreed that the price was equal to the experience.

Soon the band's coffers were overflowing with pieces of silver and gold — farthings sometimes, but more often deniers and groats. Indeed, the outlaws were beginning to amass so much money that they had to convert one of the caves into a treasury to hold it all until the money could be properly divided amongst the poor.

Robin tried to spread the wealth as much as possible, sending purses first to Ancaster, then to Warsop, then to Mansfield — even to Nottingham. Initially, the peasants were suspicious of the gifts and would sometimes chase off the men she had sent with knives or other implements.

I suppose I cannot blame them, Robin mused after one such report. *When has anyone ever just* given *them money? Always, people are trying to take it away.*

To help keep her men safe while still enabling delivery, she directed them to hide the money where it could later be found and began to do so herself. She hid coins amongst hen eggs, under doorways, and on the seats of carts. For the most part this tactic worked perfectly, but one day as she went to leave a few shillings on the windowsill of a daub-and-wattle cottage, one of the coins slipped off the thin ledge and tumbled to the floor, striking against a chamber pot as it fell.

The lady of the house whipped around at the noise, caught sight of the coins on the sill, and dashed over just in time to see Robin darting away.

"Wait!" she called. "Please, wait!"

The woman's tone was imploring rather than alarmed. Intrigued, Robin halted, fidgeting her weight onto her toes so she could leap into flight again at the slightest need.

"It is just as Frank Miller said," the woman breathed, leaning out the window for a better look. "A man in green — you are one of the men of Sherwood! You might even be —" she gulped and made a miming motion with her hands, as though pulling something over her head, " — Robin Hood himself!"

"My lady," Robin affirmed with a bow. The woman gasped.

"Will you please come in?" she begged. "To have Robin Hood in my home . . . ."

"I would, my lady, but there are others who have need of my coin."

"Of course, of course! Go," she called, "and God bless you, Robin Hood!"

Robin was still pondering the encounter when she arrived back at the outlaw camp. As she sank onto her favorite bed of moss, Nicolas came up to greet her, looking rather debonair in his new Lincoln Green suit. With only a few outfits remaining to be made, nearly everyone had their new clothes by now.

"The Sheriff sent soldiers into the forest again today," Nicolas was saying. "They did not even get as far as Apple Road this time before one of your patrol teams discovered them. A few threatening arrows in their direction, and they decided they had business somewhere else."

"The team did not kill anyone, did they?" she asked.

She could swear that Nicolas rolled his eyes. "*No*, Robin."

"A curious thing happened today," she mused. "A lady saw me leaving money on a window ledge and called to me by name — Robin *Hood*, she called me. She acted like I was someone special — like I was royalty!"

Was it her imagination, or was Nicolas refusing to meet her eyes?

"Funny, that," he said.

"Ni–ck . . ." she protested.

"Well, what did you expect, Robin?" Lot asked, looking up from the stag he was roasting. "The people want someone to thank. You have done more for them than any sheriff or lord. What do you think we answer, when they ask us who we are?"

"We are the Merry Men of Sherwood," Shane called from somewhere high in the branches of Old Tryst. "Humble vassals of our jaunty leader, Robin Hood."

"You are not my vassals!" Robin reproved.

"But we are," Nicolas informed her. "We swore to you when we agreed to follow you, and you have given us no reason to gainsay you. We are well recompensed for our service, and more importantly, by helping us to right the wrongs we have all suffered, you have given our lives pur-pose, and a noble one at that. We are proud to be known as your men."

Robin shook her head — it embarrassed her to be treated with such deference. She had not given out of a desire for recognition and would have preferred to remain anonymous, or to at least let her men take the credit. Still, it was clear that her band would not permit that. Humbled by their loyal conviction, she let the matter drop.

To Robin's confused pleasure, small gifts began to appear along the verge of the forest — a loaf of coarse bread, a small bag of flour. The people of Nottinghamshire had little they could spare to give their enigmatic benefactors, but they still felt the need to thank those whose gifts of coin meant their families could endure for another year. While these tokens of appreciation were usually half-spoilt by the time one of Robin's scouts stumbled across them (Robin, for her part, suspected there were many more such gifts that hungry woodland creatures had ensured they would never find), the sentiment remained unmarred.

One day, a pair of scouts returned to say that a merchant convoy was making its way from Mansfield Town toward the High Road; Robin and her cadre of elite archers (with the exception of Lot, who preferred his role as camp cook) set out to intercept.

The panicked whinnying of horses was the first indication that something was amiss. Raising a hand to warn her archers to silence, Robin crept forward through the bracken to peer at the road.

Three guards were trying to steady their mounts as they clustered around a laden wagon; their swords were out in their hands and they wore expressions of fear and loathing on their faces. A fourth man lay dead in the dirt before the wagon, an arrow shaft through his chest and his head half-crushed where his horse had trampled him in terror.

A hundred paces down the road, an archer was holding the entire convoy at bay, threatening them all with his drawn bow. He had a hood pulled up over his face.

"Surrender!" he shouted. "Surrender to Robin Hood!"

Robin's eyebrows shot up to her hairline. Gasps of indignation came from the others, who had come up behind her to peer through the bracken as well.

"The gall of the imposter!" Glenneth hissed in rage. "Taking on your name and hunting on our turf!"

"Does it matter?" Nicolas asked. "He is not doing any different than what we usually do."

"But we give our money away to the poor! Who is to say he will not keep it all for himself?" Shane demanded.

"And 'e killed a man!" Will Stutley piped up. "'E definitely killed a man!"

"Hey, I know him," Murray interrupted, looking not at the archer but at the merchant in the cart. "I used to run errands for him before I became an outlaw. He is a good man and an honest mercer — the only one I knew."

"We surrender!" the merchant called, leaning halfway out of his cart to place a restraining hand on the shoulder of a guard who looked ready to charge down the archer, never mind that he would surely be slain before his horse could take a dozen steps. "Only, kill no more of my men!"

Robin had witnessed enough. "Shane, Glenneth, I want you to flank that archer from behind. The rest of you, come with me. We are going to put a stop to this villainy."

She strung her bow, as did the others, keeping one eye to the scene playing out beyond the verge. The imposter was creeping forward along the road, his gazed fixed on the wagon with unadulterated greed. He kept his bow drawn and his arrow trained on the merchant, though Robin could see his muscles trembling from the unaccustomed strain of keeping it pulled back. If he were not careful, he was going to loose the shaft by accident.

Robin gave the twins just enough time to reach the archer before she stepped out onto the road. "Halt!" she cried, letting loose an arrow at the same time. It struck the archer's bow and knocked it from his hands, causing his arrow to whiz off harmlessly to the right. With a frightened cry, the man scrambled for his weapon, seized it and stood up, only to find himself surrounded on all sides by men in Lincoln Green.

The merchant and his guards gaped at the newcomers, at

first too startled to react; slowly, their expressions changed from fear and shock to utter hopelessness. Robin gave them a reassuring smile.

"Please do not fear," she said. "We mean you no harm."

"Who are you?" the merchant demanded, his voice wavering.

"I am Robin Hood," she said. The imposter let out a low groan and sank to the ground.

The merchant had experienced too many shocks that day and when he spoke next, his tone was merely weary. "Of course you are. Just take it all. But please, do not kill my men."

"Robin Hood and his band never kill except in defense," she said sternly, not so much to the merchant as to the man who was sitting with his head in his hands. "And we only take from those whose actions towards others are unjust or cruel. I have it on good authority that you are ever kind and honest in your dealings. As such, you have nothing to fear from us. Take your goods and your dead and continue on in peace, for none shall waylay you again."

Though clearly suspicious, neither the guards nor the merchant wished to question this unexpected turn of events. Two of the guards warily dismounted and picked up the body of their slain comrade, wrapping him in burlap from the wagon and laying him inside.

The third guard rode a little ways along the road and returned after a moment leading his companion's horse, which had only fled around the bend. Within minutes, the entire convoy was under away.

"See that they make their destination safely," Robin told the three men standing beside her. They nodded and disappeared into the trees.

Robin walked over to where Shane and Glenneth were guarding the would-be brigand, who was still sitting on the road with his head bowed in despair. She squatted down in front of him.

"Why did you do it?" she asked in a voice that was terrifying in its tranquility. The man began to shake, but when he finally looked up, his voice was defiant:

"Why should I ne do it? Why should ye be the only ones to steal from the rich?"

"Do you think we just take from whoever we feel like it?" Robin demanded coldly. "We have to be certain that their fortunes are ill-gotten. We have to *know* them. Do you think I do not know who is who and what is what? I tell you that I do; and furthermore, my people never take a life to take a purse."

"I did ne mean to take his life," the man said, a sob breaking through the cock in his voice. "He had a crossbow, and I was so scared . . . ."

Robin took a closer look at the imposter and saw that he was only a couple of years older than she. His face was thin to the point of gauntness, and underneath his bravado of manner, he was clearly terrified. Pity warred with Robin's ire, and in the end, pity won out.

"I know what it is like to kill a man without intention," she commiserated quietly. "It haunts you, or it should. You can never make it right—all you can do is try to ensure that it never happens again."

"I just wanted to feed my family," he whispered. "You left us some coin, but it all went to our lord—we owed him so much in rent; and the children are so hungry . . . ."

"Go home," Robin advised him, rising to her feet. "You cannot help your children if you are an outlaw or dead. As it is, you are fortunate that the convoy could not see your face, and so cannot identify you." Reaching out her hand, she helped the man to stand, but did not let go right away, ensuring that she had his full attention for what she was about to say. "But lest you be the first of many, let it be known to all that Sherwood Forest is Robin Hood's territory and that he will deal harshly from now on with any man found to be masquerading under his name, or who waylays its thoroughfares without his permission, or who takes the lives of any within its bounds—including those of the rich."

The man nodded anxiously that he understood and scurried away the instant she released his hand, hastening down the road in the opposite direction as the convoy. With a troubled sigh, Robin turned away from him and examined the scene of the encounter with a sorrowful gaze. Something glinted beneath a bush by the verge, catching her eye.

This time when Robin strode into the tailor's shop, he was standing in front of the reed partition with her bundle in his hands as though he had been waiting for her.

"That is new," the tailor remarked, indicating a silver bugle adorning Robin's right hip.

Finding the bugle had been the only bright moment in Robin's encounter with her imposter. Most likely, the instrument had fallen from the slain guard's belt and had been kicked aside by his bolting horse, skittering off the road to land beneath a bush. The convoy, distracted, had not noticed it fall, and in the haste of their departure, the bugle's presence beneath the hawthorn bush had been overlooked.

Robin had kept the bugle with her to remind her of the influence she could have on others — both for good and for bad — though she soon found herself carrying it for its own sake as well. It was a sweet, lithe instrument with a mirthful voice that traveled far, and she used it now to sound her raids, rather than bellowing. This caused her band to joke that her voice was not deep enough to resonate through the trees on its own, so she needed the bugle to do her shouting for her. Robin did her best to laugh at such jests, even though they gave her concern. How long before someone truly gave thought to her peculiarities: her whiskerless face, her leaner thews, her odd habits? She had no false illusions — only the ingrained belief that a woman could never achieve (and would certainly never try to achieve!) what Robin had done prevented her people from suspecting her gender. If ever they should have cause to doubt that assumption . . . .

"Yes, it is," she told the tailor simply, indicating with her tone that the subject was closed.

He nodded. "Forgive me. I notice a man's accouterments out of habit."

He handed her the bundle containing the last of the Lincoln Green suits she had ordered, but rather than disappearing behind the screen as was his habit, the tailor lingered.

"Our account is settled, is it not?" Robin asked, puzzled by his odd behavior.

"What? Oh, yes . . . yes, it is."

Robin waited several seconds, but when he said nothing more, she murmured, "Well, good day," and turned to leave.

"Ye will have heard of the Sheriff's archery contest — " the tailor spoke up suddenly.

"Archery contest?"

"Ye have not heard of it?" He looked as though he regretted raising the topic.

"I have heard of it now. Tell me."

"It seems," the tailor said slowly, in the manner of one weighing the impact of his words, "that a company of outlaws is making trouble for our good Sheriff. He has put a price of £200 on its leader's head and £50 on any of his men; strangely enough, no one has even attempted to claim the reward. Perhaps people are afraid to undertake the warrant — it is said that these outlaws can appear and disappear at will, so perfectly do they blend into their surroundings. Or perhaps the people's lack of interest is more . . . charitable."

Robin's gaze sharpened on the tailor. How much did he know or guess?

"The Sheriff has proposed an archery contest," he went on, "to try to attract men who might be willing to take up his warrant. The prize for the winner is said to be an arrow of solid gold."

"A tempting reward," she allowed noncommittally.

"Yes, indeed. These outlaws are reputed to have fine aim and their leader the finest of all. If ye ask me, I think the Sheriff intends to attract more than bounty hunters — I think he intends to attract the bounty itself."

"Surely, no outlaw would be foolish enough to walk into such an obvious snare," Robin remarked.

The tailor had yet to take his eyes from her face, shadowed as it was within the depths of her hood. "Indeed, we must hope not."

She gave the man a small bow of farewell, acknowledging his warning. Clearly, he had guessed who she was and just as clearly, he had no intention of turning her in. It was good to be acquainted with such a man.

"Good day, Master Tailor," she said, hoisting the sack over her shoulder and heading out the door.

His reply was almost inaudible as he closed the shop behind her, "Good day . . . Master Archer."

Her men exchanged exasperated glances across the fire. They had been trying for the last quarter of an hour to dissuade Robin from attending the Sheriff's tourney — without success.

"Robin, 'tis a trap! Eadom — you know Eadom, the innkeeper at the Blue Boar Inn — he told me that some soldiers were in there drinking the other day, and they as good as said so. You will be putting your own head in the noose if you go into Nottingham for this contest."

"*Tsk, tsk*, Lot, will you quaff away all your money?" Robin demanded with mock ferocity, attempting to change the subject. "We will not lend you more just so you can go and drink it all away."

"Robin, this is serious," David insisted, refusing to let her divert their concern. "I was there, too, and I heard the same. Do you value your neck so little that you would risk it for pride? Have you thought about what will happen to us if you get caught?"

Robin made a face, instinctively balking at his suggestion that it was pride that goaded her actions. *Well, perhaps it is a little*, she admitted to herself. *But it is more than that. It is about standing up to the Sheriff. He needs to know that he cannot rule me or intimidate me. Flouting him to his face will merely be an added bonus.*

"I am certain that you would all survive without me," she

assured her friends, holding up a hand to stave off their pro-
tests, "but as it is, I have no intention of being captured. *When
I go to Nottingham, I promise that none shall know me for
Robin Hood. Will that satisfy you?"*

David scowled. "Do we have a choice?" His voice bespoke
resignation.

She gave a merry laugh. "None at all."

⚔ **10** ⚔

THE GOLDEN ARROW

THE LANCET GATEWAY through the wall around Nottingham Town was crammed with people all trying to shove their way into the burg. Their discordant voices hurt Robin's ears and the crush of their bodies made it difficult to move. What little space she had instantly disappeared as a horse and litter wedged their way into the passage, forcing those on foot to squeeze together against the tunnel walls to keep from getting trampled.

As soon as the nobles' conveyance had passed, the peasants expanded into the gateway once more, carrying Robin along with them. A wave of sound slammed into her as they spilled into the town, making the tunnel rumpus seem like a soothing whisper by comparison.

"Pasties! Get yer hot pasties!"

"Sweetmeats! Barley sugar! Quarter farthing a strip!"

Robin staggered as an overeager vendor bumped into her.

Rather than apologizing, he shoved a pasty in front of her face, hollering the price.

Desperately muffling her ears with her hands, Robin stumbled away from the man and towards the leftmost edge of the horde, opposite the current of the crowd. After living in the quiet greenwood for nearly a year, the frenzied commotion and the clamor of peddlers were almost too much for her to endure.

"Certain you will not change your mind, Robin?" David cried, battling his way toward his comrade, his voice barely audible above the din.

She shook her head, but the motion was lost amidst the jostling of the throng; at last, the two friends broke free and stood together in a fallow field, panting hard.

David had accompanied Robin into Nottingham in spite of her protests, as had Shane, Glenneth, and several of the others. It was their risk to bear, they had argued, and worth the danger to see their leader trounce the Sheriff at his own game; but Robin knew their real motive was to be on hand in case something went wrong. Their concern gratified her, but she still would have preferred they had stayed behind.

At least they had agreed to don disguises. David, for instance, was wearing a farmer's knee-length tunic. Right now, it was crooked from his battle with the crowd and the skirt had gotten spattered with mud; still, the dishevelment only added to his country peasant look.

Robin craned her neck to see if she could spy any of her other friends — a challenge since none of them were wearing their usual Lincoln Green. At last, she caught sight of Will Stutley animatedly flirting with a flower girl. The poor lass seemed torn between succumbing to his relentless attention and ignoring him completely.

"That boy would try to woo the Queen Mother herself," Robin laughed, her tone not altogether approving.

"Wooing the Queen Mother would still be safer than shooting before the Sheriff," David insisted.

Robin let out an exasperated sigh. "David, you are my friend and I know you are just worried, but enough already! I have made my decision and you can either support me in it or not, but stop trying to change my mind!"

"I have always supported you, Robin," David said softly. "You know that."

Robin felt her ire subside. "I do," she admitted. "And I am grateful for your concern . . . truly I am. But honestly, David, do you really expect the Sheriff to recognize me in this?" She held up her arms in an orator's gesture and spun in place.

Instead of her suit of Lincoln Green, Robin was wearing her suit of brilliant red. Over her head was a scarlet hood, and one ragged patch covered her left eye. Only the nondescript quiver on her back, the small sack at her hip, and the longbow in her hand were familiar accouterments.

David gave a rueful laugh. "*I* barely recognize you in that getup. Perhaps this ploy of yours will succeed after all."

Robin smirked. "I intend it to."

In order to reach the tournament, however, she would have to navigate the tumultuous crowd once again; the very thought made her head reel. To buy herself some time, she surveyed her surroundings.

She was standing in a field to the left of the town gate — the first in a long series of pastures and houses. Beyond the houses were strips of tilled dirt, speckled with budding crops. The road through the gate traveled straight for a hundred paces before broadening into the town square. Atop a small rise in its center stood a gallows tree, surrounded almost indecently by the stalls and shops of the market. Somewhere in the distance a church bell tolled, and more fields could be seen lining the eastern border of the town. The archery range was to the right of the gate, but it was the tall sandstone ridge just beyond it that caught Robin's eye. Upon this steep precipice perched Nottingham Castle — the formidable home of Sheriff Darniel.

"Nasty thing," David said, following her gaze. "People say it is impregnable — the cliffs guard it on three sides, and the fourth wall has only one gate. Well, secure it may be, but I find it horribly bleak — I am almost sorry for the Sheriff, cooped up inside there of nights. I am glad *I* do not have to live there."

As am I, Robin thought. There was no comparing a castle's stone walls and cruel ceilings with the bright and sprightly boughs of an unfettered Sherwood. To think that she had almost been mistress of Darniel's dreadful fortress made her shudder.

"Come on," she said, hoping David had not noticed her reaction. "We have a tournament to win."

The archery range was a long, rectangular field covered with fine fescue grass. Whitewash had been painted on the ground to mark where the archers would shoot from, and six targets were arrayed a hundred paces beyond this line. Each target had been dyed into three sections — a white outer ring, a black inner ring, and a white core — with each section being half the width of its predecessor. At the very center of each target was a small black dot.

To the right of the range, near the town wall, the lords and their ladies took their seats upon wooden risers. Colorful banners streamed from the guardrails, and off-white kerchiefs fluttered in the air as women waved gaily at the arriving competitors. There were no seats to the left of the range, only thin rails to keep the peasants and lower-class tradesmen from spilling onto the field. A wooden dais with a purple canopy stood on the far end of the field; this was where the Sheriff and his party would eventually sit. For now, it was empty.

At the head of the range rose the archers' tent—a huge, enclosed structure where the participants could rest between bouts. Brilliant-hued ribbons and heraldic pennons fluttered from its roof, a few detaching beneath the talons and beaks of curious birds. In front of the tent stood a small trestle table, and a squat man in purple livery sat behind it, listing the competitors on a piece of parchment.

"Names?" he intoned as Robin and David approached, his gaze already discounting the rough-clad peasant and the one-eyed lad in red.

"Jack. From Tamworth Town," Robin invented. "My companion is not competing."

"Then he is not allowed in the tent," the scribe told them rudely. "He can watch the tourney from behind the rail with the other rustics."

His brusque tone made Robin bristle and she opened her mouth to protest his impudence, but David cut her off.

"It is all right, R–er–Jack. Find me when you are done." He cast an appraising look at the crowd and added, "If you can."

Robin watched her friend disappear into the throng. Then with an aquiline glare at the scribe, she pushed aside the thick canvas of the tent and stepped inside.

It was like walking into a warren. Over two hundred archers had come to answer the Sheriff's call, drawn by the

generous gold prize and the lure of recognition and employ-
ment for those who shot well.

Most of the competitors were examining their equipment
for any defects they might have overlooked; their greetings to
each other were genteel, but terse — there would be time for
talk later. The majority of the chatter came from a score of
young men whose evident reason for entering the tourney
was to impress a lady-friend.

Behind Robin, the tent flap opened again and a herald
stepped inside. In a voice trained to resonate over all other
noise, he called out the heats for the first round. Each heat had
ten men, assigned in the order of their arrival. Since Robin
had been the last to arrive, she was in the last heat.

At first, she waited calmly, listening with interest to the
sporadic roar of the crowd and trying to guess by their cheers
or jeers how well someone had shot. After each heat, the
archers would return to the tent — those who had performed
poorly to collect their things and leave, the rest to settle down
and await the next round. Of those who had remained, some
glowed with pride, while others bore supercilious smiles.
Robin knew it was the ones who showed no emotion at all
that were the greatest threat: content to let their skill do their
boasting, they were the ones who had skill to boast of.

As her turn drew near, Robin felt her calm self-assurance
slipping away and her heart begin to hammer. She tried to
relax, whispering to herself that she had nothing to fear, that
she would certainly pass such an early round . . . but in spite
of her best efforts, her nerves were stretched taut by the time
her heat was called.

Swallowing hard, Robin took her place on the white-
washed line and strung her bow. The crowd, seeing her,
began to jeer. Might as well be lame in the hand, they called,

than to try to shoot at a target with only one eye — let alone the right eye at that! Was this archer so foolish as to think he could still judge distance accurately? What a jest his effort would be!

So concerned were they with Robin's eyepatch that they spared not a glance for her mouth — if they had, they would have been startled by the small grin of confidence growing there. They had no idea that their taunts, instead of distressing the scarlet archer, were soothing away her tension instead.

It was true that for most bowmen, being blind in one eye would have been a grave handicap. The left eye especially was needed to sight the target, and without it, determining distance would be nearly impossible. But as a child, the vision in Robin's right eye had been blurry. Young though she had been, she had logicked that if practicing archery could strengthen her body, then practicing vision should strengthen her eye, and had taken to wearing a linen rag over her left eye whenever she had trained with her bow, forcing herself to use only her right. Though her cousin had teased her and called her the "one-eyed oddity," Robin had persisted, and within a year her blurring had disappeared and she had gained the ability to sight a target as confidently with one eye as with two, much to Will's chagrin.

This crowd is in for a surprise, she thought.

With renewed assurance, Robin nocked an arrow and raised her bow, drawing back the shaft so that the fletching touched the corner of her upturned mouth. The crowd's jeers turned to startled cheers as her arrow whizzed through the air to lodge neatly in the white core, automatically advancing Robin to the next round.

With each round she advanced, the targets moved back another fifty paces and the number of contenders dwindled.

At last, there remained only thirty archers, out of the original two hundred. Of those thirty, only ten would progress to the penultimate round, and of those ten, three to the finals. Robin intended to be one of those three.

She glanced at where her rivals now stood in small groups within the archers' tent, quaffing the free ale brought in to slake their thirst and nattering to relieve the tension. Robin herself had chosen to abstain from both activities, preferring to keep her mind focused, her vision clear, and her reflexes uninhibited by drink. Instead, she leaned back against the wall of the tent and closed her eyes, trying to shut out the ambient noise and calm her nerves.

Once again, Robin was the last to shoot. This time, she had to battle a strong wind that blew the shouts of the spectators into garble and threatened to tear the arrow out from her fingers. The capricious breeze had already wreaked havoc with the aim of several archers, changing its course just when they had assumed they had the old wind judged.

Now, Robin's days spent practicing in the Sherwood stood her in good stead as she awaited the almost imperceptible slackening of the breeze — the prelude to a momentary calm before it renewed its charge in a different direction. When that instant came, she did not hesitate, but let her arrow fly through the transfixed air to land with seeming ease near the center of the target.

The herald presented her with the yellow ribbon that signified she was one of the ten to move on, and then the Sheriff stood, signaling a short recess. Those bowmen who had not advanced to the next round gathered their equipment and left the range, nearly all of them heading for the rails to observe the outcome of the match. The spectators already there shifted aside to make room for the archers, deferring their places to those who had contributed to the day's entertainment.

Robin ducked back into the tent where the other semifinalists were awaiting the next round. After holding so many people all morning, the shelter now seemed disquietingly bare.

In the hustle-and-bustle of the earlier rounds, she had not attempted to assess her rivals. Now, she looked them over as critically as she saw they were doing to her.

The most easily recognizable was the Sheriff's chief forester, Gilbert o' the Red Cap. He wore the Sheriff's purple livery, but atop his head perched a red hat from which he took his surname. It clashed terribly with his outfit, but the forester wore it proudly. His skill and cocky confidence made him the crowd favorite, as their cheers had so deafeningly announced each time he had taken his turn. Unless something unexpected occurred, Robin was certain he would be one of the finalists.

She cautiously dismissed a short man in blue: his eyes were cunning, but his hands quivered like a nervous rabbit. True, he had to be an adept archer in order to have made it this far, but if he continued to tremble with tension, Robin did not see how he would be able to aim well enough to make it to the next round.

Two of the men were peasants — she had seen them shoot and they were indeed very good marksmen. Robin hoped one of them would carry the day if she could not, but she had to concede that it was unlikely — not because their skill was insufficient for the task, but because as the day had progressed, they had seemed to become increasingly cowed by the adroit company they kept. Even now, their gazes kept shifting sidelong to the four men standing in the middle of the tent, and Robin turned her head to peer at them as well.

These four yeomen were well attired and carried them-selves with the relaxed confidence of archers who had been to and triumphed in many such tournaments. They seemed well acquainted with each other and conversed amiably about the day's shooting. Looking at them, Robin felt her own confi-dence begin to waver. It had not really occurred to her until that moment that she might not make it to the finals, but as she considered the archers before her, she had to admit that it was more than a slight possibility. Seeking a distraction, she shifted her gaze to the last archer.

She had not seen him before amidst the press of competi-tors and the bustle of the tourney, but now he stood apart from the others with a quiet aloofness. Recognizing him so unex-pectedly made Robin drop her bow, her muscles suddenly weak. Several of the archers turned to look in her direction, their stares changing at her clumsiness from speculative to dismissing. Blushing within the folds of her scarlet hood and avoiding all eye contact, Robin silently scooped up her bow and stood against the tent wall, wishing she were invisible. Her mind was still in shock. What was *he* doing here?

Lords did not compete against peasants — he himself had said it led to overfamiliarity and encouraged people to chal-lenge their lord's authority. Heaven help her, what if he recognized her? Hastily, Robin double-checked her hood and eyepatch.

Lord Locksley, preoccupied with his own turbulent thoughts, had taken no notice of the scarlet archer's disturb-ance. He was dressed as the commoners around him, but he was no commoner, and it shamed him to compete in a tour-nament for such a plebeian reason as pecuniary need.

He had never been particularly wealthy, but he had al-ways managed his manor well and had never expected to face true financial distress. But when his eldest daughter had run off so unexpectedly, he had been left to pay the wedding forfeit ... enough to make even a rich man's coffers grow tight. A solid gold arrow would go far toward dispelling his manor's fiscal strain.

At least, he thought gratefully, the Sheriff had been willing to forgive some of the mulct he was owed, provided he still received his desired alliance with the Locksley family. Soon the whole rotten deal would be closed.

And who will be left for me then? Lord Locksley gloomed.

The summons of a trumpet interrupted his thoughts, calling them all back to the range. Robin was the first out the tent flap. As the archers lined themselves up on the field, she made certain to position herself as far from her father as she could.

Her gaze turned toward the Sheriff, who was leaning forward in his gilded chair and watching the archers with far more intent than he had thus far that day. From this distance, Robin could not see the features of his face, but it was easy to imagine the Sheriff's frown of displeasure as he realized none of the ten wore the hoped-for Lincoln Green. He bent his head towards the herald at his right; whatever the man said, Robin felt certain the Sheriff's frown only deepened.

"You will shoot two arrows each," the herald at their end was instructing. "The finalists will shoot three. Closest to the center of the target wins."

The archers nodded and strung their bows, their faces set; even the blue-clad yeoman looked poised. Robin attempted to match their expressions as she strung her longbow. She had to try twice — the first time her fingers, suddenly slick, slipped.

During the earlier rounds, the crowd had booed and cheered for their favorites, hooting wildly at the foul shots and hurrahing a shaft well aimed. Now they were silent, eerily so. The only sound was the twang of strings as the archers took their shots one-by-one, and the distant *fwumps* as their arrows struck the targets.

Twenty twangs and twenty *fwumps* later, the spectators on both sides of the range broke their silence with an enormous roar of appreciation. Surely, these were ten of the finest archers in all of England! At 250 paces, all ten had managed to lodge their arrows within the middle ring of the target. What a shame that only three could advance!

From where Robin was standing, it was impossible to tell which arrows lay the closest to the target's center. Her heart told her she had shot well, but was well good enough?

Her gaze cut towards her father; he was the very picture of serenity, calmly leaning against his bow as he awaited their results. She wished her thoughts could be as serene, but instead, doubt plagued her; the words he had spoken to her during their last real conversation together echoed in her ears:

"You seem to think you are a man . . . . You are nothing but a girl, and it is high time you faced that fact."

What if her father was right? What if she was wrong to compete like this, to think of winning against men like this, she, a mere girl? She knew society would find her so, that she would be shunned, imprisoned, perhaps even killed if the truth were known. If she lost (*when she lost*, a part of her whispered) would her people surmise that she was not all she pretended to be? Would they desert her?

A runner arrived bearing the arrows of the three most accurate shooters; Robin accepted hers from his hand, slightly dazed. Those who had not qualified were falling back, their role in the tournament finished. Rather than leaving the range, they lingered behind the finalists, waiting to see who would take home the golden prize.

Robin glanced at the other two finalists left on the field. Gilbert o' the Red Cap was one, looking very smug. The other man was her father.

Once again, Robin was twelve, preparing to do battle with her father for the right to learn the archer's art. As with that time, she would shoot well. As with that time, she would lose. Exuberant cries told her that Gilbert had shot the first of his three arrows. It was her turn.

"Come on, Robin, you can do this," she muttered to herself. But instead of focusing on the target, she allowed her eyes to flicker toward her father, who she saw was watching her keenly. The pressure of his gaze made Robin hurry her shot, and she misjudged the wind; her arrow, instead of landing in the middle of the white core, blew aside to land a finger's breadth further from the center than Gilbert's shaft. Cursing herself for her clumsiness, Robin watched her father methodically draw back his bow and shoot, his arrow piercing the white core precisely opposite that of the Red Cap's.

The herald gave a short blare of his trumpet, and the three prepared to shoot again. As she awaited her turn, Robin grappled with her concentration, reclaiming it with some success just before she shot. This time, her arrow landed two finger-lengths closer to the center of the target and several barleycorns in front of Gilbert's second shaft; her father's next arrow landed slightly behind hers.

The Red Cap stared at the target: the scarlet archer's last shot was perilously close to its center. To be assured of the win, Gilbert would need a bulls-eye.

Taking a deep breath that whistled through his wide-spaced teeth, he nocked his arrow, placed the tip of his bow

by his instep, and drew the string full back to his ear, all
without taking his eyes off the target. When he let go, his
arrow flew straight and true to lodge in the black center dot.

"Oh, my," Robin gasped, stunned by such marksmanship.
Lord Locksley glanced at her sharply, but said nothing.

The crowd was cheering wildly — they were certain that
Gilbert had won. The herald gestured for Robin to take her
final shot.

She took up her stance and nocked her arrow, drawing
back her bow. The target seemed to quiver in front of her —
but no, that was only her hand shaking her bow. With great
effort, she let the string go slack and unnocked her arrow.

Fully cognizant of her father's gaze, Robin struggled to
push aside all the fears and doubts that his presence had
raised within her. She pushed aside, too, the surprised murmurs of the crowd as they wondered at her hesitation.

I am Robin, she chanted to herself. *I am Robin Hood. I lead
the Merry Men of Sherwood. I am an archer in my own right . . .
and I will win this day!*

So swiftly did she move then that men later swore they
could not even blink in the time it took her to re-nock, draw,
and loose her arrow. Their first indication that something had
occurred was the unexpected sound of splintering wood.

"My God," the Red Cap gasped. "He done split my arrow!"

Silence suffused the range for a moment longer as the
crowd registered what had happened; the next instant, they
let out a colossal cheer. The tumult was so great that the
herald could not make himself heard, and he gestured almost
apologetically to Lord Locksley for him to take his shot.

Lord Locksley gazed at the upstart clad all in scarlet, disturbed by a familiarity he could not name and would puzzle

over for weeks to come. "Nay," he said at last into the crowd's eager hush as they watched him unstring his bow. "I will shoot no more this day. Yon lad has beat us all." Without another word, he turned and walked away.

At this display of gallantry, the crowd's ebullient shouts rose so high that people as far away as Radford Town looked into the sky to wonder at the sudden thunder.

Gilbert hesitated, his expression warring between upset and awe, and then he shook his head. "Well done," he conceded, clasping Robin's hand.

After that, everything happened very fast. The herald seized Robin by the arm and propelled her across the field toward the Sheriff's tent. People strained over the wooden barriers as she passed, fighting to touch her sleeve and craning to better see the winner. Robin felt her head spin at their praise and her heart pound with pride at her accomplishment.

They came to a halt in front of the Sheriff, who did not stand to greet her, but sat surveying Robin with a calculating stare. Phillip Darniel was just as she remembered him: a wolf, for all his chiseled features. Suddenly, his mouth contorted into a feral grin.

"Masterful shooting," he announced loudly, making Robin collapse inside with relief. She had feared for a moment that he had recognized her. "My friend, Sir Amyas, insists he has never seen its like in all his eighty years." The Sheriff gestured to a wizened old man on his left, who beamed at Robin happily.

Sir Amyas opened his mouth to say something, but the Sheriff cut back in. "The prize is yours," Darniel informed Robin, handing her a heavy silk cloth. She pulled the wrappings back and held up the weighty gold arrow for all to see—the resulting din was deafening—and then rewrapped it and tucked it inside her quiver. The Sheriff watched all this from beneath hooded lids.

"An archer of your caliber need not be content with such a paltry reward," he declared without warning. "I have a bigger prize to offer you."

"What is that, sir?" Robin inquired, feigning innocent interest.

"There is an outlaw who has been harrying my people. He has no respect for rank or title, and the common people fear him so much that none will undertake my warrant. I will give you your weight in gold if you will bring this bold outlaw to me."

Robin struggled not to laugh as those within hearing range gasped. "Forgive me, sir, but I must disoblige you. I answer no warrants but that of my stomach, when it demands a hearty meal to fill it and stout ale to quench it."

The Sheriff's eyes narrowed as the crowd exclaimed again at her refusal.

"Do not be a fool. A reward like this would make you rich, with more money in your purse than some lords have in their whole coffers. Will you serve me?"

Robin shook her head emphatically. "I will not. No man shall be my master."

"Insolent fool!" the Sheriff snapped, his face blotching purple as several people began to chuckle. "Begone, before I serve a warrant on *you!*"

With a curt bow to the Sheriff and a wave to the crowd, Robin turned her back on Darniel and strode across the range, unable to keep a smile from spilling across her face.

I wager no one has dared tell him "no" in years. Poor Phillip. He did not seem to take it very well.

Robin returned to the archer's tent and grabbed the bag she had left there, tying it securely to her belt. When she stepped back outside, David was waiting for her, along with a horde of spectators.

"That was some masterful shooting, *Jack*," he called to her, his eyes twinkling with merriment.

"Well, you would know," she joked back as she worked her way to his side. Unlike most of her band, David's archery skills were abysmal.

Robin steeled herself to battle her way through the sea of admirers, but like Biblical waters, the crowd parted before their champion, allowing the two friends easy passage into Nottingham proper.

Now that the tournament was finished, Robin realized just how hungry she was. But when she and David tried to buy pasties from a baker and wine from a wine booth, neither vendor would accept their coin—it was their pleasure, they said, to gift their wares to the champion archer and his friend!

Buoyed by this unexpected generosity, the two chose to wander through the dusking streets of Nottingham, peering at shops, eating their meat pies, and passing pleasantries with those who occasionally stopped them to offer their congratulations. Once, Robin felt a tap on her shoulder and turned to see a heavyset soldier looming behind her. Believing she had been recognized and was about to be arrested, Robin's fear turned to astonishment when he instead requested some archery tips he could give his young son. Somehow, she managed to choke out an answer and wait until he had left before bursting into laughter.

"I thought for certain he had realized who you were," David admitted, relief etched all over his face.

"So did I," Robin agreed. "All the same, it *is* a shame that the Sheriff went to all that effort to lure me out of the woodwork, and yet he believes himself failed."

"I suppose so," David said.

Robin's mouth curled into a mischievous smile. "I would not want him to think me a coward," she continued.

"Well, it is not like you can tell him," David insisted, beginning to grow alarmed.

"Hmm," Robin mused, not really listening. "The Sheriff will be sitting down to supper right about now."

She took off her quiver and handed it to David along with the golden arrow, but retained her bow and one of her shafts. "Find the others who came with us and wait for me just inside the forest. I shan't be long."

"What are you planning, Robin?" David demanded, but she was already weaving through the milling throng.

It did not take her long to find a public scribe, and a silver penny bought her the use of some linen paper, a quill, and iron gall ink. The scribe was a little shocked to find that she wanted to write her own letter, since even the nobility usually had to dictate their correspondence; a peasant who knew how to write was practically unheard of. Another penny and she saw him shrug away his curiosity and turn to other business.

Robin sucked thoughtfully on the tip of the quill, considering what she wanted to say. When she began to write, the words flowed smoothly from her mind onto the paper as though she were recalling the words to a popular song, rather than inventing them as she went along. With one last flourish, she was done.

Robin looked over her letter carefully, perusing its contents while the black ink dried. She felt extremely satisfied—

her message was short, it was merry, and it rhymed; it would drive the Sheriff mad:

> *I often take ill-gotten gold*
> *So folk won't starve or feel cold*
> *But gold today was rightly won*
> *When you named me your champion.*
>
> *So learn this lesson well today*
> *My warrant you will never pay*
> *For like arrows, Robins fly free*
> *None shall my master ever be.*

It was not difficult to learn where the Sheriff was taking supper. Robin had been to the Guild Hall only once before, when another Sheriff had governed the shire, but she remembered the conventional layout. Two long tables stretched the length of the hall, with a shorter one upon a dais near the back. That was where the Sheriff would be sitting. It was perhaps twenty paces from the front door. There was one small window near the roof to let the air pass through. It would be more than big enough for her purpose.

Robin ducked behind a stall and rolled her letter around her arrow, tying it into place with the yellow ribbon the herald had given her. Taking out her dagger, she chopped off the arrow's head so it would do little harm if she misjudged where it should fall — she would be shooting blind, after all.

The guard stationed by the door gazed about with a bored countenance, his eyes taking in and passing over the scarlet archer who had just stepped into the street — merely one of the hundreds who had flocked into town for the tourney. In that brief moment of inattention, Robin strung her bow, nocked her arrow, and sent the clothyard shaft soaring through the Guild Hall window.

Then she took off running. Behind her, the guard gave an inarticulate shout of surprise and pursued.

Robin dashed through the streets, the shouts behind her growing louder as more guards joined the pursuit. People turned to regard her with various imprecations as she darted around them, but no one tried to stop her forward progress.

As she neared the edge of the town, the crowd began to thin, and Robin risked a quick glance behind her. She was perhaps twenty rods ahead of her pursuers — it would have to be distance enough.

Jinking between several houses, she found herself in a small, abandoned alley. Hastily, she dropped her bow and reached into her sack, pulling out the shapeless dress she had bought in case of this very situation. As swiftly as she could, she drew the garment over her head, pulled out her braid, and tucked her hood into her sack. At the last second, she remembered she was still wearing the false eyepatch and tore it off.

The pounding of feet signaled the soldiers' arrival. Trying to appear nonchalant, Robin stepped in front of her bow, trusting to the growing darkness and her skirts to hide the weapon.

"Where did he go?"

"He just disappeared!"

"You! Woman! Did you see a man run by here?" the Guild Hall's guard, no longer bored, demanded of her crossly. The soldier was panting heavily and clutching at a stitch in his side. "He was dressed all in scarlet, with a patch over one eye and a bow in his hand."

"Scarlet? A man? No man has passed by here, sir," Robin averred, remembering almost too late not to deepen her voice. She cowered away as if the guard frightened her.

The soldier took in her disheveled appearance, and a look of scorn stole over his face. "I doubt that," he mocked, but he had no time for a woman and hastened down the street, beckoning the others to follow him.

Robin waited until the sound of their footsteps faded away and then picked up her longbow, checking with her fingers to see if it had come to harm when she had dropped it. Relieved that it had not, she ambled off in the direction of Nottingham Gate, feeling utterly invisible in the skirts that lapped at her ankles.

The gate porter peered down at her from his perch, intrigued by the sight of a woman exiting the city alone with a longbow in her hand.

"Halt a moment, maid. How comes ye to be carrying a weapon like that?" he called.

"Me man forgot it, the drunken sot. Forgot me too, come to that."

The porter smirked. "How foolish of him! Surely, ye need ne hurry back to such a man? Come join me up here for a while, and I will show ye how to properly work a shaft."

Robin shook her head. "Nay, sir, I am already well learned on that score. Besides, me man will be desiring me presence."

"I am sure he wol," the gatekeeper laughed, waving her through. With a smile concealed by the darkness, Robin walked through the gates and out of Nottingham, a free woman.

✁ 11 ✁

A LESSON IN POWER

FOR THE NEXT FEW WEEKS, the people of Nottinghamshire talked of little else but the exceptional tournament . . . and the arrow that had fallen through the Guild Hall window to pierce the Sheriff's mutton supper. Though the enraged Sheriff had threatened to execute any person who relayed the incident, the tale had still gotten out and by the next evening, the entire town had known that not only had the Sheriff failed in his ploy to trap Robin Hood, but he had not even recognized the bold outlaw when he had stood before him to receive his prize!

Ballads about the daring archer's latest coup quickly spread throughout the shire, and Phillip Darniel — rightly feeling himself to be the laughingstock of the entire county — coldly decided that he had had enough. Putting aside his prodigious pride, he rode out in company to London Town to beg the King for help in ridding the Sherwood of that loathsome outlaw, Robin Hood.

"Ne only did the King refuse to help," Eadom, the inn-keeper, boasted to his guests shortly thereafter, when several members of Robin's band stopped by the Blue Boar Inn for tidings and refreshment, "but he — that is, the King — he said that if the Sheriff could ne catch Robin Hood — heed this! — that he would need to find another sheriff who could! That set ourn Sheriff off right quick, ye can be sure, in a mood as dole as a midwinter sky."

Those present had laughed then at the foolish man who sought to capture the bold archer, but humor soon turned to frustration as Phillip Darniel began to send every soldier he could spare into the forest to hunt down whatsoever outlaws they could find.

Fortunately for Robin and her band, their camp was locat-ed deep within the heart of Sherwood, and though the Sheriff could order his men into the forest, he could not govern how far they ventured therein. As it was, no soldier dared to tramp too far within the Sherwood, lest night should fall before they could return to the High Road; they knew that with their senses blinded by darkness and their disadvantage com-pounded by the unfamiliar terrain, those who hunted outlaws could easily become their quarry's prey.

This wariness served the soldiers well, for though some of her men begged permission to shoot down the invaders, as long as the soldiers maintained their distance from the camp, Robin's edict against killing remained firm. Only to defend their lives would she permit her men to fight, and that was not needed . . . yet.

So for a fortnight, Robin's band reluctantly laid low, wait-ing for the sounds of the soldiers' horns to fade away. Finally, after three days of silence, Robin decided that the servicemen had gone and that it was safe to venture through the forest once more.

"But what if there are still some of the Sheriff's men lurking about?" Nicolas demanded, catching her arm as she was about to leave. "At least take one of us with you."

"Nonsense," Robin told him briskly. She was itching for a bit of freedom, and there was only so much of *men* that a girl could take. "Look, if I get into trouble, I shall sound my horn, all right? Three blasts, so you will know it is me."

"I like it not," Nicolas asserted, but he reluctantly let her go. As she strode away into the trees, he shouted after her, "Remember, three blasts! We will be listening."

Robin did not even hear him — her mind was already skipping away from the camp and into the vastness of the forest, her body following only a little slower behind. With every step she took, Robin felt the cares of her leadership and responsibilities falling further away, lifting a weight from her shoulders that she had not even realized was there.

With a happiness that was almost giddy, she plucked a pied daisy from the ground and wove it through her hooded hair, behind her ear. There it adorned out of sight, its unseen presence buoying Robin's spirits — she had almost forgotten what it felt like to enjoy girlish fancies. Putting on that dress in Nottingham had made her realize that she missed skirts and loosed hair more than she would have thought possible. Living in a camp full of men had certainly been educational, but while she insisted that they abide by some standard of hygiene, their appearance was hardly that of the dapper young men who tended to inhabit lords' halls. Not that she missed the company of lordlings, but sometimes it was nice to look on a handsome youth and to feel handsome herself. Such a self-discovery amused her.

Imagine what Darah would say to find me pining after such things!

With a laugh, Robin plucked the flower from her hair and let it flutter to the ground.

She spent the rest of the morning meandering through linden groves and stands of fragrant pines, through goldenrod thickets and through carmine meadows, letting each place breathe its life and peace into her soul. How she loved this border of the seasons, when spring merged with summer and filled the air with the sumptuous scents of flowers and sun! What other time of the year was the greenwood so bursting with brilliance?

Unbidden, the words to her favorite childhood ditty wove through her head: "For the sun is shining bright, and the leaves are dancing light, and the little fowl sings he is near . . ."

Feeling full of delightful folly, Robin sang the last part aloud, even as her feet carried her to the top of a low crag. From there she could see the wide spread of the forest: trees undulating in small dips and rises that marked its valleys and knolls, patches of ever-present fog merging with the clouds, and the faint bluing of smoke — nearly indiscernible even to her keen eyes — that lifted from her camp a mere half mile away.

She stood still for a moment, gazing out over the forest with an air of possessive pride. *My Sherwood*, she thought with contentment. *My home.*

With the ease of a bounding deer, Robin leapt off the ledge in sudden abandon, skidding down the rocky slope and coming to a halt by the verge of a pellucid river.

This particular river emanated from the same watercourse that fed the stream by her camp, but its waters were much wilder than those. In the winter, it ran deep and broad, with roiling currents that could pull a man underneath in seconds. It was a gentler being in the summer, its waters less rushed and thick; but no matter the season, it never lost its glacial chill.

From where Robin was standing, her camp was but a short walk beyond the river. Going back the way she had come would require another quarter day, and while Robin did not mind the trek, she was starting to feel hungry and was ready to return. Still, she would have walked to London and back again before she would have voluntarily forded those icy waters! Fortunately for her, nature had provided a third solution.

Long ago, a giant pine had fallen across the river, its roots tying it to one bank and its tip binding it between two tree trunks on the other. In this way, it was kept from being swept downstream by the fierce current and was the only reliable means of crossing the river for miles.

And it was close by. Light-hearted, Robin wended her way along the silt bank, singing her ditty softly to herself while her boots squelched to the beat.

All at once, she stopped short. The tree-bridge had come into view, and Robin could clearly see that there was someone already on it.

At first, she thought that it was a very short, very broad sort of person just standing in the middle of the log, but no. On closer inspection, she realized that it was really a large man who was in fact not standing at all, but was sitting with his back to her and with his legs drooped over the side of the trunk, idly twirling a large staff through his fingers like a giant baton.

"Good day," Robin called.

The person did not respond.

"I say, do you mind moving? I desire to cross," she called again, a little louder this time.

No reply.

"Fine," Robin muttered and began to stride across the log, slipping a little on some particularly wet patches of wood.

When she reached the man, she stopped, tapping her foot impatiently.

"Move please," Robin requested through gritted teeth.

It was as if the man could not hear. Was he deaf?

"Move!" she commanded, losing her patience and giving the fellow's shoulder a hard shove.

He barely budged, but her action succeeded in breaking him out of his doleful thoughts, and he whirled to face her with a look of anger and fear — emotions that quickly transformed into sheer astonishment. "Robin?"

Her astonishment was just as great. "John — John Little? Whatever are you doing here?"

John Little got to his feet, causing Robin to take a step back; she had forgotten just how tall he was. "Hiding. Is that not what you have been doing? You were smart to run into the woods after we clashed with those foresters," he told her bitterly. "I thought I would be safe enough in my own village, but a few days ago someone tipped off the Sheriff's soldiers to my presence, and I had to make a run for it."

"The Sheriff's soldiers — but *you* did not kill anyone," Robin protested, not understanding.

He shrugged. "We fought the foresters together, and which of us actually killed his nephew makes little difference to our Sheriff."

"John, I am so sorry," she apologized miserably. "If I had not —"

"If you had not, I expect I would be dead by now," he said gently, resting one large hand on her shoulder. "I do not blame *you*, Robin."

His kindness only intensified her feeling of guilt. She could see now the changes his outlaw status had wrought in him: his clothes and beard were ragged, and his face was not as carefree as it had been the last time they had met.

"Where will you go?" she asked with concern.

At her question, John looked a little uncomfortable. "I have heard tell of an outlaw leader who haunts these woods. He and his men are not like other criminals — they steal, but only from those who acquire their wealth unjustly, and then they give their takings away to the poor. It is said that their leader will not condone murder and is kind even to the people he steals from. If I am forced to live as an outlaw, I would like to be an outlaw such as he."

Robin shook her head, incredulous. "Do you mean to tell me that you sought refuge in Sherwood Forest in order to join Robin Hood's band?"

"If he will have me."

Robin laughed. "Oh, he will have you."

John Little looked at her sharply. "Do you know him, then?"

"I should say so," she smiled, indicating herself with a sweeping gesture.

John quirked a quizzical eyebrow, but then made the connection. "Of course! You are dressed in Lincoln Green — you must be one of his men!"

"One of his men? Really, is that what you think I am?"

"Are you not? Then how do you know . . . ?" John Little paused suddenly; when he spoke again, his voice was kind. "Oh — oh, I understand. He gave you the clothes out of charity, but not a place in his band. Look, lad, if Robin Hood turned you away, then he is not the man I thought him to be. Well, who needs him, anyway? I can look out for you."

Robin's jaw dropped.

"You do not need to thank me. I know how hard it must have been for you to survive on your own for this long."

"I have done quite well for myself, thank-you-very-much!" she sputtered indignantly.

"True, you do look well fed."

The ridiculousness of it all left Robin reeling, and she announced with some desperation, "Can you not see that *I* am Robin Hood?"

"Robin Hood? You?" John Little gave her a smile of compassion. "Look now, I understand why you might be mad at the fellow, but pretending to be someone you are not is hardly the way to go. Besides, he has promised to punish anyone who takes on his title, and though you may share the same forename, that will not save you from his wrath. Trust me, it is not worth the consequences."

"I tell you that I am Robin Hood!"

"Then where is your beard? Everyone knows that Robin Hood is a great bearded fellow," he told her, half-teasing, half-serious.

"They what?" Robin's hand flew to her face, affront filling her at such an inaccurate description. Then she had to chuckle at the irony: she, who had wished to remain anonymous in her role, now sought to convince someone of her identity.

She stroked her chin, affecting a woeful countenance. "Nope, no beard — though not for want of trying."

John let out a bellow of surprised laughter and slapped Robin so hard across the back that she almost tumbled into the river.

"Lad, you have spirit, I will give you that. Lead me on to this band of yours then, and I will most humbly crave your pardon when we arrive."

"After you," Robin said with amused anticipation, indicating the opposite bank.

Still chortling, John Little turned around and marched across the arboreal bridge, cheerfully twirling his staff through his hands so fast that it whistled.

"How do you *do* that?" Robin asked enviously. "Murray has been teaching me some basic moves with the quarterstaff, but I—".

"Murray? From Mansfield?" John interrupted, pausing with one foot on the bank and one on the tree. "How is it you have come to know *him?*"

"He is one of my men."

"Naturally," John Little said with a shake of his head. "Do you mean to tell me that you have been learning how to cudgel from *him?*"

"Murray is a very good teacher," she defended.

John scoffed in obvious disagreement.

"Do you think you can do better?" Robin challenged.

John Little looked her over, taking in the attentive stance of her body and the half-daring, half-hopeful expression on her face.

He smirked. "Your first lesson starts now."

John waited patiently in the middle of the bridge while Robin fashioned a makeshift cudgel for herself, cutting down a six-foot oak sapling with her sword and then using her dagger to trim off its scions and branches. Leaving all of her weapons upon the sandy bank except for the staff, she stepped back onto the fallen bole.

"Tell me again why we are not doing this on firm ground?" Robin asked as she tested her footing. Although years of use had worn the top of the trunk nearly flat, it was quite slippery and provided at best a hazardous perch.

"Balance is the first thing a good fighter must learn," John informed her. "Surely, a swordsman knows this? Or do you carry such a weapon simply for the pleasure of it?" he quipped.

Before Robin could answer, John Little struck. Hastily, she moved to block his blow, but it had been a feint. She felt his staff rap her lightly on the ribs. He went to strike again, but this time she succeeded in parrying his blow.

"Better. Strike me a good one if you can!"

Robin tried, but John Little swept away her blows as easily as though he were swatting mayflies.

"Surely, you can do better than that! How does a man become such a powerful leader when he has such weak arms?" he twitted her, testing to see if words could distract. Robin refused to be sidetracked.

"I may not have your physical power, but I empower people," she panted, warding off another blow. "My character is my strength."

John's eyes glinted appreciation of her answer, even as he casually struck aside her staff. He was clearly taking Robin through her paces, discovering just how much she had learned and offering a tip here or there whenever he found a weakness. And he seemed to find many. As exhaustion started to creep over Robin, seeping into her sinews and making them ache, she began to resent John's cavalier appraisal of her skills. She waited for an opening and when it came, struck John Little a hard blow to the ribs.

The breath went out of the man with an *oomph!* and he staggered, reflexively swinging out at Robin with more force than he had shown her in the entire past hour. His staff hit her squarely in the side, knocking her off her feet and into the frigid river.

It was fortunate for her that she had been knocked upstream and that John Little recovered his senses in time to seize her by the ankle before the current could sweep her out of reach. He pulled her, sputtering and sodden, back onto the tree trunk, and then helped her over to the bank where she collapsed among the sedges, coughing up water and relearning how to breathe.

"Sorry," John apologized, leaning guiltily against his staff. "You surprised me."

"I must remember not to do that again," Robin gasped. A violent shiver wracked her body — glory, but that water was cold!

Sitting up, she used her hands to wipe as much of the water and mud off herself as she could, wringing a small rill from the bottom of her tunic and tightening her liripipe. Her hand passed over the silver horn at her waist, but though she shook it hard, it failed to dislodge the liquid inside. Unhooking it from her belt, she blew a quick triad, sustaining the last note until she was certain that the sound was clear.

"That is a handsome bugle," John Little noted, watching her with concern.

In response, she handed the trumpet up to him to examine. He took it, his eyes never leaving her face.

"Are you certain you are all right?" he asked.

"I am fine," Robin announced with more force than she had intended. In a calmer tone, she added, "Truly, I am.

Really, John, you need not look so worried — my ribs will heal from the bruising you gave them, and I am not one to hold a grudge. If it makes you feel any better, I promise not to oust you from my band before you have even officially joined! Of course, if you ever wallop me like that again . . ."

John Little laughed, as she had meant him to, and handed her back her horn.

Just then, there came a terrible crashing sound of breaking branches and snapping shrubs. Robin gazed with instant comprehension at the horn in her hands.

"Oh, my," she expressed, but before she had the chance to say anything more, Nicolas, the twins, and half-a-dozen Lincoln-clad men burst out of the bracken. They took one look at the titan looming over their sodden leader and leapt at him in indignant attack.

A lesser man would have fallen beneath the sheer weight of their numbers, but John Little was not a lesser man. Startled though he was, his staff was soon spinning in a series of sweeping arcs, knocking men left and right until at last they drew back, rubbing their cracked crowns and bruised ribs and wondering how in the world they were to overcome.

"Enough!" Robin called, finally able to make herself heard over the chaos. She had climbed to her feet and now placed herself between the fighters, her arms outstretched. "Nicolas, stop! John . . ." she warned as he shifted his purchase on his staff.

"What is going on, Robin?" Nicolas demanded, his suspicious glare never leaving the stranger. "Did you not sound your horn for help?"

"I sounded my horn," Robin admitted, "But I did not mean to call for help when I did so. This here is John Little. He has asked to join our band, and I have agreed."

"Then you really are Robin Hood," John Little exclaimed, still incredulous.

"I am indeed. I believe this is the part where you crave my pardon?"

John gave her a rueful scowl. "I most humbly and abjectly apologize for my doubt . . . Robin *Hood*. As for my request, perhaps I need to rethink it if your band is made up of varlets such as these."

Robin flicked some mud off her shoulder at him. "Ease up a little, John. They meant no harm."

"Yes, John, ease up a *l-i-t-t-l-e*, John," Glenneth grumbled to his brother.

"Little John! I like that," Shane burst out. "He is, after all, such a very little man."

The other bandsmen laughed loudly, delighting in that vengeance on the stranger who had bruised their bodies so.

"Call me that again and I will cut *you* down to size," John growled, his fists tightening upon his staff and his already towering presence seeming to dominate still further.

"Nay, forebear," Robin said, chuckling a little herself. "After all, if people believe Robin Hood to be a great bearded fellow, then surely in their eyes you must be a Little John! We shall have a feast to celebrate this christening. Come!"

So saying, she picked up her weapons and led the way through the forest. Cheers greeted them as they entered the camp, for all had heard the bugle call signaling Robin's distress and had feared the worst. They gazed with curiosity at the stranger—head and neck taller even than Robin—who followed at their leader's heels and who stared back at them without a smile.

"John!" Murray cried in surprise, hurrying over. "You scoundrel, whatever are you doing here? And Robin, what has befallen you that you are all wet?"

Robin sighed dramatically. "This scoundrel, as you so aptly called him, took umbrage with my cudgeling skills. He gave me a drubbing and a dunking that I did not expect."

"You should teach your students better," John Little told Murray sternly, his demeanor uncharacteristically harsh. Then to Robin's surprise, his scolding expression melted away into a grin of pure delight, and he pulled Murray into a hug. "It is good to see you again, brother."

"Brother?"

Robin looked from one man to the other — there could not have been a more dissimilar pair. John was tall and his complexion fair as flax; Murray was brown of hair and skin, with a fighter's stocky build.

"Half-brothers, actually," Murray said, speaking from somewhere behind John's chest. "But we have never worried about such technicalities. I have not seen him since before I was outlawed."

"I am an outlaw now myself, thanks to your fair leader," John informed him. When Robin opened her mouth to apologize yet again, he waved her off with a wink.

Seeing that the two brothers desired to talk, Robin excused herself, grateful for the opportunity to head to her cabin to change into a dry set of clothes. When she emerged, the two men were still standing where she had left them, chatting animatedly. Rather than interrupt the brothers, Robin wandered over to the bonfire, eager to rid her bones of the river's chill, which persisted in spite of her fresh clothes.

A few feet away, Lot and David lingered by the smaller cooking fire, conferring together over a brace of does. The designated cooks by their own choice, they were responsible for preparing the communal feasts. Right now, David was roasting one doe while Lot butchered the other, casting its meat and some of Edra's herbs into a pot for some stew. They smirked to each other when they saw Robin warming herself by the fire—already the tale of her dunking had spread throughout the camp.

I have a feeling I will be hearing this story for a long time, she sighed.

By the time dinner was ready, Robin felt toasty enough to part from the bonfire and to snag two trenchers of meat. Murray was trying to pull his brother into line for the victuals, but John held back, uncertain.

"I have your plate," Robin told him, indicating with her head that John should follow her. "Come on, I am hungry."

With a shrug, Murray let his brother go and nipped ahead several places in line. Chuckling at his audacity, Robin led John over to the Trysting Tree.

"Sit here," she said, sinking down onto her preferred spot and indicating that John should sit at her right.

He was not looking at her, however—his gaze was fastened on the golden arrow dangling from the oak tree.

"Is that what I think it is?" he asked, incredulous.

Robin's smirk was answer enough. "Are you going to eat, or not?" she demanded. "A fine thing it is, when the guest of honor will not partake of his own feast."

John sat down carefully on the mossy seat and accepted the trencher she held out to him. But rather than eating the meat, he just stared at it. Though he knew that by fleeing the Sheriff's soldiers, he had made himself an outlaw, his heart had yet to accept that fact. To partake of this meal would be a willing violation of the King's law—something he had sought all his life to avoid.

Robin noted his reluctance and, guessing the cause, said to

him kindly, "Out here, we abide by the King's law as best we can. Even so, we must survive, and sometimes that does mean breaking the rules. If society were to afford us another choice, we would certainly take it, but as it is we do our best to live as honorably as we can, while ensuring that we do indeed live."

John nodded that he understood, and with the air of a man committing himself fully to his new path in life, sank his teeth deeply into the meat, tearing off a large piece.

"This is very good," John Little remarked when his mouth was free again. "But you did not need to hold a feast for me. I have done nothing to deserve it."

"Robin holds a feast for everything," Murray remarked, sinking down heavily beside his brother. He toasted Robin with his bowl of stew as he explained, "If you are a lord, you get a feast. If you are an abbot, you get a feast. If you devise a new ditty, you get a feast. If there is no one to hold a feast for, Robin orders a feast because the sun is shining."

"And when it rains, he orders a feast for that, too," Shane chimed in from his place at Robin's left. "When you have five-score people to feed, every day becomes a feast day."

"I see," John said blandly. "In that case, I accept the honor."

Robin laughed.

Murray kept up a steady stream of talk as the outlaws ate—John for his part mostly listened, absorbing the details of the band's exploits. Robin attended the tales with wry amusement, fascinated by how much the events changed in the telling.

"So, when might we christen this bonny babe?" Shane whispered to her during one such rendition, waggling his eyebrows at John.

"I nearly forgot!" she whispered back. Standing up, she detached the horn from her belt and blew a low note that gained everyone's attention. John looked up at her, puzzled — she could see that he, too, had forgotten his promised naming. A small smile tugged at her lips for the jest she was about to play.

"As all of you are undoubtedly aware by now, today I received a most unwelcome dunking." A wave of knowing chuckles greeted her announcement. "The man responsible for this outrage is sitting here beside me. His name is John Little, and he has asked to join our band. I know John Little to be a valiant man, a kind man, and — I believe — a good man, so I have agreed — on one condition." Robin turned to face John. "He must undergo a dunking in turn."

At this signal, Shane and Glenneth seized a startled John under his arms and hauled him towards the bonfire that blazed in the center of the diners.

John glared furiously at the twins, the muscles in his shoulders bunching under his tunic as he prepared to buck them off. But before he could, he caught a glimpse of Robin's face; she was laughing. So, too, he realized, was everyone else — not cruelly, but as an older brother might laugh when fondly teasing a younger sibling — as Murray had often laughed when he had teased him as a boy. John stopped struggling and allowed the twins to push him to his knees.

Robin stepped in front of John — she was holding a pot of ale. "Who bringeth this babe for christening?" she inquired loudly, affecting a high, dignified manner.

"We do!" came the jubilant replies, one from each of the men who had rushed to her aid earlier that day.

"And what shall be his name?" she asked.

"Little John!" Shane shouted.

John Little let out a low groan.

Robin forced herself to stare at John's forehead — she was

afraid that if she met his eyes, she would double up laughing and not be able to stop. Setting her face into a stern mask, she announced in a solemn voice that cracked only a little: "Thou camest to us but a little while ago, John Little. Little knew you of the world, and thus lived you but little. Now, you shall live indeed, a member of our fine company. Changed you are, and changed shall be your name. John Little is no more—Little John, I christen thee."

Then, with a glance to make sure that he was still firmly restrained by the twins, Robin took the pottle of ale and slowly, methodically, poured it over John's head.

A great cheer arose from the camp as Little John shook the thick rivulets of ale from his mane, sending froth flying. The twins released their hold on him and he rose stoically to his feet, gazing around at the applauding crowd. At last, he turned to face Robin.

For a moment, she was afraid that he might be angry, but no, he was smiling—a small grin that soon broadened into a hearty smile as he let out a rumble of laughter that amplified to soar above the cheers. Relieved, Robin handed John another tankard of ale, this time to drink.

"Welcome to the band!" she said.

Those men who had sponsored Little John's naming came up to congratulate him on his new status. Murray, his head reaching only to John's chest, stood with his hand upon John's shoulder, telling anyone who would listen about the youthful exploits of his "little" brother.

So loud was the chatter and festivities that it was a while before anyone could hear the approach of distressed shouts. One by one, heads turned toward the surrounding forest and voices quieted; Robin's hand fell without thought to the hilt of her sword.

With an inarticulate cry, a gangly youth stumbled into the now silent clearing, panting hard to catch his breath. It was Andrew, Nicolas' son.

"'Tis Will Stutley," the lad wheezed. "He has been captured by the Sheriff!"

✢ 12 ✢

A HANGING

"HE IS TO HANG TOMORROW," the boy explained, his voice trembling with fatigue and distress. Someone shoved a tankard of ale into his hands, but he did not drink. His eyes met Robin's, begging her to do something to save his friend.

Panic rose up in Robin's throat like bile, but she choked it down and led the youth over to the oak tree, sitting him down in her own spot while the others gathered around.

"Tell me," she said, her voice sounding distant even to herself.

The boy's story was simple enough. Will Stutley, buoyed by Robin's decision to venture into the Sherwood, had decided it was safe enough to venture back to Nottingham. It seemed that during the archery tournament, he had met a girl he fancied —

"The flower seller?" Robin interrupted.

"No, 'twas another. She had the seat next to the Sheriff's."

—and some kind of promise had been made between the two. When Will, accompanied by Andrew, had returned to collect on that promise, the Sheriff's guards had appeared. Will had been captured; fleet-footed Andrew had barely managed to escape.

"But Will has no warrant on his head! The Sheriff had no cause to arrest him!" Murray protested, his words rising over the dark exclamations of the band. Robin ignored their outcries, intent on obtaining every last detail about her friend's capture. At last, there was no more she could learn, and the youth's words petered away.

"You have been a brave lad, Andrew," she told him. "Get you to bed now."

"But Will? What about Will?" the youth asked desperately as Robin turned and walked away.

"Robin will take care of it," Nicolas reassured his son. "He always does."

"I do not understand," the newly christened Little John murmured to David, who was standing beside him. "Why would the Sheriff arrest this boy if he has no warrant?"

"Because Will, that foolish youth, cannot leave well enough alone! He tried once before to woo the Sheriff's daughter, and for his efforts Phillip Darniel had him beaten. Now, it seems the Sheriff has caught him at it again, only this time, Will Stutley was dressed in Lincoln Green . . . and all of Nottinghamshire knows what that means." David shook his head in dismay. "The Sheriff needs the prestige that catching one of us—one of Robin Hood's men—will bring him, especially after the tournament and the King's public doubts regarding his competency. It does not matter whether Will has a warrant on his head or not—the Sheriff will hang him tomorrow before the noon bells ring, simply for being caught wearing Lincoln Green."

With that dire prediction, David strode over to where Robin was standing apart from the group. Not knowing what else to do, Little John followed him.

Robin stared into the darkening forest, thinking hard thoughts. She had grown complacent with the success of her band, had come to believe that the cat-and-mouse game she played with the Sheriff would produce no casualties, that her people could never be captured. She was paying for that complacency now — *Will* was paying for it now.

But what was it Nicolas had said? "Robin will take care of it." Her people's faith that she would save their friend was both frightening and affirming. The time had truly come to be the leader she had promised to be, and now that it had, she was afraid. Will Stutley's life — and the lives of his rescuers — depended on the decisions she would soon have to make.

But fear could be deadly, fear made mistakes. With a deep breath and a colossal effort of will, Robin pushed aside her fear enough to focus on the task before her. She knew that her worry and anxiety were still there, but for the moment, they were frozen and unimportant. What was important was Will, and how to rescue him.

Robin raced through possible plans in her mind, weighing one scenario against another and immediately discarding them both for a third.

John and David exchanged glances.

"What are you going to do?" Little John finally asked.

"We," David corrected quickly. "What are we going to do?"

They both drew back slightly as Robin turned to face them. Her eyes were like shards of fire — blue stars that blazed

within the shadows of her hood. When she spoke, her voice
was like steel. "*We* are going to get him back."

A hanging was usually a festive occasion for Nottingham
Town, one where its citizens could rejoice to see justice well
wrought and could garner a little entertainment from the
execution as well. But this time the crowd filing into the town
square was strangely subdued. It was one thing for a man to
hang when his crime was deserving of the sentence, but this
condemned youngster had no warrant on his head, and if — as
the Sheriff insisted — he were indeed one of those men who
willingly served Robin Hood, then who here did not owe him
their gratitude? Seed had been purchased and overdue taxes
paid with the money that band had left for them. Their children played at being Robin Hood and begged to practice with
their longbows every day, not just on Sunday as the law required. How could they rejoice to watch one of their heroes
hang?

"'Tis a ruddy outrage," one man said, scowling fiercely at
the gallows.

"A shame — the Sheriff should be ashamed . . ."

". . . hanging for nothing . . ."

". . . had to leave my children at home — they would ne
stop crying . . ."

". . . an outrage . . ."

Robin heard the mutters floating around her and breathed
them in like a balm. Though she had succeeded in repressing
for the moment her trepidation for her friend, she had not
been able to prevent recrimination's dark voice from echoing
through her mind. If Will had not been wearing her colors

yesterday, the Sheriff would not have had an excuse to execute him. If she had lain low, had not robbed so many corrupt
abbots or tyrannical lords, her friend might not even now be
preparing to hang. Against this self-accusation, the crowd's
unwitting support was a solace, reminding Robin why she
had done as she had in the first place.

No, she could not afford to doubt herself or her decisions — certainly not now when so many lives were depending
on her. She needed composure; she needed to think. She had
to prepare for every eventuality. If her plan today failed, Will
Stutley would not be the only one to die.

Robin gazed out into the crowd, searching for familiar
faces. David and Little John stood near the gallows, each
clasping a cudgel like a walking stick. Further in the distance,
Shane and Glenneth lingered near the town gate, talking
innocently with the porter.

The others, however, she could not find. Panic began to
rise up within her, but Robin fought it down. *They are here,
surely they are here. It is only that they are so well hidden that I
cannot find them*, she convinced herself.

She had come in disguise, as had the others, dressed in
old peasant's clothes that allowed them to blend in with the
crowd. Those who carried swords had concealed them beneath their cloaks, and those who carried bows had been
instructed to linger in the shadows near buildings and stalls
so as not to draw attention to themselves.

It troubled Robin that this venture to save one man's life
could end up costing so many others — both those of her
people, and of the Sheriff's. She had directed her band to use
their weapons only to distract, but she knew that in the confusion of a fight, anything could happen. The guards would
certainly believe they were being attacked, and what began as

a distraction could in an instant become a fight to the death.

Once again, Robin searched the crowd for her men, but it was useless. She would just have to hope that they were in their positions and that the information the prison guard had given her proved true.

She had not considered before that he might have lied.

She had arrived at Nottingham Town well before dawn, but had forced herself to wait until its gates had been open for at least an hour before ambling into the burg. Her purpose was to reconnoiter; her men would follow later, a few at a time so as not to excite suspicion. She hoped that by the time they started trickling into town, she would be able to present them with a solid plan. They would not be able to meet all together without drawing unwanted attention, so Robin intended to relay her instructions to the first group to arrive after she did, and trust each group to do the same.

The town square had not undergone any great change in the two weeks since the archery tournament, and Robin quickly memorized its layout, reflecting ruefully that the information would prove useless unless she knew the exact details of the execution. She needed to know where the Sheriff's men would be stationed, how Will would enter the square, and how many guards there would be to interfere with their retreat. Somehow, she would have to find a way to obtain all these particulars, and right now she could think of only one way to do it.

Ducking into an alleyway, Robin pulled out a dress from her waist sack and donned her woman's disguise, too intent on her mission to register the irony that she now thought of women's garb as the guise, and not men's. If she had considered it, the thought would have disturbed her, but all her attention was focused on Nottingham Castle.

Robin climbed the winding pathway up to the castle and stood in front of the gatehouse for several minutes, just staring at the portcullis. Finally, a guard came out and demanded to know her business there.

In a slightly awed voice, Robin explained that she had heard that a fearsome outlaw had been captured — could it possibly be Robin Hood? The soldier scoffed at her naiveté, saying it was merely one of his now not-so-merry men. How did he know? Robin inquired. Why, he had helped capture him.

Robin let her eyes grow big. "*You* captured him?" she breathed, intimating that she thought him solely responsible. She allowed her eyes to travel over the soldier the way she had once seen a kitchen maid flirt with the butler.

The soldier absorbed her admiration like a sponge, puffing out his chest and straightening his spine. A few more compliments from Robin and the man's tongue began to flow like the River Severn as he boasted his knowledge with regards to the prisoner — how he would be conveyed to the gallows, the probable number of guards that would escort him there — even the dearth of defenses at the town gate.

As Robin fluttered her eyes and listened attentively to all he was saying, she could not help feeling a little surprised at the success of her wiles. She had never cared to study feminine charm, and it gratified her that her first real attempt was such an apparent success. At the same time, it made her feel a little ashamed of herself, but since the flirtation was done solely to save Will's life, her contrition on the matter was brief.

Robin finally excused herself to the guard, coyly hinting that although she wanted to secure a good spot to watch the execution, she would not object to renewing their conversation at a later time. Turning her back on the guard's smug expression, she wove her way down the steep castle road and back to the town proper. Ducking into the shadowy crevice between two houses, she pulled off her dress so that her peasant's attire was revealed once more. Stuffing the gown into the bag at her hip, Robin drew out her hood and pulled it on; then with a quick glance at the climbing sun, she hurried back to the town wall to await the arrival of her men.

Was the guard lying? she wondered now. She had not questioned his veracity before, but the more she pondered their conversation, the more it seemed that he had divulged his information far too easily. Had he somehow sensed that something was amiss and misled her? No one in the history of Nottinghamshire had ever attempted this sort of gallows rescue before, and Robin had assumed (reasonably, her mind defended) that such an action would not be anticipated. But if the guard had suspected her — if he had informed the Sheriff to be on the alert — then her people could be walking into a trap!

No sooner had Robin reached this discomforting conclusion than a cacophony of noontide bells erupted through the town. Over the sound of their resonant peals arose the blare of heraldic trumpets — at first barely discernable, but growing steadily louder as the Sheriff's company drew near the square.

Robin unhooked her own trumpet from her belt; there was no time to change her plans now. Instead, she sent up a quick prayer asking that the Sheriff remain in ignorance of her plot, reciting her mental "Amen" a mere instant before the gallows party arrived.

The Sheriff came first, looking resplendent atop his dappled white stallion, his suit of purple-and-black satin enhancing the complacent expression on his face; his mouth was curled up in a victorious grin. His entire demeanor crowed that he had caught one of Robin Hood's men, and it would only be a matter of time before he snared Robin Hood as well!

The Sheriff's horse seemed to sense its master's triumphant mood and snorted loudly, tossing its head. With a dark chuckle, the Sheriff spurred his stallion on ahead of the guards, forcing people to throw themselves out of the way to avoid being trampled. At the very last second, he reined in his steed next to the scaffold not ten feet away from where Robin was standing.

Behind the Sheriff, two-dozen guards followed at a more sedate pace on foot. Although these soldiers wore swords, they kept their weapons sheathed, and their air was alert but unconcerned. In the middle of the escort, a large cart rumbled, its deep wooden frame lurching wildly with the hauling hackney's every step.

Inside the cart stood Will, his hands lashed to the front rail. Even from a distance, Robin could see the way the ropes cut into his wrists and the deathly pallor of his face. The youth tried to stand tall, but a heavy noose hung around his neck and his shoulders slumped forward despondently. Will's eyes as they swept over the crowd were devoid of hope; he did not see her.

Robin felt as though icy steel were replacing the blood in her veins, freezing her worry into hard determination: Will was not going to hang today!

The cart lurched to a halt. Two soldiers stepped forward to unhook the back wall of the wagon and lower it ramp-like to the ground, while a third waited patiently for them to finish so he could procure Will from the cart and lead him down to the gallows. But before he could do so, someone else got there first.

"It is not very nice to go off to die without telling your friends goodbye," Little John quipped, leaping into the wagon. The boy gasped as the strange giant whipped out a dagger and slit the bonds that held him, but Will did not let his surprise slow him from pulling the *noose* off his neck or leaping out of the cart, his rescuer close behind him.

Little John's brazen action had stunned the guards, as Robin had hoped it would, but they were quick to recover. As a unit, they drew their swords and advanced on her friends while the crowd watched in confusion. Robin saw Little John seize Will by the shoulder and pull him under the shelter of the cart; it was time—she sounded her horn.

Silver blades flashed in the sun as her bandsmen drew their swords and those nearest began engaging the soldiers. Up by the gate, the twins quickly overpowered the lone porter. A shower of clothyard arrows fell harmlessly upon the cart from all directions, the thud of their shafts making the guards run for cover.

Screams echoed throughout the square—screams of fear, Robin thought, until her ears registered that they were cheers. Someone knocked into her from behind, shouting, "A rescue! A rescue!" and another, "Hey for Robin! Loyal Robin!" and half the crowd now seemed to have joined the fray, pummeling the guards with their fists or whatever was at hand. More arrows fell from the sky, aiming for the empty cart, but the wind caught one shaft and it fell on the hackney's rump; with a shrill squeal, the horse bolted down the street, the wagon fishtailing behind it and striking a guard to the ground.

It was chaos.

Robin could not see Little John or Will anymore, could not tell if they had been struck down by the guards or the wild cart. She could only pray that they had taken advantage of the confusion to duck away into the mass of fleeing people and were not lying dead in the street.

Raising her bugle to her lips, she sounded the retreat. The Sheriff was in front of her before the first note could die away, hacking down at her with his sword, striving to fell the commanding bugler.

Robin threw herself backwards and the Sheriff's sword shrilled through the air above her head. But now she was on the ground and people were scrambling around her, and the Sheriff was reining his horse ever closer, its hooves flailing toward her with deadly accuracy.

A rescuing arrow whistled through the air towards the Sheriff, flying so close to his face that it left a thin red graze across one cheek. With a bellow of rage, the Sheriff reined back his horse, and in that instant Robin was on her feet and running through the crowd. When she reached the border of the square, she risked a glance behind her just in time to see the Sheriff wheel his horse around on its hindquarters and spur it toward the safety of his castle, not minding who got trampled along the way.

"Time to go," Nicolas yelled, appearing suddenly at Robin's side. Together, the two of them raced for the gate while a last flurry of arrows convinced any remaining guards not to try to follow their retreat.

It was an exhausted but exultant party that gathered in the greenwood that night, returning in twos and threes throughout the course of the evening. Many of them bore minor wounds from the fray, and Edra was kept busy plying them all with unguents, but miraculously, none of those who had gone had failed to come back.

"I am so sorry, Robin," Will told her, shamefaced, as he nursed a swollen cut over one eyebrow. "I thought she wanted t' run away with me, but she told 'er father 'bout me instead; 'tis 'ow 'e knew where t' catch me. I ne'er 'oped ye would — I mean, I did ne expect — I thought I was done f'r."

"I understand, Will," Robin told him gently, and she did.

Now that the peril of the day was over and all her men were accounted for and being tended, Robin felt the cold calculation that had sustained her begin to melt away. She started to shake.

"Are you all right, Robin?" Nicolas asked with concern, pausing on his way to fetch Edra some hot water.

"Yes, yes, I am fine. Nice shooting," she diverted. He beamed at her and gave her a mock salute.

By turns congratulating those men who had fought with her and accepting their own congratulations, Robin managed to work her way out of the camp and into the surrounding wood. She strode through the quiet trees, not knowing what she was looking for — only aware of a rising panic growing inside her chest.

Suddenly, her knees could hold her no more, and she dropped to the ground, the fear and anxiety she had suppressed all day breaking free at last in a torrential flood that left her gasping.

For a moment more she struggled against it, but the stress of the day demanded release, and she simply could not hold it back any longer. Alone in the forest Robin knelt, head bowed, and surrendered herself to the quivers that shook her frame long into the night.

She returned to camp the next morning haggard and spent, but able to manage once more the strain of the day before.

As she made her way to her cabin, it struck her that none of the men who had chosen to sleep outside in the warm summer night showed any trace of the catharsis she had undergone; all looked contented and relaxed, and some of their faces even bore the remnants of a triumphant smile.

Robin felt a flurry of anger rise up within her, that they could so easily dismiss the fear — the tension — the *danger* of yesterday's rescue. Were they so shallow that such an event could leave so little imprint? Part of her wanted to scream, to yell, to demand some recognition of what could have occurred — that they saw it as more than just another adventure — that she was not left to deal with its aftermath alone . . . .

A hand came down to rest on her shoulder. "Are you all right?" Little John asked. He looked as though he had not slept, and she recalled with a start that he had joined her band only the day before. So much had been asked of him since then, and he had done it all without complaint or qualm. He had risked his life for a person he did not know — not out of a desire for adventure or a need to impress, but because it had been the right thing to do. His tone and his expression evidenced that the events of yesterday did not sit lightly on his conscience, and Robin felt greatly relieved to know that in this she was not in fact alone. If anyone could understand what she was feeling, it was he. Yet she hesitated, reluctant to ask this near stranger for more of himself, even if it was just for his conversation.

"Do you want to talk about it?" Little John asked, seeing the desire in Robin's face.

"I do not wish to burden you—"

"It is no burden. I, too, would be glad of the chance to talk."

She nodded gratefully. "Walk with me?"

He dipped his head in assent, and the two of them turned their backs on the insensate sleepers and stepped together into the forest.

⚜ **13** ⚜

SEEING RED

THE REST OF THAT SUMMER passed like a golden dream: a rare, sunlit season of memory in a world too often tinged with gray.

Will Stutley's audacious rescue — not to mention the arrow that scarred Darniel's cheek and for all he knew, nearly took his life — frightened the Sheriff so much that for a time he kept his soldiers tight around him, leaving the Sherwood virtually free of their presence. Unburdened by the threat of incursions, the people of Sherwood found themselves able to enjoy their pursuits without anxiety.

At Robin's request, Little John continued to teach her how to use the cudgel — on solid ground this time, much to her relief. Over the next few weeks, the muscles in her back and shoulders ceased to ache from wielding a seven-foot staff for hours on end, and her ribs and head bruised less and less often as she became more proficient at blocking blows. Sometimes Murray would join the two in a recreational bout, but cudgeling held little interest for him except as a lighthearted hobby, and he never stayed long; he was more than willing to let John take over the rigors of Robin's training.

The other band members, well accustomed to their leader's prodigious skill at archery, were fascinated to see her struggle to learn the staff. It provided no dearth of amusement to them that even the spindliest lad felt brave enough to challenge Robin to a bout during the evening games, and a refusal from her only doubled their mirth.

Their laughter and friendly taunts only encouraged Robin to work harder, and not a day went by when she and Little John could not be seen practicing together at the edge of the glade. He taught her how to use speed and cunning to win strikes against stronger opponents, how to plant her feet and still her muscles so they would not reveal her next attack, and how to absorb a blow. The first time she felled an opponent during the evening games was a victory sweet indeed.

As the months came and went under his expert tutelage, Robin began to triumph in bouts more and more often, until by summer's end she could fell even Lot of Lincoln, and he was the camp's best cudgeller after Little John. Robin never attempted to fight Little John outside of the discipline of their lessons, however — she remembered all too well the power he had shown her during their first bout and had no desire to repeat that drubbing.

Little John, for his part, knew next to nothing about archery, and Robin was eager to teach him . . . but she quickly discovered just how recalcitrant a student Little John could be.

"*Everyone* has to know how to use a longbow," Robin contended for what felt like the hundredth time. "It is the law!"

"I never bothered with it when I was a law-abiding citizen, and I fail to see why I should bother with it now," Little John argued petulantly. "A blackthorn staff is a good enough weapon for me."

"All my men have to learn," Robin argued back. "It is common sense. A cudgel is next to useless when robbing a convoy or hunting for food."

He shook his head in stubborn refusal.

Robin switched tactics. "Look at it this way: I let you teach me how to cudgel, it is only fair you let me teach you how to shoot."

"Learning how to cudgel was your choice. *Not* learning how to shoot is mine."

"Well, it was *your* choice to join *my* band," Robin announced in exasperation, "and if you want to stay here, then you are going to have to learn how to use a bow!"

At the stubborn set of his chin, Robin stormed away, angry at having to bully her friend in order to benefit him.

She avoided Little John for the rest of the day, both out of annoyance and because she was afraid that he would be vexed with her for having lost her temper. She could not have said why it bothered her so much — she did not have a problem giving orders to any of the others, even when they questioned them (as they sometimes did). But the contretemps with Little John had left a taste like sour curds in her mouth, and for some inexplicable reason, Robin felt guilty.

Little John finally had to ambush her attention, plopping down from the long boughs of the oak tree right in front of her and making her drop the brace of rabbits she had been handing over to David to cook.

"So, are you going to teach me how to use a bow or not?" he demanded, arms akimbo.

Robin tried to gather her startled wits. "Well, I suppose if you *insist* on learning," she drawled.

The fierce expression on Little John's face crinkled into a small smile.

Relief flooded through Robin that he had forgiven her their argument. Picking up the rabbits, she handed the brace to a confused David and then seized Little John by his shoulders, propelling him with effort toward the camp's makeshift range. "Your first lesson starts now."

"I thought killing the King's deer was against the King's law?" Robin teased Little John the first time he succeeded in bringing down a doe.

"Mayhap it is," he answered, returning her smile.

Robin surveyed his kill with interest, noting how little blood there was — the arrow had gone straight through the heart, dispatching the deer instantly.

"Sometimes, I think I made a mistake in teaching you how to shoot," she informed him, shaking her head. "You may rival me yet."

To everyone's surprise, not least of all John's, the giant had turned out to be a natural bowman. Within a week of nocking his first arrow, he had surpassed some of those who had been practicing archery their whole lives. Within a month, he was outshooting the twins two times to one. Only Robin could still beat him consistently, and even then, not always. Fortunately for her, Little John's rate of improvement seemed to be leveling off, so she might yet retain the title of Master Archer.

Her friend's archery skills were not the only thing to improve that summer, though the other band members saw the change in Robin before she noticed it in herself. Whereas before her sense of good humor had always been checked by a sober gravity, now her smile rarely faltered and her laugher rang out constantly. One day, David remarked to Robin that she seemed especially merry of late, and that evening as she lay in her fern bed, she reflected over his words.

It was certainly true that she felt happy . . . but why should that have inspired special recognition? Had she not always been happy? Deeper introspection revealed that no, she had not. She might have professed cheery spirits and brandished bright smiles, but they had only served to mask the loneliness she had felt. Though she had friends — lots of them — those she had felt closest to had others who came first. David had his wife and child, Will Stutley had his circle of rambunctious friends, and the twins, of course, had each other. The other outlaws saw her as their leader first and foremost, and though they liked her and admired her, they were always a little distant from her, too.

With Little John, however, things were different. There was no distance between them. He was never reserved with her, as he could be with others, and he sought out her company even over his brother's, delighting in a friend who took as much pleasure from the world as he did. Often, they would hunt together, bypassing herds of deer just so they could perpetuate a conversation. At mealtimes, he would sit at her right hand and they would banter and tell jokes and stories long after the others were done.

The camaraderie each felt was as natural as it was strong, and Robin realized now how much it had filled the void inside her. With a sigh of deep contentment, she rolled over and fell asleep, her last conscious thought a prayer of gratitude for her friend.

The summer waxed on as peacefully as before, but to Robin's dismay, her feeling of fulfilled friendship did not—it started to change. Alarmed, Robin tried to push away the strange sensations John was awakening inside of her—the faint jolt in her stomach each time their eyes would meet, the way seeing him automatically made the day seem brighter—without discernable success.

It is just friendship, she told herself sternly. *Of course that is all I feel. John is my friend, my truest friend. It is useless to feel anything else — he thinks I am a man, for goodness' sake!*

What would he say if he knew the truth? she wondered one night in a reckless moment. *What would he* not *say!*

Robin pummeled the ferns that made up her bed. She needed to squash these yearnings right now! Already they were threatening to burst out from within her, and to let them continue to grow was to risk revealing her identity and shattering the life she had built for herself.

Yet the more she fought to ignore her longings, the more her mind refused to let them go.

"Are you *sure* you do not need any help with that, Robin?" Little John called from his comfortable seat on the riverbank, not bothering to hide his amusement as he watched his friend's futile efforts midstream.

"I may not be a — brawny — giant — like you," Robin panted, "but I can certainly — manage — to free my own — sword — thank you — very — much."

She gave another fierce tug on the hilt of her sword, but it was wedged too deeply between the river boulders to come free. She could not even wiggle it from side to side. A scourge on rivers and their slippery rocks!

John let out a low chuckle.

"Fine," she called at last, unhooking her sword belt and stepping back onto another boulder, taking care not to slip again. Her sword stuck out from between the tight rocks like the ancient Excalibur, her belt dangling unceremoniously from the scabbard. "You have a try."

With a show of extreme languidness, Little John got to his feet. Nimbly, he navigated the rocks that formed the river crossing, halting in front of her captive sword. With one effortless tug, he extricated both sword and sheath from the rocks.

"Show off," Robin grumbled. "Next time, I will just have someone carry me across the river and save myself the trouble." She took the apparatus from him and examined it carefully. The sword appeared to be undamaged, but the bottom of the scabbard had several large rents running through the leather, exposing nearly a foot of cool blue steel and delicate silver etchings.

"Pity, that," Little John said, seeing the look on Robin's face as she fingered the ruined scabbard.

"I suppose I shall just have to find another," she sighed, clipping her belt back around her waist. "Maybe there is one back at camp that will fit." She doubted it, though. The swords they took from the caravan guards tended to be large, thick-steeled broadswords; hers was the thinner weapon of a noble.

"I cannot see why you bother carrying that thing around with you, anyway," Little John said as they started back across the river. "If you are close enough to a foe to use a sword, then you are close enough to use a cudgel, and a thick wooden staff will snap a blade like that any day."

Robin shrugged, but Little John was watching his footing on the slick stone surface and did not notice. "Not everything is about fighting, John. A sword has a lot more uses than to simply skewer a man. You cannot cut down a sapling with a staff, or gut a deer."

He grunted an acceptance of her logic, though Robin sensed he would always favor a stout cudgel over a blade. Of course, she knew there was another, truer, reason why she kept her sword by her side, but in spite of all the tales she had shared with Little John, including the fierce despondency of her initial days in the Sherwood, she could not bring herself to discuss with him Will's sword. Not that it mattered. She wore the blade out of habit now, rather than from conscious thought. If it also served as a reminder of the cousin and home she had left behind, well, that was nobody's concern but her own.

"Are you coming or not?" Little John demanded impatiently, already on the bank. Robin finished crossing the last few rocks and leapt down to where he was standing.

"I doubt that Eadom has better customers in all of Nottinghamshire than the two of us," she said as they strolled through the forest. "Are you going to be able to fit enough ale into that sack of yours? The men will not be so willing to forgive us if we run short a second time."

"They will fix their brewing barrel the quicker for the lack of it," he replied, unconcerned.

The sun had reached its apex by the time they attained the High Road. From this point, the Blue Boar Inn was a mile's easy walk, and the two friends' long strides began to make short work of the distance.

"Who do you reckon that popinjay is?" Little John asked with interest as they neared the Inn, pointing to a figure ahead of them on the road.

Robin peered at the traveler, amusement growing within her as she surveyed him. The man was walking in the same direction as they were, but at a slower pace, his steps ambling and measured. His gait seemed oddly familiar, but for the life of her she could not place him. Robin was certain she would have recalled a character like this!

From head to toe, he was covered in scarlet cloth; his hose was a deep red, his jacket and tunic a slightly brighter shade. He reminded Robin of a vermilion floret, so starkly did he stand out against the dusty countryside. A long feather loped backwards from his crimson cap, its tail tickling the edges of his honey-hued hair.

Rather than swinging his arms about like a normal traveler, his hands were occupied in front of him, and his elbows kept lifting every few moments as though he were holding something up to his face. As they rounded the last bend to the Blue Boar Inn, they grew close enough to guess at what he held.

"Is that a . . . *flower* . . . in his hands?" Little John asked in a slightly strangled tone, as though he were trying not to laugh. "Have you ever seen such a dandy fellow?"

Robin did not bother to check her own chuckle. Whether because the man had heard them or merely because he had reached the inn yard, he halted. With a heavy sigh, he let his arms drop, and Robin saw the flower he had held flutter to the ground. Then, showing more intention than he had the entire time they had observed him, he disappeared inside the inn.

As she and Little John reached the yard in turn, Robin glanced down to see what the man had dropped.

It was a white primrose, more specifically, a cyclamen. Robin recognized the telltale petals from her youth — a bush of them had grown just outside her window. As she recalled the childhood rhyme associated with the flower, she felt a surge of sympathy for the scarlet dainty:

> *If you want to keep a merry fellow*
> *Then dare to give a primrose yellow*
> *But if his love is not for you*
> *Then white's your color — alas, adieu.*

"Back again, are ye Robin?" Eadom asked her conversationally as she approached the counter. "That cracked cask of yorn is ne fixed yet?"

"They are carving another vat even now," she explained. "I reckon it will still be a day or so before Nicolas can get the beer brewing again."

"Not that Nick's brew could ever trump a cup of *your* humming ale," Little John informed the innkeeper loyally.

"Humph," Eadom responded, looking pleased. He took the sack of empty skins from Little John as Robin fished around in her waist sack for some coins.

"Never have to worry with ye, do I, Robin?" he said, taking the money from her. "Ye and yer men always have coin to pay yer bill, and then some."

"People been giving you a hard time, Eadom?" Robin inquired, leaning against the counter.

"No more'n usual. People come here to drink away their woes, but usually just end up drinking themselves into more of them."

"And by woes, you mean debts," Little John said shrewd-ly. He drew out another coin. "I know those skins take a while to fill, so why not hand me a flagon of Malmsey in the mean-time—I am in the mood for a drink myself."

"This one is on the house, then," Eadom said, handing him a flask with a grin that was absent several teeth.

"Thanks, Eadom," Robin said as Little John took the flask. "Give our regards to your lady."

Little John was preparing to sit down at a table, but Robin caught his arm.

"Let us go sit outside," she suggested. "It is too pleasant a day to stay in here."

"We are always outside," he complained, but followed her out the door and into the yard.

Rather than sitting on the benches in front of the inn, Rob-in chose instead to recline on the soft greensward by the path, out of the shade. The day was pleasurably balmy, and the unfiltered sun felt delightful on her upturned face. The sun's rays simply could not *reach* through the branches of Sherwood like this.

John gave a deep groan as he settled his long limbs onto the ground next to Robin, who used that moment of distrac-tion to seize the flask from his hands and take a long swig.

"*I* paid for that," Little John protested affably, seizing back the wine before she was done.

"And who do you think pays *you?*" Robin retorted, stretching out upon the grass with one hand thrown over her eyes to dim the light; she chose not to point out that the wine had been free. "Wake me up when Eadom is finished."

She did not really intend to go to sleep, but after a while she began to drift off. The sound of birds calling to each other kept flitting in and out of her consciousness, punctuated by the occasional clop of a horse ambling into or out of the yard. At one point, she thought she heard Little John murmur something about checking on the ale and the crunch of gravel as he got up and walked away.

Minutes later—or was it hours?—Robin grew dimly aware of a returning crunch and the sound of footsteps halting beside her. Without warning, she was lifted off her feet by the neck of her tunic and slammed painfully into the wattle fence that surrounded the yard.

"Where did you get that sword?" a man hissed in accusation. Robin blinked against the sunlight, her mind half-dazed, black spots dancing across her vision as she tried to fathom what was happening. Her attacker's grip on her liripipe tightened, choking any possible answer.

Suddenly, Little John was there, throwing the man off Robin with a roar.

Able to breathe once more, Robin pulled herself off the rail, straightening her tunic and her hood with one hand and awkwardly extricating her sword from its tattered sheath with the other.

What a way to wake up! She had been a fool to let down her defenses for even a moment, especially in Eadom's sunlit yard where any soldier might see her. Had she learned nothing from Will Stutley's capture?

Finally winning the blade free of her scabbard, she steadied herself and walked forward slowly, her steps turned tentative by her sun-speckled vision. Her eyesight was sufficiently clear, however, to see her assailant double over from Little John's forceful blows to his stomach, and the crowd of onlookers who had been drawn outside by the shouts.

"John, stop! Stop!" she cried. Little John landed one last punch before subsiding.

Robin walked over to the man who was now kneeling in the grass, retching dryly. It was the scarlet stranger. "What does this sword matter to you?" she demanded coldly, pointing the tip of the blade at his neck. The man's eyes fixed on the fantastical etchings.

"Sword—my sword," he gasped. "Gave it—stolen—if you—I will kill you—" His words were broken, his tone despairing even as he threatened. Robin's knees began to tremble.

"Who are you?" she breathed, seizing the man by the chin and forcing him to look up.

It was Will.

⚔ **14** ⚔

REUNION

"WILL? OH, MY GOD," Robin gasped, covering her mouth as realization hit her. "Will *Gamwell?*"

She dropped to her knees in front of him.

"How do you know—who are—Robin?" Will wheezed, meeting her eyes in confusion as the familiarity of her gaze vied in his mind with the pitch of her voice and her attire. After a moment's anxious scrutiny, recognition registered upon his face, and he gave her a grin of delighted relief.

"You know this varlet, Robin?" Little John demanded from somewhere to her left, watching warily as his friend aided her attacker to his feet. Robin came back to herself with a start.

"He is my cousin. We have known each other since we were little . . . little boys," she explained. She tightened her hold on Will's arm as she said the last part, hoping he would realize her word choice and not give anything away. His eyes widened slightly in bewilderment, but she saw that he understood.

"I thought when I saw—that is, I did not expect—I thought you were in London," Will said hopelessly, still dazed to find Robin standing before him.

"Plans changed," she said succinctly, keenly aware of the guests from the inn who had gathered to watch the fight, and who were now attending their conversation with interest. "I will explain everything shortly, but not here. Did Eadom give you the ale?" she asked, redirecting her attention to Little John.

"Yes," he growled, retrieving the sack he had dropped to come to her rescue; his suspicious glare never left the scarlet-clad man. "Your cousin, eh?"

"*Later*," Robin insisted. With one last glance at the gawking guests, she gripped Will by the shoulder and steered him out of the yard and down the path, Little John trailing closely behind them.

"You mean to tell me that *you* are Robin Hood?" Will demanded in an incredulous whisper, still not able to believe it.

The two cousins were back at the camp, sitting in the bower beneath the great oak tree and talking in low voices. Robin had filled Will in on all that had transpired for her, and he did not seem to know whether to be scandalized by her charade or impressed that she had pulled it off.

"Believe it, fair cousin," she said, stretching out a hand and indicating the camp with a grin. That grin faded slightly as she caught sight of Little John. He was sitting stiffly on a log a respectable distance away, carving a new staff and casting dour looks at Will. When he perceived Robin watching him, he glanced away.

"I do not think he likes me very much," her cousin noted, following the direction of her gaze; he winced a little as he moved, his ribs still sore from Little John's well-placed punch.

"Well, you *did* try to strangle me," Robin pointed out.

A rueful grimace twisted Will's mouth. "I suppose I did lose hold of myself when I saw that sword. You have no idea what I thought had happened to you — no, keep it," he said, raising his hands to deter Robin's guilty motion as she made to return his blade.

"But it is yours," Robin protested, even as her hands clutched at the scabbard. Will saw the faint whitening of her knuckles and shook his head.

"You will need it now more than ever, with the company you keep. Although if you keep mistreating it, I may just change my mind."

"I do not mistreat it!" she denied vehemently, and then saw his mouth twitch. "You are impossible," she sighed, and laid the sword back down. Without realizing it, she glanced over to the side — Little John was watching them again.

"Your friend seems . . . very protective of you. You are just friends, are you not?" Will demanded, the mock ferocity in his voice not quite masking the genuineness of his inquiry.

Robin laughed, trying to appear nonchalant even as her stomach leapt and her cheeks warmed within her hood at the question. "Of course, we are! As if we could be anything else. Anyway, he is my right-hand man, and he is probably just trying to make sure you do not attack me again."

"Or perhaps he fears that with your cousin here, you will no longer need him as much," Will supposed, entirely serious.

Robin shook her head at the absurdity of that notion. "Do

not be ridiculous. But, speaking of odd behavior, it is high time you told me why you were headed toward the Blue Boar Inn—on foot—dressed in *that* and sighing like someone just died."

To her surprise, it was Will's turn to blush. "I was going to London," he confessed. "I could not stay, not when—I mean, I could not bear—surely, you understand?" he demanded, strangely defiant. "I could not stay, knowing that *he* would be there."

"That who would be where? What on earth are you talking about?" Robin asked, completely confused.

Her cousin stared at her in amazement. "You mean you have not heard?

"Heard what?"

"That Marian is to marry the Sheriff of Nottingham."

"WHAT?"

Robin leapt to her feet, her voice far from hushed. All around the camp, people turned from whatever it was they had been doing to stare at her outraged eruption; John half-rose to his feet. Desperately, Will tugged at Robin's hand, pulling her back down onto her seat.

"I thought that you knew," he said in a fast whisper. "The whole shire knows. When you ran away and broke your engagement, your father was forced to pay recompense to the Sheriff, and Darniel demanded that Marian be part of it. He still wanted his blood alliance with Lord Locksley, you see, and Lord Locksley felt honor-bound to comply. The marriage was postponed for a while—I am not sure the reason why. But now Darniel stands to get everything."

"Everything?"

"The manor, the manse—everything." Will gave a dark chuckle. "Even my woodward suits belong to your father, and thus one day to the Sheriff. What I wear on my back is all that was mine to take."

"But you are his nephew! You should be the one to inherit—"

"It does not work that way. I am only Lord Locksley's nephew through marriage. Your father has no son of his own, so all of his possessions pass on to his son-in-law. To Phillip Darniel."

Robin gazed at her cousin in horror. "Then my sister is already married?"

He shook his head in denial, but his expression bespoke no hope: "Her train leaves for Nottingham in the morning. By dusk tomorrow, she will be the Sheriff's wife."

They fell silent, Robin chaffing at her fingers in thoughtful agitation, Will gazing at the relaxed bustle of the camp without really seeing it.

"We have to do something, get Marian to break the engagement somehow—" she pondered aloud.

Will's laugh was bitter. "Do you think I have not tried? She is not you, Robin—she would never put her own happiness first."

Robin felt her face flame. "Do you blame me for leaving?" she demanded defensively.

"No! I am glad you left, glad you got away from that limb of evil while you still had the chance. But Marian will not run away, not when having to pay a second reparation would ruin your father."

"We could give him the money—"

"And say we got it where? No, Robin, your father would never accept it. Even if he had the money to pay off the Sheriff, he would not do so. Lord Locksley promised Darniel he could marry his daughter, and he counts that promise more important than his daughter's happiness," Will explained with acridity.

"Then we will just have to take the matter out of his hands. Who is escorting Marian tomorrow? My father?"

"No," Will said, uncertain where her questions were leading. "Lord Locksley rode ahead to Nottingham to oversee the preparations for the after-party. Marian's journey tomorrow will be guarded by the Sheriff's men . . . . *Why* are you smiling?" he demanded as a wry grin began to spread over his cousin's face.

"My dear Will, I am afraid that I have developed this awful habit of taking things the Sheriff does not wish me to have. I usually stick with coin, but in this case, I am willing to make an exception. The Sheriff can hardly force my father to pay restitution for a broken betrothal if it is his own men who lose the bride-to-be!"

Captain Arthur o' Nottingham was hot and thirsty. To make matters worse, a wind had arisen which swept dust into his face and made it difficult to breathe. He shifted his grip on his reins so he could use one arm to protect his face, but it made little difference. In the end, he allowed his hand to fall back to his lap.

If only they could go a little faster and put an end to this uncomfortable journey . . . but no, they were forced to travel at this plodding pace, lest they injure the Sheriff's precious "cargo." At least the inn was near. Surely, the Sheriff would not begrudge his men a few cool drinks to soothe their parched throats.

Arthur was just beginning to dream of the bracing comfort of a bottle of Malmsey when a figure in dazzling scarlet appeared, walking straight down the middle of the road. His head was bent toward something in his hand, and he seemed utterly unaware of the company's approach.

"Whoa. Whoa!" Arthur ordered, reining in his horse lest he trample the stranger. Behind him, he heard the carriage creak to a stop and the grumbles of his men as they brought their ambling horses to a halt.

"You, there," Arthur irascibly called. "Stand aside!"

The scarlet popinjay looked up. He was holding a flower, the soldier observed in annoyance, and seemed to be completely surprised by their presence before him.

"Oh, fair morning to you," he called cheerily. "Pleasant day, is it not?"

"Not for you if you do not move out of our way," Arthur growled. "We are escorting a bride to her wedding and will brook no delay."

At this, the man positively beamed. "A wedding? How wonderful. Please feel free to continue on your merry way. Only," he added, as Arthur raised his hand to order his company forward, "I am afraid that the bride-to-be shall have to stay."

Before Arthur could work out this perplexing statement, wild hoots and laughter sounded from the verge, and at least two-dozen Lincoln-clad men capered into the road.

"Well done, Scarlet!" one of them cried, slapping the man in red on the back. "I have never seen a train waylaid so easily before. We will make an outlaw of you yet!"

"This is an outrage," Arthur blustered. "We are servicemen to the Sheriff himself! You cannot hope to get away with this." He tried not to look disconcerted by the score of arrows pointing in his direction.

"Of course, we do not *hope* to," Glenneth told him proudly. "We *plan* to."

"We have no coin for you to take!" a soldier behind Arthur spoke up suddenly, sounding desperate. "Nothing!"

"We are here for something far more precious than your purse," Will explained.

Arthur's eyes bulged with understanding, and he let out a string of expletives that made young Will Stutley's eyes widen with awe.

"You know, you really are quite wearying," Robin informed the captain, stepping forward and speaking up for the first time. "You have five seconds to leave, or else we will put an arrow through you." The man opened his mouth to argue. "Five . . ."

"I am not leaving without my charge!" he yelled.

"Four . . ."

"You unprincipled knave, I will rend —"

"Three . . ."

Robin drew back her bow.

It took until "Two" for Arthur to comprehend that she might actually mean her threat; with a last curse of outrage, he spurred his horse into a gallop and disappeared down the road in a cloud of dust.

"That goes for the rest of you, too," Robin announced. With fearful glances at the outlaws and their many drawn bows, the remaining soldiers decided that the wisest course of action would be to abandon their charge and follow their leader out of sight. With eager kicks, they spurred their horses down the road, one of them pausing briefly to allow the carriage driver to climb onto his horse.

Will Gamwell had begun striding toward the carriage before the last of the soldiers had thundered away, but even so,
Shane still got there first.

"Come out, fair lady," the twin called, opening the door
with a gallant bow. "We mean you no harm."

A moment passed, then another. At last, a delicate foot,
accentuated by a creamy satin slipper, stepped out onto the
rung. Robin heard several involuntary gasps as the young
lady, clad in a rich blue gown and a slightly lighter kirtle, her
brown hair unbound and streaming in the wind, stepped out
of the carriage.

"Why have you stopped us?" she demanded haughtily.
To a stranger, her uplifted chin and the tight set of her mouth
would have been mistaken for aloof pride, but Robin knew
that her sister had no such hauteur — Marian was quite simply
terrified and was trying not to show it. "What sort of man
attacks a lady's convoy?"

"The sort of man," Will said, stepping forward, "who
would not see that lady marry someone she does not love."

"Will!" the girl gasped. He handed her the dandelion he
had been holding, and Marian took it, fingers trembling. "I–I
do not understand. Who are these men?"

"Friends," he said, shooting them a considering glance.
"We have come to save you from having to marry the Sheriff."

"But–but my father — I cannot — I mean, I must — "

He took her hands in his. "Your father will be fine. The
Sheriff will not dare to fault him for this. You are free, Marian."

"Free? But I — oh, I must sit down," Marian said, sinking
onto the carriage step and holding a hand to her head as she
tried to absorb the unexpected turn of events. Several men

stepped forward in concern, and she shot them a nervous glance. "These men are . . . friends, you say?"

"Friends, yes," Will told her, taking her hands up again and speaking without thought. "They are Robin's men."

Robin instinctively started at the sound of her name, causing Marian to glance toward her. "Robin?"

"Robin Hood," Will hastily amended, but he was too late. Marian's mouth had dropped into an "O" of astonishment, and she was peering intently at her sister, who had hung back in the hopes of avoiding such recognition until they could be alone. "Robin!"

Tearing her hands free from Will's grasp, Marian darted over to her sister, flinging her arms around Robin's neck; the dandelion she had held wafted to the ground.

"Robin! I thought you were — but how did you — ?"

"Not here!" Robin told her desperately, placing a hand over Marian's mouth to still her dangerous converse. At the depth of her sister's voice, the questions burning in Marian's eyes seemed to intensify, but she masterfully restrained them, obediently letting go of her sister with one last squeeze. Out of the corner of her eye, Robin saw her men trade supposing smirks.

"Is there anything of yours you would like us to bring?" Robin asked, trying to regain control of the situation. She peered into the carriage. "Where are your things?"

"My things? At the manor . . . the Sheriff only wanted the wedding to be in Nottingham, you know — he wanted to flaunt his new connections — but we were going to live at the manor, it is so much nicer than his castle. All my things are there," Marian babbled. Her eyes shone bright with disbelief. "Do you really mean I do not have to marry him?"

Marian's reaction to Robin's story was much the same as her cousin's had been.

"*You* are Robin Hood?" she exclaimed.

"Hush! Keep your voice down!"

They were in Robin's hut and had been for over an hour now. Robin had known that her sister's inquisitive nature could not endure silence for long, so she had escorted her there the instant they had reached the camp. Sure enough, Marian's questions had tumbled out in an excited welter that would have given away Robin's identity several times over if they had remained out in public. Even now, an hour later, she was still bubbling with more.

"Is it hard, pretending to be a boy?" Marian wondered, intrigued.

Robin shrugged. "Not really. They tease me sometimes about not having a beard yet, and of course, my muscles are not as big as theirs, but no one seems to think it might signify something. They just accept it as the way I am."

"Ah, well, people see only what they expect to see," Marian said wisely.

Robin stared at her sister. "I guess."

"So you have lived here the entire time?" Marian turned in a circle to survey the sapling walls and the fern bed. For the first time, Robin became aware of how spartan her home must look to someone accustomed to the comforts of a manor. Then another thought struck her.

"Do you even want to be here?" she asked her sister, aghast at her own thoughtlessness. "When Will told me whom you had to marry, I just assumed — but if you would rather go back . . . ?"

"Are you in jest?" Marian cried, flinging herself onto the bed of ferns with reckless abandon. "A *hovel* would be better than being married to Phillip Darniel!"

"I do not think this place is *that* bad," Robin laughed, flopping down beside her sister. She sobered. "I am just glad that Darniel agreed to postpone the wedding as long as he did. I do not know what I would have done if he had already married you."

"Oh," Marian said dismissively, giggling a little. "Well, he did not really have much choice. He had to wait until I was a woman, after all."

"You mean to tell me that the Sheriff could not marry you because you did not have your monthly yet?" Robin laughed again. "That must have annoyed him!"

"Not as much as my abduction is going to annoy him!" Marian said gleefully. "I almost wish I could see his face when his soldiers arrive at the church without me!"

When Robin and Marian finally emerged from the hut, it was to a lavender sky and the first shimmering stars of twilight. Those men who had marked the pair's reappearance nudged those who had not and exchanged with each other half-hidden grins.

Robin looked at her sister. Though Marian was now wearing the rough peasant dress Robin had used as a disguise, rather than her bridal silk gown, she still looked breathtakingly beautiful. Robin could not blame the men for noticing.

"I am going to ask Edra if you can share her cabin," she informed her sister, loud enough for them to hear. She would have liked for Marian to stay with her, but as her sister had reminded her, it was just as scandalous for a maiden to sleep in a "man's" hut among outlaws as it was among the gentry. Of course, that caveat did not apply to family, but they had both agreed their relationship needed to be kept secret. Marian was obviously a lady, and announcing that she was Robin's sister would raise awkward questions about Robin that she did not care to answer.

Fortunately for them both, Edra was overjoyed to receive the request and instantly agreed that Marian could live with her. ("As long as she does not mind the smell," the woman warned.) As the camp's only herbalist and medicine savant, Edra kept a large botanical supply within her hut. The spinster had originally shared her lodging with her younger brother, but he had quickly moved out, claiming he could not endure the overbearing odors any longer. Since Edra's skills were in constant demand, she had been allowed to keep the dwelling for herself, and her brother had been forced to build himself another.

Robin led Marian over, but her sister hesitated in the doorway, her senses reeling from the pungent scent. At Robin's look of consternation, however, Marian whispered to her, "Anything is better than Phillip Darniel," and thanked Edra warmly for welcoming her into her home.

With that settled, Robin and Marian hastened to join the line for supper, which was queuing through the clearing. Several of those who were waiting in line immediately deferred their places to the highborn girl, and a few gave her a tentative greeting of welcome, but most of the men seemed unsure how to comport themselves before a noble lady and awkwardly avoided her gaze.

Marian pretended not to notice their discomfort and lavished the people around her with bright smiles, keeping up an enthusiastic stream of chatter with Robin as they waited their turn for their food. Once they had obtained full trenchers, she readily followed her sister over to the oak, and when Robin sank down upon the moss, Marian followed suit without any hesitation. For a moment, she just sat and looked around her, taking in the hearty scene with a feeling of contentment. Then picking up her roast, she prepared to take a demure bite, but paused, cognizant of the people watching her out of the corner of their eyes. Giving them an affable smile, she raised her meat toward them in a small toast, and then tore into it with such ferocity that it made several of the band laugh to witness. Robin sensed their discomfort beginning to ease.

"Whatever happened to the girl who was always so proper?" she asked her sister, bemused.

"She became an outlaw. When an outlaw, do as the other outlaws do," Marian told her happily, indicating the other voracious eaters with her piece of roast.

"I am not sure I like this new outlaw," Will Gamwell teased, stealing into the space at Robin's right side so he could talk to them both at once. Little John, who had been walking toward his customary spot before this unwitting usurpation took place, froze in his tracks. No one noticed. "She is messy."

Marian rolled her eyes in a very unladylike manner and caught sight of a disturbance by the bonfire. "Ooh, what is happening?" Marian asked with concern as several men began to wrestle. "Why are they fighting?"

"They are just having fun," Robin reassured her. "Every night, the men compete in wrestling, cudgeling, or archery matches; it provides us with entertainment and gives the men a way to show off their skills and to let out their energies. Look, that one match over there just finished. See how the wrestlers are smiling?"

"Not really," Marian admitted, craning her head for a better look.

Robin frowned at the obstruction. "Little John, could you please step aside? You are in the way."

He obeyed without a word, taking his trencher to the far side of the fire.

"They are definitely showing off," Will whispered to Robin, not altogether approving. The men were certainly being more flamboyant than usual, performing extravagant moves and maneuvers, followed by quick glances at the brunette maid to see if she were impressed.

Soon the other wrestling bouts ended as well, and Robin waited to see if another affable match would begin.

"Scarlet!" a loud voice boomed, commanding everyone's attention. It was Little John, looking very formidable. He was standing in front of the fire with his legs spread apart in a challenging stance, twirling his new cudgel viciously fast through his hands. "Do you plan to recline at your ease all evening, or are you man enough to face me in a bout?"

"He *definitely* does not like me," Will told his cousin as he rose to his feet.

Robin bit back a protest as Murray tossed Will a staff. Little John might be all patience in her lessons, but in a fight he showed no such restraint. If he were not careful, he would hurt Will. Why was he behaving like such a dolt?

Little John and Will Gamwell began to circle each other like riled dogs, sizing each other up for weakness. Without warning, Little John struck. A terrible crack rang through the forest as Will brought his staff up to block the blow.

"This is still just in fun, right?" Marian asked in an undertone, her expression worried. Robin did not answer.

This was no playful match, she knew that without a doubt.

Both fighters were straining too hard, their lips curled back and their muscles stretched taut as they aimed to fell their opponent. The clearing echoed with the sound of their blows, and Robin felt Marian seize her hand for comfort, her eyes widening with anxiety and terror as the two men strove against each other.

In spite of Robin's terrible fear that one of them would get hurt, she could not help admiring the fighters' skill. She had never seen Will use a cudgel before, but clearly, he was no stranger to the weapon. Little John, who usually finished off an opponent within minutes — if not seconds — of starting, seemed equally surprised by the strength and stamina of his scarlet foe. He gritted his teeth and renewed his attack.

Half an hour later, the two men were pouring sweat, each glaring fiercely at the other. The spectators watched them in awe — no bout had ever lasted this long before!

If only I did not care for these two challengers as much as I do! How I would love to cheer this duel on, as everyone else seems to be doing, Robin agonized. Instead, she stood with her heart in her throat, her hand clutched in Marian's, fearing the crippling blow that would strike down one of her two men.

A shout went up — Will had barely managed to duck under a blow, and Little John's staff had instead struck the fire, knocking forth a brand. Hot sparks peppered Will, and in that moment of distraction, Little John struck again. His blow caught Will upside the head, and he fell in a daze to the ground. Eyes gleaming with triumph, Little John readied his staff for the winning blow, his eyes shooting for the barest instant to where Robin was standing . . . and in that moment, Will flipped back onto his feet and rammed the end of his staff into Little John's stomach.

The air went out of John with a *whoosh!* Will did not wait.

He hooked his staff under Little John's cudgel and wrenched it from his grasp; with a final swing, he smote John a blow upon the head so hard that it sounded as if someone had felled a tree, and Little John crumpled to the ground and did not move.

"Is he dead?" Marian asked, sounding close to tears.

Dead, dead, dead. The chorus rang through Robin's mind as she blindly forced her way through the crowd, trying to get to Little John. At last, she broke through the circle of onlookers and immediately skidded to a halt, not certain if she could endure any more shocks that day.

Will had laid down his cudgel and was helping a grimacing Little John to his feet. Both men were gingerly touching their crowns; their fingers came away bloody. Without warning, Will stretched out his hand, and after a second's hesitation, Little John took it, their bloodstained palms sealing their peace.

"Well done, Scarlet," Little John rumbled amidst the cheers. "Well done."

Then, with their arms around each other's shoulders like the best of friends, the two men staggered back to the Trysting Tree and to an anxious Marian, leaving an astounded Robin to watch them go.

⚜ 15 ⚜

MANY SECRETS

"SO, WHAT IS GOING ON between you and Little John?" Marian asked curiously, wiping a strand of wind-tossed hair out of her eyes. She was kneeling in an amber meadow, hunting through the blazing autumnal leaves for herbs and roots for Edra. Her arms and face were streaked with dirt, but Robin, who had offered to help her, was still mostly clean and was staring into the shrouded sky for the fifth time that hour, her gathering forgotten.

Robin's meandering thoughts flew back to herself with alarming haste. Marian had ceased in her collecting and was innocently weaving a rich green sprig of maidenhair fern through her hair; she watched Robin's reaction to her question with avid interest.

"There is nothing going on," Robin replied a shade too quickly, standing up and dumping the few scraggly plants she had gathered into Marian's basket. "Nothing at all."

"Ah, I see. And is that the same sort of nothing that was going on that time I caught you making doe-eyes at the miller's son?" Marian teased.

"I have not been making doe-eyes at John!"

"Protest all you like, dear sister," Marian replied, getting up and looping her basket over one arm while she dusted stray leaves from her skirt. "Even *he* noticed you staring at him last night."

Robin blushed. She certainly had not *meant* to gape. She had just lost track of her thoughts until John, feeling her eyes on him, had turned to her and raised an inquiring eyebrow.

Ever since the fight with Will, her friendship with Little John had grown even stronger — especially once Little John had realized she had no desire to replace him with her cousin. But that closeness meant Robin was even more hard-pressed to control her feelings toward him, and last night, she had let her defenses lapse.

"It was just a stare," she protested dully. "Nothing more. And Little John accepted my excuse easily enough."

"Because he thinks you are a man," Marian filled in.

"Exactly."

"If you told him the truth about yourself, he would not see you that way anymore."

"I—" Robin snapped her mouth shut, afraid that if she said anything more, if she listened to that calm voice of encouragement, she would be tempted to do just that. And there were a thousand reasons why telling John the truth would be a terrible idea.

"Just think it over, all right?" Marian asked, wrapping an arm through one of Robin's. "Love is a wonderful thing; we should not have to hide it."

Back at the camp, Marian unloaded her basket of herbs in Edra's hut while Robin waited outside.

"I hope no one is at the stream right now," Marian exclaimed when she returned. "I cannot wait to wash this stink off me!"

"How can you stand the reek?" Robin asked, wrinkling her nose at the cabin. A mere whiff of the interior was enough to give Robin a headache; she could not imagine having to live there.

"Oh, you get accustomed to it after a while. But my skin is covered in the smell right now, and I want to be able to sit among people tonight."

With a small wave, Marian headed for the stream, climbing down the granite rocks to the shallow pool that the men had dammed off for bathing.

Robin was about to turn away when a light giggle caught her attention. She turned back just in time to see two small figures disappear into the bushes that topped the rise.

"Are your heads so *thick*," she demanded imperiously, snatching hold of their collars and dragging them out of the brush, "that you think they can withstand a walloping? Or perhaps your parents will do the honors for me, when I tell them that I had to outlaw their already outlawed sons for spying on a woman bathing!"

"We meant no harm, honest!" one of the young boys cried, twisting in her grasp. His friend nodded furiously in agreement.

"Well, I *do* mean harm if I ever catch you peeping again. Now, git!" Robin commanded, flinging them back in the direction of the camp.

Still they lingered. "Please, Robin? Just this once?" they begged.

"No! Marian is off limits. Now, you have two seconds to disappear before I take a cudgel to your backsides!"

They scampered, exchanging nudges of smug surmise and stifling snickers as they went.

Robin kept guard at the top of the rise until Marian returned, smelling strongly of lye and attempting to weave the sagging fern frond back through her sodden locks.

"Even in an outlaw camp, the boys cannot seem to keep their eyes off you," she teased, helping Marian over the last few rocks.

"Boys? What boys?"

"Just a couple young lads." Was it Robin's imagination, or did Marian look faintly disappointed? "Remind me sometime to show you where *I* bathe—I will not always be around to chase off your admirers."

"Am I such an inconvenience to you?" Marian asked wistfully.

Robin turned to face her, shocked. "No! I am pleased that you are here. Truly I am."

"It is just, you are so busy—so many people rely on you here. You have made a whole life for yourself, and I do not really feel like I am a part of it. I try to help Edra . . . but I do not think that anyone really wants me here."

"*I* want you here," Robin insisted, seizing her sister's hands. "You belong here as much as anyone."

"And I suppose you think that is comforting?" Marian challenged, a teasing gleam in her eye. Robin laughed, glad to let drop the subject of not belonging.

As autumn began to merge into winter, several more be-draggled families found their way into Sherwood Forest, each bearing a tale of eviction at the hand of the Sheriff's new captain—a man so vicious he made even the most heartless of mercenaries pale by comparison. With nowhere to go and still reeling from the brutality of their treatment, they had sought refuge with the only protector they knew: Robin Hood.

Robin had no choice; basic human decency demanded that she take them in. As winter progressed, the sight of a weary stranger staggering into her camp, guided by a man in green, became an all-too-common occurrence, one that never failed to send a surge of frustration coursing through Robin. No matter how she tried to disperse the monies her band obtained, it seemed there was always someone who fell victim to a poor harvest and the Sheriff's unrelenting taxes.

"Just imagine how many *more* families would be camped around our fires if not for the money you leave them. You cannot save everybody," Little John told Robin one day.

"But look at them!" she cried, indicating a recent addition to the camp whose family make-up included an infant and two unsteady toddlers. "They do not *belong* in the greenwood. They belong in their own house—not crammed into a little hut in a wintering forest, with naught but the clothes on their backs to call their own. It is not *right!*"

"Since when has our Sheriff ever concerned himself with what is right? Look, Robin," Little John said, "why do you think they come here? It is because you are the only one who seems to care what right *is*."

"Stealing is not right," she argued inimically. "It is a crime."

"Stealing a person's home because they cannot pay an

unjust tax is a crime — *not* returning that tax to the people it was taken from. You taught us that. Have you forgotten?"

"No," Robin admitted. She knew that Little John was right, but for once, his words did not comfort her.

"You are a hero," Little John insisted.

But looking into the eyes of the families clustered by the fire, Robin did not feel very heroic.

Robin supposed she should have seen it coming. A man would have known *exactly* what was going on when some of the new, unattached girls who had sought haven in the Sherwood with their fathers or their brothers began to take it in turns to bring Robin her meals. They would have seen the truth behind the shining eyes, the giggling whispers, the innocent run-ins, and the earnest greetings. But Robin, consumed with her own secrets, failed to recognize theirs until it was almost too late.

"Are ye sure ye will ne have more stew, Robin?" a girl named Valerie asked for the third time in as many minutes. Robin let out a deep sigh of impatience. It was one thing to be proud of one's cooking, but honestly — how much did these girls think she could eat? She had already had her fill and then some, but still they pestered her to have more. A serving rotation had been Marian's idea, since she had hated standing in line, but now Robin was beginning to yearn for the days when each person had obtained their meal for themselves.

"No, thank you," she repeated, struggling to stay polite. "Truly, I cannot swallow another spoonful of your excellent repast."

"Oh, but—"

"If he does not want it, I do!" Shane exclaimed, jumping up and snatching the bowl out of the woman's grasp. He gave her a dazzling smile.

Flustered but unable to protest, the girl stalked away. Shane watched her go, a trifle disappointed. He looked down at the soup in his hands. "Does anyone want this?"

When they shook their heads, he collapsed back down onto a log with a sigh, setting the bowl aside. His eyes never strayed from Valerie as the girl returned to her friends (the young women immediately huddled together, conferring urgently).

"Let us have a song, Allan!" Shane suddenly cried, leaping back onto his feet. "One that will set our toes to tapping and our feet to dancing!"

Allan, a slim slip of a boy, obediently picked up his lute and drew his hand across the strings, causing a cascade of tones to thrill through the air. Allan was one of the band's more recent additions, and though shy and quiet most of the time, an emboldened self seemed to spring from within him whenever he was called upon to sing. Suddenly boisterous and jolly, his voice — a surprisingly rich tenor — would surge forth as strong and pure as a stream born of melting snows.

"Nonny, hey Nonny, beauteous and bonny, come and dance with me . . . . We will spin through the meadows and romp in the shadows beneath the greenwood trees . . . ."

The transformation Allan's voice wrought in her band never ceased to amaze Robin. For the moment forgetting all their worries and cares, her people would grab as partner whoever was close at hand, dancing merrily with them in the twilight. Against the blaze of the fire, their silhouettes flickered black and red, accentuating their movements and making her dizzy just to watch them.

"Come on, Robin!" Marian called, appearing suddenly from out of the sea of dancers. "Dance with me!"

"I do not dance —" Robin began, but Marian would hear no protest. Seizing hold of her sister's hands, she pulled Robin into the cavorting circle. Robin had to move then or risk being crushed by the prancing feet and flailing arms. One moment she was dancing with Marian, the next Will had her by the waist and was spinning her in circles — Shane caught her by the arm then and began to perform a high-kicking step that she did her best to mimic; David seized her by the shoulder and they capered around each other, clapping to the beat. For one brief instant, Little John held her — his arm was wrapped in hers and they were dos-á-dosing around each other, and Robin could not remember why she had ever hated dancing before — this was wonderful, this was real, this was *right* — and then suddenly, Little John was gone and she was dancing with Valerie.

Robin's mind was still whirling from her brief moment with John, and maybe that was why she did not realize the impending danger until it was almost too late. Before she could register what was happening, Valerie had the edges of Robin's hood wrapped in her fingers and was pushing it back, stretching onto her tiptoes as she did so to kiss Robin squarely on the lips.

It was Robin's instinctual reaction that saved her — a split second before Valerie would have pulled down the hood and Robin's disguise along with it, she caught the girl's wrists and flung her away from herself in harrowed disgust.

Valerie fell to the ground; the men nearest to Robin were staring. Snatching at her slipping hood and feeling like she was going to be ill, Robin turned and ran out of the circle. Behind her, she heard someone call, "Do not bother with him — he is saving himself for the Lady Marian!" and thought that it might be Shane.

"You certainly know how to make an exit," Marian told her sister the next day, once Robin finally heeded her pounding and let her into the cabin. "Poor Valerie is quite distraught."

"Oh, *Valerie* is distraught?" Robin seethed, her voice rising slightly as she shut the door. "*She* kissed *me* — which, by the way, is an experience I would like to forget, thank-you-very-much — and she almost gave away who I truly am as well!"

"Just because you have no clue what to do if a woman kisses you does not mean she jeopardized your identity. Lots of men would have reacted the same way. Although running away was perhaps a bit much," Marian added thoughtfully.

In irritation, Robin yanked off her hood, revealing her thick yellow braid. "*This* is what she almost did," she announced hotly.

Marian's eyes widened in surprise. "You mean you have not cropped your hair yet? Robin! Of all people, how could you be so foolish?" she scolded. "Think of all your hard work, and all it would take is some rogue knocking your hood from your head to destroy it! You have gone to such lengths to disguise your voice and amend your habits, why in the world have you kept your hair this long when it is the one thing you could easily change?"

"It has worked brilliantly for me!" Robin answered with vehemence. "It has let me slip into and out of Nottingham more than a few times ... and it helps protect my head against buffets from John's quarterstaff!"

"It is too risky, Robin. If you intend to keep up your charade, you must cut it."

Robin turned away, but as much as she tried to resist the truth of Marian's words, she knew that her sister was right. She had kept her hair long as her one vanity, not for any of the reasons she had listed — those had merely served to excuse her not shearing it.

"Let me do it," Marian told her, her eyes softening a bit at the look on Robin's face. "I promise to be quick."

Robin tried to think of some argument she could give, some further reason not to cut her hair . . . but Marian was right: it was too risky. Valerie had proven that. With a nod of surrender, Robin dug beneath her bedding for her dagger and handed it to her sister with great reluctance. Marian took it, but hesitated; even she seemed loath to cut the golden locks.

"Just do it," Robin whispered, her eyes closed tight.

The blade began to saw at her braid; as the heavy strands fell away, Robin felt some vestige of the woman she had been — Robin of Locksley, daughter of Sir Robert of Locksley; a noblewoman — to which she had so stubbornly clung fall away at last.

Finally, the shearing blade grew still. Tentatively, Robin shook her head — wisps of gold fluttered around her neck, and her head felt strangely light. She touched the bottom of her hair — the ends curled up softly around her fingertips, freed of the weight that had dragged them down for so long.

Robin turned to her sister. "What do you think?"

"You will pass," Marian said thoughtfully, looking her over. "Although I doubt there is a prettier boy in all of Nottinghamshire. You had better get used to the girls wanting to steal a kiss."

Robin blanched.

After Marian left, Robin sat for a while turning over her hood in her hands. It made her feel peculiar to know that she did not need to wear it anymore to protect her identity. She reached up to touch her short hair. How would her people react to seeing her with her head uncovered for the first time?

Part of her wanted to get it over with, to face their startled exclamations and thus free herself of her hood's shadowy confines, but she was not quite ready to cast her namesake aside. At last, she pulled on her hood with a sigh. *I will go without it tomorrow*, she promised herself reluctantly.

True to her word, Robin deliberately left her hood aside the next morning, stepping into the sedate bustle of the camp with her head completely unadorned. She felt highly self-conscious and waited expectantly for someone to notice her newly cropped curls.

Expectation soon turned to astonishment, however, when for the first time in over a year, no one raised their arm to her in greeting nor came up to her to share some tale. In fact, no one gave her more than a passing glance, clearly dismissing the youth with the shaggy gold hair for just another recent arrival.

Marian was right, Robin thought with wonder, gazing around. *People really do see only what they expect to see!*

Her anonymity tickled Robin's humor, and she decided to see how long it would last before someone would recognize her. For the better part of the day, she worked at various tasks around the camp, marveling at how its inhabitants would pass her by without a second glance. Once, when Little John was walking just a few yards away, she deliberately dropped the bundle of wood she had been carrying, attracting his

attention. While he did pause and stare at her for a long moment as she gathered up the logs — puzzling perhaps over a
certain familiarity — in the end, he could not make a connection and moved on.

By afternoon, the fun was starting to wear thin. When the
scent of roasting venison began to fill the camp, Robin betook
herself to the oak tree to await the meal, collapsing down onto
her habitual spot.

"Boy."

She nearly looked up, but refrained at the last moment;
Little John was looming before her.

"Boy, I suppose you are new here so maybe no one has
told you, but that there is Robin Hood's spot. He will not
thank you for usurping it."

She quirked an eyebrow and smiled.

"Perhaps, he does not understand," Nicolas suggested,
coming up beside John. Speaking slowly, as though she were
a simpleton, he reiterated: "You — are — sitting — in — Robin —
Hood's — spot."

Still, she did not answer. By now, Lot had joined them.
"What is this?" he demanded. "Does this young whippersnapper need to be taught some humility?" He cracked his
knuckles menacingly.

Robin could not refrain from laughing any longer. "Peace!
Do you know me so little that I can sit right before you, and
you can talk to me, and yet you do not recognize me?"

They gawked at her. "Robin?"

Now that they thought to look, they recognized the firm
yet pale jawline of their friend, the dancing blue eyes behind
the wafting bangs, the slightly crooked nose, and the high
cheekbones. But for the first time, they could also see an

aureole of hair curling upon her neck, and a face unmasked by shadows.

"I have never seen you with your hood down before," Lot apologized. The others grunted their assent. Robin's hood was so much a part of her that seeing her without it was like seeing a king without his coronet — odd, and slightly disconcerting. And though they had always known that Robin was young, it was startling to see the proof before them that the man who lurked beneath the hood, the bane of the purloining rich, was just a slim-faced lad!

"Sorry, Robin," Little John told her abashedly, sinking down beside her. "I did not realize that you were you." This strange sentence just made Robin laugh harder, and Little John look more rueful.

"Trouble yourself not a whit!" Robin told him cheerily, seizing the excuse to buffet Little John lightly upon his arm as the others returned to their places. "I am well pleased to find my seat defended so loyally against usurpers!"

At her impish grin, even Little John had to laugh.

⚔ 16 ⚔

GUY OF GISBORNE

TIME PASSED, AND WINTER did, too. In spite of having had nearly twice as many people to feed this year as she did last year, no one in Robin's camp had starved . . . though there had been some nights when everyone had been very hungry indeed.

As with last winter, there was one red hart that eluded everybody's efforts to bring it to table; Robin, for her part, was certain it was the same deer. Over the summer, the stag had grown into a sage ten-pointer, and as she watched it leap away from her questing arrow, some part of her was glad that the brave hart had escaped yet again. Like Robin, the stag's continued reign in the forest depended on dodging the hunters who sought to bring it down. Fortunately, with the Sherwood in full awakening and animal life beginning to burgeon as much as the flowers, there was now no need to chase after such evasive game.

With a contented smile, Robin unstrung her bow and strolled through the blooming forest, breathing deeply of its warming mists and sweet perfumes. It was barely past noon-tide, and though she would eventually have to find another contribution to the evening meal, there was no need to hurry.

She came upon a river and hopped happily across, taking care not to slip on the spray-drenched stones. She pranced merrily onto the bank and into the greenwood, thoroughly enjoying how the lush green grasses muffled the sound of her footsteps into silence—such a difference from the crisp crunching of winter snow! As she meandered among the trees, Robin sought out the most sun-drenched paths, rejoicing in the warm rays that fell upon her face. She still wore her hood up at times, partly out of habit, and partly to maintain the expectations of her reputation, but today she had let it slip back completely so she could fully bask in the sun's radiance.

It was as Robin was dancing from one dappled sunspot to another that a tremendous belch reverberated through the trees, making her heart jump in her chest even while her body instinctively froze. Chances were the noise had originated from one of her bandsmen, out hiking or patrolling, but still . . . it never hurt to be cautious. An eructation that brash could very well have come from a forester, or even from one of the Sheriff's soldiers sent to prowl the forest for outlaws. If the latter proved the case, she would need to warn her people.

Reluctantly, Robin crept through the trees, searching for the source of the giant belch. When at last she found it, she could hardly believe her eyes.

What in God's good creation is that? she marveled in alarmed amazement, peering surreptitiously from behind a wall of ferns. Just beyond the bracken lay a small glade, and leaning against a bordering ash tree was the strangest creature that Robin had ever seen. Grotesquely misshapen and large, its design did not seem to follow the rules of nature. It was only when a tawny hand unfurled itself from its side and raised a sun-dried strip of meat to its mouth, and yellow teeth parted to rip off a piece before letting out another belch, that she realized she was gazing at a man.

Yet what a man! From head to toe, he was clad in black horse skin, tanned into leather with the hair still on it. Even his hose was made of the bristly skin. He wore a hood over his head, and from this hood protruded two horse ears, pricked upwards as though they could still listen. He was sitting on the ground with his legs stretched out before him, and his scabbard — also covered in horsehide — stuck out from his hip like a third leg. He seemed to be more beast than man and was altogether a frightful sight.

But it was the malice and danger the man seemed to exude that made Robin want to back away without delay; only her sense of duty kept her in place. As Sherwood's leader, it was her responsibility to protect the forest and the people within it. She could not turn her back on a potential menace — she must know what he was about.

Before she could rethink her decision, Robin strode into the glade and gave the man her most cavalier hail: "I must say, I have never seen a fellow like you in all my life! Who are you, and why in the name of all holiness are you decked out like a sable horse?"

It took all of Robin's willpower to maintain her smile as the seconds ticked by and the man made no answer. At last, he cast back his equine hood, revealing sharp, raptorial features that seemed oddly familiar, though Robin could not recall ever having seen him before. Two deep-set ebon eyes glared in her direction, even as they squinted at her against the sun, and his pinched mouth curled into a cruel sneer.

"Few fools are bold enough to approach me so insolently. I have half a mind to skewer you where you stand."

"I do not skewer so easily," Robin said, letting her hand rest on the hilt of her sword. She felt her heartbeat — already fast — quicken further.

The beast-man gave a short bray of laughter. "Boy, you would not last five seconds against my blade. I have slaughtered men for less trouble than you are now causing. You may thank your tender years and my good mood that I spare your life today."

Robin did not relinquish her grip on her sword. "I will thank the ground I stand on and the outlaws who guard it — Robin Hood and his band do not take kindly to murder in their honest Sherwood," she warned, trying to keep her voice light.

"But murder is why I have come," he said, his lips twisting in a feral grin. "The Sherwood shall be the more honest yet, when its leader lies dead from my sword."

"You are here to kill Robin Hood." She began it as a question, but it ended as a statement. She recognized the man now, despite his equine attire. This was Guy of Gisborne, the man who had sought to control the people of Sherwood and who had threatened to have her killed. He had stormed out of the forest the same day she had ascended as its leader, and since that time he had become almost as well known as she, though for vastly different reasons. Deadly and savage, Gisborne performed terrible deeds for anyone who had the coin to pay him. The people of Nottinghamshire lived in fear of him, his cruelty engendering their hatred as intensely as Robin's charity engendered their love.

"Of course," Gisborne smirked. "The Sheriff would hardly seek out someone of my talents to dispose of a mere sycophant.

Rage burned in Robin's chest at his words. This . . . *loathsome* . . . man had dared to violate the sanctity of Sherwood — her Sherwood — for a purpose so vile as murder! That it was to be hers bothered her less than his clear contempt for the people she valued.

Anger warred with rationality, and Robin fought to remain calm. Gisborne clearly did not recognize her; if she were careful, she could exploit his cocksure temper to gain important information without giving herself away.

"How will you know Robin Hood when you find him?" she forced herself to ask.

Gisborne laughed. "I remember his build, and though I may not recall the face he shadows, it is all the better for me: I will simply kill every likely man in the Sherwood until there is none left who might be he. After all, be it one murder or one hundred, it makes no difference to me, and each outlaw I kill will fetch its own reward. Why should I be selective and risk missing my prize when I can earn a Wolf Head's bounty on them all? So run away, little boy, before I decide your stature reminds me too much of that hooded man's and you should die this day as well."

His callous words drenched Robin like a cascade of boiling oil. Before she knew what she was doing, she had cast her bow aside and drawn her sword, her anger squashing the voice within her that screamed she was being a fool and to flee while she still could!

"If someone is to die today, Guy of Gisborne, it will be you," she told him in a voice that shook with fury as she stepped towards him out of the sun's glare. "I have killed only once before, and remorse for that death has haunted me every day since. But you . . . you kill without mercy, for pleasure and for pay. How many lives have you destroyed? And now you come here to destroy again. Well, I will not let you. I will fight you, Guy of Gisborne, and I will slay you if I must to protect the Sherwood and all those within it. Stand up and draw your sword, if you are a man, or else I will whip you like the gelding you are, for I am Robin Hood!"

Astonished by her hot words, Gisborne could only stare. Then with a roar of recognition, he leapt to his feet and drew his sword, swinging out at her with flashing might.

Robin barely got her sword up in time. Pain lanced through her arm as she blocked the forceful blow, her whole body trembling as she strained to hold off the heavier man. She thanked all the days she had spent in cudgeling practice, which gave her the strength now to fend off his attack. But how many more such strikes could she block? This was no comrade she sought to fell, and while a rap from a cudgel might mean a bruised rib, a rap from this sword would mean death. As Robin parried Gisborne's crippling blows, she feared that he would indeed bring about her end before this bout was finished.

Suddenly, miraculously, Gisborne seemed to stagger, and Robin hastily lunged in for the kill—but it was a feint! She tried to correct her stance, but it was too late. Overbalanced, Gisborne's next blow sent her tumbling, her sword knocked from her hand. Desperately, Robin scrabbled for the dagger at her hip even as her left hand swept the ground for her sword. Out of the corner of her eye, she saw the flash of Gisborne's sword as it arced down towards her, and instinctively, Robin raised her outstretched arm to block it. Her reflex and the bracer she wore saved her life — although the blade bit deeply into the leather, the arm guard deflected the blow and the sword sank not into her heart, but into her shoulder instead.

She screamed, and as she screamed, Robin lashed out with her right hand, and her dagger scored deeply across Gisborne's face. With a yell, he wrenched his sword out from her shoulder. One hand clutching at his bloody face, he raised the blade high with the other, prepared to loose the fatal blow.

A great staff descended through the air, whistling shrilly as it struck the blade from Gisborne's hand. The staff whistled again and dealt a blow that would have cracked a greater man's skull, and would have cracked Gisborne's if he had not been wearing a cowhide cap under his hood that absorbed most of its force. Instead, the blow sent him staggering. Blinded by blood and by pain, he lurched away from this new attacker, not even bothering to reclaim his sword as he fled.

Little John wanted desperately to chase after the man and finish him off, but Robin moaned, and he dropped to his friend's side. Robin's face was taut with pain, her breathing shallow and gasping.

"It is just a scratch," she choked out. "I am all right."

"Of course you are," Little John said, panic rising within him as he tried to stem the flow of blood blooming against Robin's chest. "As you said, it is just a scratch."

But there came no reply.

When Robin awoke, it was night, and only the gentle twinkling of stars through the treetops separated this darkness from the realm of the unconscious. Stars, and the hiss and pop of a burning fire, commingled with the scent of roasting rabbit convinced her senses that she was alive.

"John?" she croaked, straining to sit up. Immediately, her shoulder exploded in agony, pain clawing its way into her stomach and making her head reel. Robin saw the stars begin to disappear again, and she struggled mightily to hold on to consciousness.

"I am here," he said. "Be still."

There was something odd about the way he spoke the words, but Robin could not distinguish the change through the roaring in her ears. All that mattered was that Little John was here.

"How did you find me?" she coughed. If she held herself very still, the roaring in her head quieted and the pain in her shoulder subsided to a dull shriek.

"I was on my way to Lincoln Town. I heard the battle and went to see who was fighting with *swords* in the greenwood. Then I heard you yell."

"It is lucky you came by when you did," she sighed. Talking was torture, but she had to know. "And Gisborne? What happened to him?"

"Was that who it was?" Little John asked, startled momentarily from his mood. "He has gone. Run away."

"He will have gone back to the Sheriff," Robin brooded. She turned her head as much as she could without moving her shoulder, trying to bring Little John into better focus. He was sitting on the far side of the small fire, his face masked by shadows. Though she could not see his eyes, she felt the force of his gaze boring into her; without any perceivable reason, she suddenly felt uneasy.

Something niggled at Robin's mind. She pulled in her chin as best as she could to look at the wound that had almost taken her life. Little John's cloak lay over her like a blanket; it had fallen away slightly when she had tried to sit up, and no longer quite concealed the strips of her tunic — now stained a dark crimson by clotting blood and antiseptic wine — that had been used to bind her wound.

"Oh, dear," she gulped, realization striking her as painfully as had Gisborne's sword. "John — "

"Who are you?" he asked, his tone so cold it made her heart freeze.

"Robin," she replied.

"Do not lie to me!" Little John shouted, losing control at last and jumping to his feet. Robin braced herself to keep from cowering away, ignoring the pain in her chest. "I trusted you, and you have been lying to me from the first."

"I did not lie!" she answered hotly. "You just assumed the day I met you that I was a boy."

There. She had said it. In all of her daydreams and night dreams about telling John the truth, she had never imagined that it would come out like this.

They glared at each other across the fire.

"An easy assumption to make, when you go around dressed as a man and acting like one," he said in icy anger.

Robin bit back a heated reply. He was right to be upset, but she could not endure the betrayal she heard in his voice. An acrid scent distracted Robin — she glanced over at the fire and saw that the small coney was alight, its flesh charring before Robin's eyes.

"Your rabbit is burning," she said, trying to match the coldness in Little John's tone.

He started slightly at her statement, her words echoing through him like a half-forgotten memory. With one booted foot, he kicked the rabbit away from the fire, knocking down the makeshift spit and causing the logs to erupt with sparks.

"Do not change the subject," he said.

"What would you have me say?" she asked. "Yes, I lied! My father wanted me to marry the Sheriff, so I ran away. I did not ask for you to join my campfire that night, or for Will Stutley to follow me home, or for all those people to come to me, or for you to join my band. It just happened! And I have been dealing with it all as best I can."

"What kind of band is led by a woman?" he demanded in disgust.

"Would you rather it have been led by Gisborne?"

He was silent. Robin pressed on:

"Look me in the eyes and tell me, John, that I have not done well by all of you. Tell me that you were all better off without me. Tell me that you would still have sought to join our band if it were not the band of *Robin* Hood!"

Robin was wheezing; the effort of speaking so forcefully left her racked with pain and short of breath. Still she held Little John's eyes, refusing to look away as he studied her. Finally, his shoulders relaxed just the tiniest bit, and he sat back down.

"I may not be a man," she went on, speaking softer, "but I am still the Robin you knew. Do not throw away everything we have worked for, everything we have achieved, just because my gender is different than yours." She was speaking of their friendship as much as the band, and she saw the awareness of that in his eyes.

After a moment, Little John reached over and picked up the singed rabbit, brushing celadon grass off the meat.

"Would you like some?" he asked, his tone carefully bland.

Robin tried not to look surprised and considered whether eating was even possible at the moment. Her wound made flame lance through her chest with every breath she took.

Swallowing was agony. How in the world would she manage food? "Please," she said at last.

Little John helped Robin into a sitting position, leaning her back against a tree and pulling up the cloak where it had fallen. He touched her no longer than he had to.

It was a struggle to eat, but Robin managed, more for the comfort of the familiar task than because she felt truly hungry. The last time she and Little John had sat around a campfire eating rabbit like this, Robin had used the time to study him; now, it was Little John who studied her, and she was not certain he approved of what he saw.

"So," she asked at last, when the silence had stretched on for longer than she could bear, "am I to be let live?"

She deliberately posed the same question he had asked of her the night they had first met. She tried to say it lightly, but there was too much truth in the query. What was he going to do?

He frowned. "I do not know what to make of you, Robin. You are not who I took you to be, and I cannot forgive you for that—but everything that mattered about the Robin I came to the Sherwood to seek . . . all the reasons why the Sheriff hunts you and the people love you and your men follow you—you are still all that. I think."

"So you will not tell anyone?" she asked, unable to prevent a note of begging from creeping into her voice.

He considered for a long moment. "I cannot promise you that," he said at last. "I need time to think. But I will not mention anything to anyone for now."

Robin could hardly have expected a more positive response, and yet she had, and she felt her stomach twist with disappointment and anxiety. Still, Little John had promised to safeguard her secret for now, which was something. She would have to be satisfied with that.

Horrified gasps met the pair when they returned to camp, Little John carrying Robin in his arms, wrapped inside his cloak. Within seconds, anxious onlookers had surrounded them, their voices rising as they demanded to know what had happened, offered their aid, and loudly promised vengeance on Guy of Gisborne and the Sheriff as the story spread.

To Robin's relief, Little John took her straight to her cabin. He helped her lie down on her fern bed, the effort of reclining bringing tears to her eyes as her wound split open anew.

"I will go get the healer," he offered, rising back up.

Just then, Marian rushed in, followed closely by Edra.

"I will tend to my — to Robin," the girl announced loudly, dropping the armload of unguents, herbs, and cloths she had been carrying onto the ferns. She then began to push Edra and Little John out the door, insisting over the healer's protests that she would attend to Robin herself.

Before Little John left, he gave Marian a long, appraising look. After his promise to Robin last night, he had kept mostly silent except to ask a few questions, which Robin had answered as truthfully as she could. He now knew that Marian was her sister and that Will was indeed her cousin, and that she had been born well-off, although he did not know that her father was Lord Locksley.

Whatever Little John saw in Marian's face must have satisfied him, because he gave her a small nod of acknowledgement and stepped outside, shutting the door behind him. Through the walls, Robin could dimly hear him telling Edra that the wound was very minor, and that Marian's presence might do more to speed Robin's healing than any herb could do.

Thank you, John, she wept in silent gratitude as Marian began to peel away her bandages, which seemed to have welded themselves to her skin. *Thank you for that much.*

Days passed. At first, the agony of her wound left Robin too exhausted to do anything but sleep. She roused only to drink the broth that Marian brought, or when her bandages needed changing.

As her body began to heal, however, Robin found unconsciousness beginning to elude her, and she would lie awake for hours on end, unable to move and with nothing to do. Soon the confines of her hut began to oppress her, and she fretted so much that Marian, exasperated, finally agreed that Robin could go outside if she promised to sit quietly under the oak tree and *not* exert herself. Will dutifully carried his cousin to her moss-strewn spot, propping her up against the tree trunk and giving her one of the new deerskin blankets that Murray had tanned especially for her.

The sight of Robin sitting in her old spot raised her people's spirits tremendously—rumors had been blazing like wildfire through the camp that she was mortally injured, or had even died. Robin thought this was silly since David and Mara (accompanied by little Hannah, who had gazed at her with solemn eyes) had been in to see her several times, as had the twins, Will Stutley, and several of the others, and they had all announced to the camp that she was mending well. But fear gave rumors strength, and they had persisted until Robin's presence proved them false.

Little John, she noted bitterly, had not been by since he had returned her safely to the camp. Robin tried not to brood over this, but could not succeed. Marian claimed that Little John inquired often about how she was doing . . . but if that were true, then why did he not come to see for himself? If he were still her friend, then surely he would have come. No, it was far more likely that the discovery of her deception had destroyed his feelings of friendship for her, and his inquiring—if indeed, he really did inquire at all—was merely out of courtesy, nothing more.

Such thoughts had plagued Robin's mind through her long, inert days spent recovering in her hut, and she had feared that even out here in the sun, they would persist. However, her people's relieved expressions when they saw her back at her perch, and the eagerness with which they came up to talk with her, babbling on about the weather and other camp inanities in their need to speak, heartened Robin tremendously; she found that she could not remain gloomy for long. Their anxious concern buoyed Robin through her frustrating days of incapacity, as her muscles reknit themselves and her tissues healed, until at last the day came when she could pick up a bow again for the first time and send a goose-fletched arrow winging through the trees. Though the strain in Robin's chest made the arrow veer wide of its mark, the cheer she received echoed all the way to Mansfield Town—the whole camp had turned out to watch their brave leader bend a bow once again.

But in spite of Robin's mending body, her spirit stayed wounded; Little John alone remained aloof throughout her recovery. He still sat beside her at meals, but he chose to converse with Will Stutley and David rather than with her. Whenever they passed each other by in the camp, he was cordial, making no obvious effort to avoid her presence, but making no effort to seek her out, either.

One night while Marian was changing Robin's bandages—unnecessarily, as it turned out, for her wound was almost fully healed and in spite of the day's activities, had not wept—Robin could not help venting some of her frustration.

"I do not know what to do! If only he would give me some sign, one way or the other, then I could decide what action to take—but I cannot tell what he is thinking! And I dare not ask, in case he decides against me. It is driving me mad!"

"Are we still talking about the fact that Little John knows you are a woman now, or are we talking about something more?" Marian asked as she gathered up the wrapping.

Robin's response was muffled, her head suddenly buried in her arms. With a tender smile, Marian reached out to stroke her sister's short-cropped hair.

"Why not just tell everyone who you really are?" she suggested for the hundredth time. "You cannot stay a fair-faced lad forever. John knows the truth, and he is still here. You said yourself that he admitted you were a good leader. Your friends will support you."

Robin shook her head, rejecting her sister's words.

"Would it be so terrible if they did find out?" Marian asked again.

"Yes," Robin groaned. "It would be the end of everything!"

Helpless in the face of such illogic, Marian gathered her healing supplies into her basket. She wished she could provide an anodyne for her sister's heart as she had for her wounds, but this was something that Robin would have to work through herself. With a kiss to the top of her sister's prone head, she exited the hut, leaving Robin to struggle with the pain in her chest that no ointment could heal and no bandage could contain.

⚔ 17 ⚔

A MEET DIVERSION

AFTER HER LONG convalescence, Robin was grateful for any excuse to stretch her legs, so when the time came for the twins to go disperse the month's monies to the needy in Cuckney Town, she gladly chose to accompany them.

Although she had not really thought she would need it, Robin had heeded Marian's advice and brought along her cudgel for use as a walking stick. Now, after a day spent hiking through the forest and the farms of Cuckney Town, she found herself fully appreciating its aid. Even though Marian had declared her to be completely healed, Robin's trip left her feeling more tired than she had supposed she would be — it would clearly still be some time before her body would regain the level of fitness it had possessed prior to her injury.

"What is he doing?" Glenneth demanded harshly, interrupting Robin's musings.

"Poaching our good King's deer!" came Shane's snarled reply.

Robin turned to look at them, startled by their sudden ire; just a few moments before, the twins had been chatting lightly together as they walked through the greenwood. Now they were halted, their expressions indignant. Following the direction of their gazes, she saw what they had espied: a stranger stalking a herd of deer.

Now, someone not from the Sherwood might have wondered why this sight should have so concerned the trio — after all, Robin's band poached deer often enough themselves. But whereas her band hunted to survive, the sturdy attire of this unknown tracker and his well-fleshed appearance bespoke a secure if moderate existence. Clearly, he had no need to hunt the King's deer, and whatever one might say about Robin and her band, no one could claim that they were not loyal to the King. Her band viewed themselves less as poachers and more as unofficial foresters, granted the right to vert and venison as long as they protected the King's land and all those within it.

If the King's deer were in danger, then it was Robin's duty to protect them, in spite of her desire to avoid a confrontation. Also, there were the twins to consider — as their leader, she needed to provide the proper example. This poacher could not go unchallenged.

"Hold!" she shouted, marching forward and startling the man from his perch in the bracken. The deer, also startled, leapt away.

"Wassat?" the hunter growled, rolling to his feet with a wrestler's grace. He immediately adopted a defensive crouch, casting a regretful glance after the fleeing deer as he turned to face Robin. "Who are ye to tell me, 'Hold?'"

"We are the King's foresters," Robin said, widening her stance and deepening her voice even lower than normal in response to his challenge. "And we cannot let one such as yourself steal our good King's deer."

"I am no thief!" the man cried, surprised. "I admire the deer, and I like to watch them graze — indeed, I like it more'n anything. I was *ne* hunting them!"

"A likely tale!" Glenneth scoffed.

But now that Robin looked closer, she could see that the man carried no bow — only a thick quarterstaff clenched tightly in his white-knuckled fist. Robin cast around for a way to apologize without losing face, even as her hands tightened upon her own cudgel in instinctive response.

The man, misinterpreting her grasp on her staff, raised his own in defiant threat. "I care ne who ye are, ne whom ye purport to be — no one has ever made Arthur a Bland cry 'Mercy' before, and ye shall ne today!"

"Is that so?" Shane demanded. "Thief or not, your tongue has earned you a drubbing! I would delight in the task myself, but I cannot deny my master the pleasure." He gave Robin a short bow. "He will give you a drubbing that will knock all the pretty words loose from your head, 'Mercy' included."

"Ye call this *boy*, 'Master?'" Arthur a Bland sneered, raking Robin with his gaze and dismissing her just as quickly. "I will break him beneath the first blow from my staff."

He began to circle Robin, who — seeing there was no longer a way to escape from a fight — reset her grip on her cudgel and settled into a small crouch.

A faint whistle signaled the start of the bout as Arthur's staff shrilled through the air. Robin moved to block the blow and struck back quickly with her own staff; the man parried her attack effortlessly. So they went, each warding the other's blows until sweat dripped from their brows and their hands began to slip on their staves.

A deep ache was growing steadily in Robin's left shoulder; her muscles, softened from her recovery, protested the strain of the battle. She began to guard her movements, trying to ease the pain, until at last she moved too slowly to block a blow, and her opponent's staff smote heavily upon her ribs, forcing the air from Robin's lungs and leaving her gasping for breath.

Arthur a Bland swung then what he was sure would be the winning stroke, but to his patent surprise, his opponent blocked it. With more strength than she had shown yet, Robin struck back, the pain in her side fueling her determination to end the bout. Just as she unleashed the blow that would fell her opponent, her shoulder seized in a crippling spasm, jerking her cudgel and causing it to strike the other staff at a ruinous angle; her stave jarred horribly in her hands for a moment and then broke in two.

"Blast," she said, and then ducked as her adversary cast another blow at her head.

"Foul!" Shane and Glenneth cried together, racing forward to defend their unarmed friend. Her opponent backed away, spinning his cudgel menacingly.

"Come on, then!" he snarled. "I may just be one man, but even if ye prove as stout as this fellow turned out to be, I will fight ye all to the bitter end! I will ne cry 'Mercy' to anybody!"

"Enough!" Robin shouted, seizing the back of the twins' tunics simultaneously. When it seemed as though they would ignore her command, she repeated it again with stern emphasis: "*Enough*."

Reluctantly, they obeyed her, relaxing their aggressive

postures and taking a step back — Glenneth first, and Shane a moment later. "Aye, Robin," they submitted, the disappointment in their voices clear.

"Robin?" Arthur a Bland gasped. "Robin Hood?" His gaze passed from one Lincoln-clad man to the other, coming to rest on the flaxen-haired youth he had just fought, the boy the dark one had called, "Master." Arthur's grip on his staff grew weak as he made the connection, and the wooden pole clattered to the ground.

Robin flinched and then winced, her shoulder and side still throbbing from the match. To add to her vexation, the man she had just fought was now gazing at her in disbelief and apparent awe. "What?" she demanded crossly.

"I did ne realize," he began, his voice quivering a little. "I would never have wanted — never have dared — to raise my staff against *ye*. Forgive me."

Bewildered by his abrupt change of demeanor, but unwilling to look a gift horse in the mouth, Robin seized the opportunity to salvage her reputation and her pride.

"There is nothing to forgive," she informed the man. "We were wrong to accuse you of poaching, and there is no shame to admit it. I, for one, am glad of any soul who is stout enough to defend against injustice."

The man beamed at her self-consciously. "'Twas nothing."

"Indeed, it *was* something," Robin said, barely masking the rueful note in her voice as she touched her tender ribs. "You keep fighting against injustice, Arthur a Bland, no matter how small it may be. We have great need of such men."

Her words stunned Arthur, but he quickly recovered. "Oh, let me join ye!" he begged. "To live a life in the forest I love, to see the dun deer always, and to have brave men like ye for my companions is the height of my desire! Yessir, and if ye will forgive me my impertinence, I would be most willing to join yer band!"

The force of his unexpected response took Robin aback. She had been speaking of society in general, not of her band, but this man had clearly misconstrued her meaning. Still, she could not very well take back her words—there had been enough misunderstanding between them for one day. Even so, she tried.

"No one in my band would be here if they had anyplace better to be. Either they have lost their homes due to taxes, or they cannot return to them because they are outlaws. You still have a place in society. Consider well the riches you possess before you abandon them."

Arthur a Bland gave an indifferent shrug. "I have no family to miss, and what is a house to me? Merely a place to sleep, and I can do that here as well as anywhere else. Let me join ye!" he beseeched.

His choice baffled Robin, but she nodded.

Immediately, Shane and Glenneth came forward to clasp their new comrade on the shoulder, buffeting him with their accepting laughter, their natures as quick to forgive as they were to attack. They spent the rest of the return journey through the Sherwood tossing the tale of what had just happened back and forth between them as they walked, all the better to recount the occurrence once they reached the camp. Amazed by how the story was aggrandizing before her very ears, Robin followed the threesome at a more sedate pace, shaking her head in silent wonder.

Shane and Glenneth took to Arthur a Bland right away, for all that he was a cudgeller and a wrestler and not a bowman like they. He was brash and coarse, with a streak of naughty humor that other men seemed to delight in.

Not everyone attended to the new arrival, however.

"What is *his* problem?" Arthur asked the twins one day in a whisper meant to be overheard. He gestured to the ridge overlooking the river, where a man had been sitting all morning. It was Little John, staring silently into the distance and pondering many lonely and troubled thoughts. His back stiffened slightly at Arthur's comment, but he ignored it.

Shane shrugged and glanced over at Little John. "Who knows? Ever since spring began, it has been like he is only half there."

"Ah," Arthur said wisely. "Of course."

"Of course, what?" Glenneth demanded. It irritated him to have to guess at others' thoughts.

Arthur paused for effect. "Yer friend is undoubtedly suffering from . . . spring fever!" he announced. When this diagnosis was met by blank looks, he expounded impatiently, "Spring fever—the feeling of hot vigor rushing through yer blood after a winter's restraint; the desire to prove yer vitality again—to pursue, to conquer! The fever that can only be allayed by the tender ministrations and submission of the fairer sex."

"In English?" Glenneth asked.

"Yer friend needs a girl," Arthur exclaimed, exasperated. He strode over to where Little John sat and seized his shoulder. "Come, my good man. Let us take ye into town—I know a couple of wenches there who are always welcoming, and whose hospitality is everything a man could desire."

"I have no need for such hospitality," Little John told him coldly, brushing the man's hand off his shoulder.

"Nonsense," Arthur blustered, beckoning to the twins. "We will get ye a girl, or we will not return home tonight!" He seized one of Little John's massive arms, and Shane and Glenneth impulsively seized the other, and between the three of them, they managed to haul Little John to his feet.

Little John's face turned red with anger and he was about to throw them off, but like a sword being doused in water, his ire abruptly cooled, giving way to a sense of exhaustion. He could not battle these men and his own thoughts, too. With a sigh of resignation that bespoke the turbulence of his mind more eloquently than any words, he allowed the trio to steer him towards the edge of the clearing.

Robin, just returning to camp from one of her forest rambles, gazed curiously at the quartet as they passed her by. Shane and Glenneth were chuckling boisterously at something Arthur had said and did not notice her; Little John, caught up in the midst of the group, faltered for a second when he saw her, but then averted his gaze and strode on.

It matters not, Robin lied to herself, trying to brush off the hurt of his evasion. Seeking a diversion, her gaze fixed on Will Stutley, who was sitting with an air of utter dejection upon a nearby rock, his head bowed disconsolately.

"Anything the matter, Will?" she asked, walking over and sitting down beside him. "Why the long face?"

"Shane and Glenneth are takin' Little John t' town t' get a girl, but Arthur will ne let me come along. 'E called me a little boy! I am ne little — I am a man, and I 'ave as much right to a girl as anyone!" he exclaimed defensively.

"Oh," Robin said faintly. "Oh, I see." She felt as if someone had just rammed a quarterstaff into her gut for the second time that week; all at once, she could not breathe.

"'Tis ne fair," Will complained petulantly, not noticing her distress as he buried his chin in the palm of his hand.

An inexplicable anger filled Robin, pushing aside the pang in her stomach and releasing the constriction that bound her lungs, allowing her to breathe once more. She got to her feet. "No, it is *not* fair, and I, for one, will not sit here pouting while the others go out and have their fun. We will find an adventure of our own, shan't we, Will?"

"Will there be girls?" he asked hopefully.

Robin gave a bitter laugh. "I will see what I can do."

They made their way through the Sherwood, Will trusting that Robin had something wondrous in mind to soothe his wounded spirit, and Robin knowing only that she needed to find something to distract her mind from Will's dismaying news before it could overwhelm her.

How can Little John just go off like that? Has he no self-respect? Or is the lure of female flesh more important than our feelings?

"Oh, whom am I fooling?" she said aloud. There was no *our*.

"Wha' were that, Robin?" queried Will from a few paces behind her.

She waved a dismissive hand to show that it was nothing.

Yes, nothing. John has made it very clear that he wants nothing to do with me — with the woman, Robin. And it is not as if I ever told him how I feel. I have no claim on him.

"It is his choice — his life," she muttered angrily, her voice too soft for Will to hear. "I cannot — I mean, I have no *right* to stand in his way."

The thought did not comfort her.

Eventually, Robin's aimless trudging led the pair to the High Road. As she hesitated over where to go, a cart ambled down the highway. The smell of ham and mutton, steak, and goat meat hit her nose hard — the driver was obviously a butcher on his way to Nottingham's market to sell his wares.

On a whimsical impulse, Robin stepped out into the roadway. "Good sir, halt a moment," she called. The surprised butcher obediently reined in his horse.

"Good morning, friends," he called blithely, looking down at the pair with cheerful curiosity. "Why have you stopped me?"

"My name is Robin Hood —" she began, but she got no farther than that, for the butcher let out a low moan and dropped his reins, drawing back in his seat in fright.

"Please, sir, I am an honest man!" he cried. "I am on my way to Nottingham to sell my meat so I can provide for the dear lass who has pledged to be my bride. I have done you no harm, sir, and I have cheated no one, so if you are the man I have heard tell about, I beg you, sir, take naught from me!"

"Calm down," Robin implored, although the man seemed inclined to do no such thing. "You are to be wed?" she asked, trying to set him at ease.

"Next Thursday," he replied, anxiety etching deeper into his face.

"Well, sir, I have never robbed an honest man, least of all one who was about to be married. I would like to buy your meat from you, and your cart and your horse, too, if you are willing. How much is their value?"

Will shot her a questioning look—was this part of the adventure?—but he did not interrupt.

The butcher was also puzzled. He stammered as he answered, "F-four marks for everything, but less if I cannot sell all my meat."

"I will give you six marks," Robin told him, pulling from her purse more money than a common man could earn in a year. The butcher gaped at the silver coins. "Consider the balance a gift to help set you upon your married life."

The butcher clambered down from his seat, stuttering his thanks. He took the coins from Robin and quickly slipped them into his own purse, shoving the pouch deep within his tunic. Robin climbed into the cart and helped Will up beside her. With a flick of the reins, the horse ambled off toward Nottingham, the incredulous butcher watching the outlaws depart with his mouth agape.

Robin flicked the reins again, inciting the horse into a trot; she was eager to get to Nottingham and to the diversion it promised.

An avid crowd had gathered around the butcher's market, their necks craned in an attempt to catch sight of the wondrous new vendor. The other meat-sellers' stalls were devoid of customers, and the butchers behind them glowered at the newcomer and muttered darkly to themselves.

From behind her butcher's bench, Robin—clad in the bloodstained apron she had found in the back of the cart—cleaved contentedly at the butcher's meat. When one slab was done, Will would whisk the pieces away for sale and lay another slab in its place.

Every now-and-again, Robin would pause in her cutting and cry out in a loud voice,

"Meat, meat, now who will buy my meat? Fat priests and greedy merchants stay away—I like you not and will make you pay twice what my meat is worth. The common man may choose to buy, it matters not to me—I will charge you three pennies for three pennies worth of meat. Now, the goodwives among you have a friend in me—I will give you three pennies worth for just one penny. But the pretty maids among you will like us best—you get the choicest meat for the price of just one kiss."

Laughter turned to astonishment as the crowd saw things were just as Robin said, for Will would hand a man his money's worth of meat, but a lady would walk away with three times the meat she had paid for. As for the girls, they swarmed around the stall, accepting tender cuts from the handsome Will and giving his lips a savory kiss in return.

Robin was more than happy to let Will handle the exchange, laughing inside at how the lad's eyes would light up with each maid he espied. Some of the girls were disappointed that the handsome butcher was letting his brother do all the work, but Will quickly made them forget their dismay.

"This is wonderful!" he told Robin during a brief lull. "Can we do this ag'in t'morrow?" He did not wait for an answer, for a fetching young woman had just approached the stall, and he turned to trade her some meat with a broad grin on his face. Robin chuckled and returned to cleaving the meat with a grin of her own. This charade was far more diverting than she had expected it to be, so much so that Robin soon forgot the bitter mood that had driven her out of the Sherwood.

It gave her a horrible start, therefore, the next time she glanced up, to recognize those waiting in line for her meat.

"Ye cleave a pretty bargain, Robin," Arthur a Bland said cheerfully, "but as ye can see, I already have all the morsels I need." He had his arms wrapped around two buxom ladies — one blonde, the other brunette. The brunette winked at Robin saucily.

Looking beyond him, Robin saw Shane and Glenneth, each with a lady clinging to their forearm. John, she noted with selfish relief, walked alone.

Catching her gaze, Arthur misinterpreted its meaning. "Yes, 'tis a fair shame, is it ne? Fool man refuses to have anything to do with these heavenly beauties. Oh well, the more for me and the merrier I shall be. An oath is an oath, and I shan't be coming home tonight!"

With a laugh, he and his ladies sauntered away, the twins and their partners following closely behind him. John paused for a moment as if to speak, a faint blush tingeing his cheeks, but then he closed his mouth and trailed after the others, his tall frame causing the crowd to part around him to allow him through.

Will, occupied with a shapely redhead who had been more than generous in her payment, laid a new slab of mutton in front of Robin with a breathless smirk — he had noticed nothing.

Before long, the duo had sold all their meat, and the people began to disperse. As Robin mopped up the stall with her apron and Will said a poignant farewell to the redhead, a thickset man approached their cart.

"Apologies, sir, but I am all out of meat," Robin informed him over her shoulder as she tossed her cleaver and apron into the cart.

"So I have noticed," the man replied dryly. Robin turned to look at him and saw that he wore a butcher's apron much like hers, although it was lacking in a day's fresh stains. "Never have I seen a butcher like you, so willing to make loss instead of profit. If I did not know better, I would say you were a thief who had stolen your wares . . . but when did a thief ever give away his goods? You must be some foolish prodigal who does not know or care for the value of things and thus parts with fine meats for a pittance."

"You have seized the matter by the nose," Robin told him merrily, tickled to encounter this rare man who had clearly never heard of Robin Hood. "May I help you in some other way, good sir?"

"The Sheriff has invited our guild to a feast this afternoon," the stranger reluctantly told her. "The victuals will be good and the drink hearty. However you came into this trade, it seems you are a butcher now and if you should like to attend, you may."

"That sounds . . . fine indeed," Robin replied, a clever idea springing into her head. "It is certainly meet for a butcher to feast on the Sheriff's meat. I will see you there."

The butcher nodded, then paused, having registered her pun, and at last walked away, shaking his head.

"Ye are not plannin' t' go, are ye, Robin?" Will asked, standing suddenly at her elbow.

"Indeed, I am," she answered with a crafty gleam in her eye. "Though on second thought, you had better not—the Sheriff knows you by sight now." Robin's mouth quirked at Will's obvious disappointment, and she pulled him close, dropping her voice to a mere whisper. "Listen, I want you to return to camp and tell the others . . . tell them I have a brilliantly stupid idea!"

⚒ 18 ⚒

A COSTLY BARGAIN

WHEN ROBIN WALKED into the Guild Hall an hour later, the feast was already well underway. She paused in the entrance for a moment, carefully assessing the locale. The conventional room was much as she remembered it, with two long tables spanning most of the hall. A third, smaller table sat across the head of the room; this was where the Sheriff was seated, surrounded by a few of the more prominent butchers. A ray of light from the window illuminated the Sheriff's face, and Robin smiled, remembering the uproar last summer when her arrow had sailed in through that selfsame window, bearing her triumphant message.

The same sensation of rebellious power that had filled her then filled her now as she stepped into the wolf's very den. She was wearing her suit of Lincoln Green, and while there were enough butchers dressed in similar hues to keep her attire from standing out, she still felt very brazen as she gazed about the room, undisguised.

Just then, a servant — blinded by the large roast pig he was carrying — knocked into Robin, and she hastily jumped aside ... but that put her into the path of several footmen, each intent on refilling goblets and replacing empty platters with new ones. Somehow, she managed to avoid a collision and to find a free seat at the leftmost table. She had barely begun to lade her trencher, however, when someone tapped her on the shoulder.

"Beggin' yer pardon, sir, but my lord requests yer presence," a harried servitor informed her. It was just the summons that Robin had been hoping for, but she put on a face of surprised flattery and followed him to the head table.

The Sheriff beckoned her over to the seat at his left hand, and the butcher who had held that spot shifted over grumpily, irritated at having his position usurped.

"Master Bostock here has been telling me about your exploits in the market today," Sheriff Darniel told her, nearly shouting to be heard over the multitude of boisterous voices. "He claims that you sold your meat for only one penny, although you could have charged three pennies for it and done well. And that a pretty lass had but to kiss you, and you would give her the meat for free."

"All true, my lord," Robin confessed, not bothering to correct his last statement. "I would rather have a kiss than three pennies any day."

The Sheriff roared with appreciative laughter. "Indeed, indeed. I daresay you got the better end of the bargain! You may have to change your prices," he added, addressing the Chief Butcher, "or else risk losing all of your custom to this brazen lad!"

The butcher gave her a sickly smile. "Where is your help-er?" he asked, trying to shift the conversation away from his day's poor sales.

Robin saw her opening. "My brother had to return home to tend our land and our beasts."

"You must have many beasts, and much land, in order to forgo your coin so willingly," the Sheriff guessed, a greedy glint in his eyes.

"Yes, indeed," Robin confirmed, warming to the subject. "We have over five hundred horned beasts, but alas, we cannot find buyers for any of them. If things keep going as they are, I shall be forced to butcher them one by one, just to feed my family. As for my land, I have never bothered to take its measure."

"Just so, just so," Darniel murmured, envisioning five hundred plump steers. "Well! I like you, lad, and I would help you out of your trouble, if you will permit. Tell me, how much do you value these beasts of yours at?"

"I imagine they are worth at least ... five hundred pounds," Robin told him, biting into a thick pasty and pre-tending not to see the look of cold calculation that flashed across the Sheriff's face.

"Five hundred pounds is a lot of money," he said slowly. "But for three hundred pounds in silver and gold, I will take these beasts off your hands."

"Three hundred pounds!" Robin protested, feigning out-rage. "Five hundred beasts are worth twice that amount! Or do you think to kiss me and get half my beasts for free?" The Sheriff flushed a dark vermilion, and the Chief Butcher's mouth fell open at Robin's audacity.

"All right," Robin said, halting whatever words the Sheriff might have found to say. "I will accept your offer, if only because my brothers and I need the coin to maintain our merry lifestyle."

"Very good," the Sheriff replied, the thought of such a rich bargain excising all ire at the youth's effrontery from his mind. "I will come with you today to inspect your horned beasts."

"As you wish," Robin said. "But mind you bring your money with you. I do not trust a man who offers so shrewd a bargain."

"Of course," the Sheriff assured her, and then changed the subject to a more mundane topic.

As soon as the feast ended, the Sheriff returned to his castle to collect his monies, and Robin followed the other butchers out into the Hall's paved courtyard. The Chief Butcher was the last to leave; he looked around, caught sight of Robin leaning carelessly against the wall, hesitated for a moment, and then walked over.

"Lad, I do not know who you are, but leave now before the Sheriff returns," he advised Robin in a low tone, glancing this way and that for sight of the Sheriff. "It is a scurvy trick he has played on you, agreeing to buy your beasts for so little a sum. I bear you no ill will and would not have him beguile you."

"He has not beguiled me," Robin assured the man, pleased that despite his impression of her, he had character enough to try to warn her. "My brothers and I know the value of our beasts—we will ensure that the Sheriff pays proper value for the meat he receives."

Bemused, the butcher opened his mouth to argue, but just then the Sheriff reentered the quadrangle astride his blood bay mare, accompanied by several guards.

"Very well," the butcher said. "On your own head be it.

I have never met such a mad youth in all my life." With a nod of acknowledgement to the Sheriff, he walked away.

"Shall we?" the Sheriff asked, indicating for Robin to lead the way.

Robin shook her head. "I will lead you to my home as I have promised, my lord, but not these men. My brothers dislike soldiers."

"They come to protect me," the Sheriff scowled.

Robin spread her hands as if to indicate, *I am helpless in this.* "I merely repeat what I know my brothers will say: if your men come, they will have nothing to do with you. It is your decision, my lord," she added when he hesitated. "I am sure there is someone else out there who would be willing to buy my beasts."

That settled it — the Sheriff simply could not let a deal this good pass him by. "Remain here," he ordered his servicemen. Although Robin saw doubt reflect in their eyes, they were too well trained to argue and obediently fell back.

"Follow me, sir," Robin said, walking away before the Sheriff could change his mind.

Once outside of Nottingham, they did not pass many people by, but those they did pass turned often to stare at the sight of a youth in Lincoln Green walking next to the Sheriff's horse. Robin's lanky legs came in handy now as she was forced to take long, striding steps to match the mare's gentle amble. To her regret, she had sold the butcher's horse and cart before going to the feast, and the Sheriff had not thought to offer her the use of a mount.

Well, what did I expect? Robin mused. *Since when does our Sheriff consider* other *people's needs?*

At least the Sheriff had been quick to forget his abandoned guards; in fact, he was in a rollicking mood. Phillip Darniel fully expected to earn at least four hundred pounds through his canny bargain, and it had put him in such a good humor that he scarcely noticed when Robin led him off the High Road and onto one of the lesser paths traversing Sherwood Forest. Instead, he regaled Robin with long-winded tales about his judicial exploits and talked animatedly about the new taxes he hoped to implement next autumn. Robin gave his words her full attention, nodding politely when required and chuckling occasionally at his jokes.

All at once, the Sheriff stopped talking and gazed around at his surroundings. They were deep within the shades of Sherwood now, in a part of the forest he did not recognize. "Heaven preserve us," he said, casting an alarmed glance at Robin and reining in his mount. "Are you lost, boy, to take us so deep into the woodland where that varlet Robin Hood dwells?"

"Not at all!" Robin insisted. "We must pass this way to get to my home. Do not fear, you are safe with me!"

The Sheriff peered uneasily into the dark foliage, far from comforted by the youth's reassurance, but at last the thought of the profit he would forfeit if he turned back now overwhelmed his anxiety, and he allowed Robin to lead him further into the forest.

They had not gone more than another half mile when Robin suddenly halted, putting one hand upon the Sheriff's bridle rein and pointing ahead with the other. "There are my horned beasts, good Sheriff," she trolled. "Have you ever seen such fine-looking animals?

The Sheriff followed her pointing finger to a small cluster of red deer chewing contentedly on the bronzing grass. "Is this a jest, lad?" he demanded angrily.

Robin looked at him steadily. "Not to me."

Alarm coursed through the Sheriff as he met those intense blue eyes. For the first time, he registered the Lincoln Green apparel of his guide.

"Let go of my horse," the Sheriff said, fear tightening his voice as he attempted to pull the reins free from Robin's grasp. "I do not know who you are, but I know that I like not your company any longer! Go your own way, sirrah, and let me go mine."

"That I cannot do, lord Sheriff," Robin told him, tightening her grasp on the reins. "My brothers would never forgive me." So saying, she unhooked the silver bugle from her belt and blew a ringing triad that made the Sheriff's heart quiver within his chest.

The Sheriff drew his sword. "Stand back, cur," he commanded Robin, "or I will trample you beneath my horse and blade."

Robin let go of the reins and stepped out of the Sheriff's way. Phillip Darniel wheeled his horse around, preparing to gallop out of the greenwood with all possible speed, but his way was blocked by a score of archers. He spun his horse on its hindquarters back toward Robin—the horse, alarmed, kicked out with its forelegs before coming back down on all fours, almost striking her—but his way was blocked by another half-score of archers there, too. Seeing that there was no way out of the trap, the Sheriff held his horse very still and sat stiffly upon it, waiting with obvious trepidation to see what the outlaws would do.

Robin held out her hand for the Sheriff's sword, and he gave it to her without protest.

"Shall we kill him, Robin?" Little John asked from the head of one group, his face expressionless. The Sheriff felt his throat close up; he began to wheeze.

"You ask that of *me*?" Robin queried quietly. "For shame. This is the Sheriff of Nottingham," she announced, turning away from Little John. "He has taken the time out of his very busy day to come and feast with us. We are honored, are we not? Put down your weapons, men, for he is to be our guest!"

The archers reluctantly let their bowstrings go slack. The Sheriff, realizing that they were not going to shoot him — not yet — found that he could breathe again. The giant who had asked if they should kill him came forward and took the reins from Robin. The Sheriff knew there would be no escaping from this outlaw — he looked quite capable of holding back a surging horse if so required.

With another trill of her trumpet, Robin led the party off the narrow path and into the twisted trees of the forest.

The Sheriff's hands clenched into fists of hatred in his lap as his horse ambled after the jaunty youth. No wonder he had never caught Robin Hood before. He could scarcely believe that this scurvy lad, this . . . this fair-faced *boy*, was the bane of his existence, the scourge that had plagued the good folk of Nottinghamshire and himself for so long! If word of this got out, he would be a laughing stock. It would mean the end of his career as sheriff . . . assuming that he survived the night. It galled Darniel to no end that the only reason he was still alive right now was because his foe had ordered it.

These thoughts so preoccupied the Sheriff that he scarcely noticed that his outlaw captors — rather than reveling in their victory — were walking beside him in somber silence. No one seemed inclined to look at the Sheriff directly, preferring to shoot him surreptitious sideways glances instead.

At last the procession came to a halt, and the Sheriff was startled out of his brooding by the sight that met his eyes. Phillip Darniel had never troubled himself to imagine what an outlaw camp might look like, but if he had he would have pictured men strewn about the ground in drunken slumber, half-eaten carcasses littering the turf, and golden coins winking in the sunlight. The orderly, peaceful hamlet that greeted the Sheriff was completely beyond anything he might have conceived.

Its residents had obviously been waiting for him. The men stood at silent attention beside their cabins, their womenfolk kept slightly behind them. The people's noiseless stares sent prickles down the Sheriff's spine. Even their children watched his passage quietly — one man held a young toddler who gazed at him with wide brown eyes, a plump fist stuck in her mouth.

"Please sit," Robin said, giving Darniel a small bow and gesturing toward the base of a tall oak. Her voice seemed overloud in the silence.

The Sheriff hesitated for a moment, feeling the weight of ten-score eyes upon him and then he dismounted his horse, taking the seat that Robin had indicated. A glint of yellow caught his gaze — dangling above his head was a golden arrow. A taunting rhyme began to dance through his mind, and the Sheriff glared at its author with newfound hatred, his mouth tightening into an impossibly thin line.

Seemingly undisturbed by his glower, Robin sank down onto the ground beside him. The Sheriff flinched away; she pretended not to notice. "Come, men!" she called. "Where is our hospitality? Our venerable Sheriff provided me with a lavish feast this afternoon, and I shall be shamed if we of the Sherwood cannot do the same for him!"

As if her words were the countercharm to some great spell, the camp's strange stillness abruptly broke. Those on serving duty immediately began to bustle about, seizing wooden platters and placing slabs of meat upon them, filling

horns full of sack and ale, and finishing the supper preparations. Those who were not on duty that evening took their
seats; Will Gamwell sat down in his normal place at his
cousin's left, and Little John settled on the Sheriff's right side
like a guard. Both of them shot Robin dubious looks that
seemed to question the sanity of her actions, but neither of
them voiced their doubts aloud.

Marian had no such reservations. "Why did you bring
him here?" she demanded in a too-loud whisper as she handed Robin her food. "Now, he knows where to find us; he will
bring back his men and hunt us down—"

"I was very careful," Robin assured her sister, patting her
hand. "He will not be able to find his way back here. Trust me
to know what I am doing."

The Sheriff watched their interaction, his gaze growing
blacker as he realized that his abducted fiancé was in fact a
willing consort to Robin Hood. He ignored the trencher of
meat that another server was holding out to him; exasperated,
the man set it down on the ground in front of the Sheriff and
stalked back to the fire.

Sneering at Marian, the Sheriff demanded loudly, "Tell
me, *Lady* Marian, do you serve all the men of Sherwood, or do
you save such tender meat for Robin Hood alone?"

Marian flushed and drew away from her sister. Will half-
rose out of his seat, but Robin seized him by the arm before he
could stand and issue a challenge, pulling him back down.

"I would mind my manners if I were you, lord Sheriff,"
she suggested in a nonchalant tone. "Steel blades cut deeper
than steel tongues." Robin took a deep bite from the meat on
her trencher, deliberately letting its golden juices run down
her chin. "Do eat up, Sheriff. You would not want to insult
our hospitality."

With a mouth puckered so tight that it was a miracle he could fit aught inside it at all, the Sheriff of Nottingham picked up the meaty bone and took a contemptuous bite. Robin pretended not to see his expression alter over the next few mouthfuls from mutinous compliance to delighted consumption. Phillip Darniel was neither a forester nor nobility and had no more right to the King's deer than a peasant — venison was not meat that *he* would scorn to eat with impunity!

And venison was just the start of the meal. Rabbit-and-onion pasties, boiled capon, and a delicious honey-and-curds dish soon followed in succulent succession. It was a fine feast indeed, and Robin wished that her people could be as lively and merry as they usually were at their mealtime gatherings, but the strange quiet that had gripped the camp ever since the Sheriff had entered persisted even through their supper.

Have I made a mistake? Robin wondered, not for the first time. She had wanted to show the Sheriff the livelihoods he had stolen — to make him see her people as children, wives, and husbands, not outlaws. She wanted him to feel some remorse for those he had ousted from their proper place in the world and to engender some respect for the lives they had managed to forge here. But the Sheriff looked only at the food he was eating or at the space above the congregation's heads. And her people, with their quiet whispers and sidelong glances, were hardly the picture of a happy and healthy community.

Somehow, I have to make him see them as I see them, Robin thought desperately. *I have to make him at least* look *at them.*

Robin nudged Will with her elbow and stared meaningfully at the cudgel lying propped up by Little John's side. With a sigh, Will Gamwell put down his unfinished pasty and got to his feet.

"Shall we have a bout, Little John?" he asked loudly, helping his friend up and handing him his cudgel. Immediately,
the atmosphere in the camp shifted. A fight between Will
"Scarlet" and Little John was always a treat, and lately a rare
enough occurrence that the mere suggestion was enough to
enliven the people with eager anticipation.

Will led Little John over to the sparring ring in front of the
fire, accepting a cudgel from David along the way. As one, he
and Little John settled into their stances, their eyes locking on
each other with an intensity that suggested their camaraderie
would not prevent them from giving their best to the contest.

Indeed, the match was everything that a sportsman could
desire. By the fourth or fifth cracking blow, even the Sheriff
was riveted, his food lying forgotten in his lap.

When Little John seized the victory a half hour later, Robin was relieved to hear the Sheriff's boisterous baritone join in
cheering the prowess of the fighters. Other sparrers sprang up
to replace Will and Little John, engaging in their own spirited
bouts of wrestling and cudgeling. The people applauded their
antics, glad to have a focus for their attention that was not the
Sheriff. Darniel, for his part, cheered and groaned right along
with them. He was a sportsman at heart, and shrewd fighting
never failed to fill him with heady gladness, so that he unwittingly cried, "Well struck! Well struck!" and forgot for a time
that it was outlaws he was praising.

Robin wore a small, satisfied smile as she felt the tension
seep out of the camp. Maybe this plan of hers would prove to
be more brilliant than stupid after all.

Eventually the sun began to set, and the bright harvest
moon began to rise majestically in the sky. Aware of the
growing shadows, the Sheriff stood; those nearest to him
broke off their conversations first, with those further away

soon following suit. Quickly, the happy laughter of the camp faded away into silence, and those left fighting immediately broke apart to see what would happen next.

The Sheriff took a deep breath, fully aware of the eyes upon him, and that whatever he said next might mean his life or death. For this reason, he affected a cheerful tone: "Thank you all for the generous hospitality you have shown me and for the merry entertainment you have provided. It heartens me to see such respect for the King and I, his deputy, even in the heart of Sherwood. But I must go now, for the day wanes late and I have neglected my other affairs for far too long."

"Of course!" Robin agreed, also getting to her feet. "How thoughtless of us to have kept such a hardworking man from his duty. But before you go, there is something you seem to have forgotten."

"I have forgotten nothing," the Sheriff insisted, his face going as white as the fist that clutched for his absent sword.

Robin smiled kindly. She would have preferred to avoid this, but she knew that letting the Sheriff leave the Sherwood with a full purse would be too much for even her band to endure. "I understand how a man with so many important affairs weighing on his mind might fail to recall our fee. Poor innkeepers that we are, we must insist that our guests pay their worth for the food, drink, and merry entertainment that we provide. We in the greenwood *are* known for our charity, but I would never insult *you*, lord Sheriff, by presuming that you need it."

"Understandably," the Sheriff said through clenched teeth. "And even if you had not asked, I would surely have given you a score of pounds for the merry time you have shown me."

"Oh, but I would never treat you so disrespectfully!"

Robin protested. "Imagine what the King would say if he knew his sheriff was of so little worth. I cannot in any conscience value a magistrate of the King at less than three hundred pounds."

"Three hundred pounds?" sputtered the Sheriff over the startled exclamations and guffaws of the band. "Think you that your measly entertainment was worth three pounds, let alone three hundred? I will not pay your fee!"

"Careful, Sheriff," Robin said, closing the distance between them and speaking in a soft voice. "Look around you. Right there is Will Stutley, whom you had beaten and later attempted to hang for the crime of courting your daughter. That big man there is David — you threw him and his pregnant wife off their land because they could not afford your impossible taxes. Shane and Glenneth there, you outlawed for a brawl your soldiers instigated; Shane almost lost the use of his arm in that fight. And I . . . I you tried to assassinate. I assure you, lord Sheriff, that everyone here has a story to tell regarding your hand in their lives. None are pleasant.

"We do not wish to be at odds with you, Sheriff, but you have left us no choice except to support ourselves in the only way we can. Perhaps in the future, you will remember this day and consider whether mercy might be more profitable than greed. But for now, realize that your actions have left my people with only contempt for you, and much anger, and know also that I may not be able to restrain their ire much longer. Be advised by me — pay your value without more ado, if your life is something you value."

Darniel blanched. Slowly, he reached inside his tunic and withdrew a heavy purse, letting it tumble from his fingers to the ground with a clunk.

"Little John, please count the monies," Robin requested,

not tearing her eyes from the Sheriff's face. Was he ruminating even a little on the more profound things she had said? Based on the hatred radiating from his gaze, it would seem that he was not. She sighed. "It would be tragic if the Sheriff misjudged his purse."

Little John obliged her, counting the coins aloud in a booming voice while the Sheriff stood by stiff as stone. When the last of the silver and gold sat upon a wooden trencher and the tally read three hundred pounds, Phillip Darniel turned away without a word and mounted his horse.

"Nicolas, go with him," Robin commanded. "Night is nearly upon us, and I would not have our guest lose his way in the forest."

"No!" the Sheriff bellowed, visibly alarmed. "I have no need of guidance."

That was an obvious falsehood, but Robin, seeing the fear in the Sheriff's eyes, understood why he might not want to be alone with one of her men.

"Then I will lead you myself," she announced. Seizing hold of the horse's reins, she led the placid mare into the trees. As she wended her way along invisible forest paths, doubling and occasionally tripling back until Darniel could not possibly keep his direction, Robin wondered if the Sheriff might not spur his horse into a canter and trample her beneath its hooves or try to stick a concealed dagger in her back. She was almost surprised when they reached the High Road to find that she was unscathed.

She handed the reins back to the scowling man. "Farewell, Sheriff. Go in peace and remember your feast in the forest the next time you seek to cheat a man." With that valediction, she slapped the horse on its hindquarters, startling it into a forward leap. Without waiting for his beast to settle down, the Sheriff kicked the horse into a gallop, racing down the moonlit road until all that Robin could see were clouds of silver dust.

Robin exhaled slowly and turned her gaze away from the road. Facing the slumbering shadows of the forest, she called out loudly into the darkness: "Come out, then, whoever you are, and tell me why you are following me!"

⚔ 19 ⚔

THE LANGUAGE OF FLOWERS

WILL GAMWELL stepped out of the shadows.

"Whatever are you doing here? I did not ask to be followed," Robin rebuked him as she recognized her cousin, but she tempered the reprimand with a smile. "Still, I suppose I should be thanking you, since I suspect the Sheriff would have tried to retaliate against me if not for your presence. Likely, he sensed you behind us as I did and chose not to risk it."

Will quirked his head, as though her words surprised him. "If so, I am glad I was present, though I must confess that my guardianship was accidental. I wanted to talk with you."

Now, it was Robin's turn to quirk her head. "I am glad to know you have such faith in my ability to self-protect," she told him dryly. "Could your conversation not have waited until I got back to camp?"

"I wanted to talk to you *away* from the camp."

Robin frowned and walked back into the Sherwood, Will falling into step beside her. "Well, we certainly are 'away.' So talk."

Her cousin's tone grew stern: "You have gotten caught up in this role of yours — in being Robin Hood. You have forgotten how it affects other people."

"Of course, I have not forgotten!" Robin exclaimed, taken aback by his censure. "That is why I brought the Sheriff here, so that he might see us not just as outlaws, but as *people* — deserving people who need a sheriff who will do rightly by them. If the Sheriff shows leniency to even one family as a result of today's experience, then bringing him here will have been worth all the risk and displeasure. I thought you of all people would understand that."

"I am not talking about the Sheriff!" Will seized Robin by the arm, halting her forward progress. "I am talking about Marian."

"What?" Robin blinked at her cousin, completely confused. "What does Marian have to do with this?"

"You heard the Sheriff earlier, what he thinks she has become. And he is not the only one. If you keep up this charade, you will ruin Marian's reputation."

"She is living in a camp of outlaws. Technically, her reputation is already ruined," Robin pointed out pragmatically.

"Not to me!"

Will's explosion startled several birds from their sleep in the trees; Robin jumped at the sudden outburst, and even her cousin seemed surprised at himself. He continued on in a more controlled tone, "Did you never wonder *why* no one has questioned your right to steal Marian away in the first place?

Why no one has even dared flirt with her since she came to live here? They think the two of you are in love!"

Robin gaped at him, shocked. "I never thought—I will straighten them out, tell them there is naught going on between us . . . ."

"You cannot!" Will took a deep, steadying breath. "Try to understand: no one is going to make a bid for her if they think she is Robin Hood's lady. You are the only protection she has here. But it kills me, the smirks and the whispers and the jokes, each time they see the two of you alone together."

He sank down onto a lichen-covered log as he spoke, almost collapsing through the rotten wood. Will scarcely noticed, however, and buried his head in his hands. Robin, bewildered and alarmed, bit back the urge to demand further explanation and simply waited.

"I thought you and I would always be together, you know?" Will declared suddenly, still not looking at Robin. "Even after you ran away, I half-envisioned myself going to London Town to find you there. But those were the dreams of a youth, with a youth's focused attachment, and I know better now. I care for you deeply, Robin, and I always will, but I love Marian. I love *her!*"

The abruptness of this revelation should have startled Robin, but oddly, it did not. Back at the manor, she had sensed Will's friendship toward her starting to change into a deeper attachment, but she had pushed the awareness aside, afraid to acknowledge a devotion she could not return. Now, she was relieved to hear that those sentiments no longer prevailed.

"Have you told her?" she asked with solicitude, sitting down on the soft grass in front of her cousin, rather than risk the crumbling wood.

"Yes. That is the problem," Will sighed, fingering the wilted aster stuck through his buttonhole. Robin saw it and wondered at its presence—as a youngster, Will had always shunned such frippery, yet ever since he had come to the Sherwood, he constantly seemed to have some sort of flower upon his person. She had stopped noticing it, but now the oddity struck her anew.

"You two have been speaking with flowers," she said in sudden realization. "That white primrose you dropped in the road by the Blue Boar Inn—that was from Marian, was it not? She always did like that sort of romantic foolery."

"She gave it to me when she thought—we both thought—that she would have to marry the Sheriff. To tell me farewell. And now that she is free to return my affections . . . now, it is I who must refuse *her*."

"But why?" Robin asked. "If you two truly love each other, then why should you not be together?"

"Because I am an outlaw, Robin!" he burst out. "Even if the Sheriff does not know by now that Will Gamwell and Will Scarlet are one and the same person, what kind of life can I offer Marian, without title or deed to my name? She was meant for more than a peasant's life; I cannot give it to her."

Robin scowled at such stupidity, but she kept her voice level. "You cannot really think that Marian cares about all that. If you truly did, you would have let her marry the Sheriff."

"Mayhap I should have," Will moaned. "Maybe I was wrong—"

"I am going to whip you with the flat of my blade if you do not start acting sensible," Robin announced, forsaking empathy and rising to her feet. "For shame, Will Gamwell! Blaming *me* for Marian's reputation because you are too lackwit to marry her. *I* am not the one who should be her protector — you are. And if you refuse — if she gives up on you and falls for someone else — then you shall have only yourself to blame!"

Robin strode away, leaving a stunned Will alone with the echoes of her words. *Let him chew on that for a while*, she thought, pleased with herself. *He will come to his senses. Men just like to make things difficult.*

Robin did not have to wait long for Will's decision. She was sharpening her sword by the river the next morning when Marian came flying into her.

"Careful!" Robin cried, dropping the sword and throwing one hand behind her to keep from falling over as Marian seized her in a desperate hug. "Never, ever grab someone when they have a sword in their lap!"

"Look at this!" Marian cried, ignoring Robin's rebuke and thrusting something under her nose. Robin blinked and craned her head back until whatever it was came into focus.

It was a small bouquet of blue violets bound together with an ivy vine. So Will had made up his mind, then — but was his resolution what her sister wanted to hear? She chanced a glance at Marian's face: it was shining with happiness.

"Will has asked me to marry him!" Marian exclaimed.

Robin smiled, taking her sister's hands. "How wonderful!"

"You do not mind?" the girl asked tentatively, some of the excitement leaving her eyes as she sat down next to Robin. She lowered her voice to a whisper. "I know that Will used to like you, so I thought perhaps you might, even if you do like Little John now . . . ."

"I do not mind in the slightest. I am very happy for you both," Robin told her sincerely. "When will you have the wedding?"

"In the spring, when all the flowers in bloom. It seems only right, considering how much they helped us when we could not freely speak of what was in our hearts! And what are a few more months to one in love?" She kissed her sister on both cheeks. "Oh, Robin, I am so *happy!*" Then Marian bounded back onto her feet and skipped away, leaving a startled and slightly lonely Robin to watch her go.

The band did not know what to think about Will and Marian's unexpected engagement.

"But Marian is *your* girl!" Allan protested to Robin, bemused and a trifle disappointed — he had almost finished composing a song about the two outlaw lovers, and now he could not use it. "I mean, she is, is she not?"

"The *maid* Marian," Robin emphasized, not for the first time that week, "is no more my girl than she is yours. We were friends in the before time, as we have been ever since — that is all. I am quite pleased that she is with Will."

Still, Robin understood the confusion the outlaws felt at the betrothal — it was strange even for her to see Will and Marian together as a couple. She mentally kicked herself for not noticing the signs of their affection before. How could she have missed the tenderness with which Will treated Marian, or her sister's radiant smile every time his eyes met hers?

She watched the two of them now from where she stood, half-hidden by a tree. She should have left the glade as soon as she stumbled upon them, but something about their blissful innocence had gripped her heart and held her fast. They were just standing together, Will weaving sprigs of grass through Marian's hair while her brown locks flowed in the breeze. His fingers combed through the strands and caught.

Just then, something snagged in Robin's own hair, and she spun, surprised. Little John blinked down at her, his hand poised in midair.

"It suits you," he said lightly, lowering his arm and looking beyond her toward the small clearing, where the couple was now walking away, hand in hand. Robin reached up and gingerly felt the object in her hair — it was a flower, which came away in her hand when she touched it. A shiver ran down her spine.

"John?" she began, but the eyes he turned toward her were blank, and the words she wanted to say died away in her throat. "What made you change your mind?" she asked instead.

Little John frowned and plucked at a loose thread on his tunic. "I suppose it was you bringing the Sheriff to our camp and then letting him leave again. No one else would have done it. Every person here hates the Sheriff, and nothing — not even three hundred pounds — could have made them give him up once they had him in their clutches. Nothing but you. For *you*, they let him go. He owes you his life, and he knows it."

"I never thought of it like that," Robin admitted. "I wonder if that was the real reason he did not stab me in the back ere he left."

"He may try to yet," Little John warned. "He is a wily one, that Sheriff."

At that moment, a small motion distracted their attention — a doe was peeking its nose into the now-empty glade. Robin felt a small tug on her quiver as Little John pulled out an arrow, handing it to her. "Did your father truly want you to marry him?" he asked with affected indifference.

"Mmm," Robin murmured, slipping the pansy she was holding into her quiver and stringing her bow. "Yes. But *I* did not much care for the idea." Her arrow sailed out, passing through the shrubbery to strike the deer's hidden heart.

Little John helped her gut the kill and then insisted on carrying the carcass back to the camp. She argued with him briefly before giving in, simply to hear them talk. She had not realized until that moment just how much she had missed Little John's company; by the look on his face, neither had he.

They walked together to deliver the deer to Lot, Robin teasing that if she did not accompany him, Little John was certain to steal credit for the kill. Lot grinned at the two of them as he accepted the beast, and those standing nearby wore a smile on their faces as well, glad that the pair's tacit estrangement had ended. No one had liked seeing Robin Hood and Little John at odds, whatever their reason might have been.

"We should go buying!" Marian exclaimed later that afternoon, startling her sister, who had been lazing by the river with a dreamy smile on her lips.

"What? Why?" Robin asked, sitting up far too quickly and making her head spin.

"To celebrate you reconciling with Little John, of course!" Marian said. "All you ever wear is that green suit of yours. You should get something pretty, something bright . . . especially if you want to draw his eye."

"I hardly think a suit would do that," Robin commented wryly, even as she remembered his hand placing a flower in her hair.

"But a dress would," was Marian's wicked reply.

"Marian! I am not getting a dress." Robin lowered her voice, even though there was no one nearby to hear them. "How would I explain it?"

"Well, a new suit then," her sister conceded. "Or have you something better to do?"

"Not really," Robin admitted. "I suppose I am due for some new clothes. All right then, when do you want to go?"

"First thing tomorrow!" Marian announced.

But the next day when Robin went in search of her sister, she was nowhere to be found. Just when she was about to give up looking, Marian came running up to her, her face flushed with excitement.

"Will wants me to go patrol with him! Do you mind?"

The abrupt change in plan took Robin aback, and she found herself feeling a trifle disappointed — she had begun to anticipate the excursion — but she quickly regained her composure. "Of course not. We can go some other time."

"Some other time? Do not even think of it!" Marian replied. When she saw that Robin was about to defer, she grew stern. "Robin, it is high time you acted for yourself and not for other people. Just go get the suit, all right? You can thank me later."

"Yes, my Lady," Robin said with a smile, sweeping her sister an elaborate bow. Marian laughed and gave Robin a peck on the cheek, and then dashed off to find Will.

It had been several months since Robin's last visit to Lincoln Town. The burg was much as she remembered it, with one exception — when she got to the tailor's shop, there were purple-clad guards lurking out front.

She ducked back behind another shop before they could notice her. Why were these soldiers stationed here, so far from Nottingham? Most towns had their own colors for their guards — purple identified those men who answered directly to the Sheriff. Had the tailor requested the protection? But why not from his own town, if such security were needed . . . and why would the Sheriff have granted his permission?

The small snap of a cracking branch made Robin look up in alarm. A young boy, dressed in filthy, yet well-cut clothes, was peering down at her through the boughs of a tree. Without warning, he tumbled down and dashed towards the guards. Robin made a grab for him, but missed. Desperately, she turned to take flight, but a tremendous bellow of pain made her halt mid-step. Turning toward the sound, she risked a curious glance around the corner.

Rather than alarming them to her presence, the boy had run up to one of the guards and kicked him in the shin. The second guard was already in pursuit while the first, still yelling curses, drew his sword and hobbled after the lad as well as he could, using the blade as a cane.

Amid this turmoil, the tailor appeared in the doorway of his shop, peering furtively around. When he espied Robin peeping out from behind a nearby building, he beckoned to her. "Quickly!" he mouthed. With one last glance at the retreating guards, Robin hurried over to the shop.

The tailor pulled Robin into the back of the store and tugged the reed divider closed between them, leaving her alone in a small chamber. The room was sparse, possessing a hearth and two pallets in one corner, some cookware, a few personal belongings, and not much else. There were no windows or doors. Completely bewildered, Robin put an eye to a crack in the screen, wondering if she had made a mistake in trusting the old man.

After a few moments, she could hear the loud imprecations that marked the return of the guards, and their threats of what they would do if they ever caught the boy. The tailor inquired something to which the guards snarled a reply, and then he closed the door to his shop.

"Brutes," the tailor said, reappearing from behind the screen. "Keep yer voice down."

"Why are they here?" Robin asked in a whisper.

"The Sheriff sent them. A week ago, he got clever and decided that since *I* am the only dyer who can produce cloth in Lincoln Green, if he put guards around my shop, then he would catch one of ye when ye came to buy. Never mind that those boors scare off my customers in the meanwhile!" He spat on the floor. "Of course, if the Sheriff were a *tad* bit cleverer, he would have hidden his guards like I hid my Roland, and not posted the purple peacocks in broad daylight where ye can espy them a mile off." The man was seething. He seized a jug from one corner of the room and took a swig, offering it to Robin when he was done. She thought it best to take it.

"Who is Roland?" she asked after she had taken a polite drink.

"My son. It was he who distracted the guards outside so I could bring ye here. I had him watching for anyone in Lincoln Green ever since those clods arrived, just in case."

"Your son could have told me all this," Robin pointed out, still suspicious. "Why bring me here?"

"Roland is mute," was the tailor's blunt reply.

"Oh. I am so sorry."

The man shrugged. "God's Will be done. But here now, ye shall have to stay until nightfall. They switch the guards then, and the night pair always sneaks off to the alehouse mid-shift. Ye can get away then."

Robin nodded. "I will warn my people not to come here for a while."

"And deprive me of my best custom? Do not ye dare!" the man growled. "I will have my boy stay near the town gate. He may not be able to speak, but he is not deaf. He can take yer orders and bring them to ye — just let him know when ye will be coming around to get them."

"But if he cannot talk, then how can you — "

"We have a system worked out," the tailor said. "Trust me, yer clothes will be as ye order. And speaking of order, what did ye come to buy today? I assume that ye came to buy."

Robin assured him that she had and described the suit she wanted.

"A change from Lincoln Green, to be sure," he said slyly. "Ye're sure ye do not want it in red this time?"

She smiled at his keen memory. "Not red," she concurred.

When Robin tried to pay for the clothes, the tailor refused her coin outright. "Consider it my vengeance on the Sheriff, if ye must. I am that vexed," he said when she insisted. His mouth was set in a thin line, and Robin knew better than to argue further. She let the matter drop.

With night came the change of the guard, as well as Roland. The lad seemed, if possible, even filthier than when Robin had last seen him, and he listened to his father's lecture on the subject with a bowed head and an impish gleam in his eyes. As soon as his father relented and handed him a bowl of stew, Roland began to "talk," using a mixture of signs and pantomimes to relay the adventure he had had earlier with the guards, while somehow managing to eat at the same time.

At last, the tailor led Robin into the front of the shop. Opening the door the barest crack, the two of them peered outside. The guards were gone. With a last murmur of thanks and plans to meet the boy a week later to pick up her suit, Robin shook the clothesmaker's hand and disappeared into the streets. When the guards returned to their post an hour later, they found the street quiet; all they could hear was the faint shearing of cloth as the tailor worked inside his shop.

❧ 20 ❧

A SORROWFUL KNIGHT

ROBIN DID NOT MAKE IT back to the Trysting Tree until late that afternoon. Since the evening meal was only an hour distant, she chose to wait until everyone was gathered together before telling them about the guards in Lincoln Town. Though they laughed when she described Roland's mischievous means of distracting the Sheriff's men, they acknowledged the warning within her story. All agreed to be extra cautious should they go into town.

That night, there was a beautiful autumn thunderstorm, the first of the season. There was no wind, and the rain fell gently upon the roofs with faint patters. Every few minutes, light would blaze through the chinks in the walls and thunder would shake the cabins. Many people propped open the doors of their huts to watch the flashes, a few of them comforting frightened children as they did so. Robin had not slept for nearly two days, but even so she was one of the last to close her door and turn her thoughts toward sleep.

The next morning when she stepped outside, it was as if to a different world. A lustrous silver fog hung close to the forest floor, eddying through the trees like a lazy stream. Everything looked softer, yet brighter at the same time, and the air smelled fresh and clean; the aroma of wet leaves and damp soil mingled pleasantly in Robin's nose with the scent of smoke from the fire.

I do so love the forest after a rain! she thought with a smile, taking in a deep breath of luscious air. She felt utterly invigorated, but one glance at the half-awake camp evidenced that she was the only one to feel that way. All around her, people were moving slowly, the fog's languor seeping deep into their marrows and making them desire nothing more than to relax. Little John actually growled at her when she suggested they scout themselves some mischief.

"You go lose yourself in that ruddy soup if you want to. I am quite comfortable where I am at." He drew a deerskin blanket closer around his shoulders in emphasis and hunkered down next to the fire.

"Where is your sense of adventure? It is hardly the time to hibernate yet!" she laughed, but she let him be. No one else seemed inclined to venture from the camp, either, so Robin set off on her own into the misty forest.

Within the fog's silvery veil, time seemed to stand still, as though the land had been transfixed by some spell. Only Robin moved within the silent Sherwood, slipping occasionally on the sodden leaves that littered the forest floor. Their orange and amber hues formed a shimmering carpet beneath her feet, decorated with gossamer embroidery that glistened in the mist. A slight wind picked up, brushing coldly past her cheeks. Robin drew up her hood to help protect against the chill.

The white fog and chiaroscuro transmuted the forest from her familiar woods into a strange land of light and shadows, exotic and mysterious. Robin's breath swirled out before her as she gazed about in wonder. The splendor around her was captivating, and even if she were to live in the Sherwood for a hundred years, she knew she would never grow tired of it.

Robin trekked on, enthralled with her surroundings, until a flicker appeared ahead of her through the mists. She halted, and the flicker came once again, like a large shadow moving through the drizzle. She was certain it was not a deer. Perhaps a wolf? Not planning to hunt, she had not brought her bow, but the comforting weight at her hip reminded her that she did wear her sword. This Robin drew, the cool metal whispering quietly as she slid it from its sheath.

A horse whinnied softly; for an instant, the breeze drove the mists apart, and Robin saw that she was standing near the High Road and that a man and his horse were ambling toward her. Yet there was something very wrong with the picture they made, and she puzzled over it as the mists closed again. The rider was dressed in rich satin clothes, but he wore no jewels or gold chains — ornaments those of his obvious standing rarely went without. He rode unaccompanied but sat his horse like a noble, though he did not hold himself like one. Instead, his head drooped disconsolately against his chest, and his hands were slack on the reins — even his horse plodded with its head hung low, mirroring its master.

A burning desire to know the truth of this enigma made Robin forget her caution.

"My lord," she called impulsively, sheathing her sword

and stepping towards him out of the fog. "Stop a moment, sir, for I would speak with you."

"Who are you, that you would halt a strange traveler in this manner?" the man asked her wearily, looking up at last.

It was her father!

Robin froze. Lord Locksley was waiting for an answer, and knowing him, he would not wait much longer; in fact, Robin was amazed that he had stopped at all. She forced herself to think. Her father did not recognize her, that much was obvious, and the daughter in her *had* to know what was causing him distress.

Sinking her chin into the depths of her hood, she withdrew into her woodland persona. "Who I am depends on who you ask. Some people say that I am a charitable man, while others call me a thief. Some name me their friend; to others, I am their enemy. Yet any whom you ask will tell you these two things: I am an outlaw, and I am known as Robin Hood."

"Are you indeed?" His moustache twitched, as though suppressing a smile. "I have heard of you, Robin Hood. We have met before, in tourney . . . though I am certain you do not remember."

"How could I forget a man who shoots so well and loses with such grace?" She bowed, grateful that her tongue could be so smooth, even when addressing her father. *See, Darah, I have learned a courtier's glibness after all!* "I would be greatly honored if you would join me for a meal in the greenwood today."

Now the knight did smile, a sorrowful twisting of his mouth. "Ah, yes, I have heard that you and yours keep a mighty inn — one that is almost worth the fair purse you ask in exchange. But I am afraid you would find me a disappointing guest; I have no money. You had best let me pass on in peace."

"What?" Robin gasped, momentarily forgetting herself. Quickly, she resumed the attitude of her *nom de guerre*. "You jest, Sir Knight. Lords like yourself always have purses upon their persons, though they may hide them well."

Sir Robert's face turned red. "If any other man were to question my word thus, I would demand recompense for the insult. But I can see why you might think as you do. It shames me, but I speak the truth when I say that the ten shillings in my pouch are all the money I possess in the world."

He reached inside his tunic and handed a stained silk purse to Robin. She knew before she opened it that it would be as he said.

"How can this be?" she asked, bewildered, handing him back his purse. "Unless the trappings on your horse deceive me, you are Lord Robert of Locksley, cousin to the King himself. Everyone knows that your estate is the grandest in all of Nottinghamshire."

The bitterness in his voice shocked Robin. "Soon it will be my estate no longer . . . the Prior of Emmet has seen to that!"

"My lord, if you would find it in your heart to tell me your troubles, I may be able to help," she offered.

He looked at her strangely. "Why would an outlaw wish to help a lord?"

"Sir, you say that you have heard of me. Then you must know that I steal only from the rich and the wicked that I may help the poor folk they have wronged. I have yet to hear of you despoiling your tenants in any way or of you mistreating your people. Please come with me into the greenwood and tell me what ails you, and I will do what I can to aid."

Her father sighed. "I do not know what good it will do to tell you, nor what aid you might provide, but I will come with you as you ask and explain."

Robin led Lord Locksley into the forest, listening with growing guilt as he told her the tale of his two daughters — how the first had broken her engagement to the Sheriff by running away, and how the second had been stolen away by outlaws on her wedding day. As if losing his two children had not been misfortune enough, the Sheriff had appeared at his doorstep only a week ago to demand recompense for the twice-broken engagement.

"I am not a rich man, Robin, though I have always managed my estate well. I emptied my coffers to pay the engagement penalty when my eldest daughter ran away — her name was Robin, too. Yes, Robin, though the priest who baptized her refused to give her a boy's name at first, claiming it would make her too headstrong. And she was strong, my Robin. If I had been fortunate enough to bear a son, I would have called him Robert, but God gave me a daughter instead. Well, His Will be done, and at least I had a child to carry on my name.

"But forgive me, I digress; I was telling you about the Prior. I had to pawn my estate to him in order to afford the betrothal damages a second time. I *have* paid the Sheriff his recompense — I can say that much at least! — but now I am penniless. Even so, in three days time I must repay the Prior all that I owe him, or else I forfeit my estate to him forever."

"But by what right could the Sheriff demand payment?" Robin exclaimed, horrified by her role in her father's ruin and outraged at Darniel's greed. Obviously, her words to him in the Sherwood had had the opposite of her intended effect. "You told me yourself that it was *his* men who had charge of your daughter on the day she was kidnapped. Is not the fault for the missing bride his?"

"Yes, well." Lord Locksley's keen blue eyes slid sideways to look at Robin. "Apparently, he had an unfortunate encounter with a band of outlaws the other day, and my daughter was there among them. Since she made no attempt to throw herself on the Sheriff's mercy — in fact, she complained about his being present — he concluded that she was there voluntarily and that the kidnapping had been staged to break the engagement. According to the bylaws of Nottinghamshire, he has the right to demand recompense."

Lord Locksley's tone and words were neutral, and his face revealed nothing as he turned his gaze into the forest, but Robin knew as surely as if he had shouted it that he was aware she had orchestrated Marian's disappearance. Shame filled her for not having confessed to the action the first time Marian's name had been mentioned. Now, it was too late. Robin braced herself for her father's wrath, but it did not come.

"You do not blame me?" she asked at last, bemused by his lack of rancor.

He did not answer her question directly, but merely said, "I shall be glad to see my daughter again."

Robin felt even worse.

The sun was high in the sky and the fog dissipated by the time they reached the camp. It was much as Robin had left it, full of torpid men reclining at their ease. Even John was still at his place by the fire, staring drowsily into the flames. Had so little changed in their world? It seemed like a lifetime had passed since she had first espied her father on the road.

"Look lively, my friends!" Robin called to her men. "We have a guest."

They turned to stare lethargically at the strange knight in their midst — at his rich clothes and his discrepant lack of jewels — who did not seem at all discomforted to find himself in an outlaw camp. Something about his demeanor sent them stumbling to their feet, and several of her people touched their hand to their forelock in an instinctive gesture of respect.

Robin led Lord Locksley to the base of the wide oak tree, stealing the blanket off Little John's shoulders as she went. To her band's surprise, she gave Lord Locksley her own place of honor, laying the skin on the ground for him to sit upon. Without being bidden, Lot sent two boys to the knight with a bowl of stew and a trencher of capon.

"Father!"

Marian ran over from across the clearing to hug the sitting man, almost making him drop the food he held in his hands. To Robin's surprise, he let her hug him and even patted her lightly on the back in return, not seeming to mind that those around him were watching the display with avid interest.

"Father, what are you doing here? Did Robin bring you? Did Robin tell—?" but Robin coughed at that moment, and when Marian turned to look, she shook her head at her slightly. Disappointment swept over Marian's face, but she bit off her question and turned back to her father with a smile.

"How are you, my child?" he asked when Marian finally let him go; his voice was strangely rough. "Do they treat you well?"

"Oh yes, Father!" she cried, sinking down onto the moss by his feet. Tears filled her eyes, and she hung her head. "I am so sorry to have worried you."

"Never mind that now. You are safe when I had feared you were dead; that is all that matters to me."

Robin was stunned; she had not realized that Marian and her father had grown so close. When had it happened? He had certainly never regarded *Robin* with—was that love?— shining in his eyes. She found she could not bear to look at them for long and turned her head away, accidentally catching Little John's gaze. His face showed a clear comprehension of who this man was as he looked from Lord Locksley to Marian, and then back to Robin. Feeling self-conscious, Robin glanced away.

". . . and are you happy here, my Marian?" her father was asking in a voice almost too low to hear. The girl beamed at him and nodded, but before she could expound on her answer, someone stepped up behind her and put a possessive hand on her shoulder.

"Will! So you are here, too?" Lord Locksley asked, quite surprised.

"Yes, sir," he bowed. Marian tilted her head up to look at Will and reached to cover his hand with her own. Lord Locksley watched the tender gesture with astonishment.

"What is this?" he demanded.

Will gave a guilty start and quickly withdrew his hand from Marian's shoulder, but replaced it a moment later with the air of a man steeling himself for a confrontation, clasping Marian's fingers tightly in his own.

"I have asked your daughter to marry me, Lord Locksley. It would mean a lot to me — to us both — if you would give us your blessing."

Sir Robert looked down at his daughter, who was gazing at him with hope and anxiety in her eyes. Her face had bloomed with light at Will's determined declaration, and Lord Robert of Locksley remembered the way his own wife had looked the day she had agreed to marry him.

"Of course," he said thickly, clearing his throat. "You will surely be a far better husband to my daughter than the one I had chosen for her." Will's shoulders sagged with relief, and silent tears slipped down Marian's cheeks as Lord Locksley stood and kissed them both upon the brow.

One youngster let out a cheer, and to Robin's surprise, Lord Locksley actually laughed. The rest of the band took that as permission to come up and clap Will on the back and to offer Sir Robert their congratulations.

"I thought you might insist on taking Marian back with you," Robin murmured once the well-wishers had dispersed, squatting down next to where her father had resumed his seat.

He looked at her, his expression changing from one of fatherly pride to one of resigned sadness. "In three days time, even a forest home will be more than I can offer my daughter. Besides, she is happy here, and Will is a good man. They love each other deeply, that much is plain. It is best for them both that she stays."

"Most lords do not care about their children's happiness when it comes to marriage," Robin said carefully.

"Most lords have not lost what I thought I had lost." He gave Robin a wan smile. "All that I wanted was to secure a future for my daughters. Instead, my decisions stole both of my daughters from me, drove away my nephew, and lost me my estate. I have learned, too late, the value of happiness."

"Well, at least you have Will and Marian back now. That has to be something," Robin offered gamely.

"Yes . . . that is something."

The melancholy in his voice was almost too much for her to bear, and Robin nearly blurted out her true identity right then and there. Only two years of carefully guarding her secret managed to stay her tongue. There was no point in revealing herself now, she reasoned, especially since it was likely that her father's sorrow stemmed merely from the impending loss of his estate. Yes, that was it—he was concerned about the Manor; it had nothing to do with her.

"How much do you owe the Prior?" Robin asked him quietly, lowering her voice so that Marian, who was sitting nearby, would not hear.

He sighed. "Four hundred pounds."

"That is all!?" Robin struggled to keep her voice from rising. "You are to lose your estate over a paltry four hundred pounds?"

"So says the outlaw," the knight remarked dryly.

"What about your friends, the other nobles? Can they not help you? Can not the King?"

"The friends that I had when I was well-off have left me now that I am poor, and those who would have stood by me fear to do anything that might antagonize the Sheriff. As for the King, he is going on Crusade to Jerusalem and has no money to spare for a poor relation."

When Robin went to speak again, her voice shook with anger. "It is a sad day when the only friend a lord can boast is an outlaw. Someday, I will make the Sheriff pay for all the ruination he has caused." Lord Locksley stared at Robin, startled by her fury, as she got to her feet and sounded her horn. Heads snapped around to look at her, and those further away paused in what they were doing and wandered toward the center of the clearing to better hear what she had to say.

"My people! This honest knight has suffered cruelly at the hand of the Sheriff, and I would help him if I may," Robin announced. "I wish to give him five hundred pounds from our coffers to buy back and reestablish his noble estate. I am well aware of the enormity of the sum I am asking, so I desire to know: does anyone protest my decision?"

The outlaws looked at each other. It was a shame for any man to lose his home, but five hundred pounds could feed five-score families for a year. Could they justify giving that sum to one man, even if he was Marian's father?

Finally, David stepped forward. "Robin, you have always led us well. If you say that this lord is an honest man and deserves to have his lands, then it must be so. Do as you think is right."

Affection for her people welled inside Robin as they murmured their agreement, and she had to turn away for a moment to hide her sudden tears. "Thank you," she began, but her father interrupted.

"I protest," he said, rising to his feet. "When I was wealthy, I treated five hundred pounds like it was a pittance. Now that I am poor, I know the value of the coin you offer. I cannot accept such a gift when your charity could help so many others who are in need."

It was easy to see that he was sincere. His candid words filled the outlaws with awe, giving them hope for a future in which nobles could be so humble. Robin, overwhelmed with pride for her father, shook her head. "Sir, your refusal does you honor, but please consider: I am responsible for stealing Marian away from you and for placing you in this predicament. You must allow me to remedy the situation. Furthermore," she continued loudly, when he opened his mouth to interrupt, "you must not forget the many families and tenants who live on your lands. Though the Church is supposed to help people, it is said that the Prior is a cruel master, and your people are sure to suffer under his rule. Refuse to accept this money, and the Prior and the Sheriff will accomplish not only your own ruination, but that of your people as well."

Lord Locksley stared at Robin for a long moment, his brows furrowed in contemplation. Finally, he spoke. "I think, Robin, that you could convince the devil himself to leave off sinning if you so tried. I will accept the money you offer and use it to pay off my debts, but only on the condition of a loan," he emphasized. "I will pay back your money, on my word as a gentleman and a knight."

"Then I need not fear to see it again," Robin said.

At her request, Will Stutley went down to the band's treasure cave and brought back the agreed-upon monies. As he handed the bags to her father, Robin could not keep a slight smirk from appearing on her face — one of the bags was the Sheriff's velvet purse, which had been taken during his recent visit to their camp. The second sack had — until two days ago — belonged to the Bishop of Hereford, by far the band's least pleasant guest; Robin would never forget the hatred effusing his face when he had addressed her. It seemed appropriate that it was their gold that would help to pay her father's debts, since it was the Sheriff and a Prior of the Church who sought to despoil him.

Her father received the contributions with stately gratitude, looking as though a thousand worries had been lifted from his shoulders. Holding his head high for the first time that day, he laid the monies aside in order to laugh and joke with her people, asking about their lives in the camp with genuine interest. Logan and Bentworth wrestled for his entertainment, and when the archers began to shoot, Lord Locksley took a turn and beat them all, although Robin declined to compete.

At last, he insisted that he could stay no longer, and Robin rose to lead him back to the main road; to her surprise, several of her men rose with her.

"We have been discussing the matter," Little John informed them both, "and with your permission, we would like to accompany Lord Locksley to the Priory in case the Sheriff or the Prior gives him trouble. We shall return as soon as we are satisfied that he and his estate are safe."

"Of course," Robin granted, touched by their concern.

Lord Locksley seemed unable to speak. Finally, he said in a voice that trembled, "When I set out this day, I never thought to meet with such kindness. I cannot tell you how much I—" He tried again. "It means so much that—" but again, words failed him. In the end, he contented himself with, "If any of you are ever in need, come to me. I will lose my estate and all that I own before I let harm come to any of you."

Robin brought over his horse from where it had been grazing, while Lord Locksley kissed Marian and Will on both their cheeks, promising to return for their wedding in the spring. Then he mounted his horse and allowed Robin to lead the way back through the woods, accompanied by a retinue of outlaws.

"Fare you well, sir," Robin said when they reached the High Road, handing him back his reins. "Good fortune and God's blessings be yours."

"And yours also, Robin of the Hood. Someday, I will find a way to repay you for all you have done." Then, placing one hand on her shoulder to steady himself, he leaned down from his saddle and kissed her on the forehead as a father might kiss his son. It was the first time he had embraced Robin since before she could remember, and her mouth fell open in astonishment. Lord Locksley gave her a small smile, and with a *tsk* to his horse, ambled off towards Emmet Town, Little John and her men walking at a comfortable pace behind him.

⚔ **21** ⚔

A FATEFUL DECISION

LITTLE JOHN and the others did not return to Sherwood for several weeks, but when they did, it was with great elation over the outcome of Lord Locksley's dealings with the Prior.

"That old man has some of your cunning, Robin," Shane remarked to her in admiration, unaware of the truth of his own assertion. "Lord Locksley never lied once, yet wove his words in such a way that the greedy Prior felt certain he would own his estate before the day was through. The Prior even lowered the quittance price to three hundred pounds, so as not to seem completely without mercy!"

"You should have seen the Prior's face when Lord Locksley made good on that three hundred then and there!" Glenneth chimed in. "He turned as green as a basil leaf."

"Any man who can get the better of the Prior is a man indeed!" Murray hailed, staggering to his feet and raising his tankard in a toast.

The outlaws and Robin cheerfully agreed, "Hear, hear!"

Their cheerfulness soon vanished, however, when a capricious turn of nature caused winter to strike before autumn had a chance to fully develop. One day the weather was sunny and mild, the next it was cold and wet, with scarcely a pause in between.

This premature shift in season took the people of Sherwood completely by surprise, and they had to scramble to prepare their camp to survive a lengthy winter. The carpenters among them worked day and night to patch and reinforce those huts that had fallen into disrepair over the summer. Ten men were kept busy at all times gathering firewood to store in the granite caves, out of reach of the blustery rains. Another ten exhausted themselves stocking the winter larder with venison and rabbit, while the tanners worked to convert the pelts into much-needed blankets. Pairs of runners made surreptitious trips to Lincoln Town to purchase wool clothing for the winter as well. Everyone aided where they could.

"'Tis an omen," Lot mulled one day, blinking through sodden bangs at the gloaming sky from where he sat thatching a roof. "It has to be. Winter has never come this fast before."

"Nonsense," Robin snapped, her temper made short by the storm and her menses. She was eager to finish the roof and get out of the rain. "It is just bad weather; omens have nothing to do with it."

Time seemed to prove her right, for in spite of nature's attempt to catch them off guard, her people quickly surmounted their chores, and December found the outlaws as prepared for a Sherwood winter as they had ever been.

Little John struggled to keep sight of his friend as they wended their way through Nottingham's crowded streets, but it was difficult without the hue of Lincoln Green to guide him — Robin's simple grey attire blended in with the drove all too well. Attempting to hasten his steps did not help, either. Little John's bulk usually made people part around him like Moses parting the Red Sea, but today no one was standing aside. Instead, his size served to impede him as gaps in the throng of last-minute shoppers disappeared before he had a chance to squeeze through. Even so, he had almost managed to catch up to Robin when a small patch of ice made him slip; desperately trying not to fall, Little John staggered into the smithy's yard.

"Could you not have slowed down a *tad?*" he complained as Robin seized him by his tunic to help steady him. He quickly regained his balance, and Robin let go; Little John straightened his rumpled tunic, his cheeks tingeing slightly as he glared at his friend.

Robin's gaze was unrepentant. "You know that everything closes early today."

"Then you should have done the sensible thing and finished your shopping days ago!" Little John scolded.

"This is the last stop, I promise."

"Are yeh two gonna keep squabbling, or get whatcha came fer?" the blacksmith demanded. "I close in twenty minutes, whether yeh be ready or ne."

With a small wink at John, Robin turned away to describe to the smith why she had come. In spite of himself, Little John felt his own lips twitch up in response. It was impossible for him to feign ire at his merry friend for very long.

The blacksmith disappeared inside his shop to retrieve Robin's order, and seeing that he was not needed at the moment, Little John meandered over to a nearby bakery whose appetizing aroma had been taunting his nose ever since he had turned onto the street.

Robin watched Little John weave through the crowd without envy, glad to be out of the way of the increasingly desperate passersby. Soon all of the shops would close for the twelve-day Christmas holiday — indeed, many stores had already shuttered their doors — and the crowd was hastening to those still open to buy last-minute goods.

Robin glanced at the sack she was holding in her hands. Like the people in the streets, she had foolishly put off making own her holiday purchases for a little too long.

In her bag were masks for mumming and playacting — her peoples' favorite Christmas-tide pastime. Just before dawn on Christmas Day, the outlaws would don their masks and homemade costumes in the darkness of their huts and then wait until Robin passed by their door, singing and dancing and calling for them to come out. What began as one mummer would quickly grow into a procession that would cajole from hut to hut until everyone had joined, at which point they would gather under the giant oak tree and perform nonsensical theatricals for each other's amusement. Though the masks in Robin's sack were less elaborate than they might have been had she bought them weeks ago, they would more than suffice for such entertainment.

Robin's bag also held her New Year gifts, which she had ordered through Eadom before winter had struck. There was a beautiful amber-and-glass necklace for Marian; a chess set for David, whom she was teaching how to play; a book of carols for Allan; a bottle of vintage wine for Lot; hammered tankards for Will Stutley and the twins; and sundry trinkets for the others. The item the blacksmith had gone to fetch was her cousin's gift, the last of her commissions.

Robin should have felt satisfied, but instead she felt anxious; the stores were almost all closed for the holiday, and she still had no idea what to get Little John. No gift she had thought of seemed right.

Perhaps something store-bought is the wrong way to go, she sighed, running a discontented finger along the blacksmith's anvil. *Well, I still have six days left until New Year's. Surely, I can think of something to give him before then.*

The blacksmith returned. Hastily, Robin snatched her hand off the anvil and wiped it on her tunic, leaving a large sooty streak behind.

"This here beauty was a real pleasure to make," the blacksmith told her proudly, smiling through the grime on his face. He angled the sword in his hands to show her the dragons and fairies he had carved into the steel, their engravings filled with gold. "I do ne get much call fer etchings like these. Too expensive, fer most."

His grip on the sword suddenly tightened, as though it had occurred to him to wonder how a forester was going to pay for such a weapon. Robin withdrew a placating purse from her tunic and dug out some coins, which she placed on the anvil.

"Four shillings as agreed, and another for making you rush so close to Christmas."

"Er, that sounds about right," the blacksmith said, blinking at the size of the tip. He snatched up the money quickly so that Robin could not change her mind, and disappeared into his forge. A moment later, he returned carrying a black scabbard with faded gold etchings on it, into which he slid the sword. Then he wrapped them both in cloth as carefully as if he were swaddling a baby and handed the bundle to Robin.

With a nod of thanks, she took her cousin's gift from him and stuck it under her arm, heaving the sack with the rest of her presents over her shoulder and knocking her quiver askew in the process. Biting back an oath, she resettled her pack, wishing she did not have her own weapons to juggle as well as her gifts . . . but with winter came wolves and despite the inconvenience, it was wise to be prepared. Still struggling to balance her load, she wished the blacksmith a Merry Christmas and went to find Little John.

He was waiting for her outside the bakery a few yards away. In his hands were two oaten cakes, one of which he handed to Robin. Without asking, he plucked her purchases out of her hands and placed them inside his own large sack, already laden with barley sugar for the youths and wassail honey for the adults. He hefted the bulging pack over his shoulder as if it held but a feather.

"I was managing fine on my own," Robin protested self-consciously.

John raised an eyebrow at her. "Do you want them back?"

"No!" she said hastily. "I will let you carry them—just to teach you your folly," she teased, taking a large bite from her cake. "Shall we go?"

They had almost reached Nottingham's western gate when the deep tolling of bells resounded through the town, bringing Robin to a sudden halt.

"What is it?" Little John asked, puzzled.

"The bells . . ." Robin began wistfully, a half-forgotten desire gripping her heart.

Little John waved a dismissive hand. "They are just marking the four o'clock. It is nothing to worry about."

Robin shook her head. "Those are church bells. I have not attended Mass in such a long time . . . . I had not realized how much I missed it until I heard those peals. I know that service is not for a few hours yet, but it *is* Christmas Eve; I would like to go."

John gazed at Robin as though she had gone daft. "Those bells must have affected my hearing — for a moment, I thought you said that you wanted to go to church. Only, I know you of all people would never suggest such a foolish thing."

"Well, I did," Robin defended. It hurt her that Little John was so quick to dismiss her desire. "I want to go, and I mean to go. I will be back in time for the boar hunt in the morning, worry not."

Little John grabbed her by the arm before she could take more than one step away. "Was there more in that cake that I gave you than oats?" he demanded. "You cannot go into church, especially not on Christmas Eve! Do you know how many nobles and soldiers will be there? I will not let you."

With difficulty, Robin shrugged off his arm. "It is not your choice," she snapped. "It is mine, and I will thank you to remember that!" Before a stunned Little John could protest further, she turned and stalked up the road toward St. Mary's church.

Little John narrowed his eyes after her. "Women," he muttered, and turning his back on Robin, he strode out the gate and down the road towards Sherwood Forest.

Robin's temper had cooled by the time she reached the road leading up to the church, but though she regretted her sharp words to Little John, she did not regret her decision to stay.

She lifted her gaze toward St. Mary's church, which stood upon its knoll like a sentry overlooking the town. It was too dark by now to distinguish much beyond its torch-lit entrance and its glowing windows, but Robin could feel its stern presence looming beyond her in the dusk.

The doors to the church were open, but Robin temporarily deferred its invitation. It was still a few hours yet until Mass, and now that she knew how to get there, she could pass the time until its start in a more comfortable locale.

Robin wandered back through the town, searching for a warm place to wait. Nearly all of the shops were closed by now and their customers returned home. At last, she found a small inn where a penny bought her a place by the hearth for as long as she cared to remain. For three more pennies, she could have bought a nice meal and a tankard of mead as well, but Robin's conscience was already bothered by the oat cake she had consumed; not having planned on attending church, she had not thought to abstain.

Then again, what is a pre-Mass repast when compared to the sin of armed theft? she mused.

Robin sent up a quick prayer for forgiveness and signaled the innkeeper for some food; she hoped that God would be so pleased to see her in church again that He would absolve her for failing to fast.

The wait until Mass was long, but the inn was crowded with holiday travelers who plied Robin with stories and music and who did not seem to mind that she talked little in return. Eventually, the innkeeper's candle-clock had only one stripe left, and Robin thanked the loquacious peasant who had been telling her about his daughter's ringworm and wended her way through the guests and out into the night.

It was freezing outside. Robin pulled her hood tight and

tucked in her chin, blessing the new wool garments she wore; thick and warm, they did much to keep out the frigid air. They did little to protect her face, however, as a small white droplet clearly emphasized by splattering on Robin's nose. She looked up towards the sky just in time for another droplet to land in her eye. Uncertain whether to be irritated or pleased by the unexpected Christmas snow, Robin quickened her pace through the town's abandoned streets.

The snow was slushy at first, but soon it changed into solid flakes that peppered Robin's face like cold sparks. In spite of her discomfort, Robin took great pleasure in watching the world around her turn white. The snow dazzled where moonbeams struck, and the holly and ivy bedecking the houses glistened through the growing blanket of ice. Still, it was with relief that Robin mounted the slick stone steps of St. Mary's church, thankful to be out of the weather.

Doffing her hood out of respect as she stepped inside, Robin glanced curiously around. Though she was nearly half an hour early, the church was already beginning to fill. Rather than entering the nave to join the rest of the congregation, Robin headed for a small vestibule off to the left—she had some respects to pay before Christ's Mass began.

The Bishop was tired. He had ridden all the way from Hereford at the Sheriff's request to celebrate the Midnight Mass, and he would have to ride all the way back to Hereford to celebrate the Dawn Mass in the morning.

At least the Sheriff was paying him well for his service.

The Bishop set down the heavy purse he had been holding and pulled on his pontificals—a white alb and chasuble, a pointed miter for his head, and a stole for his shoulders woven with real gold thread. The motion caused the ring on his third finger to glitter in the candlelight, and he paused to admire the huge ruby carbuncle. He had acquired it upon his rise to the bishopric; its price could buy a small fiefdom.

A low gonging reverberated through the room as the bells called the faithful to Mass, startling the Bishop out of his admiration. Hastily, he picked up his purse and shoved it into the deep inner pocket of his robe. Seizing his shepherd's crosier from its stand, he exited the vestry, making his way through cold corridors to the narthex entrance at the back of the church, where the ceremonial procession would commence.

The pealing of bells brought Robin out of her reverence. Her knees ached from kneeling on the icy stone floor, but she had needed that moment to pause and to pray. There were so many things on her mind of late.

The statue of the Virgin Mary smiled kindly down at her daughter. Maybe it was because Robin had no mother of her own, but she had always felt a special connection to the Virgin. It was to Mother Mary that she told all of her secrets and asked for guidance in her life. She knew that Heaven's King did not mind this intimacy—Mary was one of His envoys, after all.

The bells rang again and with a small groan, Robin got to her feet, the chill of the stone biting into her hands as she pushed herself upright. She glanced at the statue again, her gaze directed this time at her bow and quiver peeking out from their imperfect hiding place behind the stone figure. She hated to leave them there, but she could hardly take them into the church proper. It was one thing to retain her sword — nobles and soldiers wore their blades into church all the time—but a bow would draw far too much attention. She should have just handed the weapon off to Little John before going her separate way, but pride at his commanding words had lost her the opportunity. Now, she had no choice but to leave her bow and quiver in the prayer room until the Mass was finished.

No sense in dwelling on it now, Robin thought, forcibly pushing the concern from her mind as she exited the vestibule and navigated her way into the main body of the church. The seatless nave had filled during her prayers and was now so crowded that Robin could scarcely squeeze inside.

At least with everyone standing so close, I will not be cold for long, Robin reflected. In fact, the chill that had seeped into her bones while she had been praying had already begun to withdraw.

As the choir in the chancel began to sing, Robin blessed her uncommon height, which allowed her to see over the heads of many of the people standing before her. Widening her stance as much as she could, she settled in for the long Midnight Mass.

Little John emerged from the black tangle of trees and stepped into the camp unnoticed. The outlaws had clearly decided not to wait until Christmas Day to start their revelries, and were wassailing around the bonfire with much noise and cheer, tipping back pots of spiced ale and shouting on occasion, "Drinkhail!"

"Little John!" Will Scarlet called out, barely audible over the festive music. He danced away from the fire and toward his friend, his face glowing red from merriment and heat. He made a grab for Little John's pack.

"None of that, now," John rebuked him sternly. "Those gifts are from Robin, and you are not to see them until New Year's Day."

"Where is Robin? I want to show 'im me costume," Will Stutley cried, bounding over as well. "Did ye bring the masks?"

"Robin decided to go to church," Little John said sourly, trying to make his way over to the blazing fire through the growing circle of revelers.

"Church? On Christmas Eve? That lad has more guts than a butcher's pail," Lot laughed, watching with amusement as Little John tried to fend off Will Stutley and the twins, who had joined forces in an attempt to pull the sack from Little John's shoulder.

"All right!" Little John bellowed, reaching into his pack and tossing a sheaf of disguises onto the ground. "There are your blooming masks!"

"Crab Apple," Will Scarlet called him fondly, picking up the masks and passing them around. "I know just the thing to sweeten your temper." Seizing Little John by the shoulder, he drew him towards the ale tun.

Five minutes later, Marian came running up to them, her eyes alight with pleasure. "It is snowing!" she cried, just in case they had not noticed.

"Merry Christmas, darling," Will smiled fondly, seizing Marian in an embrace and dipping her down for a kiss.

Little John felt a sharp stab of loneliness. Mumbling an excuse to Will, he ambled toward the far side of the fire where the celebrants were fewer and it was quieter. Behind him, some of the outlaws had slipped into costumes and masks and were knocking on the doors of the empty huts, dancing and caroling as if a whole town were watching.

John felt their revelry wash over him like the queasy feeling one gets when they have had too much to eat. Turning away from the merrymakers, Little John found himself searching for the presence of a nimble figure amongst the skeletal boughs of the forest, even though he knew it would be hours yet before Robin would begin her journey home.

"... and it is at this moment—the darkest moment of the darkest night—that the light of salvation appears. When all hope is gone and your hearts shrivel with despair, that is when God makes himself manifest. He is a mewling infant, crying out for your attention in the night. Seek him, nurture him, and He will grow within you into a man whose Word will renew you and whose Spirit will guide you ..."

The Bishop lectured on without paying much attention to what he was saying; after thirty-odd years as a bishop, he knew his speech by heart. While his lips were expounding on the Sacred Birth, his mind was busy contemplating the vast feast that would be his in Hereford Town only a few short hours from now. As his hands began to prepare the Eucharist, his mouth was envisioning the succulent taste of Christmas boar.

That earthly vision disintegrated, however, the instant he descended the steps leading down from the altar in order to give Communion to the people. Their grimy natures disgusted him; he hated being so close to the low populace. As he placed the Holy Wafer in their mouths, he shuddered at the touch of their breath on his fingers. Still, the rewards of his station more than made up for the unpleasantries, and for tonight at least, he would only be tasked with giving Communion to the men — Nottingham's own priest could bother himself with the chore of serving when it came the women's turn.

By turning his mind back toward the upcoming feast, the Bishop managed to endure his repulsive duty. Soon, there were only a few men left to serve. As the Bishop held the Host up for his final invocation, he looked into the face of the one standing before him and saw familiar blue eyes staring back at him — eyes that mocked him in his dreams and made him relive the indignity of being robbed.

Robin Hood — for that was who it was, the Bishop was certain, despite the grey woolen garb and lowered hood — was clearly concerned; he had hesitated too long in giving Communion. Hastily, the Bishop of Hereford murmured the ceremonial blessing and dropped the Host on Robin Hood's tongue. As soon as Robin turned away, the Bishop scurried up to the altar, leaving St. Mary's priest to present the Sacrament to the women of the congregation.

Under the guise of clearing the altar of its Eucharistic implements, the Bishop beckoned over an altar boy.

"I am excusing you from the rest of the service," he whispered fervently. "Go through the vestry and into the nave, and find the Sheriff as quick as you can. He is sitting with his guard in the front row, on the left-hand side. Tell him that Robin Hood is here, and if he acts fast, he may catch him!"

⚔ 22 ⚔

NOTTINGHAM CASTLE

ROBIN WAS CERTAIN that the Bishop had recognized her. The startled look in his eyes and the hatred that had flashed across his face before he had thought to disguise it had been unmistakable.

Little John was right – I was foolish to have come here, she berated herself, shaking her head in dismay.

Robin followed the line of returning communicants to her spot near the back of the church, her eyes searching urgently for an exit. The main entrance seemed to be her nearest option. She wavered: would it be better for her to remain hidden within the tight press of people until Mass ended, or to get out of the nave and risk the attention that would bring?

Her own anxious motions stole the decision from her. Irked by her disquiet, the people around her shifted away, leaving Robin momentarily unsheltered.

"There he is!" a voice shouted. Robin whirled around and saw the Sheriff pointing in her direction from the side aisle and several soldiers shoving their way through the crowd to get at her.

Robin panicked. Pushing people forcibly aside, she squirmed toward the west end of the church, breaking free of the multitude and sprinting toward the exit. From out of nowhere, two soldiers appeared abruptly before it, blocking her escape.

With the agility of a fleeing rabbit, Robin changed direction and darted over to the sidewall, seizing with both hands the ring of a heavy iron door and pulling it open, hoping desperately that it would lead outside.

A narrow, winding staircase appeared before her, heading toward the roof. Without a second thought, Robin dashed up the stone steps and reached for the handle of the door that awaited her at the top . . . .

It was locked.

"Mary, Jesus, help me," Robin prayed as footsteps pounded up the stairs behind her. Bracing herself at the top of the spiral staircase, she instinctively reached for her bow — but of course, it was not there. Hastily, she drew her sword instead; its blade cleared the sheath an instant before the first soldier came charging around the bend.

Desperation lent Robin strength as she fought to preserve her life, and the stones beneath her feet soon grew slick with blood as she slew her attackers. Yet even as one man would fall, another would emerge to take his place, pushing his predecessor's body aside and seeking to strike her in spite of the hampering curve of the stairs. Had she been fighting anywhere else, Robin would surely have been dead within the first few moments; only the advantage of her position at the top of the narrow staircase saved her from serious injury.

Then she overreached.

"Oh," Robin gasped as her sword lodged in the chest of a young soldier. The shock in his dying eyes matched her own as his weight pulled her off balance, causing her to slip on the blood-drenched stone and tumble forward into a soldier positioned below, whose instinctive reaction was to shove the conjoined duo aside, thus furthering their momentum down the stairs; Robin's head struck a wall as they crashed into yet another soldier who was charging up the steps — his out-stretched sword impaled his dead comrade, freeing Robin from his weight; she toppled over him and out the bottom doorway, coming to a crumpled halt at the Sheriff's feet.

"So nice to see you again," he sneered as his men pulled a quaking Robin roughly to her feet. One of the soldiers bound her wrists together while another confiscated her sword.

"Sanctuary," Robin choked out, spitting blood from her broken lip. "I claim sanctuary."

The Sheriff hesitated and turned to glance behind him at the Bishop of Hereford, who had deserted his post at the head of the church to come and watch the arrest unfold. At the Sheriff's implicit question, the Bishop gave a cruel smirk and turned his back on Robin, walking away.

"You are mine now, Robin-lack-Hood," the Sheriff grinned, seizing her short hair and flinging her toward the church's main entrance. Robin stumbled and fell, jarring additional agonies into her already bruised bones.

"But he claimed sanctuary," Robin heard one bystander exclaim as a series of kicks and shoves propelled her outside. The protestor was quickly hushed.

A soldier brought over the Sheriff's horse, and Darniel turned away from the lieutenant he had been addressing to mount it. With Darniel prancing triumphantly at the head of the escort, Robin was led away through the town streets while the rest of the congregation watched from the church steps, conversing together in wary whispers.

Robin scarcely noticed her surroundings, too dizzy to pay much attention to anything besides her footing. Only once did she look behind her; her bloody footprints gleamed black in the moonlit snow.

Not my blood, she thought dully. *Theirs.*

By the time the contingent arrived at Nottingham Castle, Robin was nearly frozen from shock and from cold. A pair of castle guards, not yet relieved from duty for the holidays, took charge of her from her soldiering escort and followed the Sheriff into the Great Hall, where a blazing fire roared. In keeping with her misfortune, they halted her just outside the reach of its warmth.

Now that she had stopped moving, Robin could not keep from swaying where she stood. The reeling in her head had abated only a little, and she had to struggle to focus as the Sheriff's lieutenant strode into the room and began to speak.

". . . my men did a thorough search of the church like you ordered. We found no other outlaws, but we did find this."

He offered Robin's bow and quiver to the Sheriff.

"Well, well," Phillip Darniel gloated, taking her bow in his hands. His fingers caressed the pied wood. "So, this is the bow of Robin Hood."

The guards next to Robin let out startled gasps, and in spite of her situation, Robin could not help but be amused. Clearly, they had not realized the identity of their charge. With looks of commingled fear and awe, they inched away ever so slightly, despite the fact that her hands were bound.

Suddenly, the Sheriff let out a sharp hiss. His head snapped up from his examination of the bow, and his eyes burned into Robin's like black fire.

"Out!" he shouted at his men, his voice trembling with inexplicable rage.

Puzzled, but grateful to comply, they hastened from the room, leaving Robin alone with the Sheriff in the middle of the Hall.

Darniel grabbed Robin by her collar and thrust the bow beneath her nose. "Explain . . . THIS!"

Reflexively, Robin glanced at the bow, but she did not need to see its stave to know what the Sheriff had spotted. The small engraving inside the grip of her longbow was worn from use, but still very legible upon close inspection:

Robin Ann Locksley

Robin did her best to summon a cavalier smile. She must not appear afraid. "Hello Phillip. Care for a dance?" she taunted in her natural voice.

He threw her bow aside and struck Robin hard across the cheek. Only his grip on her tunic kept Robin on her feet. "The only dance *you* will be doing is a whirl with the hangman's noose," he snarled.

"How delightful. Do you plan then to tell everyone that your famed nemesis is really a *girl?*" Robin jeered, blinking back tears of pain. "Think what ballads they will sing of your heroism! Oh, but I suppose I shan't be able to hear them if I am dead — well, they say there is a blessing to everything."

"You *dare* mock me!" the Sheriff railed, shoving Robin to the floor, his eyes sparking hellfire.

What he would have done next, she was fortunate to never find out, because someone spoke up just then from the doorway.

"My lord?" It was the castle steward, the only man who could interrupt the Sheriff with impunity. He gazed in surprise at Darniel, who was kneeling over his prisoner with an expression of cruel retribution. "My lord, I see that it is true what the guards have been saying — you have indeed captured Robin Hood! May I offer my congratulations, sir, and shall I dispatch a courier to the King?"

Darniel's face twisted with displeasure at the interruption, and Robin felt the grip on her collar tighten. Pulling her forward so that his lips brushed against her ear, he menaced, "One word about any of this, and I will have you drawn and quartered."

He let her go and stood up. "Yes, send a courier. And have the guards take this varlet to the pit. He will be executed at high noon — that will give us time to announce his capture at the morning Mass."

"Noon, sir? But it is Christmas —"

"NOON!"

It took no less than five prison guards to escort Robin to her cell. These were not the same guards who had stood with her in the audience chamber — the ones who had seemed to both fear and revere her. These were hard men, fit for little more than managing the underground prison.

They did not talk as they walked through the tunnels, not even to each other. The only sounds were the squelching of their footsteps and the hiss of sputtering flames as water dripped from the stones overhead to land on the torches. The touch of falling droplets was like tears on Robin's face, mingling with the ones that came there naturally.

At last, the procession stopped at the lip of a pit. The lead guard grabbed Robin's arm and drew her to its edge, letting his torch flare down beneath them so that she could see into the cavernous depths. The pit was deep and shaped like a jug, with concave mud walls that would be impossible to climb. The stench of rancid decay reached Robin's nose at the same instant that she discerned the remains of what had once been a man.

"Enjoy your new home . . . while you can," the guard taunted as another one cut her bonds. Then with a hard shove to her back, he pushed Robin into the pit.

For one brief moment she was weightless, suspended in the air like the bird whose name she bore. Then she was falling through rank darkness, her hands uselessly thrown out in an attempt to forestall the crippling force of landing.

Little John prodded at the fire with a stick, watching the consequential red sparks shoot into the air with disinterest. Mass was certainly over by now — it would have been for at least an hour. Robin would be on her way home. So why was he so uneasy?

Little John was a sensible man, not given to wild flights of fancy or to overindulgences of the imagination. But since the moment he had turned his back on Robin, he had felt a deep sense of misgiving. Only pride had prevented him from turning around and accompanying her to Mass.

Her. Would he ever get over the tightness in his chest each time he thought of Robin and that word?

It was only worry that his tongue would slip when talking with others, he was sure. He always had to be so careful now not to do or say anything that would seem strange or . . . improper.

How much longer could their charade last?

A dim, high note interrupted his musings. Little John leapt to his feet, listening intently.

"Is it Robin?" David asked in joyful expectation, coming up beside him.

Little John shook his head as another bugle joined the chime. "No. It must be soldiers."

"Here? Now? But it is Christmas! No one seeks for out-laws at Christmas," David laughed. "Besides, if they cannot find us in the daytime, surely they must know they have not the least chance of finding us in the dark!"

"They are not trying to find us," Little John realized in sudden alarm, his heart pounding against his ribcage as the bugles sounded once more. "They are trying to ensure we do not leave. Robin is in danger!"

Robin lay curled against the earthen wall as far from the fetid corpse as she could get. The smell of rotting flesh choked her breath; she had already been sick two times. At least the darkness hid the sight from her eyes.

The pit was frigid and dank, but Robin tried not to shiver. Though the corpse had broken her fall, part of her weight had fallen onto her outstretched arm, dislocating her shoulder instantly. Any movement at all sent a wave of agony coursing through her body.

Still, aside from her shoulder and groggy head, Robin had managed to come through her ordeal relatively unscathed. Granted, her body felt like one massive bruise, and her arms were sticky with dried blood, but she was fairly certain that the majority of it was not hers.

She tried not to think about the people to whom it *did* belong, but their faces kept running through her mind. Did they have wives ... children? How many families had she destroyed tonight?

"God, if I am to die anyway, why could you not have let me fall beneath the first swordsman's blow? What purpose did this night serve, tell me that? Tell me!" she shouted in despair.

He did not answer.

❧

"Are you not due back in Hereford, my dear Bishop?" the Sheriff asked.

"I would not for my soul miss the hanging of Robin Hood," he replied.

"To have caught that unprincipled knave at last! It is the most perfect of gifts — and it is not even New Year's yet."

"Perhaps we should have Christmas gifts from now on," the Bishop joked.

"Indeed! But come, I believe I promised you a feast. Let us go and rejoice as no men have done before and revel in the capture of that thief!"

❧

Robin did not remember falling asleep, so when she awoke, it was in sudden panic. How long had she been insensate? The pit was as dark as ever; there was no way to tell if she had been unconscious for five minutes or five hours.

At least the dizziness she felt had abated, that was something. But she was still so tired. A deep, dragging weariness weighed her down and forced her eyelids closed in spite of her best efforts to stay awake.

When she awoke once again, the pit felt different; Robin realized that she could discern the slime-encrusted walls and the heap of rotting flesh. Looking up, she saw orange light splayed across the ceiling in the corridor above, growing steadily stronger. Someone was coming.

Robin pushed herself to her feet with her good hand, biting back a moan as bruises left in one position for too long made her nerves scream and her shoulder blaze. She fought against the pain, determined that when the guards arrived, they would find her standing and composed; she would face Death with her chin held high.

Two shadowed figures appeared at the top of the pit—but only two. *Not an execution party, then*, Robin sighed in relief. The first shadow squatted down by the edge of the pit to see her better, directing the light from its torch into the hole and allowing Robin to see its leering visage.

"Well, well, we meet again . . . Robin Hood," Guy of Gisborne mocked, his scarred features turned hellish by the torchlight. "At last, you are in the kingdom you deserve."

"Hello, Guy," Robin replied, sitting back down despite the pain that the motion caused. She would not do this *cur* the honor of standing. "Have you come to ensure that I am still alive? What a pity to see that you still are—although you do look a sight better than the last time I saw you. That scar I gave you does wonders for your complexion. Of course, the darkness aids a great deal as well."

Gisborne laughed, which surprised her. She had hoped to make him angry. "Even you cannot vex me now, Robin. Your wings are clipped. In a few hours time, you will sing your tune for the hangman's noose."

Had he really said . . . hours? Relief filled Robin, contrary to his intent. She had yet a while to live!

Emboldened, she retorted: "Really? How interesting. I seem to recall that the last time the Sheriff attempted to hang one of my men, it did not go so well for him."

Gisborne's smirk was savage. "He will succeed with this hanging, never fear. You will not be executed in the town square — your gibbet will be the castle wall itself. No one will be near enough to save you, but all will be near enough to see your end."

How astute, Robin ruefully acknowledged to herself, but what she said aloud was, "Do you really think that will stop my men from rescuing me?"

Gisborne laughed in contempt. "*My* men have been combing the forest ever since your arrest — your people will have gone to burrow like the vermin they are. By the time they learn that you are here, it will be too late."

Robin flinched, her relief disappearing in an instant. She had known in her heart that there was no chance of rescue, but to hear Gisborne actually say it was a crippling blow. Still, she would not give him the satisfaction of knowing how deeply his words had struck her.

"Poor Guy — after all this time, you are still searching for us? What a pity you did not think to remember the way to our camp when you chose to leave," she taunted, hoping to mask her distress with a jeer.

"I remember," he hissed, his glare darker than the shadows of the pit.

"Then why have you not told the Sheriff?" Robin asked, surprised. Guy did not answer her, but someone else did.

"Because I will not let him."

Robin squinted up at the second man, trying to make out his face in the flickering torchlight.

"Who are you?" she queried.

"John of Nottingham. You knew me as Johnny."

"Johnny?"

"Silence, boy!" Gisborne growled.

"My father and I," Johnny continued, ignoring his father's command, "do not get on well. I do not approve of his thirst for power, nor the means by which he obtains it. But power is meaningless without someone to leave it to, and I am my father's only heir."

"I will beget another, just you wait and see. Then you will regret all the times you have defied me!"

Johnny shrugged. "Perhaps. Until then, our accord stands—I do not inform the Sheriff that you are pilfering from his coffers, and you do not divulge the location of Will's home."

Robin could scarcely believe what she was hearing. *This* was young Johnny, Will Stutley's best friend, who had so meekly followed his father away from their camp without even a word goodbye? Yet there was nothing meek in his tone now. And if what he had said was true, then out of love for his friend, this boy — no, *man* — had defied his father and saved Will and the entire camp from capture at the Sheriff's hands.

"It is a shame that you left. You would have made an excellent Merry Man," Robin told the youth. It was the highest praise she could think of.

Gisborne spat.

"Do not insult my son. Merry Man—Merry *Wo*man is more like it," Gisborne sneered. Robin froze. Had the Sheriff told him her secret? She would have thought him too proud, but—.

"Fair-faced youth—you are not even a man yet, are you? It is said you have never possessed a woman, not even the one it is rumored you love." He laughed in disdain. "Oh, the Sheriff was in a rage when he heard that you had stolen away his bride-to-be. For that insult, he was prepared to have you flayed alive; I fail to understand why he has now changed his mind. Personally, I was looking forward to hearing your agonized screams."

"Funny, I am sure there are many who would say the same thing about you. How *did* you get the Sheriff to dismiss your warrant?" Robin demanded caustically.

Gisborne bit at the change in subject. "Any warrant can be forgiven . . . for the right price. I just had to pay the Sheriff's."

"And the price?"

"You," he sneered

So that was what inspired our last run-in, Robin realized. *I should have guessed.*

"The Sheriff must have been so disappointed when you failed," she goaded. "I am amazed to discover that you are still around."

"I have other uses. Someone has to recollect the taxes your men so disobligingly steal. And the Sheriff knows that my means are . . . effective."

Robin spat. The satisfaction it brought her was worth the pain in her swollen cheek. "You and Darniel deserve each other."

"*Tsk, tsk*. Compliments will get you nowhere."

Before Robin could think of a retort, the thin notes of a distant bugle filtered through the dungeon walls, announcing to the town, "All is well!" The notes seemed to startle Gisborne from his verbal sallies.

"Come," he ordered his son. As he turned away, he flung one last taunt at Robin, "See you in a few hours."

Gisborne disappeared into the tunnel, taking the light with him. Johnny lingered a moment longer, his face inscrutable. Robin opened her mouth to say something — what, she had not yet decided — when he, too, turned on his heel and left, leaving her alone in the darkness once more.

✄ 23 ✄

THE COMING OF DAWN

SOMETHING IN THE AIR roused Robin and alerted her to the arrival of day. It wasn't anything definable — the pit was just as dark as ever, and she could hear no distant sound; yet Robin knew that at that moment, dawn was stretching across the land like a hangman's noose, reaching forth slim tendrils of light to choke the life from her . . . .

Stop that! Robin ordered her mind. *Just . . . just stop that.*

But panic had her in its grasp, and she felt like she could not breathe. With a sob, Robin buried her head in her knees. *God, I am not ready to die.*

Something skittered through the silence — a pebble kicked across one of the puddles in the dungeon tunnel. Robin looked up. Torchlight flickered against the ceiling, and the faint patter of footsteps grew into echoing drumbeats as several guards drew near. This was no gawking foe — this was an escort. The Sheriff must have changed his mind and decided to have her executed at dawn. Or perhaps he wished to continue his earlier interrogation . . . the thought made Robin shudder.

What if I just refuse to get out? she pondered as the guards tossed a rope ladder over the side of the pit. But when it came down to it, she would rather stand on the castle wall with a noose around her neck and have one more moment in the light—and be able to glimpse the distant trees of her Sherwood home one last time—than to spend her remaining hours moldering away in this abyss.

Robin stood with aching slowness and wrapped her good arm through a rung on the hempen ladder, grasping its side firmly with one hand. "Pull me up," she called, not quite able to keep her voice steady.

She had expected a taunt or a challenge, but none came as the ladder gave a sharp jerk and began to rise. The motion sent a wave of nausea and pain coursing through her, and it took all of Robin's strength and resolve to maintain her grip on the rope and not fall. The pit was wider at the bottom than at the top, and the ladder swung back and forth like a pendulum, threatening to dislodge her; it nearly succeeded, too, when her feet slipped off their rung and she went into a dizzying spin, her boots scrabbling for purchase against the slimy walls. The soldiers dragged Robin over the lip of the pit not a moment too soon; her good hand seized spasmodically and let go of the ladder, its strength gone.

With nary a moment's respite, Robin was pulled to her feet and herded through the tunnel, her escort as silent now as it had been before. The only sound she heard was the pounding of her heartbeat—like time, it was speeding up, speeding towards the end . . . .

"Stop," came the leader's imperious command. He handed his torch to another guard and cracked opened the prison door, peering outside. Whatever he saw must have satisfied him, because he opened the door just wide enough to slip through and then closed it firmly behind him. The low murmur of voices seeped through the stone, and a minute later the guard returned, tucking a weighty bundle inside his tunic; as it settled against his chest, Robin thought she heard the dull chink of shifting coins.

At his curt signal, Robin was thrust forward and out the door. Pain blinded her — one of the soldiers had unwittingly shoved against her shoulder — and for a moment, Robin's world went black. With a burst of sheer will, she shoved the darkness away. Only then did she notice that none of the guards had followed her through the doorway and into the castle corridor; the door's solid bulk was closed against her back.

Just then, someone stepped forward from the opposite wall, and Robin forgot all about the guards.

"John!" she cried in disbelief, her knees growing weak. Only the presence behind Little John kept Robin from flinging herself into his arms. Instead, she reached out with her good hand and clasped his forearm as tightly as he did hers, trying to convey with her fingertips what it meant to see him again.

"I brought Will Stutley," Little John said in a strangled voice. "He knows the castle layout; he knew that we could bribe the guards. The others wanted to come, too, but we thought — I thought — that the less the better. Just in case we could not get out of here alive."

"You should not have come," she whispered, unable to keep tears of relief from spilling down her cheeks.

"A simple 'thank ye' will suffice," Will Stutley grinned. "But ye can say it later. Fer now, I would rather ye focus on gettin' us out o' 'ere alive."

"I thought that was *your* job," Robin replied with a ghost of her old smile, sniffing back her tears.

Will's grin widened, and with a short bow, he gestured for them to follow.

The passageways that wended from the bowels of the castle up to the main level were completely deserted; even the servants were gone, released from their obligations these twelve days of Christmas to be with their families. No one was around to see the trio sneak their way through the large tower that formed the castle keep.

At first, Robin was grateful for the complete absence of people, but soon the lack began to worry her. They should have run into *someone* by now. What if the guards had only pretended to accept the bribe, and she and her friends were walking into a trap?

To her surprise, when Robin ventured this concern to her companions, they both began to snicker.

"The Sheriff called a castle-wide feast to celebrate your capture," Little John explained. "Last we saw, he and every-one else were dead asleep in the Great Hall, clutching empty tankards in their palms."

Will gave a snort. "'ow I wish I could 'ear 'im rage when 'e wakes up t' find ye gone!"

"Believe me, you are better off not having that wish come true. His rage is a pretty terrible thing," Robin said softly.

Will reached out then and opened an exit in the side of the keep, exposing the yard of the surrounding bailey. Sunlight blazed in through the open doorway, its brilliance magnified by the reflective snow. Robin tilted her face up toward the sky, rejoicing in the blinding glow she had thought to face only from the other side of Heaven. For the first time, Little John and Will Stutley got a good look at their companion.

"Dear God!" Little John exclaimed, halting abruptly and reaching a hand towards her face. "What did he do to you?"

Robin blushed under his scrutiny, conscious of what he must see. Based on the way her face ached, the left side was bruised a solid purple sheen from when the Sheriff had struck her, and her lip was swollen and split down the middle from her fall. Her clothes were covered with muck and decay, and there was clearly something wrong with her arm — she was holding it against her body at an odd angle, and her shoulder was unnaturally square.

"I am fine," Robin declared firmly, stepping away from Little John's touch. "We should be going."

"What is wrong with your shoulder?" Little John persisted.

"It is only out of joint," Robin informed him, glancing self-consciously behind them down the corridor. "Really, people are going to start waking up, and we had better not be here when they do."

"If I get my hands on that Sheriff —" Little John fumed.

"Would ye like me t' fix it?" Will Stutley interrupted.

Robin looked at her friend in amazement. "You can do that?"

Will smiled wryly. "I 'ave 'ad some experience."

Robin glanced nervously once more back down the corridor. As much as she wanted the pain to abate, they could not afford to linger. "Not right now — I would rather have a disjointed shoulder than the disjointed neck we will receive if we get caught."

Without waiting for a response, she turned and plodded down the steps of the keep, forcing her friends to follow her across the bailey yard. She ignored the worried looks that Little John kept casting in her direction as they walked, all of her senses on the alert for a witness to their presence or a foe . . . but the bailey was as empty as the castle had been, and they reached the gatehouse without incident. The stone building was dark; Little John squinted around for the porter.

"He said he would be here," Little John murmured anxiously. "Twenty pounds he took, and twenty more to let us back out again . . . ."

"Money cannot help a man who is dead," a cold voice suddenly cut in.

It was Gisborne, standing in front of a corpse in the corner, a bloody sword blade in his hand.

"Beautiful craftsmanship, this sword." Gisborne gloated, angling the blade so that Robin could see the familiar line of etchings underneath the red sheen. "It was wasted in your hands, but it will serve me well in my new capacity as the Sheriff of Nottingham."

"You are mad," Robin snapped. She felt Little John step behind her, using her body to shield his motions as he loosened his sword from his waist.

"Am I?" Gisborne asked carelessly. "The King already feels feels that Darniel is losing his grip after letting you roam the countryside free for so long. Just imagine what he will say when he finds out that the Sheriff caught you at last, only to let you escape! He will need a new sheriff, and who better than the man who slew Robin Hood and two of his Merry Men?"

"But I am defenseless," Robin said, spreading her arms in an open gesture to further shield the movements of Will and John. "You would be committing cold-blooded murder."

"It would not be the first time," he remarked with a wicked smile. "Even my son will forgive me my killing his friend —" he indicated Will with a nod of his chin " — when he reaps the rewards that will follow."

"Then ye know little about friendship," Will retorted hotly.

"Friends are for the weak," Gisborne snapped. "Power — and what one is willing to do to get it — is the strength of true import. I will rise after this night in power and glory both, whereas the lot of you will descend into nothingness."

"Mighty imaginings," Little John snarled, speaking up for the first time. His naked blade shimmered in his hand as he stepped in front of Robin. "But even a dastard like yourself should be able to count high enough to grasp that there are three of us and only one of you. Your so-called strength will not avail you."

Guy of Gisborne laughed. "The archer is unarmed and injured; Will Stutley, I could beat blindfolded, and you — you do not even know the proper way to hold the sword you brandish."

Robin winced. Her cousin had only just begun to teach Little John how to use a broadsword. Clearly, he had not been as quick to master that weapon as he had been to master the bow. She saw Little John hastily readjust his grip, his face flushing at his error.

Gisborne saw it, too. His bloodthirsty grin widened. "Brave as well as stupid. This should be fun."

Without another word, Gisborne swung his sword in a cutting arc and lunged into attack.

Robin backed away, pressing herself against the gatehouse wall as Little John and Guy of Gisborne hewed at each other. Will attempted to join the fight, but Gisborne's back was to the opposite wall and Little John was standing between them, so all Will could do was dance around behind his friend, too afraid of striking Little John to risk attacking Gisborne himself.

"Get away from there!" Robin hissed. "You are just getting in his way!"

Hastily, Will backed away and joined Robin against the wall. "They are goin' t' kill each other!" he cried.

Memory flashed unbidden through Robin's mind of the time she had revealed to Little John the deep depression that had overtaken her after killing the Sheriff's nephew. "Life is our most precious gift," Little John had told her, gazing into the distance with the expression of a man who has given the subject much thought. "Only as a last recourse should we ever consider taking a life, and then only to preserve another. I am glad that you preserved mine, Robin, but gladder still that you grieved for the one you took. The day we can kill without sorrow is the day we cease to be human."

"John will not kill him — not if he can help it," Robin told her friend without tearing her eyes from the battle. She felt utterly, maddeningly helpless. Nothing in her existence had prepared Robin to stand idly by and watch the man she loved fighting for his life!

There was no question in Robin's mind as to who was the better swordsman. Only Little John's swift reflexes and brute strength saved him time and again as Gisborne lashed out at him. Little John's hasty blocks and frantic attacks left large openings in his guard — openings that Guy of Gisborne intentionally ignored.

He is toying with him, Robin realized. She began to grow angry.

"Give me that," she said, snatching the two-handed broadsword out of Will's grasp. She almost dropped it — it was thrice as heavy as her own lighter sword, and she could not use her injured arm to help hold it aloft; her shoulder was already screaming at the strain.

"Robin, no!" Will gasped. He snatched at her, his fingers just missing her tunic as she managed to hoist the weapon with one hand, and dashed forward.

Rather than joining the fight, Robin hovered just out of reach of the whipping blades. As Gisborne sneaked in a cunning blow that Little John only half-managed to block, leaving the collar of his tunic rife with blood, Robin seized her chance. With all of her might, she heaved the heavy sword past Little John and into Gisborne's legs, causing him to stumble and careen into Little John. The two opponents tumbled together to the ground.

Gisborne struggled to get up, but Little John rolled over on top of him, his long form pinning Gisborne's to the floor. Robin kicked her sword out of Gisborne's hand and picked it up, leveling it at his throat. Will snatched up the brand she had hurled at Gisborne and did the same. Guy held very still as Little John clambered to his feet.

"That was a dirty trick," Gisborne glared.

Robin shrugged. "I cannot say that I am bothered. Get the key from the porter," she commanded Will, who reluctantly lowered his sword and began to search the slain man for the key.

Gisborne laughed, the contemptuous motion of his throat making the tip of Robin's sword jostle slightly against his skin. "There is nowhere for you to go. I ordered my soldiers placed all around the outside of the castle to keep the crowd from making a scene at your execution. You will be caught before you can get ten paces down the road."

"Is this true?" Robin asked Little John.

His brow creased with concern. "We slipped up here

when they were changing the watch. There were only a couple of men then, but they could have brought out more."

Gisborne let out a low, vicious laugh. "You are all dead."

"There is another way out," Will spoke up suddenly. Robin, Little John, and Gisborne all turned their heads to look at him. He flushed at their attention. "Nella — the Sheriff's daughter — she told me 'bout it. There is a 'idden tunnel in one o' the guardhouses. It lets out into the caves at the base o' the castle."

"Why did you not tell me this before?" Little John demanded.

Will shrugged. "'Tis always locked. Only the Sheriff 'as the key."

"Then it is useless to us," Little John said bitterly.

Robin rubbed the bridge of her nose with her forefinger, thinking hard. "Give me your clothes," she commanded Gisborne abruptly.

Gisborne stared at her. "What?"

"Your clothes," she snapped. "Your tunic, your hose — give them to me now."

When Gisborne did not move, Little John let out a low growl, "Either doff them yourself, or I will do it for you."

With a malicious glare, Gisborne began to pull off his horse-skin hose.

Will stepped in to guard him again as Robin handed her sword to Little John and took the garments from Gisborne. The clothes reeked of horsehide and sweat, although she supposed they were pleasant odors when compared to the noxious stench of the pit that clung to her still.

Guy of Gisborne was much of a height to Robin, but broader, which meant that she could draw his clothes right over her own. Even so, she almost fell as she tried to pull on the loose hose with one hand, fire lancing through her shoulder.

"Um, a little help?" she gasped at Little John, trying and failing not to blush.

With an expression like stone, he helped her dress; the revolting tunic with the horse-ear hood was the last piece they went to pull on.

"My arm is stuck," she murmured after a moment, her tone one of apology. "It hurts too much to lift through."

The muscle in Little John's jaw tensed, but he bent to examine the problem, and as he did, Robin heard rather than saw Gisborne drive his fist into the back of Will's knee, sending the boy sprawling. With one swift motion, Gisborne seized Will's sword and leapt at Robin, who—entangled in the tunic—could do nothing to stop him.

The next instant, Robin was flying through the air as Little John's hand slammed into her, pushing her out of the way with enough force to smash her into the opposing wall. She heard something crack, and the agony in her shoulder flared into white-hot fire, choking her so that she could not even scream. A moment later, it subsided to nothing more than a sharp ache; the force of the blow had rammed her joint back into place.

With a grateful sob, Robin rolled to her feet and yanked down the tunic that was blinding her, only to find herself staring into the gaping eyes of Guy of Gisborne. Blood trickled from the corner of his mouth and spilled from his chest where the hilt of her sword was protruding.

Holding on to the hilt was Little John, who had jammed the blade through Gisborne's chest with enough force to splinter through his breastbone and out his back. Realization of what he had done seized John, and he let go of the sword as if it had seared him.

In the background, Will was picking himself up off the

floor, apologizing over and over again for letting down his guard. Tentatively, Robin placed one hand on Little John's muscled shoulder; he turned his head away.

Robin turned to stare at Gisborne's body. Regret welled up inside her; as much as she had loathed the man, she would have preferred to avoid his death. More than anything, she would have preferred for the stain of that death to be on her soul, not on Little John's.

Reluctantly, Robin went to pull her blade from Gisborne's body. It was stuck. Doing her best not to shift the corpse, she attempted to shake the sword free. It would not budge.

A large, callused hand wrapped itself over hers, making her shiver. With a single tug, Little John pulled the sword free from Gisborne's body; he immediately let go her hand.

"We should leave," Robin murmured into the silence.

The journey back through the sunlit courtyard and up the stairs leading to the castle keep seemed to take forever. The encounter with Gisborne and its deadly result had shattered what little nerve Robin had left after her ordeal; only the presence of her friends gave her the strength to throw her chin high and strut across the greensward as Gisborne would have done — with the arrogant confidence of a man accustomed to getting his way without qualm over how. She needed that air of confidence about her if she were to succeed in getting into the Great Hall and stealing the Sheriff's key without being stopped. No one who might see her could suspect her of being anyone but Gisborne, or all would be lost.

Such was her focus that she reached the keep door and had her hand stretched out toward its handle before she registered that it had already begun to move; just as her fingers grazed the metal ring, the door swung open of its own accord, and the Sheriff stumbled out.

"Gisssborne?"

The Sheriff blinked at Robin, trying to make out her features as his eyes adjusted to the light. He held one hand to his head to soothe the ache that came from a night of drinking; his tunic was soiled with the stains of wine and meat.

His presence, so utterly unexpected, evoked in Robin a terrible panic. Their last encounter was still fresh in her mind, and her cheek stung with the pain of recall. Behind her, she sensed Will Stutley and Little John tense.

"My lord," she began in a hoarse tone, struggling to regain her poise. Her tongue stumbled as her mind frantically sought to weave some story. "I was just on my way to find you. I have something terrible to report—"

"Father, that is not the stairwell," a feminine voice interrupted, her words growing more audible as she caught up with Darniel.

The Sheriff turned to look at her, and in doing so revealed the maiden behind him, but Robin did not need Will's indrawn breath to confirm her identity.

It was Nella.

The girl's mouth curled in revulsion as she observed the person standing before her father. Her eyes took in Gisborne's horse-eared hood and did not look to the face beneath it, sliding instead to the men behind Robin and widening as they fixed on Will Stutley's face. Nella's hands flew to her mouth, but she did not say anything. Her eyes darted from Will, back to Robin—clearly not Captain Gisborne! she saw now—to her father, and back to Will again.

The Sheriff, still befuddled from too much drink, did not notice his daughter's reaction. He frowned at Robin.

"Whassat?"

Robin licked her lips; her mouth had gone dry. She swallowed hard and continued to speak, trying not to think of what she would have to do if Nella sounded the alarm. "I just discovered that the gatehouse guard has been stealing from your treasury, sir. When I confronted him, he tried to run, so I slew him."

"Waz a f–far better deathh than he dessserved," the Sheriff slurred.

"Just so, my lord. With your permission, I will take your keys and return what he pilfered to its rightful place, and then resecure the treasury."

Darniel's brows knit together. There was something not quite right about this request, but wine had made his mind slow and he could not process what it was.

"My keeyss?"

"Yes, sir."

The Sheriff unhooked the key ring from his belt. Robin reached for it, but the Sheriff did not let it go. He peered at her closely, his bleary gaze struggling to focus on Robin's face beneath the horsehide hood.

"Gisssborne?" he questioned again.

"Father!" Nella spoke up sharply. Robin tightened her grip on her sword. "Father, come. You must rest and refresh before the execution. Nottingham must see what a powerful sheriff it has."

"Yess, yes, it musst see . . . ."

The Sheriff let go of the key ring and turned away, staggering back into the keep. Nella stared at the trio for a moment longer, her gaze locking with Will's; she gave him a small smile and closed the door.

Robin exhaled in a *whoosh* of relief.

"She loves me after all," Will stammered. "She really loves me!"

"Or else she did not want you murdering her father," Little John pointed out.

"I think you are right, Will," Robin said to forestall an argument. "But I would rather not wait to see if she summons any soldiers or not. Where is that secret passageway you spoke of?"

According to what Nella had told him, the tunnel was hidden inside an unused guardhouse at the edge of the bailey. Though they found the place quickly enough, they had to linger in the open for several uneasy minutes before Robin could find the appropriate key; at last, they gained access to the room.

The place was small, made much smaller by the large amount of clutter littering the floor. There was barely enough space for the three of them to crowd inside and still leave the door ajar to provide some light. Trying not to trip, they shoved and piled the ancient armaments and rusting equipage into tall stacks against the walls. The raucous objects would have made an excellent alarm had anyone been around to hear.

Eventually, the three of them managed to shift enough of the jumble aside to reveal a two-foot square trap door, latched to the floor with a heavy iron padlock.

"Hurry, Robin," Will encouraged as she tried to fit various keys into the lock. Just as the padlock snapped apart, the room suddenly brightened as someone pushed the door—now unimpeded by oddments and gear—open to its fullest extent.

"Hey, what do you think you are d—Father?" Johnny asked, breaking off his accusation at the sight of Robin hunched over the trapdoor in Gisborne's horsehide suit. "Father, what is going on? What are you doing?"

Only then did he register the green-clad men flanking his father, and one man in particular. "Will?" he asked, astonishment etched all over his face.

The next instant, Little John's hand was at Johnny's throat, pinning him against the wall and causing several precarious piles to crumble in the process.

"Let him alone," Robin said, dragging down on Little John's arm.

"But he knows who we are—"

"I know what he knows. Let him be."

Reluctantly, Little John released his grip on the youth but did not relax his wary stance. Johnny sagged against the wall, rubbing his throat.

"You killed my father," he said. It was not a question.

Robin nodded. "I am sorry."

"Then you are the only one." He took a deep breath and shot a nervous glance at John before fixing his gaze back on Robin. "With his death, my destiny is once more my own. Earlier, you said that I would have made a good Merry Man— let me prove to you I still can be. Let me come away with you now!"

Robin glanced at Little John, whose expression was clearly skeptical. Johnny saw this and pressed on: "I have spent years serving in this vile place, serving the greedy pursuits of the Sheriff and my father. If I stay, it will destroy me. Let me join you! I swear I will devote myself to your cause and live a life committed to philanthropy."

Robin rested her hand on Johnny's shoulder and looked into his eyes. He met them steadily. "Then you are welcome indeed into my band," she said.

He smiled at her, but his gaze was already sliding back to Will, true friendship gleaming from both their eyes. Little

John shook his head in consternation but did not question Robin further. Instead, he pushed away the objects that had fallen and raised the heavy trap door, then climbed down into the tunnel. A moment later, a dim glow flared from within; John had evidently found and lit a torch. One by one, the others descended through the trapdoor and into the sand-stone passageway until the guardhouse stood abandoned once more.

☙ 24 ☙

ROYAL REQUEST

ROBIN WAS THE LAST to step out of the dark tunnel and into the white blaze of morning. Squinting against the sudden brightness, she turned to look up at the ridge behind her; red and gold sandstone cliffs towered above her head, and at the top squatted the Sheriff's black castle. Soon its residents would realize she had escaped, but with luck, they would not think to look for her outside of Nottingham Town until she and her friends were far away.

Alert for any signs of pursuit, the foursome trudged their way back to the forest in single file, pausing only as needed to empty the snow from their boots. In spite of the cold, Robin doffed Gisborne's horsehide tunic and allowed it to trail behind her as she walked; the heavy material brushed a light capping of snow into the tracks so that from a distance, their path would be nearly impossible to discern.

They reached the boughs of Sherwood Forest without encountering a single soul, but that changed once they were inside the greenwood.

"Stay low," Little John warned, gesturing them down into the bracken. No sooner had they ducked into the cover of the fronds than a group of soldiers sauntered past.

"What are they doing here?" Robin hissed.

"Trying to make sure no one leaves to go rescue you," Johnny confessed, looking abashed. His expression brightened. "Not that they succeeded!"

"Hush!" Little John and Robin whispered simultaneously.

The soldiers paid the group no heed, too busy grousing amongst themselves about having to work on Christmas Day to hear or notice anything unusual.

Once the soldiers had passed, Robin and the others rose silently to their feet. Warily, they made their way deeper into the woods.

They had to pause often at first to hide from the Sheriff's men, but for the most part, his soldiers seemed content to meander in small groups near the forest paths, sounding their horns on occasion and complaining to each other in loud voices. The number of soldiers diminished the further the foursome traveled into the forest, though their caution meant it was still well past noon before they finally reached their home.

Marian was the first to espy them, and giving a shout of sheer delight, ran to greet her sister. Instantly, the rest of the band leapt up from where they had gathered by the fire — masks and revelries forgotten, the traditional boar hunt foregone — to await the outcome of their leader's rescue. They surrounded her now, overjoyed to see Robin alive again. As her cousin picked her up and swung her around, heedless in his euphoria of Robin's bruised and noxious state, she was aware that at that moment she might have been swinging from the walls of Nottingham Castle, and her eyes filled with tears of love for her friends.

They pressed in around her as Will set her down again, their elated shouts melding in Robin's mind with the echoes of the soldiers' cries during her fight in the church. Reality seemed to waver before her, and she squeezed her eyes shut, desperately trying to separate the trauma of the past few hours from the rejoicing of the present moment, and failing.

"We should let Robin get some rest," her cousin commanded, having observed the whitening of her face. Reluctantly, the others parted to let Will — one arm wrapped around Robin's shoulders to steady her — deliver their leader to her cabin. A pot of steaming water and a slightly soiled rag was brought for her use, and in the privacy of her hut, Robin finally wept as she washed the dried blood and muck from her body.

She had barely enough energy left to pull on her spare suit before sleep won the effort to shutter her eyes. With a grateful sigh, Robin curled into a ball on the fronds of her bed and yielded herself to exhaustion.

Her sleep was deep and dreamless . . . for perhaps ten minutes. Then Marian, with a look of intense apology, shook her awake.

"I am truly sorry, Robin, but Will Stutley says you hurt your arm; I need to check on it before it has time to set."

"'Twas my shoulder, but it is fixed now," Robin mumbled, her mind groggy with sleep. "'Twas just put out, not broken."

"Even so."

Marian helped her sister to sit up, steadying her with one hand while she examined her shoulder with the other.

"Does that hurt?"

"Just a little," Robin answered with some surprise, coming more fully awake. "Not anywhere near what it did before."

Satisfied that the joint was where it should be, Marian wrapped Robin's arm in a sling of cloth, which would keep the shoulder in place while the tendons tightened.

"I also brought this," she said, holding out a bowl of yellow-green ointment. "It will help with the swelling in your face."

As Marian began to dab on the salve, Robin could not suppress emitting a small yelp. The paste stung like a hundred bees against her abraded skin.

"You should hear the tale that Will is relaying," Marian began, trying to distract her sister from the balm's bite. "He was on his third rendition when I left, and the number of guards and perilous battles seems to grow with each retelling. From the way he describes it, you would think that Little John had killed ten men with his bare hands, and of course, you and Will both had your share of the felling."

Sadness filled Robin that the events of the night could give pleasure to anyone, and she groaned. "Can no one stop him?"

"Oh, everyone is just soaking it all up," Marian hastened to reassure her. "They are so glad you are safe; they need to celebrate. The tale just adds to their joy."

"How delightful."

"Well, I—hold still, Robin! Really, you are just as fretful as Little John. He had barely gotten back before he took off again, for who knows what reason or where. There. I am done."

Marian rocked back on her heels and surveyed Robin's face with approval. Her smile wavered. "Is something the matter?"

Robin shook her head, hastily masking her concern with

an expression of gratitude. Marian's words had filled her with a confused anxiety and had ignited in her the intense desire to seek out Little John and reaffirm that everything was all right. But she knew that in her current condition, her sister would never permit it.

So instead, she smiled up at Marian. "Thank you," she said, giving her a one-armed hug. Marian returned the affection with a careful embrace that still managed to convey her relief.

"I am so glad to have you back! If you ever do something so foolish again . . . but there, I promised myself I would not scold. Get some sleep, and we can talk more when you wake."

Taking the now-empty bowl of balm in her hands and giving Robin one last smile, she left her sister to her slumbers.

Rather than going back to sleep, however, Robin waited until Marian had made her way back to the bonfire and to the fierce celebration that was now underway, and then slinked out of her hut and into the trees. The afternoon sun illuminated the trail of oversized footprints leading away through the snow, and without hesitation, Robin followed it.

She discovered Little John sitting on the fallen bole that spanned the Sherwood's most turgid river, his posture nearly as bent as on the day she had first found him there. Robin sat down beside him, clutching around her shoulders the blanket she had brought with her in a futile attempt to keep off the cold.

"Thank you for coming back for me," she offered when Little John made no stir to speak.

Little John did not look at her, but gazed instead at the turbulent waters below their feet, where tiny cakes of ice were sweeping by and occasionally leaping up to tap the soles of their boots. "I thought you were going to die," he told her at last. "I thought they were going to hang you, and it was all my fault for leaving you behind."

"It was my decision to stay," Robin reminded him, torn by the wretchedness she saw in his face. "I should have listened to you."

"I have never killed a man before," he continued, staring at his hands. "It was so . . . easy. I should not have thought it easy."

Guilt clawed at Robin; now she understood the distress that had caused him to distance himself from the company of the camp. "John, I am so sorry. If I had only heeded your advice, you would never have been placed in a position where you had to."

He did not reply. His silence to her spoke volumes. How he must hate her for this!

Feeling utterly miserable, Robin rose to her feet, not wishing to burden him further with her presence. A large hand fastened around her wrist.

"Stay," he said, looking up at her for the first time. "Please." Robin hesitated and then sank back down onto the log.

Little John went back to staring at the river, but he did not relinquish his hold on her wrist. She almost missed his next few words, so lowly did he speak.

"It is strange to think that killing a man should have been easier for me than this seems to be. But I promised — I swore — that if God gave me another chance, I would not neglect it.

"I am seven-and-twenty years old, Robin, and in all that time I have never met anyone — any woman — like you. When I thought I had lost you, I nearly went wild. I realized . . . so many things, and I knew in that moment that I would either rescue you or hang beside you, but I could not endure a life without you."

Robin felt her breath quicken at his words, billowing out before her in brief puffs of frost. *Is he saying what I think he is saying?*

Little John was looking at her now, his eyes shining with more intensity than a summer sun. He clutched her chilled hand in both of his own, as though to secure her for fear that what he was about to say would make her bolt.

"I love you, Robin. I love you, and I need you the way the stars need the night, and the clouds need the air, and the streams need the rain. I cannot exist without you. Tell me you feel as I do, for truly I cannot bear to be nothing more than a friend to you any longer."

Robin struggled to find her voice, but the lump in her throat made speech impossible. Encountering only silence, Little John's face fell.

"What a fool I am to think that a woman like you could ever feel that way about someone like me. Please forget I said anything. I shall not trouble you again." He started to rise.

Robin shook her head and pulled on his hand until he sat back down. Her voice when she spoke trembled violently, but not from the cold. "I have desired — dreamed and prayed — for so long that you would speak thusly to me. I thought you would never, could never —"

She was unable to go on.

At her words, Little John's expression had transformed from one of wretched hopelessness to one of exultant disbelief. Unable to contain himself any longer, he burst out, "Then you do care for me! Oh, Robin, say you will be mine! Let us be together so that from this day on, whenever people think of Robin Hood and Little John, it shall never be one without the other!"

But before Robin could make a reply, Little John quickly

checked his enthusiasm, his tone turning solemn. "Only . . . Robin, you would have to lay aside your guise and declare yourself to be the woman you are — otherwise, we could never have a life together. It might mean losing the friendships you have built here and your position of leadership if the others reject you. Would you be willing to forsake all that? Then, too," he rushed on, "there is your family to consider. You are the daughter of a nobleman and thus by all that is proper beyond the reach of a peasant like myself — a fact I know I should not forget! Yet forget it I must, for my heart demands I ask: Robin of Locksley, of the Sherwood, of the Hood — will you marry me?"

Tears coursed down Robin's cheeks, so different from those she had cast earlier in her despair. How quickly she had gone from being the most pitiable creature on earth to the happiest! Her throat closed over her voice and choked off her reply, so she merely nodded, ducking her head.

Little John stood up, pulling her gently to him. His arms wrapped around her in a mantle of warmth, strong and protective. His heart beat against hers, fast and fierce — almost as fast as her own. Robin met his eyes and felt her breath catch at the naked emotion she saw there.

"Lord, who am I to deserve such grace?" he prayed, his voice husky. "You are so much more than I ever dared imagine might exist."

"I exist. I am here. And I am yours now and forever," Robin replied, finding her voice at last.

He kissed her then with so much gentle love that her bruised lips made no protest, and neither of them said anything more for a long time.

Alabaster clouds drifted upon the late-spring sky, pushed across the blue expanse by a light warm breeze that teased of summer. That same breeze sifted through the trees to ruffle Robin's hair as she tugged at her tunic and cast another anxious glance into the forest surrounding the camp.

"They are late," she said for the hundredth time that morning.

David shot her a look of compassionate understanding. "It is early yet. They will be here."

He caught her hand as she went to tug at her tunic again. "Stop that. You look fine. Very . . . very beautiful."

To Robin's surprise, he blushed and dropped her hand.

Robin sighed. It had been months since she had revealed her secret to the band, but even David — loyal, stoic David — was still uncomfortable around her at times.

She had felt so alone that day, standing under the tall oak tree and calling for everyone's attention. Little John had offered to stand up with her, but Robin had refused, knowing she needed to appear confident and strong on her own. In truth, she had never felt more afraid. The Sheriff's wrath and the battles for her life had evoked less terror in her than staring into the eyes of ten-score woodsmen and announcing to them that she was a girl.

Some of the men had been angry — she had expected that. But she had not expected the way their gazes would wound her as they changed from astonished disbelief into rage, or the way their expressions of betrayed trust would rend her heart. She had felt like the worst of traitors at that moment and had wanted to cower away to her cabin and never come out again, but she had forced herself to stand tall and to accept their indignation.

Not all of her people had reacted with fury, however. A few, like Will Stutley, had thought the whole thing a terrific joke. At first, Robin had presumed that was because they did not believe her, but the truth was clearly evident once they had cause to consider it. Their delighted laughter at her announcement had been at their own blindness and the impotency of the Sheriff, foiled time and again by a girl. Their amused guffaws had helped ease the ire of the others and had given a lighter perspective to her charade.

In the end, despite their initial shock at her announcement, the majority of the band had continued to accept Robin as their leader. The respect and honor they felt for her were rooted too deeply within them to be dislodged by even such a startling revelation, and while a few bandsmen continued to dispute the propriety of taking orders from a woman, in the face of such solid and well-regarded supporters as David, Will, and Little John, their voices were scarcely to be heard.

"They are here! Robin, they are here!" Marian cried, interrupting her sister's reflections and hastening over. Though attired in a simple rose-colored dress, her only ornament the purple amaranths braided into her flowing brown hair, Marian looked absolutely radiant, her excitement tingeing her cheeks the same hue as her gown. In the past, her sister's delicate beauty would have made Robin feel self-conscious of her own height and thew, but she knew now that in her own way, she did indeed look as David had said, "Very beautiful," in her robin's egg suit of blue, with her short golden hair held away from her face by a small circlet of honeysuckle.

At Marian's words, Robin felt the butterflies in her stomach fly up into her throat—but her sister's announcement soon proved premature. It was only Will Stutley, returned ahead of the main entourage to alert the camp of their impending arrival, now just a few minutes distant. The two girls waited anxiously for their guests to appear, Robin's hand clutched tightly in Marian's.

Lord Locksley was the first to emerge from out of the trees, accompanied by Little John and Will Gamwell, walking one on each side. Little John was talking with her father and looked as handsome and poised as she had ever seen him. He caught her eyes and smiled at her; Lord Locksley followed his gaze to where his daughters stood.

"Girls!" someone cried, but it was not their father. A carriage was clattering clumsily through the underbrush, and from its window, Darah was waving a handkerchief in anxious greeting to the two sisters. As soon as the carriage rumbled to a stop, she tumbled out and would have dashed towards them were it not unladylike to do so. Instead, she contented herself with walking as quickly as she could.

"Oh, I have missed you so! How different you look! Marian, you have grown so brown—and Robin! Whatever have you done to your hair, my child? And what on earth are you wearing? Gracious, but you do look like a boy!"

"Hello, Darah," Robin greeted, surprised to hear no rancor in her voice. She did not even mind the woman's thoughtless babble. "I am pleased to see you," she said. And she was.

"Robin," a deep voice called softly. She turned to face her father.

He had dismounted from his horse and was standing just a few feet away. His garments were clearly new, and the lines of worry she had seen on his face during their last encounter were gone. But instead of feeling relieved, his reestablished wealth made her nervous. Once again, he was Lord Locksley, presuming and noble; the humble camaraderie he had displayed to her only a few months ago was gone. What must he think of her now?

"Sir," she greeted him uncomfortably.

"I have brought you something," Lord Locksley said, appearing to be as uncomfortable as she. "I know I promised to repay your loan before the year was through, but I thought your men might prefer these to mere pounds."

He beckoned a cart forward and lifted the cover to show Robin what lay inside.

"Two hundred bows of Spanish yew," he told her, removing one and handing it to her to examine. The stave was inlaid with silver dryads that shone against the wood and were so intricately carved that they seemed to come alive in her hands.

"There are two hundred quivers as well," he added. Robin could see the stacks of rich green leather, embroidered with silver figures to match the bows. Each quiver held a sheaf of arrows fletched with peacock feathers that rippled from the depths of the cart like a thousand rainbows.

"They are beautiful," she gasped.

Lord Locksley carefully lifted out a wool blanket from the cart and opened it. "These are for you, Robin, since the Sheriff took yours.

He handed her a quiver whose arrows were innocked with gold, and a longbow with gold etchings spiraling up the burnished wood. Gold horns capped the ends of the bow, and the string between her fingers was as smooth as velvet. At the grip, in her father's script, was the meticulously incised title:

Robin of the Hood

Robin could scarcely speak, she was so overcome. "Thank you . . . Father," she whispered.

"Such nonsense!" Darah interrupted them with a sniff. "What a thing to give a daughter! Although I suppose you shan't be discouraged from it now. Well, Robin, at least you are getting married! Who would have thought? Surely not I, for I am certain I despaired of you ever finding a match!"

Robin stood under the Trysting Tree's chandelier branches, her face dotted by the brilliant light that pierced its thick crown of emerald leaves.

To her left stood Will Gamwell, decked head to toe in scarlet raiment, with a splendid white feather stuck in his cap, which trailed past his shoulder and down his back. He had one arm wrapped around Marian, and the two were gazing at each other with eyes that bespoke a lifetime of devotion and happiness to come.

To her right . . . to her right stood Little John, his shoulders seeming broader than ever, and his eyes twinkling at her with an emotion that made Robin dizzy to behold. He took her hand as the friar Will had enlisted hemmed and hawed and sought to find an appropriate Bible passage for the occasion. Out of sight of everyone, John's thumb made small circles in Robin's hand, distracting her so that she missed the first few words that Friar Tuck spoke.

". . . come here today to join these men and women in the holiest of unions . . ."

Was that Darah sobbing loudly in the crowd?

". . . to honor each other, and to love each other, and to guard each other in health and affliction, forsaking all others . . ."

Her people gazed at her with bright eyes, the obvious joy they felt for their friends lending beauty to even the most weathered of features. Even those members who still resented Robin for her concealment were not unaffected by the scene.

Robin caught the gaze of her father. His blessing on the life she had chosen touched her more deeply than she could have imagined, and some restless part of her soul that had agitated her since her youth finally found peace.

"Do you, John Little — also known as Little John — take this woman, Robin of Locksley, to be your wife in the sight of God and Man?" Friar Tuck asked, interrupting her thoughts.

"I do," Little John avowed.

"And do you, Robin of Locksley — also known as Robin of the Hood — take this man, John Little, to be your husband in the sight of God and Man?"

"I do," she affirmed, and never did she taste two sweeter words.

Friar Tuck then asked the same of Will and Marian and then handed each couple their ring.

Robin's eyes fixed on Little John's face as he lifted her hand toward himself until her fingers just grazed his chest. Everything else around her seemed to fade away; Robin's whole world was encompassed by the look in John's eyes.

"I, Little John, take thee Robin to be my wife. Through fortune and affliction, through weal and woe, for now and for eternity, I pledge eternal loyalty. In the name of the Father — "

He touched the ring to her thumb.

"And the Son — "

He tapped it to her forefinger.

"And the Holy Spirit — "

It alighted briefly on the one in the middle.

"Amen."

Little John slid the token of their unity onto Robin's ring finger, forever there to stay.

Half a furlong from the Trysting Tree, two figures threaded their way towards the clearing, unaware of the momentous event currently taking place.

The boy named Much wiped a grimy hand across his brow. He had lost his way twice already, in spite of Eadom the Innkeeper's whispered instructions and his own vivid memory of the time Will Stutley had shown him to the outlaw camp. The second misdirection had taken Much half an hour to amend — time that Eadom would not be quick to forgive. Yet through it all, his companion had followed him staunchly and without question, seeming as comfortable trekking through the bracken as he had been sitting astride his ivory mare.

Much shot another glance at the youth he was leading. The lad was garbed in bright-hued clothes of the finest cut and possessed the fresh aroma of one who bathed every day; Much, on the other hand, wore the oft-patched tunic of a stable hand and stank of the horses he tended. He had fully expected his coxcomb companion to complain throughout the journey and was still rather surprised that he had not.

"This is it," Much announced with relief as the sound of voices reached their ears. He had not taken more a few steps into the clearing, however, when an eruption of cheers shook the air, startling them both.

"Ayah —! What is going on?" Much exclaimed loudly, biting off an alarmed shout of his own.

A stately woman near the edge of the crowd overheard his question and turned to face them both with a beatific smile stained with tears. "Oh, it is Robin and Marian—they are married at last! I cannot believe it, truly I cannot. Oh, now I can die a happy woman!"

"Robin . . . Hood?" asked the well-clad youth, his green eyes focusing intently on the crowd gathered beneath a great oak tree, parsing the joyous assembly until he fixed on a couple at their center.

The stable boy followed his gaze and wished more than anything that he could linger to celebrate with the merry outlaws, but Eadom's hand was heavy when his orders were disobeyed. "Take the messenger to Robin Hood and come straight back," he had commanded, and Much had already taken far too long to carry out that task. But what a tale he would bring back with him! Robin and Marian were finally married . . . . Why, he might even earn the rest of the day off for being the first to bring Eadom the news!

His mind awhirl with the possibilities, Much bowed to his companion and accepted a silver penny from the lad's soft, lily-white hand; clasping it tightly in his own sun-browned fist, he began his trek back to the inn.

Robin finally managed to break her gaze away from Little John and turned to face her friends, laughter burbling from her lips. Lot handed her a cup of spiced wine, and she took a sip before handing the chalice to her husband.

Husband! He is my husband now, she thought in amazement. Little John lowered the cup, his lips glistening from the drink. He bent to kiss her, but just then Allan struck up a lively tune on his lute, and with a merry laugh, Little John seized Robin around the waist and swept her off into a dance.

They whirled around the greensward, each rejoicing in the feel of the partner in their arms. Will and Marian joined the dance a few moments later, and soon all the woodland couples and those who had no partner were cavorting beneath the Trysting Tree to the sound of Allan's lute.

At one point, Robin's hyacinth wreath flew off her head, but she took no notice and did not see the elegant lad who stooped to pick it up. All of her attention was focused on Little John, who suddenly stopped dancing. Taking her chin in his hand, he thrilled her lips with a kiss that tasted of nutmeg and cinnamon.

"Beg pardon," a voice interrupted.

The couple ignored the utterance, but when the interjection was repeated a second time, Robin reluctantly broke away from Little John and turned to face the speaker.

Standing before them was a stately youth, with a face fairer than Robin's own and clothes that were fairer still—a crimson tunic and hose, made of silk and lined with gold thread. The emblem of the royal household was embroidered upon his chest.

With a small bow, he handed the hyacinth wreath to an astonished Robin but turned to address Little John.

"Sir, forgive my intrusion. I am Richard Partington, page to Her Majesty, the Queen. Her Majesty has heard of your skill with the bow and of your daring deeds, and would like to extend to you an invitation. In four days time, her husband, the King, will hold a tourney in London Town in which the greatest archers in all of England will partake. Her Majesty opines it a travesty that one of your talent should not be allowed to compete simply because you are an outlaw, and if you will deign to strive against the King's most adroit bowmen, she will guarantee you safe passage to and from Court, and will venture with the King to have you and your men declared Royal Foresters and your crimes pardoned should you win. To demonstrate her good will, she bade me give you this ring."

He removed an ornate ring from his pocket and held it out to Little John.

"That is quite an offer," Little John said, making no move to take it. He looked down instead at the lady standing beside him. "But I think it is not I to whom it is made. Robin?"

The page shifted his gaze to the blue-suited woman, completely confused. His bafflement lasted only a moment, however, as a swift review of what he had seen and heard since his arrival in the camp comprehended to him his mistake. Whatever Richard Partington's personal thoughts might have been regarding the true identity of Robin Hood, his eyes remained empty of judgment, and he continued to hold out the ring.

Robin took the gold band from his fingers and cautiously turned it over in her hands, her mind weighing the dangers of the request and the magnitude of its rewards. "A very generous offer. I would be worse than a fool to refuse it."

Little John's brows knit together in consternation. With a glance at Richard Partington that warned him not to follow, he drew Robin a short distance away.

"What of our wedding day? What of our people?" he demanded quietly. "For all this page's fancy words, there is no guarantee the Queen will secure our pardon; and though she has promised you safe passage, there is no law that says the King must obey her pledge. Will you imperil your life again on a chance?"

Robin laid her hand upon Little John's cheek. "John, I understand your concern—truly I do. But this is not like Christmas Eve. You were right to try to deter me then—I was taking a foolish risk, and I should have listened to you. But this is different. The possibility of a pardon far outweighs any personal danger in attending this tournament. It is not as if I *want* to go . . . but you asked me to think of our people, and I am. I want our family—all of our family—to be raised to a life that is free."

Little John stared at her. He would not have believed that the love he held for his wife could grow any stronger, but Robin's readiness to sacrifice her life for the chance to assist others filled his heart with a crushing pride. Though he trembled inside at the thought that something could happen to her, he knew as surely as if God had spoken it that she was destined for a greater purpose than to just be his wife, or a noble, or even the leader of their band. God had spared her for a reason, and though he could not see His ultimate plan, he sensed that the journey to London Town—for better or for worse—would play an important part.

He nodded his assent. "I am coming with you," he declared.

"Of course!" Robin smiled at him, surprised. "I would hardly go without you."

With a kiss that drew from him a broad grin, she slipped the Queen's ring onto her right hand and turned back to face the page. "I am honored to accept the Queen's bidding. We can leave for London on the morrow."

"Forgive me, my lady, but there is no time. We must leave straightaway if we are to make it to London before the tourney."

The newlyweds scowled at the urgency but knew there

was little choice. "Then we shall leave in an hour, but no sooner," Robin informed him, the steely determination in her voice indicating that she would not negotiate on this point. "It is my wedding day, after all, and I intend to spend at least part of it with my friends."

"Very well," the page acquiesced, giving a small bow.

The next hour passed in the blink of an eye, and at Partington's gentle prodding, Robin and Little John gathered their few belongings into a sack and went to take leave of the band.

"Do ye really 'ave t' go?" Will Stutley asked with a mournful expression as his oldest friend bade him farewell.

Robin gave him a kind smile. "For a little while, at least. You will be in good company here, and if I win the tournament and the Queen keeps her word, then none of you will ever need fear the Sheriff again."

"I almost wish I could go with you," Allan told her enviously. "What a story I could tell of your adventure!"

Robin suppressed a smile. Allan hated to travel.

"You will just have to tell other stories," she said. "I have every confidence in your ability to turn even everyday doings into heroic feats . . . a talent you have aptly and frequently demonstrated."

"Your doings are far from ordinary, Robin. One day, they will make you legend — with the help of my ballads, of course."

"Legend?" she laughed. "Really, Allan, you must not tease a lady so. But since I know you will keep composing no matter what I think, just promise me not to embellish your tales *too* much."

"Only as will please my listeners," Allan chuckled, running a hand across the strings of his lute.

Robin shrugged, experience having taught her that she would get no better assurance. "Do as you will."

At that moment, a familiar bellow of laughter reached their ears, and Robin turned to see Little John standing a few yards away, clasping forearms with his brother and attempting to maintain a light-hearted farewell. About to head towards them, she caught a glimpse of the lingering misery on Will Stutley's face.

"Here," she said on sudden impulse, unbuckling the silver horn from her waist and holding it out to him. "Will you keep this for me until the day I return?"

Will's eyes lit up at the entrustment, and he took the trumpet from her hands almost reverently, a broad grin splitting his face.

"Ready?" Little John asked, coming up beside Robin. She nodded.

Marian had already bidden her sister farewell, but she ran up again and threw her arms around Robin's neck, soaking her tunic with her tears. Will followed his wife at a more sedate pace, but upon reaching them, seized them both in a fervent hug.

"I love you!" Marian cried, letting go of Robin at last.

She was replaced by Darah, who pulled Robin down and clutched her to her bosom like a child of five, all the while issuing advice on court protocol through her tears.

"Enough of that," Lord Locksley commanded, and Darah reluctantly stepped aside. Father and daughter gazed at each other for a long moment, neither knowing what to say. Then something melted in Lord Locksley's face, and for a brief instant, Robin caught a glimpse of herself in her father's eyes, surrounded by a golden gloriole of pride.

"God keep you, daughter. Come home to us soon." He handed Robin her inlaid bow and placed her quiver upon her back, smiling a little as the peacock feathers formed an iridescent halo behind her head. Taking hold of her shoulders, he kissed her on the forehead as he had at their last parting that foggy autumn day, and turned and walked away.

"Now, I am ready," Robin told Little John, her voice thick with emotion. Wrapping one arm around her husband's waist, she waved a last farewell to her friends and with resolute steps, led the way out of the clearing.

Behind her, the air swelled with the sweet, clear sound of a trumpet, filling the hollow space that grew in her heart as her feet carried her further away from the place that had come to be . . . would always be . . . home.

A soft *fwoosh* marked the course of two arrows as they passed on either side of her and embedded themselves in twin trees twenty paces ahead. Robin turned and saw Shane and Glenneth both raise their bows in salute, while Will Stutley puffed on her horn and the rest of her people waved until she was beyond their sight.

Richard Partington had stabled his horse at the Blue Boar Inn, so rather than turning immediately southward toward London, the small group headed east — crossing the river at the log bridge where Little John had proposed to Robin — as the most direct path to the inn. They had barely set foot upon the opposite bank, however, when Robin broke away and dashed down the silty bank toward a nearby knoll, scrambling up its spongy slope to the top.

For a long moment, Robin just stood there on its apex, gazing out at the Sherwood that had been her sanctuary and protector, her friend and wonder, for the last three years. Hope for what she could achieve in London glowed brightly in her heart, but fear of what could result if the Queen failed in her promise lay upon her like a heavy counterweight. Would she ever see her greenwood home again?

A comforting arm wrapped around her shoulders, and she looked up at Little John; wedding-day joy and parting sadness shone from both their eyes. Neither spoke, but neither had to. Each knew in that moment exactly what the other was feeling.

A small movement at the corner of Robin's eye drew her attention, and she glanced down the knoll's steep frontal slope to where the river curved its way through the trees. A royal rack was parting the bushes at the bottom, followed by the russet head and sturdy body of a Royal stag. Though she and Little John were standing upwind of the deer, Robin saw its head rise in perception and could swear that it stared straight at her, meeting her gaze with the clear recognition of equals.

"Protect them for me," she murmured to the enduring hart, dipping her chin in a nod of respect. For an instant, she thought that the stag returned her gesture, dipping its noble brow in her direction before bounding into the woodland once more.

"Did you see that?" Little John asked her, startled.

"See what?"

Robin gave Little John a quirky grin, filled with exuberance at the sudden assurance she felt that her people would be all right. Seizing her husband's hand, she turned away from the green vista and pulled him down the hill, her pace quickening into a run. "Come on!" she cried, laughter spilling from her lips as she gamboled down the knoll, down to where Richard Partington was patiently waiting, down toward the path that would take them to London, and the Queen, and a lifetime of adventure and love — down into the beginning of everything.

ACKNOWLEDGEMENTS

There are many people to whom I owe my sincere gratitude and appreciation, and without whose influence this book would never have come to be. Most especially, I would like to thank:

Mr. Schultz, who gave me a love for the English language;

Professor Kuenning, who reminded me of my own worth at a time I really needed it, and whose willingness to extend himself left a lasting impact;

Monika Rose and the other members of **Writers Unlimited**, for their unending support and critique;

Bud Hoekstra and **Antoinette May**, who undertook the task of editing my story—both my book and I are greatly indebted to their insightful comments;

Lou Gonzalez, for his generous mentorship in the realm of eBook publishing;

and finally,

My mother, who possesses a singular ability to find plot holes and inconsistencies, and whose willingness to decimate my story and then help me rebuild it is ultimately responsible for the quality of my book.

With all my thanks,
    R.M. ArceJaeger

P.S. I would be extremely remiss if I neglected to extend my appreciation to the late **Howard Pyle**, whose *Merry Adventures of Robin Hood* was my passport to the wonderful world of Robin Hood when I was growing up. *Robin: Lady of Legend* was deliberately written to complement that familiar classic, and although it assuredly stands alone, I did insert certain tidbits as a treat for readers familiar with both works. Furthermore, Pyle's extensive use of song within his book is an exquisite feature modern works seem to lack, and as a tribute to his lyrical skill, I have included a line from one of his songs in my book. See if you can figure out which one it is!

ABOUT THE AUTHOR

 **R.M. ArceJaeger** is the author of several books for children and adults, including #1 bestseller *Robin: Lady of Legend*. In 2005, she was named a California Arts Scholar for excellence in Creative Writing, and she possesses degrees in Computer Science and Education. Currently, she uses her skills to help other authors by providing eBook formatting, editing, publishing, and website design services. For more information or to contact the author, visit her website: www.rmarcejaeger.com. ArceJaeger has been writing books since she was five years old and especially enjoys making her readers rethink classic tales.

Last Name Pronunciation: R-C-J-grr

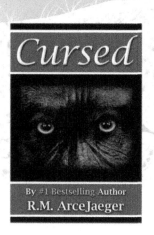

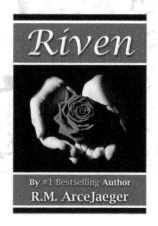

Don't Miss Our

Astounding Animals Series

Exclusively on Amazon

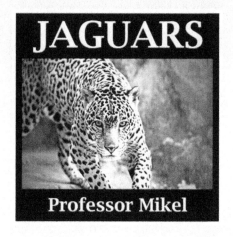

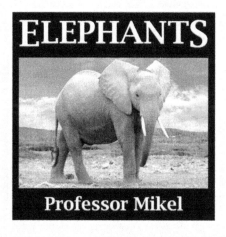